Thistle & Lion

Once & Future Book 5

Meredith R. Stoddard

Fredericksburg, Virginia

Erkita Press
P.O. Box 41173
Fredericksburg, VA 22407
www.meredithstoddard.com

Publisher's Note: This is a work of fiction. Names, characters, places, and incidents are a product of the author's imagination. Locales and public names are sometimes used for atmospheric purposes. Any resemblance to actual people, living or dead, or to businesses, companies, events, institutions, or locales is completely coincidental.

Book Layout © 2014 BookDesignTemplates.com

Thistle & Lion/ Meredith R. Stoddard. -- 1st ed.
ISBN 978-1-7333933-7-9

For my children, who forge their own paths

CHAPTER ONE

September 13, 1996
Edinburgh, Scotland

Dermot Sinclair got out of the limousine and straightened his jacket as he waited for the plane to land. It was something he'd done a hundred times before as part of his work in the security division of Alba Petroleum. Just another day at the office, or so he liked to pretend.

The nervous fluttery feeling in his stomach had nothing to do with the fact that the love of his life was about to step off that plane. With her husband. He hadn't seen her since the wedding three weeks before. Three weeks since her father had been murdered in front of them. Three weeks since she'd done exactly what Walter Stuart demanded for the sake of the people she cared about; for him, his mother, Grant MacDuff, the brother and sister she barely knew.

Three weeks of worrying about her state of mind, her safety, her heart. Three weeks of wondering how things would be between her and James Stuart. Would he have expected her to hop right into bed as if it were a normal honeymoon? Dermot's stomach churned. He didn't think James would push things forward so soon after her father's death, but James had surprised him before.

The plane came to a stop a safe distance from the waiting car. Dermot eyed the door, willing it to open so he could clap eyes on her. The seconds felt like hours before the door cracked open and swung downward, revealing the stairs. Dermot held his breath.

Fleming Sinclair, a distant cousin, and fellow Alba Petroleum bodyguard was the first to emerge. After scanning the area and giving Dermot a nod, he descended the stairs and turned to wait for James and Sarah. James came next, his shoulders filling the doorway. His dark brown hair was burnished by the sun, and his cheeks were slightly bronzed. At the bottom of the stairs, he turned to offer his hand to his bride.

Sarah stepped out of the plane and took James's hand as she descended the handful of steps to the ground. Dermot's heart flipped. She looked like a soft breeze blowing in from the Mediterranean. Her cheeks were sun-kissed and the dress she wore flowed around her calves like waves on the shore. He was equal parts relieved she appeared to be in good spirits, and insanely jealous as James tucked her hand into his elbow.

'Look at me.' He thought. He needed to see her eyes to know she was alright. 'Look at me.'

They strode toward the car with an easy grace, contrasting the muscles bunching in Dermot's shoulders. He should be doing his job, making sure there was no one approaching them, no one trying to sneak a photo from outside the chain link fence, but all he could do was watch James and Sarah as they approached. James said something to make her smile, and she leaned into his arm looking up at her husband with what looked like adoration.

'Look at me.' Dermot fairly screamed in his head. As they got closer, he opened the door to the limousine, trying not to show how affected he was by the sight of them looking like a couple.

"Alright, mate?" James clapped him on the shoulder as they arrived at the car.

"Aye, alright." Dermot hoped he was convincing.

"My love?" James stepped back allowing Sarah to get into the car first.

She stepped between them brushing a hand down James's arm as she lowered herself onto the seat. She hadn't spared Dermot a glance. His heart ached, and his throat tightened with each breath. He looked back up and met James's eyes. They were the same blue as his own, but James's were filled with sympathy, and a question. 'Would he be able to do this?'

Dermot drew in a breath and pulled his shoulders back. He lifted his chin giving every appearance of being dispassionate, in control. His eyes never left those of his childhood friend, his employer, and maybe relative. He would have to do this. He didn't have a choice.

***

August 28, 1996
Riboux, France

White flowers floated lazily across the surface of the water, as Sarah's lungs burned. Her mother's voice cooed softly in her ear. 'I'll protect you.' But Sarah knew too well she was beyond her mother's help.

'I tried, Mama.' She thought for the millionth time in the last few days. 'I tried to get away.'

Sarah's eyes stung from the chlorine, and her head started feeling light from the lack of air, but she pushed herself away from the surface with her hands wondering how long she could stay under the water. Strangely, her past torment had become her comfort.

Under the water, no one expected anything from her, not even Mama. Down there, the clamor of the world was muffled. She couldn't hear Lady Anne's passive-aggressive censure, or Walter Stuart's quiet threats. She couldn't hear the cameras clicking, or anyone talking about image or messaging.

Under the water the world was a wash of reflected light and color. She could barely see the garden around her. The white bougainvillea that climbed the pergola nearby and dropped its flowers into the pool, was nothing more than splotches of color, and her husband standing at the edge holding a towel was a blur.

She'd had no idea where they were going when they'd boarded the Stuarts' private jet on their wedding night. She had promptly fallen asleep exhausted from the long day and felt like she woke up in a dream world. A limousine ride through the countryside and mountains up a long gravel drive took them to an estate complete with a thirteenth century stone manor house, barn, pool house, and breathtaking views. She could easily imagine a reclusive local lord hiding out there while battling a generations-old curse on his family. Instead, it was the winter home of her new in-laws, who thankfully were staying away.

James had given her the grand tour the morning they arrived. Although she had been tired and had barely heard what he'd said, she had gotten the vague impression of rustic beams, stone walls, and elegant furnishings. After a brief and awkward introduction to Martine, the gorgon of a housekeeper, he had walked her to the master suite where he had given her shoulders a gentle squeeze and said, "I know you're grieving. I won't press you."

She had murmured. "Thank you."

He'd kissed her forehead and added. "I'll be just down the hall if you need me."

Without any more conversation, he had left her in the massive bedroom with its adjoining bath, closets, sitting room and balcony overlooking the gardens. Sarah was sure the room was worthy of a magazine feature on how to modernize your medieval chateau in style. But she didn't see the beauty at the time.

If she hadn't been so tired, she probably would have cried all night. Her father was dead. Her lover was back in Scotland. Her family and friends were under threat. Here she was; married to the wrong man, expected to enjoy herself on what for any other girl would be a dream honeymoon with Prince Charming.

How long did she have before he would want to consummate this marriage? How on Earth was she supposed to without feeling like she was betraying Dermot in the worst possible way?

Three days had passed. Since then, James had been kind and solicitous of her every need. He had not pushed himself on her, or pressed her to talk about her feelings, or her father. He had given her room to grieve.

Sarah looked up through the water at him, not rushing to get out. She waved her hands again to keep herself under the water until she felt her heartbeat throbbing in her ears, and her vision was rimmed in black.

***

They were married now, much good it did him. James Stuart leaned against the column watching his wife swim. Soak might be a more accurate description of what she did. Since their arrival at the family chateau three days ago, she had spent much time in the pool. She seemed to like being under the water.

None of this had gone the way he planned. He had imagined her arrival in Scotland would give him the opportunity to woo her, charm her, and get her to fall in love with him. They were destined for each other. He hadn't expected to compete with his childhood friend for her hand, nor on her clinging to the career that would have at best provided her with an unremarkable life. He definitely hadn't expected her father to die less than two days before their wedding.

She was his now, but at what cost? They were three days into their honeymoon, and she was grieving. Grieving the loss of her father, her career, her privacy, anonymity. He had the world at his fingertips, and he had no idea how to make this woman happy.

So, he was giving her space. He hadn't pressed to consummate their marriage, because it had followed so closely after the death of her father. He hadn't even proposed any activities. She was cordial with him, even friendly at times, but it was clear she didn't love him. Doubtless, she wasn't over Dermot. But she was his now, not only to love, but to take care of.

He pushed away from the column and retrieved her towel. Unfolding it, he held it up for her at the edge of the pool where she was sure to see him.

She didn't move. She waved her hands at the shoulders keeping herself under, looking up at him through the water and floating flowers. Alarm licked at the edge of his mind as he started to wonder if she meant to come up at all.

He counted twenty seconds planning to jump in after her if he got to thirty. He was nearly there when she turned her palms down and pushed herself to the surface. She took several heaving breaths before swimming to the side of the pool.

"Are you preparing for a free diving competition?" He masked his concern with a joke.

Sarah pushed herself up on the side of the pool and swung a shapely leg up to climb out. "It's quieter than my thoughts down there."

He studied her, holding the towel out. "You know you can talk to me."

She smiled at him, though her eyes held the same sadness he'd seen for the past few weeks, even before her father's death. "When I can sort my thoughts into something coherent, I will let you know."

"They'll be serving dinner soon. It would be good to get dressed. The chef doesn't like having to wait."

Sarah took the towel. She stepped around him drying herself off and slipping on her shoes. "I don't know why we have to have a set dinner time, or even a chef. It's just the two of us."

"Martine insists on keeping a routine." He watched as she rubbed the towel down one thigh. God help him. "Also, we need to show them their jobs are safe. We have some responsibility to the people we employ."

Her green eyes shot to his, and for the first time in days, she smiled. "I hadn't thought of that. I suppose I can tolerate it for their sake."

So, one way to gain Sarah's approval was to think about his employees. He tucked that observation away for later inspection. "They will appreciate it."

"Are we dressing for dinner?" She asked.

"I think not." He gave her his most winning smile, the one he'd used to charm princesses and business associates alike. Sarah was impervious to it as she wrapped the gauzy robe around her and tied it at the waist. "It is just the two of us after all."

"Right." She picked up her book and towel before turning back toward the chateau. Over her shoulder she told him. "Then I guess I'll see you in about thirty minutes."

He wondered if she had any idea what she did to him. Until a few days ago he'd been the U.K.'s most eligible bachelor. He'd been with supermodels, A-list actresses and heiresses, and this obscure academic with her petite curves pulled at him like a magnet. The pull only became stronger when she challenged him. And heaven knew there was rarely a day when she didn't challenge him.

CHAPTER TWO

August 28, 1996
Edinburgh, Scotland

Dermot's head throbbed, his eyes itched, and if his nose didn't deceive him, he hadn't showered since Saturday. Someone was banging on his front door. His breath caught as a memory zipped through his mind of the morning almost a year ago when Sarah woke him up to give him a tour of Chapel Hill. He'd opened the door of his basement flat to find her standing there with two cups of coffee and the first friendly smile she'd ever given him. He'd fallen half in love with her that day.

His heartbeat thudded in his ears as he pushed through the drowsy fog to get to the door. He knew it was impossible, but what if it was her? What if the wedding had all been for show and she was standing on his doorstep ready to run away from the Stuarts and all their Machiavellian scheming. He gave his head a shake. He knew better.

He unlocked his door and opened it to find Felicia Banks looking as smartly put together as ever. She arched a perfectly shaped eyebrow at the state of him and her nose wrinkled. "Are you hoping she'll smell you all the way in Provence?"

He coughed sheepishly. "That bad, eh?" He shuffled back from the door and let Felicia decide if she dared to come in. "I'm not good company right now."

She leaned into the flat looking from side to side. "So, I see." She cleared her throat. "And smell."

He didn't respond but lumbered his way to the kitchen to put the kettle on. "Tea?"

"Cheers." Felicia took a tentative step inside. She looked over the scene of scattered takeaway containers, empty bottles, and general disarray. "I see you're taking things as expected."

Dermot sighed. "What else am I supposed to do? At least James didna ask me to be on the security detail for the honeymoon."

Felicia made a face suggesting he should know better. "Give him some credit."

"Mmph." Dermot poured boiling water into two cups. At least he had two clean cups.

"I would ask how you are, but I think I can tell." She stepped around an empty takeaway bag to join him in the kitchen.

"How d'ye think I'd be?" He muttered before blowing across the top of his cup to cool it.

Felicia pressed her lips together, likely biting back one of her customary witty retorts. She took a tentative sip of her tea before setting it down. "You did know the wedding was going to happen. You had months to get used to the idea."

It was his turn to raise an eyebrow, irritated. "Have ye ever been in love?"

Felicia cocked her head to the side. "That's not the point."

"If ye had, ye'd know that it doesna go away over a couple of months. I had hope until last Saturday. She might have been engaged to James, but there was still a chance..." He thought about their ill-fated attempt to help Sarah escape from the Stuarts and what it had cost her. "Now, it's really over."

He looked around his flat at the mess. "Except it's not, because in a month they'll be back. And I'll be right beside James every day, protecting the man who married the woman I love."

Felicia looked at him with sympathy. "When you put it like that, I wonder he trusts you at all."

"We've known each other all our lives. I couldna hurt James if I wanted to, not really." Dermot shrugged. "And there have been a few times when I wanted to."

"I won't be repeating that to Mark Shaw." She said referring to the head of security for Alba Petroleum, who was Dermot's boss at least on paper.

"I expect he already knows it." Dermot put his cup down. "I'm sure if James hadna chosen me for his personal detail, Shaw would have me guarding an offshore rig in the Arctic."

Felicia's scanned the room. "A little distance might be the thing you need."

Dermot ran a hand over his face trying to wipe away the lingering fog. "Ye might be right. But my mother is in a care home here. I dinna like to go too far from her. The months I spent in America almost drove me mad with worry."

"I think I remember hearing something about your mother. Sarah has been visiting her, hasn't she?" Felicia picked up the paper takeaway bag and went into the living room.

"Aye, she has. Even when I was acting like a right bell end, Sarah kept my mother in mind. She's better than I deserve." Watching Felicia pluck an empty food container from a chair with her neatly manicured fingers. Dermot sprang into action. He got a bin liner from the cabinet and unfolded it. After waving it through the air to open the bag, he followed her to the living room and held the bag open for her. Felicia dropped the container in. "She's better than both of you deserve."

She had the right of it. Sarah, still in her own misery, had thought about someone else. Hell, she'd been miserable because she put the safety of the people she cared about above her own freedom. "Aye, ye're right."

They worked their way around his living room picking up rubbish until it looked almost livable.

"Cheers." Dermot said when she dropped the last bottle into the bin bag.

Felicia brushed her hands together, marking the end of her cleaning help and gave him a stern look. "You're better than this." She waved a hand as if to indicate all the mess around him. "This is not the man she stood up to the Stuarts for. You may never get her back, but you should try to be worthy of someone like her. You never know when the right person might come along."

Dermot studied her. Felicia had been a good friend when he and Sarah were angry with each other, and when he'd been angry thinking Sarah had chosen James. She'd taken good care of Sarah during her engagement as well, shielding her from the worst of the press and supporting Sarah when she and Anne Stuart butted heads.

He had wondered when he met her if Felicia was one of Walter Stuart's minions. She had told him then she was 'no one's creature but my own' and he was starting to believe it.

He didn't know whether it was gratitude, loneliness, or sheer stupidity which had him leaning toward her, his gaze fixed firmly on her lips.

Felicia recoiled. "Not me, you idiot. Don't be ridiculous."

Her tone wasn't unkind, more like a sister who was out of patience. He shook his head as if breaking himself out of a trance. "Sorry. Don't know why I did that."

"Because you're alone and miserable, and I was kind to you. Don't get confused. You'll get over her faster by working on yourself, not diving into someone else." Felicia cut right to the heart of it as she frequently did. He liked her frankness. It was often hard to come by in the upper echelon of Alba Petroleum.

He sighed and ran a hand through his hair which felt a bit greasy. He looked down at himself. He was barefoot in sweatpants and a shapeless white T-shirt. There were more than a couple of stains on the shirt in colors varying from curry to tea to HP Sauce. "God, I'm disgusting."

Felicia looked him up and down. "You really are. Go take a shower. I'll pick up a bit more out here while you put on something clean. Then we're going out for a proper dinner. You need to get out of this flat."

"I dinna much want to go anywhere, but I think ye're right."

He trudged down the hall to the bathroom dropping the rubbish bag in the kitchen. He hoped there wasn't anything too embarrassing in the living room for Felicia to find. The days since Saturday had been a blur of misery and self-pity. Felicia was right. It was time to snap out of it.

CHAPTER THREE

Riboux, France

Sarah slipped into a bottle green silk dress with folds of fabric draped across the front and fastened at the shoulders. She didn't remember picking it out, but she liked it. Now that Gillian, her stylist, had her measurements, fashionable clothes appeared in her closet, which she thought of as more of a costume closet. Tonight, she would be playing the part of a woman who belonged in a chateau in Provence with her rich, handsome, important husband. She would smile, and blush, and pretend to be happy about being James's wife, at least while other people were around.

She pinned her hair up in a French twist and tried to use the makeup Tony had given her to fix her face into something better than death warmed over. She focused her attention under her eyes, on her cheekbones, forehead, lips, anywhere but her eyes.

Whenever she caught her eyes in the mirror, everything she had seen for the last year came flooding back; Ryan Cumberland's crazy-eyed glee when he told her who Dermot worked for, Amy's misdirected fury, Dermot's eyes when he told her he loved her and when she told him she had chosen James, her father being shot in front of her, Walter Stuart's smug face on her wedding day. It was all there. She hoped she was the only one who could see it. She needed to make the best of her situation. In a fit of bravado, she had told Walter Stuart she had his king in check meaning James was hers to control now. She needed to use their time away from everyone else to make it true. She had to get James on her side. Sex would be an easy way to do it, but she wasn't ready to take that step. She was still processing the past few months.

When she finished applying her makeup, her skin looked dewy, her cheekbones defined, and her lips red and inviting. She wasn't sure anything would fix her expression. She wasn't sure she had it in her to be the person she needed to be, whoever that was. With a deep breath, she managed to pull herself together. She needed to focus on learning what she could about Walter's weaknesses and building some kind of bond with James.

Candles flickered on the dining room table. Warm golden light came from the sun setting outside the doors leading to the veranda. With the cream-colored walls, mahogany furnishings, and white accents, it looked as if the room was made to be lit by the setting sun. The effect was magical.

James waited at the bottom of the stairs to usher her to the table. He wore a button-down shirt and cotton twill trousers. He had dispensed with the sport coat because of the heat, but still cut a handsome figure.

He glowed with approval when she appeared at the top of the curved stone staircase. Sarah made her way carefully down the stairs in gold strappy heels clinging to the wrought iron railing.

"You are stunning." He took her hand and kissed her cheek.

"You are not so bad yourself." Sarah smiled at him. It was hard not to when he turned on his megawatt grin. He really was ridiculously handsome. Tall and lean with slightly tousled dark hair, deep set blue eyes, and a chiseled jaw. James was any girl's dream. Just not hers.

"I hope you enjoy seafood. The chef told me she had a delivery from Marseilles this morning." James pulled the chair to the right of the head of the table out for her.

"I love it." Sarah told him. She addressed Martine who stood sour-faced by the kitchen door waiting to tell the rest of the staff they were ready to eat. "Good evening, Martine."

Martine, a thin woman with salt and pepper hair and an attitude that was plain salty arched an eyebrow at her before exiting to the kitchen.

"She hates me." Sarah whispered to James.

"It's not you. She treats everyone that way." James whispered back as he took his seat beside her. "I'm glad you like seafood. I'm still not sure of your preferences, beyond coffee and cooking for yourself."

"I suppose I've been letting your mother tell me what to eat for the last couple of months. I wasn't really concerned with the menu." Sarah reached for the water goblet in front of her hoping she would remember the comportment lessons Lady Anne had forced her to go through. She hadn't much cared for the lessons, but she didn't want to embarrass herself.

He gave her an indulgent smile. "Let's not allow that to happen again. I want you to trust your instincts as much as I do. My mother has her strengths, and so do you. I was so relieved when you finally stood up to her. I hope the two of you can find a way to work together."

Sarah almost choked on her water. She set the glass down and lifted her napkin so she could cough discreetly behind it.

"Together. I thought she and your father would be going back to Ibiza once the wedding was over."

"I thought so too." James seemed oblivious to Sarah's horror at the idea of working with his mother. "But we had such a short engagement, my uncle suggested she stay to help you transition into the role more smoothly."

James's mother was everything Sarah was not; from a noble Scottish family, rich and schooled in all the nuances of etiquette and comportment a country girl like Sarah couldn't even fathom. Anne was an aristocrat through and through, which meant she looked down on Sarah as an uneducated peasant (never mind the master's degree).

Lady Anne's passive aggressive sniping, while treating Sarah as her own personal Pygmalion had resulted in Sarah giving her a verbal shredding. It was the adult equivalent to a child standing up to a schoolyard bully. Since then, Lady Anne had treated Sarah with slightly more deference. But Anne was also thick as thieves with James's uncle, Walter. They were no doubt plotting against Sarah as she sat there.

Sarah watched James sip his water and smooth his napkin waiting for the first course to be served. The poor man was about to become the rope in a tug of war between Sarah and his family. And Sarah did not intend to lose. "Can we make an agreement?"

"Of course." There was his megawatt smile again.

Sarah kept her tone even and used her hand to adjust the flatware beside her plate. "Can we agree that what goes on in our marriage is between us, and your parents and your uncle don't get a say?"

"Certainly," James put down his glass and laid his hand over hers. "What's between us is between us and no one else."

Sarah felt reassured. She knew she was going to be in a battle with Walter Stuart for James's allegiance. She'd rather not involve his parents as well. James released her hand. "But I don't think their assistance would be harmful when it comes to public appearances or business. They are on the board of Alba Petroleum after all."

That caught Sarah's attention. "Your mother is on the board?"

"Yes. So is my father." He shrugged. "It's a family business."

"Maybe so, but it's also publicly traded. I would think there would be fewer family members on the board." They paused while Martine brought out a pair of salads and set them in front of Sarah and James.

James didn't speak until they were alone again. "We balance our family members with other board members like your solicitor, Lyall Green, and some others who aren't related to us." He paused and thought for a second. "Well, not closely related anyway."

Sarah knew about Lyall Green and thought she might have met some of the other board members at the wedding or at a fundraiser but didn't remember any names. "How are those board members selected?"

James thought for a second. "Ah. Most were chosen by my father and uncle before the company went public."

Sarah cocked her head at him. "And they haven't changed since then. When was that?"

"We went public ten years ago. There are a couple of new members, but they are the minority." James took a bite of his salad. "You should try this. It's delicious."

Sarah followed his suggestion and took a bite of the salad. Peppery greens, sweet beets, and tangy goat cheese filled her mouth with flavor. She chewed while processing what James had told her. Then asked. "Most of the board was handpicked by your uncle and father?"

James gave her a crooked smile. "Well, I think my uncle is probably questioning his decision to add Lyall Green."

Sarah chuckled. Lyall Green had acted as her solicitor and arbitrator while Sarah was challenging whether the prophecy which had landed her in this situation applied to James or Dermot. In the end, Green's efforts to discover who was the real subject of the prophecy proved inconclusive. "I can imagine."

"There are some factions within the board." James said after taking a thoughtful bite. "Some members are more aggressive than others when pursuing new investments. After so many years, there have been disagreements. They're not as cohesive as they once were."

"Have you ever thought it might be time for some new blood." Sarah suggested, her fork poised above her plate.

James shrugged. "I honestly haven't. I haven't seen a problem with the board as it is."

Sarah finished her salad, thinking. Dermot had warned her James was a figurehead, and Walter really ran Alba Petroleum. Now, she could see how right he was. She wondered if James realized it. "So, what happens if you and Walter disagree on how A.P. should be run?"

James thought about it tapping the fingers of his left hand on the table. "That doesn't happen often, but when it does, we usually work it out between ourselves."

Their salad plates were removed and replaced with plates of fish and vegetables on a bed of polenta with a lemon cream sauce. Sarah took a spoonful of polenta. "And what does that look like, working it out between yourselves?"

James savored a bite of fish. "This really is superb." He said. "I suppose we look at the evidence for both arguments and decide what is best for the company."

"What happens if you can't agree?" Sarah pressed.

"Why the sudden interest in the business?" James asked, stabbing a tiny, steamed squash with his fork.

Sarah leaned back in her seat. "I'm only trying to understand the dynamic with you and Walter."

"I know Dermot and my uncle have had their differences, and Walter can seem a bit underhanded at times, but his heart is in the right place. He wants what's best for AP."

"And Scotland?" Sarah took a sip of the dry white wine which had been served with the fish.

"Of course, he wants what's best for Scotland." James picked up his own glass. "We all do."

"I think Walter is very comfortable wielding the power he has amassed and I'm not sure it's always in the best interests of either the company or the country." Sarah took a sip of wine.

James leaned back tapping his fingers softly on the table. "Walter took over the company after my father retired. He's seen us through exponential growth and helped push forward the study on devolution with Westminster. How can you say that?"

"I'm not questioning his accomplishments." Sarah sat forward and returned her glass to its spot on the table. "Only his methods and motives."

"Because you're an expert on the oil industry and Scottish politics?" James snapped.

Sarah raised an eyebrow. She seemed to have ruffled the prince's feathers. "There's no need to get defensive. I'm trying to understand why you value him so much."

James shook his head. "I may have studied business, but Walter has taught me everything about our business and the oil industry. Without his guidance, I wouldn't have lasted a minute as CEO of Alba Petroleum."

"I'm not saying he hasn't been helpful to you." Sarah tried to keep her voice steady. She had found in the past a logical measured approach worked best with James. "I'm only wondering if his methods are still helpful. You have to admit, his treatment of Dermot and his mother was not acceptable."

"Of course, I admit it. It was deplorable." He waved a hand as if pushing away the memory of Walter's past behavior. Sarah would love to tell James that Walter murdered her father. But Walter had also threatened Dermot and everyone else she cared about if she told him. After seeing her father shot in front of her, Sarah knew Walter wouldn't feel an ounce of guilt about murdering Dermot, or Ruaraidh, or anyone else she loved. And if she wanted to get James on her side, it would probably be best not to tell him she had tried to run away from him two days before their wedding.

There had to be something else on Walter. He hadn't batted an eye at shooting Rab in front of half a dozen people. Sarah was sure he'd done it before or worse. She had to find a wedge she could drive between Walter and James. In the meantime, she could chip away at their connection by planting seeds of doubt.

"Do you really think it's the first deplorable thing he's done? It's probably not even the worst." She watched James use his fork to flake off pieces of fish. He avoided her eyes. "Or is it that you don't mind his methods when they work to your benefit?"

His gaze flew to hers; the happy sparkle was gone. They were hard as flint and reminded her of Dermot in a temper. "I don't think I like what you're implying."

She'd struck a nerve. It was rare to see a crack in James's polished and confident persona even in private. It might not have been the best strategy to keep pressing it, but after squirming under Walter Stuart's boot for months, it felt good to feel someone else squirming. "I know you don't like his methods, but you do benefit from them."

"I don't have to defend our business practices to you." His fork clattered against his plate, and his eyebrows drew together, and the finger tapping began again.

"Well, if you mean to lead a country, you're going to have to get used to your methods being questioned and to having to defend them to far tougher audiences than me." Sarah leaned away from the table. "There's a big difference between being the boss and being a leader. Leaders have to take responsibility for their methods."

"That sounds like a naïve way of thinking." He looked her up and down, as if he wasn't quite sure who she was. "Politicians get away with all kinds of bad behavior without accountability."

"You had no idea Walter was holding Dermot's mother hostage for almost a year, or that your most trusted friend was suffering because of it, and you're calling me naïve?" Her tone wasn't so measured anymore. She leaned forward jabbing her index finger at the table in front of her to emphasize her point. "Real leaders, good leaders hold themselves to a higher standard. I thought that was the kind of leader you wanted to be."

His eyebrows rose almost to his hair line. "I wasn't aware you cared so much. Here I thought you were in it for the security and the wardrobe."

He. Did. Not. Sarah was so furious she could feel every hair follicle on her scalp tingling. Every seam of the green silk dress scratched her skin and the straps of her gold sandals felt like they were rubbing blisters on her feet. She inhaled and stood up. Her eyes blazed at him. His blazed right back as if daring her to escalate the conflict.

CHAPTER FOUR

James held his breath, wondering how a simple dinner had gone so wrong so fast. He shouldn't have said that last bit. He knew it was the furthest thing from the truth, but it was what people who didn't know Sarah said about her. She was a chancer, a climber. What was the term Americans used? A gold-digger. If anything, she was the opposite. She was put off by his money. He felt like a cad for throwing the worst rumors about her in her face. He could claim she'd pushed him to it, but that was only an excuse.

Sarah's face was frozen, but her skin had gone from alabaster to near crimson. She fixed her gaze on his, clearly fighting back harsh words. She slowly rose from her seat. When she spoke, her voice was tightly controlled. "You know damned well it isn't true. I would give back every scrap of fabric, every shoe, every carat, and every bodyguard if I could go back to my life before I met you." She drew in a steadying breath. "But that horse has left the barn. My life is broken." Her voice cracked. "I am broken. And I am trying to find my way through this maze of Machiavellian plots. So, you will have to forgive me if my questions annoy you, Lord Caledon."

She raised her hand, her napkin dangling from her fingers. Without another word, she dropped her napkin right onto the fish she'd barely touched and turned on her gold-clad heel and left.

Damn! He'd bollocksed it up in short order. "Sarah, wait."

By the time he made it to the front hall, she was at the top of the stairs. He heard the door slam before he made it to the landing. She might not like wearing high heels, but they didn't seem to slow her down.

Bloody hell! He'd put his foot in it.

James turned around and slumped back down the stairs. Martine stood in the doorway to the dining room looking concerned. He told her "Dinner is over. Thank you."

He'd lost his appetite. He walked out the French doors at the back of the house onto the veranda and out into the gardens.

Would Sarah ever stop confounding him? Countless women around the world would give up a limb to be with him. He had money, influence, and managed not to be a complete arse like a lot of the men he knew from similar backgrounds. Then again, if the evening's conversation was any indicator, he might be more of an arse than he thought.

She had cared about him once. They had been on one date when she and Dermot had been avoiding each other. She had asked about his ambitions, his hobbies, and things he found fulfilling outside of work. She'd wanted to know James Stuart the man, not James Stuart the heir, CEO, billionaire. It had been glorious. Yet when she had finally shown some interest in his work, he had lashed out like a petulant child.

He silently acknowledged the security guard who stood watch at the end of the garden before turning back to the house. He owed his wife an apology.

***

Sarah was coming out of the bathroom with a damp cloth to lay over her eyes when there was a knock at the door. She just wanted to be left alone. She didn't need Martine looking down her nose at her while offering to have food sent up, or one of the maids she'd seen gossiping in the kitchen garden sneaking a peek at *'l'Américaine'* while turning down her bed, or anything else she was more than capable of doing herself. "I don't need anything. Thank you."

"I do." James's voice came from the other side of the door, sounding chastened. "I need to apologize."

Sarah didn't say anything. She needed a different plan of attack when dealing with James. She had gone after Walter too directly at dinner. She had to work on James and strengthening their relationship before she could make any moves against Walter. James might be the handsome face of the Stuart steamroller that had flattened her life, but he was still part of it. It was clear James and Walter's relationship was deeply enmeshed both personally and professionally. Disentangling them was going to be hard. As much as she wanted out of this situation, she was going to have to play the long game.

"Please, Sarah." He pleaded through the door.

"Go away, James." She took a step forward, still not sure she wanted to talk to him again tonight. "I'm not in the mood to hear any apologies."

He was silent for a moment. "I deserve that. I acted like a spoiled child, which I suppose I am at times."

Sarah listened. James had acknowledged he was spoiled before, but he rarely admitted to behaving badly. She was still figuring out how to handle her new husband. Challenging him only seemed to make him want her more. In the past he'd responded to honesty, but tonight her honesty had caused him to lash out. She must have touched on an insecurity.

"I wish I could take it all back." His voice was quiet and came from closer to the floor. He must be sitting on the other side. "Not only what I said tonight, but all of it. I would love to go back to the day we met when you had no idea who I was, and you were happy to meet me. I would do so many things differently."

It wouldn't have changed anything for Sarah. She had already been half in love with Dermot. James and Dermot's relationship had already been fractured. Ryan Cumberland had already begun stalking her through her roommate. Sarah's mother had already been chewed up and spit out by their people to fulfill the same prophecy. Her grandmother had already fled her home in Scotland to escape Nazi treasure hunters. "I think you would have to go back generations to find a time before the damage was done."

"I suppose you're right. Both of us are the products of generations of plots and schemes. We weren't made for happiness." His tone matched hers.

Not made for happiness. How many times had she felt that? Between her mother's depression and mood swings and being an outcast in the backwater where she grew up, Sarah had never had it easy. She had started to believe she could make something of her life when the Stuarts had come for her. Since then, she'd been told she was made to preserve tradition and her family's gift. James was told he was made to carry on the Stuart name and reclaim the throne of Scotland. It reminded Sarah once again that she and James were in the same boat. James just had a more comfortable seat.

Within a few steps she had reached the door. She paused with her hand on the doorknob. "We don't have to accept it. We don't have to stick to the plans someone else made for us before we were even born."

"What do you suggest we do?" He asked. "We are who we are."

Sarah pulled the door open. James sat on the floor leaning a shoulder against the doorway. He looked up at her, his face full of misery and guilt. Sarah sat down next to him. "I suggest we become a team."

"We are. We pledged that in front of our friends and family."

"Not exactly." She shook her head. "You are still thinking about your life in terms of how to fulfill what your parents and uncle want, what they've told you you should want."

"I think you'll find it's more than my parents and my uncle." He looked thoughtful. "Or even Seonag, and Lyall Green."

"What do you mean?"

He paused, as if choosing his words carefully. "It may not be for as long as your family has, but we have been preserving a legacy for many generations. My grandparents had forgotten about it in the buzz of the early twentieth century, with the war and all. But the family here has been keeping the secret for two thousand years."

"Ah. Dermot told me your family believes you're descended from Jesus." She'd laughed it off, but this was a new wrinkle to add to an already convoluted situation. "Can you explain more?"

"It might be easier to show you." He studied her for a moment. "But I think that's a problem for another day."

She heaved a sigh. "Probably. I'm tired, and this conversation is supposed to be about us."

He reached out his hand and rested it palm-up on his knee between them. "I like the sound of that."

Sarah put her hand in his. "I know you have your team of people, your parents, your business associates, your friends. That's all fine, but we have to be each other's priorities now. We've got to have each other's backs, which might mean standing up to your uncle and your parents when what they want doesn't agree with what's best for us."

"You are right." He wrapped his fingers around hers. "That goes both ways."

Sarah tried not to let her bitterness creep into her tone. "I've left my career behind. I have no close family. You're all I've got."

He looked guilty. "And I treated you like I did earlier. I'm so sorry."

"So am I." Sarah conceded. "I want to understand something of how the business works so I can support you. I'll reserve my judgement until I know more."

He brought his other hand to cover their joined hands. "We can't go back in time, but let's make this a new beginning. Give me a chance to prove how much I care for you. Let's make this honeymoon the beginning of a proper courtship."

Sarah had to say yes. They were already married. If she was ever going to be rid of Walter and the threat he posed to Dermot and her family, she needed James on her side. "Okay. A new beginning."

James leaned across the space between them and kissed her. It wasn't passionate or practiced like their first kiss. It was chaste, and hopeful. "I hope I can be worthy of you."

CHAPTER FIVE

In the morning, Sarah was taking her coffee on the veranda when James approached her. She reminded herself they were aiming for a new beginning. She couldn't hide under the water forever. Their agreement the night before seemed to have done James some good at least. He had a new spring in his step.

"Morning, my love." He kissed her cheek. She was still getting used to his casual shows of affection. They had started during their engagement, and Sarah had told herself it was all part of the charade. They had to appear to be in love when there were others around, but James kept it up even when they were alone. Of course, James believed he loved her. Sarah reminded herself the whole reason they'd gotten married was to produce an heir. Eventually, his casual affection was going to have to be something more.

"Morning." She picked up her coffee cup and leaned back in her chair. He wore cargo pants and hiking boots with a collared shirt. "You look like you're ready for a hike."

"I thought it was time we got out to see the sights." He poured himself a cup of tea and began spreading some chevre on a slice of toast. "And I can start explaining a bit about my family's history."

"Great. Is it safe to go out?" Sarah was used to the tight security they'd had in Edinburgh, and she'd been pursued by more than one assassin since meeting the Stuarts.

"We'll have protection with us, but I'm not worried around here." He bit into his toast. "We leaked a decoy reservation for our honeymoon on Lake Como. It should be days before the press catches up to us."

"Hmm. Smart." She was relieved they didn't have to worry about paparazzi at least for a few days. "So, we're not going far?"

He raised his hand to point toward a ridge to the southwest of the house. "On the other side of that ridge is one of Christianity's most holy sites, and I think it's a good place to start exploring." He grinned. "It will be like hiking up Arthur's Seat, but at the top there's a church."

Sarah looked skeptical. Of course, she had studied enough of religion to know the brand of Christianity her neighbors in Kettle Holler had practiced wasn't the same as what was practiced here in France. The Christian world was full of variety, but in her experience, it was rarely friendly to people like her. "I don't know. I haven't had the best experiences with churches."

"Ah, but this one is in the Grotto of Saint Mary Magdalene. After being pushed out of church leadership by the patriarchy, she is one to welcome outcasts."

Sarah narrowed her eyes at him. Despite their claims, the Stuarts seemed to only be nominal Christians. "I didn't realize you were a believer."

James shook his head. "Oh, I'm not. At least not in the sense that most Christians believe." He leaned back in his chair satisfied he had piqued her curiosity. "I'll be happy to tell you about it while we walk up to the shrine. It is some fascinating and ancient folklore."

He knew precisely which button to push. "Alright." Sarah began dressing a slice of toast for herself. "I suppose hiking boots are in order."

"There should be some in your closet." He said around a mouthful of toast. "You'll want to dress modestly, maybe a skirt over shorts. And bring a scarf to cover your hair in the church."

"Do people still do that?" She hadn't heard of women covering their hair in church in decades.

"Not at most places." He admitted. "But this isn't most places, and you and I aren't most people."

***

When they arrived at the beginning of the trail outside Saint Maximin de la Sainte Baume, Sarah read the marker. "My French isn't good at all, but does this say the 'Path of Kings'?"

"Yes, I'm impressed." James said.

Sarah shot him a look. "Let me guess, you've only ever taken this path."

"It is the fastest route." He felt a blush creeping up from his collar. Her eyebrow rose in a perfect arch of suspicion prompting him to add. "And probably the easiest."

She looked around. "Where are the other paths?"

"The Canape Path starts over there." He nodded toward the hostelry serving as the main building on the compound. "On the other side of that building, and I think the Path of Giniez starts further over there."

"Right. Path of Canape it is." She started in the direction of the hostelry. "No reason why I should be the only one in unfamiliar territory."

James enjoyed the way her skirt clung to her hips and swirled around her ankles. He loved it when she pushed him out of his comfort zone. She rarely missed an opportunity.

He followed Sarah to the trail head. They waited for a bodyguard to precede them a few paces before they started their way up to the monastery. Sarah's legs seemed to eat up the trail. When her skirt got in the way on the steeper parts, she stopped and knotted it near her knees on either side. "I can take it down when we get up there."

"I can tell you grew up in the mountains. You're much better at this when you're not hungover." The last time he'd taken Sarah on a hike, she'd been suffering the aftereffects of a night on the town.

She paused with one foot on a stone step cut into the trail. "It's amazing what a good night's sleep, hydration, and a good breakfast can do. Also, the Folklore department office at Carolina was five stories up and the building only had one small elevator. I climbed a lot of stairs."

"That would do it." He motioned for her to walk on. "Shall I tell you about how Mary Magdalene came to be here?"

Sarah looked at the path ahead of them. "Not until we get up there. I'm enjoying the walk."

He let her walk in peace. Whatever peace he could give her, he would.

"I thought you said they call it the Rock of Mercy." Sarah stood at the bottom of the stone steps climbing to the rock outcrop which formed the cave. "There doesn't appear to be any mercy in this climb."

James stopped beside her looking up at the stairs. He was already feeling the heat of the Provencal summer. He was sure she was as well. "What kind of pilgrimage would it be if the walk wasn't hard? Besides, I thought you were good with stairs."

"Pilgrimage indeed." Sarah shook her head taking the first step.

"There are exactly one hundred and fifty steps to represent the one hundred and fifty psalms of King David." James told her as he started up behind her.

"Are we supposed to recite the psalms as we climb?" Sarah asked over her shoulder.

"Do you know any?" He thought she hadn't been raised in the church.

Sarah shot him a look. "I might be suspicious of religion, but I have read the Bible. Although the only psalm that comes to mind is the twenty-third."

"The Lord is my shepherd. I shall not want." He remembered from the chapel he'd been required to attend at boarding school.

Sarah continued walking. "He maketh me to lie down in green pastures: he leadeth me beside the still waters."

"He restoreth my soul: he leadeth me in the paths of righteousness for his name's sake." James came up beside her.

"Yea, though I walk through the valley of the shadow of death, I will fear no evil: for thou art with me; thy rod and thy staff they comfort me." A dark expression came over her when she recited the fourth verse. He could only imagine she was thinking about the attempts made on her life, and about her father's death. Her tone turned grim. "Thou preparest a table before me in the presence of mine enemies."

He took her hand, giving it a reassuring squeeze. "Thou anointest my head with oil; my cup runneth over."

She stopped near the top of the staircase and surveyed the view. James followed her gaze across the valley and mountains beyond. It was breathtaking. In a hushed voice, "Surely goodness and mercy shall follow me all the days of my life; and I will dwell in the house of the Lord for ever." She sighed and waved at the valley. "If there is a God, this is his house. Not some church."

"Perhaps that's why Mary Magdalene chose this place, because of the view it gave her of the Lord's house." He said.

"If you believe the legend." Sarah muttered.

"Wasn't it you who told me every legend begins with a thread of truth?" James took her elbow to help her up the last few steps.

Soon they arrived at the top and went through the stone arch serving as a gateway into the courtyard which was bounded by buildings on two sides and the mountain behind. Sarah looked around instantly curious. "What are these buildings?"

"The monastery. Monks began guarding the cave in the fifth century. They've traded off different orders over time and continued making improvements. After the revolution at the end of the eighteenth century it was left in ruins. Eventually, they rebuilt the monastery and pilgrimages resumed."

Sarah turned to face the mountain rising above them. "It's like a hood."

"Yes, my father explained it to me when I was a boy." He held up two hands at an angle meeting at the fingertips like a house. He moved them to demonstrate the movement of the plates as he described it. "Two tectonic plates meet here, and both push up until one is pushed slightly further than the other and folds over to create the cave here."

CHAPTER SIX

Sarah couldn't help thinking of the Moine Thrust at Inchnadamph, and how dramatic it is to see one tectonic subjugated under another, so striking that local legend said the devil himself made it in a fit of rage. Here, at this holy site, both plates rose together until one bent over the other almost protectively. It was an interesting contrast. She caught herself wishing her cousin Bridget was there to give a more in-depth explanation of the geology. The cave created by this formation was big enough to build a church by walling off the exposed side complete with stained glass windows topped by stone arches.

"Are you ready to see the church?" James held out a hand toward the façade.

He led her to the double doors, motioning for her to cover her head. Sarah untied the blue silk scarf around her collar and draped it over her hair, throwing the ends over her shoulders. She also untied the sides of her skirt, so it once again hung to her ankles.

Inside were all the trappings of a church. There were rows of pews, a magnificent white marble altar, and statuary. The only difference was the ceiling of rough, uneven rock and the size. Beyond the platform where the altar and pews were, the cavern extended to include a lower area and more beyond. The cave was enormous, and Sarah wondered at the idea of a woman living there, sheltered by the stone, but so high above the forest. Had she been alone? Were there followers with her?

In spite of the pews, imposing altar, statues, and candles like any other church, the air felt different there. Goosebumps rose on Sarah's arms. Her rational mind knew it had to be a result of the temperature change from the late summer outside to the coolness and dampness of the cave, but it was something more. There was a quiet energy emanating from the rock around them. Maybe it was the energy of the plates pushing against each other. Sarah felt it like a low hum under the quiet shuffles of the reverent visitors.

They watched as people prayed in front of the altar; heads bowed before the crucifix, surrounded by imposing white marble stark against the dimness of the cave reflecting every spark of light. Not for the first time Sarah admired the design. Each of the religious icons stood out from its surroundings. In a place where light was scarce, they seemed to have their own glow which someone less familiar with the materials might believe was supernatural. The chapel was designed to induce awe, and it did.

After a few moments observing the chapel, James drew Sarah to an area behind the altar platform. Their first stop was an alcove under the altar where an ornate reliquary sat behind bars. "These are the bones of Mary Magdalene. The story goes they were found in the thirteenth century and moved here."

Sarah glanced at James who kept his focus on the glass and metal container. "Do you really believe that?"

He half shrugged. "I believe they found remains of a woman and now thousands of pilgrims come to see them. If they are hers, then the veneration is justified."

"And if they aren't hers, all of these pilgrims are being duped." Sarah kept her voice low as she examined the reliquary. Behind its glass shield the ornate and macabre display included a glass capsule containing something that might be human bones. Although it was hard to tell through all the glass and decorations.

"Or they've taken a common woman who would otherwise have decayed in the ground and elevated her to holy status where her remains are revered by many. People like their symbols. They like something to rally around or revere, to travel hundreds of miles and climb a mountain to see. It's why monarchies persist." He bumped her shoulder with his. "Which explanation do you prefer?"

Sarah took a step away from the alcove. "The one about how relics like those are vestiges of pre-Christian ancestor worship."

James laughed, head shaking. He wrapped his arm around her waist and whispered in her ear. "Aren't we relics of pre-Christian ancestor worship?"

"Only if we want to be." Sarah gave him a saccharine sweet smile before pulling away to view the next item on display.

To the right of the reliquary stood a statue of Mary Magdalene being lifted up by angels. Lit from beneath by electric lights and racks of lit candles, the white marble stood stark against the dark rock behind it, a beacon to believers in Magdalene's divinity. The flickering of the candles created a warm glow around the bottom of the statue.

The flickering light danced across the flowing robes of the angels, and a feeling of peace swept over her. The ever-present hum she'd felt since entering the cave settled into her bones. James brought her a lit taper "I thought you might like to light a candle for your father."

She was touched by his gesture. "You know I'm not a believer."

His smile was soft, reflecting support. "Then light a candle and meditate on the good things you remember about him. Either way, it keeps his memory in your heart."

Sarah gave his hand a squeeze before approaching the racks of candles. It was a sweet thought. She held her hands in front of her as if in prayer and thought about her father. She hadn't known Rab Ballantyne for long, but she had read her mother's account of their affair. They had loved each other so much that Rab had mourned the loss of Molly for decades and Molly had never gotten over the heartbreak of being abandoned by him.

She had seen such hope and regret in Rab's eyes when he'd told her he was going to rehab for his drinking. She had shared his hope for success, and as far as she knew he had been successful. He had certainly been sober when he had thrown himself in front of Grant MacDuff, the father of Sarah's heart. Remembering the sudden loss of him opened a hollow place in her chest, and a tear slipped down her cheek.

No, she was supposed to remember something good about Rab. She thought back to the moment she'd known he was her father. He'd sung a Robert Burns song about a lass named 'Mally' and the crack in his voice had confirmed her suspicion, her ne'er do well Da. She'd been both overjoyed and a little disappointed to meet him, but it was a fitting way to remember her father, with a mix of emotions and a song in her heart.

When she had fixed the memory in her mind, Sarah lit a candle for him and whispered a soft. "Thank you, Rab."

She took a step back and blew out the taper. James was lighting a candle of his own a few steps away. She wondered what his was for but decided not to ask. He respected her grief; she would respect his privacy. When he turned away from the candles, his eyes lit on her and he looked a little embarrassed. He held out his hand to her, and Sarah took it.

They moved through the cave to an alcove containing a pool of dark water. The water dripped from the rock above the pool. It was blocked off from the room by bars. The hum Sarah had been feeling became more pronounced. She barely heard James say, "This is the spring of Saint Sidonius of Aix. Legend has it he was a blind man who was healed by Jesus, before coming to France with the…"

The humming grew louder punctuated by the steady drip drip of the water from the rock. James's voice faded into the background. The natural cave sounds and the hum drowned out the human sounds of talking, footsteps and whispered prayers. Sarah looked at James to see if he felt or heard what she was feeling, but he talked on, oblivious to what Sarah saw. In the dimness of the cave beyond James's shoulder, a woman in robes knelt outside the bars by the spring. Sarah followed her gaze, trying to see what she was looking at. There was nothing but the still water, disturbed only by the steady drip, drip from the rock above. When Sarah looked back, the woman was closer, standing on the other side of James. Sarah leaned forward looking around him while the woman mirrored the motion. The woman looked to be around middle age. Crow's feet marked the corners of her eyes and laugh lines bracketed her mouth. Her nose was aquiline, and slightly larger in proportion to the rest of her face. The candlelight around them sparkled in her brown eyes as she smiled at Sarah. Sarah could only look on, her head buzzing.

The woman spoke. Her voice was soft and her tone motherly, but her speech was strange. It reminded Sarah of when she had heard her great aunt Eilidh sing the lines of "The River Maiden" that she'd been unable to translate. The woman spoke in another language, but while Sarah's ears heard the foreign words her mind registered their meaning. "He is a scion of the King."

A chill crept up Sarah's spine. This had to be a hallucination brought on by the stress of the last week and the power of suggestion. She shook her head and pinched herself. When she looked back, the woman was gone.

"Your path is difficult." Sarah nearly jumped out of her skin. She whipped her head around to find the woman on her other side now. "But you are blessed."

Did the Stuarts pay her? Was this some kind of plot to gaslight her into believing she should be with James? Sarah looked at James, but he was no longer beside her. He had moved on to look at another statue. Sarah turned back to find the woman watching her. Her expression was kind. "You will be the mother of the king."

'Yeah, I've heard that one before.' Sarah thought. She whispered to the woman, "Did the Stuarts put you up to this?"

"I did not care to hear my role when they told me either." The woman took a step toward the bars blocking visitors from the spring. "You will see."

The woman stepped through the bars. Not between them. Through them. Sarah's jaw dropped. Chills raced across her skin. All she could do was gape as the woman walked into the spring fading from view with every step until she was gone. Sarah's breath caught in her chest, as if her lungs couldn't expand. Her heart raced.

***

"Are you alright?" James returned to Sarah's side looking concerned. "You look flushed."

Sarah gripped his hand and forced a breath past the tightness in her chest. She took several deep breaths trying to shake off the lingering disorientation from the vision, or visitation, or whatever it was. She tried to figure out how it could have happened and whether she could believe what she was seeing. "Yes, I'm fine. I think it's a little cool and close in here. Can we go outside?"

"Of course." He offered her his arm. Sarah took it, grateful for the support.

The sun was nearly blinding as they emerged from the cave into the courtyard. Unlike the cold damp cave, the courtyard was hot and sunbaked. Sarah headed for a nearby bench. "I think I should sit for a few minutes."

"I'll get you some water." James walked toward the monastery.

Sarah took a few deep breaths, adjusting to the change in light. Could the woman really have been a trick of her mind, a hallucination? This had to be something from her subconscious, some kind of projection. It couldn't be real. She'd had visions before, but they were always of her mother or grandmother sending images which were probably from her own memories. They didn't converse with her.

Was this it? Was this the moment when she cracked? She'd half expected to have a breakdown ever since she had come to understand what had happened to her mother. If anything would cause a breakdown, the last few weeks could do it.

"Here," James returned with a paper cup of water.

Sarah took the cup with shaking hands and drank the cold water, dowsing some of her misfiring thoughts. "Thank you. I'm not sure what happened to me in there."

"The damp can be a shock after the walk up here." James acknowledged taking a seat beside her on the bench. He waited patiently while Sarah caught her breath and let the shaking subside. After a few minutes, the goosebumps faded, and her skin started to warm in the sun. Sarah worked to ground herself focusing on concrete things like the stone bench underneath her, and the cool water. After several minutes she felt almost normal, at least physically.

"Better?" James asked.

"Yes, I think I'm ready for the walk back down." She stood with more energy than she thought she had. "You can tell me the legend of how Mary Magdalene came to live here. You know I love a good legend."

"Alright." James took the cup from her fingers and disposed of it.

The walk down the side of the mountain was considerably easier than the walk up, and they took it at a comfortable pace. The physical exertion helped to calm Sarah's nerves. Once they had crossed through the monastery gates, James began to tell her the story.

"You know Mary Magdalene was the first of Jesus's disciples to see him after the resurrection, yes?" He glanced at her checking for understanding.

"Of course."

His blue eyes twinkled. "Most of the early church knowledge comes from Paul and is decidedly skewed to his agenda."

"I'm glad to hear you acknowledge Paul had an agenda, and don't take the epistles as the only view of the early church."

He gave her a half smile reminding her too much of Dermot for her comfort. "I did some studies of my own at university. Well, some historians believe Mary was another leader in the early church. In fact, she was so revered that she was exiled from the Holy Land."

"Because Rome or early church leaders didn't like a woman getting so much attention?" Sarah warmed to the topic embracing the distraction rather than ruminating on the vision from the cave.

"I expect it was a bit of both." James offered her a hand on a spot where a stone was missing from the steps. "For whatever reason, Mary Magdalene and another Mary, Maximin," He waved in the direction of the nearby town of Sainte Maximin de Sainte Baume. "Lazarus and a 'dark-skinned' girl described alternately as a servant or Sarah the Egyptian were put into a rudderless boat and set adrift in the Mediterranean."

"A rudderless boat?" Sarah interrupted. "Hmm. Saint Mungo's mother was set adrift pregnant in a coracle with no oars in the Firth of Forth."

"I do remember reading that." James said. "He's the patron saint of Glasgow, right?"

"Yes, and if I'm remembering right, he was a bit of a politician. I wonder how much of that story was legend building. Maybe he pulled it from the Mary Magdalene legend."

"He wouldn't be the first to pull from earlier legends." James added. "I suspect this rudderless boat borrowed from the story of Moses being set adrift in a basket."

"I didn't know they taught comparative folklore at Swiss boarding schools." Sarah teased.

"Saint Andrews." James gave her a side-eyed look. "In any case, Mary's boat washed up at what is now Sainte-Marie de la Mer. They brought Christianity to France before anyone else in Europe. After founding the church, she retired to live up there."

They paused near the bottom of the stairs where the trail back to the hostelry began and looked back up at the monastery perched on the rock face like an eagle's nest.

James went on. "Local legend says she climbed to the top of the ridge seven times a day to pray. There is a shrine up there now. It has an amazing view of the land. You can see for miles. I used to think she went up there so she could see Jesus coming when he returned."

"Returned?" Sarah studied him. "Like the second coming?"

James paused. "Mmm. Something like that."

Sarah wondered what he meant but decided to stick to the subject at hand. "How long did she live up there?"

"Thirty years, and she didn't have those carefully crafted stairs to get up and down." He went back to walking the trail.

"I'm not sure how much is accurate or the early Christian church's fetishization of asceticism."

Sarah laughed. "You sound like an academic."

His cheeks turned slightly pink. "Given my family's connection to the area, I developed a fascination with local history. My reading on the subject sort of snowballed. There are some books on it in the library at the house."

"I've never seen this side of you." Sarah bumped his shoulder, enjoying the camaraderie. Even if she didn't want to be married to him, they had once been friends. If she wanted him to choose her over Walter, she needed that friendship. "I like it."

James smiled, clearly pleased with himself. He took her hand and laced their fingers together. They walked the rest of the way hand in hand.

CHAPTER SEVEN

Edinburgh

One thing he liked about his mother's new care home was that her room was on the ground floor and afforded her a view of the garden. The home Walter Stuart had moved her to when she'd been his hostage was in the city center, and although it had a courtyard garden, his mother's room had been floors above it. She hadn't been able to see much and had only been able to visit the courtyard occasionally. Now, there were walking paths where she could stroll accompanied by staff, and benches where she could take her knitting outside. They had many patients like Seonag with Alzheimer's Disease or some form of dementia, and they were staffed with people who knew how to take care of their specific needs. The place seemed a much better fit and he didn't mind the longer bus ride to visit.

It was drizzling that day, and he found his mother in a common room which served as a larger sitting room. The lounge was full of comfortable chairs arranged in groups. Seonag was in a corner facing the room knitting. Her lips were moving as she counted her stitches. She kept glancing around the room. When she saw him, her face lit up. "Hello, young man."

She didn't recognize him. She had known exactly who he was when they'd come to move her from the previous home. The job would have been a lot more difficult if she hadn't. But he couldn't be surprised she didn't know him today. The days when she recognized him as her son were outnumbered now by the days when she thought he was a nice young man who came to visit her. "Hello, Miss Sinclair. How are ye feeling, today?"

"Och. All right I suppose." She lowered her knitting to her lap and gave him with a soft smile.

"Are ye settling in then? This seems like a much more comfortable place than the last one ye were in." He glanced around at the other people in the room. There was a couple sitting on their own enjoying the large windows which looked out onto the garden, and a few families visiting their loved ones. It looked as nice as a care home could.

"It's verra nice here." Seonag told him, although he could tell she didn't quite mean it. She went back to knitting without meeting his eyes.

"Is there something wrong?"

"Och, no." She waved a hand in dismissal. "It's only an old woman worrying. Nothing to fash about."

He let the subject drop and they sat for a few minutes with only the sound of her needles clicking and sliding. "Have ye been outside? The grounds look lovely."

"Eh." She half shrugged, focused on her knitting. His mother had rarely hid her opinions from him over the years. It wasn't until the onset of her illness that she made a habit of not answering his questions and hiding things from him. If he hadn't developed the habit of reading her body language to tell when she wasn't telling him something, he might not have noticed her needles moving faster.

"Is there a problem with the grounds?" He leaned closer to catch her attention.

She turned her head to look out the window. Her fingers didn't slow.

"Seonag?" He was afraid to call her mum now. She rarely recognized him as her son, and it upset her if he tried to remind her.

She breathed deep, and he could see the debate happening in her mind. She let her knitting fall to her lap, lowering her voice. Dermot leaned forward to hear her, his brow creasing in worry. "He's out there."

An icy chill swept down his back. "Who is out there?"

Seonag's shook her head slowly. "Auld Scratch."

"The devil?" Seonag confirmed with a grim nod. His mother had never been a particularly religious person, so he was certain she didn't believe the actual devil was in the garden of her care home. "And he's in the garden?"

She nodded again, and he felt the fear radiating off her. He was clearly going to have to find out more. "Is he a resident here? Can ye point him out?"

She shook her head. "Only in the garden."

He pressed on. "Does he work in the garden?"

She raised an eyebrow. "Not likely in his suit."

"He wears a suit. A tailored suit?" He pressed on. Could it be a doctor or was someone else visiting her here. "Does he talk to anyone else, or just you?"

Seonag looked from side to side as if watching for Auld Scratch himself. "Only me. Only in the garden."

"And ye dinna recognize him?" Who was he kidding? She didn't recognize her own son most of the time. It could have been anyone she'd known before and if she hadn't seen them in a few years, she wouldn't have recognized them. "Did he give ye a name?"

She gave her head a quick shake. Dermot could see tears starting to pool in her eyes. "It's all right, Seonag. I'll have a word with the staff and have them keep an eye out for him. Can ye describe him?"

She picked up her knitting and slowly executed a few stitches, as if she was thinking. "He's old, gray hair."

"Alright. Gray hair and a suit." Could be half the doctors in the building, or someone visiting another resident. "Anything else ye can remember?"

"His voice. It was so familiar, but I couldna place it. I know I'd heard it before." She pressed her lips together in frustration.

"What did he say to ye?" Dermot hoped she could remember.

Seonag thought for a moment before shaking her head slowly. A tear spilled over and trickled down her cheek. "I can't…"

"It's alright." Dermot patted her arm. "I'll have a word with Patricia. We'll try to make sure he doesna come back to bother ye." Dermot made a mental note to talk with his mother's case manager before he left. "Now, tell me about what ye're knitting."

"Och. It's a scarf for my wee Dermot." At the mention of his name, her face transformed from worried to glowing. "Do ye know my Dermot? He's a fine lad."

"I'm sure he is." He agreed, not convinced it was true.

***

"Has my mother had any other visitors?" Dermot sat across the desk from his mother's case manager. "She's reluctant to go into the garden because of someone who spoke with her out there."

Patricia, a motherly looking woman in middle age, with a helmet of brown-gray hair and large round glasses, which she wore on a chain around her neck, turned to the computer. "Let me see." She typed a few words, clicked a few times on the mouse, and then stared at the screen while tapping the down arrow on her keyboard. While he waited, Dermot glanced around the office. A plant rested on the windowsill, framed certificates hung on the walls. In the corner an end table had a stack of magazines. On top was a copy of a tabloid, a photo of Sarah and James looking at each other in the doorway of Saint Margaret's chapel taking the prime spot.

He clamped down on the rage bubbling up inside him. He couldn't get away from them. He didn't think Patricia was a bad person, but people eating up the celebrity gossip pushed out by those tabloids were the market which kept the beast chasing people like James and Sarah.

Patricia turned back to him. "No, you're the only visitor she's had."

"Hmm. She's reluctant to go in the garden because she says a man spoke to her. She wasn't clear about what he said, but it clearly upset her. She seems afraid to go outside now."

Patricia gave him a look of mild concern. He was sure it was the look she wore whenever she talked with family members. "Was she able to describe this man?"

"Not in detail. She said he was older, with gray hair and he wore a suit. She also said his voice was familiar." Dermot lifted a hand as if to say, 'that's all I got.'

Patricia's eyebrows lifted and she looked off to the left as if trying to remember. "I suppose some of our doctors might fit that description, but I can't imagine what one of them could have said to scare her. They know how stressful her condition can be."

"I expect they would." It was becoming apparent there was no clear easy answer to his mother's problem. "Is it possible someone could get on the grounds without being in the visitor log?"

Patricia thought about it. "I suppose it's possible, but the garden is well-fenced. Some of our patients have been known to elope. We do our best with the fence and gates, but I can't say it's completely impossible."

"Could it be another resident?" He could see some of the residents saying something outrageous and mistaking his mother for someone they already knew.

Patricia gave him a sympathetic smile. "It is possible." Possible, but her tone said it was unlikely. "I don't think we have any residents who fit that description, especially not the suit." She laced her fingers together and rested her hands on the desk in front of her. "The other thing to consider, Mr. Sinclair, is that your mother's disease may be progressing. It's not uncommon for Alzheimer's patients to suffer from hallucinations or paranoia. They may see people who aren't there. Sometimes they relive bad memories which seem completely real to them. While it is possible your mother had a visitor that wasn't in the log, or another patient, or even a doctor, it's equally as likely that she hallucinated it."

Dermot sank back in his chair. He knew what Patricia was saying was the most likely story. Still, his mother's fear was real. An itch to do something spread from his shoulders down. The need to take action prickled under his skin. But there was no solution. The battle they were fighting was inside his mother's brain. "Well, thank ye for talking with me. I apprcciatc it."

Patricia walked him out with a reassuring smile. "And we will keep an eye on anyone who visits or approaches your mother in case it's not a hallucination."

"Cheers." The desk attendant unlocked the door letting him out of the patient area. Outside, he scanned the fence and front gates which were intended to keep the residents from leaving the grounds for their own safety. They weren't necessarily designed to keep people from coming into the grounds. No doubt a well-placed bribe of a gate or desk attendant could get a person in without recording their visit. Dermot knew a few gray-haired men who wore suits and had the money to do exactly that.

CHAPTER EIGHT

August 30, 1996
Riboux, France

Sarah took a deep breath and slid under the water. She thought about her mother and waited. Water filled her ears muffling the noise of the world, of the house, of her thoughts. Within a few heartbeats, her mother was with her. "They won't have you. I won't let them."

"They've got me, Mama." They did. It seemed no matter how hard Sarah tried to get away, she kept getting pulled in deeper. She'd had fun with James despite the weird experience in the cave. She had enjoyed most of the day. It felt as much a betrayal as their first kiss had. He wasn't the man she wanted. She was sure he wasn't the man she belonged with.

"You're going to be free." Her mother's voice cooed in her ear, but Sarah couldn't see her way to freedom, not with the likes of Walter Stuart around. Sarah waved her hands at her shoulders to keep herself underwater. She could inhale, breathe in the water and none of it would matter anymore. She could finish what her mother had started all those years ago.

"You are blessed." The words rang through Sarah's mind even as her lungs burned. Her haven had been invaded by the image and voice of the woman she'd seen in the cave.

"Won't let them have you." Molly's voice became urgent like it had that day in the bathtub. "Not my baby."

"Your path is difficult." The voice from the cave overlapped Molly's, but unlike her mother's increased urgency, the woman's voice was calm.

"Not my baby. Not my baby." Molly muttered again and again.

"Your path is difficult." The woman whispered.

"Won't let them have you.'" Her mother nearly screamed in her ear.

"He is a scion of the king." Sarah pushed with her feet off the bottom of the pool and shot to the surface desperate to make the noise in her head stop.

Her breathing was ragged as she made her way to the ladder. She climbed out and collapsed on the pool deck coughing and gasping for air.

Sarah looked toward the house hoping no one could see her. The last thing she needed was a maid or James fussing over her. She worked to control her breathing, eventually she was able to sit up and breathe normally again. She retrieved her towel and robe before going back inside.

As she walked, dripping through the hall, she passed the door to the library. Sarah remembered James mentioning some history of the area in the collection. She felt a familiar tickle of curiosity in her mind. It was time for Sarah to do what she did best, research.

***

James watched Sarah dive into the pool from the window in his study wondering if he should consider putting a pool in the house at Polwarth Terrace. She seemed to enjoy having one on the property, although she hadn't mentioned liking swimming so much. He wished he could be out there with her.

At least she was warming to him. They had managed to spend the better part of the day together and hadn't argued. She'd even held his hand for a time without her usual reluctance. He mentally drew a line under hiking on the list of activities they enjoyed doing together. Maybe he should plan more day trips to places which piqued her curiosity, places with hiking trails. Perhaps it was the best way to distract her from her grief and break the ice on their relationship.

He shot one last longing look outside as she sank beneath the water's surface before turning back to his desk and the work that awaited him. CEOs didn't really get vacations. In spite of leaving his uncle in charge of Alba Petroleum while he was away, there were still strategic reports to review and acquisitions they were working on. He would read those and fax his responses back to Miss Lennox before he could get back to wooing his wife.

He was deep into revenue projections for a refinery they were considering acquiring when the phone on his desk rang. He debated letting the call go until someone else answered it. On the third ring, he thought better and picked up the receiver. "Hello."

"How is the honeymoon going?" His mother's voice simpered down the phone line. He should have known she would be calling soon. It had been all of five days since she had inserted herself into his relationship with Sarah.

"It's...progressing." He was careful not to reveal too much.

"I don't have to tell you how important this is." His mother and uncle had instructed him on the importance of an heir ad nauseum since James was old enough to understand how heirs were made. Such talk had accelerated exponentially since they'd found Sarah. Of course, then she'd been a concept, and abstract entity named in a family prophecy.

Now, she was a person, one with feelings and goals, one he'd come to care for. Now, anyone outside their marriage talking about an heir made his skin crawl. What was between James and his wife should only be between the two of them. "No, you don't."

"Martine says you are sleeping in separate rooms." She said.

"Martine needs to mind her own business." His icy tone should make it clear Martine would find herself dismissed if she told his mother another thing about his relationship. He truly did not need his mother in his bedroom much less the housekeeper. "May I remind you that her father has just died. Sarah is grieving, and I will not force myself on her."

His mother's tone turned placating. "Of course, she's grieving. But moping about the chateau is no way to get over it."

James tapped his fingers impatiently on the desk blotter trying to tamp down his temper. Through gritted teeth, James said. "I wonder you even needed to call me, when Martine has clearly given you a full report."

"I'm only worried for you, and for Sarah."

"Let me worry about Sarah. I have everything in hand, mother." He seethed. "And I suggest if you want to keep Martine on as your housekeeper, you resist the temptation to ask her about my relationship with my wife again."

His mother sputtered on the other end. James didn't bother to wait for a response. He simply hung up the phone. After a moment's consideration, he picked up the receiver again and punched in the extension for the kitchen. The chef answered the phone. "Can you please ask Martine to see me in my study? Thank you."

A few minutes later, Martine knocked confidently on the study door before poking her head in. "You wished to see me."

"Please come in and close the door." James indicated the chair in front of the desk.

Martine quietly closed the door and sat on the edge of the seat. Her head canted at an insouciant angle. A petite but formidable woman, she had always reminded James of Napoleon; small but mighty, slight but commanding. Martine was a few years older than his mother and had been the housekeeper at the chateau for many years. Unlike the rest of the staff who worked only seasonally, Martine stayed at the chateau year-round acting as caretaker even when the family wasn't in residence.

She took a very proprietary attitude toward the chateau and the family. James would have to watch her and her communications with his mother. When he'd been an adolescent, he had feared Martine's wrath if he had dared to damage any part of the house. A broken window, dented wall, or damaged vase would garner one of Martine's silent but censorious looks. Inevitably, his mother would hear of it. If Martine did not feel like his punishment was enough, he would find his food was salted too much, whatever book he was reading would disappear, or the rubbish bins in his room wouldn't be emptied for weeks.

As he had grown older, he had learned to stay on Martine's good side, and she had learned to treat him like the future owner of the chateau. Today, she sat at attention looking at him expectantly.

"Martine, how long have you been with us?" He leveled a serious look on her.

Martine pulled her shoulders back and in her heavily accented English said. "Twenty years."

"That is a long time." James said. "And I believe you and my mother are close. Are you not?"

"She is a great woman. I admire her." Her tone suggested anyone who didn't admire Lady Anne, must be a fool.

"Mmm…" James walked around the desk and stopped in front of the chair looking down on her. "I am sure she appreciates your loyalty and relies on your discretion. I am equally sure my wife will come to appreciate those traits as well."

"*Certainement.*" Her head bowed slightly, but her tone was still confident.

"My wife is a very private person." He put extra weight on the word 'private'. "And she has been through a lot, most recently the death of her father only days before our wedding."

Martine did not speak but nodded her acknowledgement. James went on. "I'm sure you can imagine why I am concerned for her, and for the way she is treated here."

"*Bien sûr.*" Martine agreed. And he had effectively boxed her in.

"I am also a very private person. So, I want to make myself perfectly clear." James pinned her to the chair with a look and his tone turned cold. "If I hear again that you have told my mother what is happening on my honeymoon, you will be dismissed from our employ. Is that clear?"

Martine studied him for several seconds. He could almost picture a scale in her mind weighing who had more power, him or his mother. In the end she understood he had the ability to make her life very difficult. The look she gave him was properly obsequious. "I understand completely."

CHAPTER NINE

The library at the chateau was an interesting blend of modern books with flashy colored dust jackets, old leather and canvas bound books with spines which crackled when she opened them, and leather-bound folios holding large documents and even loose papers. It took Sarah a few minutes to get her bearings and understand the organization of them.

When she found the shelves about French history, she didn't have to look much further. There were volumes about everything from Charlemagne to Charles de Gaulle, but Sarah was looking for something older. She found those books on a shelf so high she had to roll over the ladder. After checking to make sure they were in English, she retrieved several volumes and spent the better part of the afternoon poking through them.

While many of them had mentions of Mary Magdalene's arrival in France, it was in only the vaguest terms. There wasn't much more than what James told her. Sarah knew it was all too common for women to get written out of history. She supposed it was no surprise history books talked about the Patriarch of Rome, but almost never about the Matriarch of Marseilles. Sarah climbed the ladder again looking for more. One shelf up from the previous one, she found some books which offered histories of the Holy Grail. Some of the books on this shelf were old, some were new. Sarah picked some of the newer ones and climbed back down.

Opening a book which looked promising to the table of contents, Sarah found a chapter on Mary Magdalene and began to read, until she found something she wanted to make note of. If she'd been at the university library, she would have had her index cards or a notebook ready.

She searched every drawer in the room but only came up with a stubby pencil and a couple of tiny scraps. So, she set out to find something she could use.

Not wanting to bother James while he was working, Sarah went looking for Martine, or a maid. Surely, they would know where she could find a notebook and pen. She headed toward the kitchen and followed the sound of laughter. Pushing through the swinging door to the kitchen Sarah found the two maids and chef gathered at the table.

One pretty maid with wispy light brown hair was standing beside the table, or rather slouching comically and frowning. She was obviously performing for the others, and although Sarah couldn't understand exactly what she was saying she did catch the words for American, poor, and miserable. Unsure how to react, she stood frozen in the doorway watching the joke unfold in a language she couldn't understand. She didn't think she'd been mocked in quite this way since Tonya and Ronnie Sue Corbett had made her life hell back in Kettle Holler.

"Clemence!" Sarah hadn't noticed Martine come up beside her until she barked at the maid, fury shooting from her narrowed eyes.

The women at the table jumped, and Clemence, the pretty one who had been putting on the show whirled around. When she saw Sarah standing in the doorway, she was aghast. She straightened her shoulders and smoothed down her clothes. "Oh, madame. *Je suis désolée.*"

Martine rushed into the kitchen clapping her hands at the two other maids, shooing them back to work. Sarah slowly approached the table where they'd been sitting. There was one big difference between this maid and the Corbett sisters. Sarah was Clemence's employer. For once she was the one with the power.

Martine stood next to Clemence and faced Sarah. She looked properly embarrassed, which was surprising. Sarah was sure Martine had also been looking down her nose at the new Lady Caledon since they arrived. "Madame, I will have Clemence clear out her things immediately."

Clemence sniffed, looking down at her feet. Sarah could let Martine fire the girl, maybe she should have. But Sarah knew what it was to depend on a job. She watched Clemence's fingers twist together nervously. "That won't be necessary. I'm sure Clemence has learned this lesson."

Clemence's gaze lifted to hers in surprise. Sarah met her large brown eyes with a warning look. "My French isn't very good, so I didn't catch most of what you said, but the impression wasn't bad. I am sad and miserable. You're correct. I should be enjoying myself, and my husband."

"Madame-" Clemence started to say something, but Sarah cut her off.

"You see my father died a few days ago." Sarah cleared her throat where an unexpected lump formed. "It was very sudden, and unexpected, and I—" She had never said those words to a stranger before and the emotion of it surprised her. "I'm sorry. But joy feels wrong right now."

"Of course, madame." Clemence blinked several times as if fighting back tears of her own.

"I won't bother you anymore." Sarah turned away, the lump in her throat grew painfully large. "Excuse me."

Sarah turned her back to the women in the kitchen as the tears escaped. She blindly pushed through the swinging door to the dining room and made for the stairs. She held back the flood until she reached her room. Her hands shook as she fumbled with the lock on the door. The pain she'd been pushing down and keeping to herself swelled in her chest until she thought she would explode. She couldn't let these people see her like this.

She stumbled to the closet, falling to her knees as the wracking sobs took hold. Grabbing the robe she had left on the bench in the middle of the closet, she crawled to a corner. Tears flowed like a river now, running down her face. She wanted to cry out, to scream, and rage at the unfairness of it all, but she didn't dare let anyone see her weakness. She threw the robe over her head and gathered some of the fabric in her hand pushing it against her mouth to muffle her sobs.

Her shoulders shook and her head hurt with the effort. In the delirium of her grief Sarah could have sworn she felt an arm around her shoulders. She leaned in and rested her head on a comforting shoulder. A hand stroked her hair, and a voice whispered comforting words she couldn't understand. In time, her sobs quieted, and the shaking calmed. Sarah felt wrung out, exhausted from the wave of grief which had nearly drowned her.

"You are blessed." The comforting voice said.

Sarah's eyes flew open and were met with the soft dark brown gaze of the woman she'd seen in the grotto. She was in the woman's arms. They felt so solid she would have sworn the woman was real and was sitting beside her, there in the closet. If she'd been rational, she would have been terrified by the sudden appearance. But what she felt was an abiding peace, a warmth reaching the most stricken and grief-worn parts of her heart. Sarah rested her head back against the woman's shoulder and breathed deeply, taking the peaceful feeling in and applying it like a balm to the cracks inside her.

"Madame?" Martine's voice came from the bedroom.

Sarah started, thinking she had locked the door. Of course, Martine would have a key. Sarah looked back to the woman, but there was nothing there, only the wall she'd been leaning against, and the robe which had fallen to the floor.

"Oh, madame! Let me help you." Martine rushed to help a dazed and exhausted Sarah stand. With her arm firmly around Sarah's waist, Martine led her to a chair in the sitting room.

Sarah let Martine fuss over her, getting her a blanket and pouring her a cup of something. "Herbal tea." Martine told her as Sarah wrapped her hands around the cup. Despite the late summer heat, Sarah was shivering. She sipped the tea, which tasted of chamomile and honey. It was soothing and helped warm her from the inside. "I will get a cloth for your eyes."

They did hurt, and she was sure they were red and puffy. She closed them and warmed herself inhaling the steam from her tea. After another sip, she held the warm cup to her forehead where her sinuses were starting to complain.

"Here." Martine held out a washcloth.

She set her tea on the nearby table and placed the cold damp cloth over her sore eyes. Her voice was scratchy when she said. "Why are you suddenly being so nice to me?"

Martine didn't answer immediately. She went to the closet to straighten the clothes Sarah had knocked down. When she returned she sounded contemplative. "We have a saying, 'write injuries in sand, write kindness in marble'. That's what you did today with Clemence. She will never forget your kindness." She topped off Sarah's tea. "I think you could use some kindness, *non?*"

Sarah lifted the washcloth and dabbed at her eyelids. "Whatever gave you that idea?"

Martine's laugh was low and breathy. She gave Sarah a knowing look. "I will tell him you have a headache and will skip dinner this evening."

CHAPTER TEN

The next morning after an abbreviated swim, in which she actually swam, Sarah got a stack of notebooks and pens from Martine and settled herself in the library. James had fortunately left her alone after she'd told him her plans over breakfast. He had not asked about her puffy eyes, although Sarah could tell he had noticed them. He had graciously, if reluctantly left her to her own devices. She appreciated it. She knew this wasn't what he had imagined for their honeymoon.

Thoughts of James were quickly overridden when Sarah returned to the stack of books she had left on the table the day before. By that afternoon, she had notes organized into four topics: Mary Magdalene and 1st century Christians, Black Madonnas, and the Holy Grail. She stopped, stretching her neck before reviewing her notes.

- *Mary Magdalene*
  - o *Mary along with another Mary and Martha, Lazarus, Maximin, and young girl named Sara were set adrift and landed in France.*
  - o *Mary went about spreading the word and eventually retired to her mountain hideaway.*

- o *All the castaways would eventually become saints.*
- o *Saint Sarah, the 'dark-skinned' girl who arrived with Mary*
  - ▪ *Patron saint of the Romani people and of misfits.*
  - ▪ *Black Madonna? 180 Black Madonna icons in southern France. Based on Sarah or pre-Christian deity?*
- • *Holy Grail – actual object or allegory?*
  - o *If not allegorical surely Mary would have had contact with it. Did she bring it to France?*
  - o *Joseph of Arimathea took/sent to Britain? Appears in Arthurian legend*
  - o *Grail Romances=allegorical quests for enlightenment.*
  - o *Grail/Cauldron correlation*
    - ▪ *healed wounds*
    - ▪ *provided bottomless nourishment*

There was one thing about the legends which caught her attention. The Fisher King, the guardian of the grail, who invites Perceval to his castle in Chrétien de Troyes's twelfth century romance is wounded in the leg. This reminded Sarah of the king from the legend of her people. He was beaten by the New Folk, and the cauldron had healed him, but not entirely leaving him with a limp. Furthermore, some scholars relate the Fisher King to Bran the Blessed from Welsh lore, who is described in the Mabinogion as a giant. 'In the time

before time, our people sprang from the footprint of a giant...'
Given her people's legend, Sarah was always on the lookout
for giants.

She was so engrossed in these connections and questions
she didn't notice the sun setting. She only looked up when a
chuckle came from the doorway. "I should have thought about
this earlier. The best way to draw you out is to pique your
curiosity."

Sarah looked around at the books littering the table, then at
the darkening evening outside and laughed. "You got me.
Once I get hold of a thread, I'm not satisfied until I've
unraveled the whole sweater. And I'm a sucker for legends
that subvert accepted history."

"I had planned to show some of this to you after our
conversation yesterday," He walked around the table to pull
up a chair next to her. "But I see you have already started."

"I was curious about Mary Magdalene." She looked
awkwardly at the mess on the table. "And then it kind of
snowballed."

"No bother. I'm interested to hear what you've found." His
eyes twinkled with what Sarah thought was admiration. She
couldn't help it; she felt a little flutter of awareness. Whether
she loved him or not, it was a heady thing to be admired by
James Stuart. That nagging guilt reared its head. She wasn't
supposed to enjoy being admired by James.

Sarah broke eye contact looking back at the books which
littered the table. "If you ask anyone in the English-speaking
world, they would tell you Mary Magdalene was a prostitute
who Jesus saved from a mob, not a leader in the early
church." She reached for one of the newer books. "This one
even theorizes she was married to Jesus and had his child."

"As to that…" James cocked his head to the side giving her a look of confirmation.

"I've heard your claim." She said before he could finish. "Do you really believe your family is descended from Jesus?"

"Do you believe you're descended from a tribe of people living thousands of years outside of modern society to preserve their bloodline?"

"Actually, I still struggle with it. Even with everything I've seen, it's hard to believe." She confessed.

"Let me show you the family history."

The more Sarah learned about what the Stuarts believed, the better. It might help her make sense of the things she'd been reading. And there might be something she could use in her battle against Walter Stuart. "Alright. But shouldn't we get something to eat?"

"Yes, we should. In fact, it's probably on the table right now."

"Let's have dinner and then you can show me what you've got." Sarah pushed her chair back from the table.

He gave her a rakish smile which Sarah was sure would charm many women. "It may take all night. There is a lot to explain."

***

"I expect you have questions." James said as Martine set their plates in front of them. He was surprised to see the housekeeper give Sarah's shoulder a friendly pat before leaving. "That's a change."

Sarah glanced over her shoulder toward the kitchen door. "Oh, I think we understand each other a little better now."

So, his talk with Martine worked. Good. At least he could help make Sarah's adjustment easier. "So, what are your questions."

Sarah's brows drew together in thought. He loved the way she looked when she was turning a problem over in her mind. He wanted to kiss her right there, between those eyebrows, where the working of her mind showed on her face. "It's honestly hard to process all of what I've been reading. I went looking for more information on Mary Magdalene and I feel like I've uncovered so much more than I expected. And I still have very few answers about her."

"I'm not surprised. It has rarely been in the church's best interest to elevate a woman to the level of the other disciples." James took a sip of his wine.

"And yet Catholics revere the Virgin Mary almost as much as Jesus." Sarah took a bite of her food, her face transformed into one of delight. "This is so good. I'll have to tell the chef."

"Ah, but that Mary is pure." He tipped his water glass in her direction. "She manages to be the example of motherhood and purity at the same time. She's the measure by which all women are judged."

"So that Mary becomes a tool of the patriarchy, whereas Mary Magdalene is made into a whore?" Sarah raised a skeptical eyebrow. He loved how animated her face was when she talked about things which interested her.

"And that bit of bad press comes courtesy of the Council of Nicea where fourth century clerics sorted through all the early Christian texts and chose what made it into the Bible and what didn't. Through some trick of juxtaposition, the whore Jesus saves from stoning and Mary Magdalene get conflated."

"And any evidence to the contrary fades into obscurity." Sarah finished eyebrow raised cynically.

"Obscurity by mainstream western standards." James felt warm, and it wasn't only the wine. He was enjoying their exchange, a rare moment when they felt in tune. He lived for moments like this. "Some of those texts have been preserved by other sects. Coptic Christians, for example have some of them. They even have a gospel of Mary which seems to support the idea that Jesus and Mary Magdalene had a special relationship, if not marriage."

Sarah's eyes went wide. "Really? I'd love to see it."

"We might have it in one of those books in the library." James offered. "If not, I'm sure we might be able to find it in the library at the university in Marseilles."

She bit her lip in thought. James drew in a breath resisting the temptation to kiss her. "So, for the sake of argument, let's say Mary and Jesus were married, or at least had children. And Mary brought those children with her to France, and they set to building a church. If we accept the legend about Mary retiring to live in her cave, then what happened to the children?"

"I think that's a conversation for after dinner when there are visual aids." James picked up the bottle of wine from the table and poured some into her glass. "In the meantime, you should try this sauvignon blanc. It's one of my favorites."

Sarah tasted it. He watched her lips as she sipped it and enjoyed the taste. "That's very nice. I know precious little about wine."

James leaned closer as if sharing a secret. "To be honest, I only know what I like. We should visit one of the nearby wineries. I'm sure they'd be happy to educate us."

"Sounds like fun." He got a smile from her.

"I'll have the security team see what can be arranged." He felt like she'd just agreed to a first date. Maybe they were turning a corner. "I'm glad you're feeling better this evening. I missed having dinner with you last night. "

"I'm sorry. Everything kind of hit me at once yesterday." She set her glass back on the table and looked down at her plate obviously remembering the night before. "I had a good cry, and I think I feel a lot better, or at least better than I have been."

"I'm so sorry. You know you can always talk to me." He covered her hand with his. "I meant it when I said, for better or worse."

Her eyes lifted to his, and he was caught in their green depths. He thought she might share something of her feelings. She might let him in. Then her eyes were shuttered, and his heart sank. "Well, believe me yesterday afternoon was definitely worse. You did not want to see."

James let the subject drop. Instead, they chatted about other things they might do in the time they were there. Perhaps the night before had helped her. She seemed enthusiastic about planning outings. It almost felt like they were a couple.

CHAPTER ELEVEN

After dinner, they returned to the library. James closed the door behind them. "I know you think I've been raised to believe this prophecy, but I went through a skeptical phase too. It's hard to sit through a British history lecture and not compare what historians told me with the family legend. I had to research things for myself."

"And your research confirmed what they told you?" After a couple of glasses of wine, she had a hard time keeping a note of doubt out of her voice.

His laugh was throaty, sexy. "There were some things in my research which lined up with the family legend, and we have some documents supporting certain aspects of it. I'll show you."

He turned to a bookcase which stood against an interior wall at the far end of the room. He pressed some spot Sarah couldn't see, and to her surprise a little handle popped out of the side. James pulled the handle and the bookcase swung away from the wall.

"I'm having serious Nancy Drew flashbacks." Sarah muttered to herself as she went for a closer look. Behind the bookcase, there was a room no bigger than a closet. Inside were shelves of books, rolled parchments and folios. It seemed like a treasure trove of old documents and texts. "This is like something out of a gothic novel. Are you going to show me the dark family shame? Is there a secret wife hiding in here?"

James laughed. "No secret wife, but I will swear you to secrecy on what I'm going to show you." His tone turned serious. "The public isn't ready to hear some of this. It would not go well, not to mention our AP shareholders would think I'd gone mad."

"Don't worry." Sarah told him as she scanned the closet. "I don't think anyone would believe me if I told them."

James selected a couple of folios and a leather pouch before backing out of the room and pushing the bookcase back into place. Sarah followed him to the table where he spread out a folio to reveal a family tree which started with Jesus and Mary Magdalene. "You asked what happened to their children. Here it is, well at least one of them."

Sarah perused the document in front of her. It was old, but certainly not first-century old. Below Jesus and Mary were three names; Sara, Joseph, and Tamar, but only Sara had more detail. According to the chart, Sara married after coming to France. "I'm afraid I don't know enough about French history to know if these names should be familiar to me."

"I doubt most French historians could even remember some of these names." James flipped to the next large page to show the line of descendants continued. "Maybe you'll recognize someone on this page."

Sarah followed the generations from one line to another. Eventually, there were titles listed under the names, which helped a bit. It was when she saw a fifth century King of

Burgundy Sarah started to understand. Sara's descendants were interwoven into the families of major houses, and those houses became the nobles of the small regional kingdoms which eventually became France.

Sarah traced the line through the Kings of Franks, Aquitaine, and Austrasia. It all started to blur together. She turned the page, and continued following the trail until she found a name she definitely recognized, Charlemagne. "So, Sara's children became part of the French royal family."

"And through the Auld Alliance married into Scottish families including mine." James opened the other folio he had pulled out. This is my family tree from my father back. You can trace our line from him, back to the French kings and Dukes of Burgundy."

She traced a finger through the lines of the family tree. 'Where is the connection to Charles Edward Stuart?"

James chuckled. "I should have known you would ask. It's here. When he was in Italy almost thirty years after the Rising of 1745, Charles married Princess Louise of Stolberg-Gedern. By most accounts, their marriage was miserable and tempestuous. Eventually, Louise left Charles and after alleging abuse was effectively granted a separation and half of Charles's pension. That was almost unheard of then." He paused, staring at the yellowed paper in front of them. "What most history books won't tell you is Louise was pregnant with Charles's son, who she kept hidden from Charles and much of the world for his own protection. By then Charles was eaten up with bitterness at being robbed of his throne and I expect some shame from his failure in the Rising. He was abusive to Louise and had been to his previous mistress, Clementina Walkinshaw. Louise didn't want to risk his abuse or his ambition falling onto a male heir. Ironic, as the pursuit of a male heir was the whole reason, he had married her."

"So, what happened to the heir?"

He gave her a half-smile. "Well, Louise, who I think you would admire, spent a couple of years with her son, Thomas, in a convent. A few years later, she went public with an ongoing affair she was having with an Italian named Alfieri. She and Alfieri became social pariahs among the Italian nobility although they were very popular with artists and intellectuals. They raised Thomas in relative obscurity. Some even assumed he was Alfieri's son. Thomas's children and grandchildren were spared ambitious marriages and fortunately, the wrath of various anti-royal movements which nearly put an end to European monarchies in the nineteenth and twentieth centuries."

"Not unlike Mary Magdalene bringing Sara here to France and not telling anyone whose child she was." Sarah connected the two threads of their conversation. "And not unlike Arthur, being raised in obscurity only to rise to the throne."

James flipped a few pages back in Henry's family tree. "That connection is more than just thematic. Arthur, the real one, was a warlord in the lowlands in the sixth century. He was a contemporary of a pagan mystic named Merlin."

Lyall Green had told Sarah and Dermot that merlin was more of a title than a name, but Sarah thought she would keep that to herself. "Did Arthur or one of his contemporaries search for the Holy Grail?"

"I think that was a construct of the troubadours." James laughed flipping back in the chart another couple of pages. "The grail as characterized in legend is mainly a metaphor for the bloodline itself." He pointed to the name Arthur on the chart with the date 560. Sarah followed as he dragged his finger up the list of antecedents until it stopped on a woman named Tamar, and her parents. "Arthur was also of the bloodline."

Sarah shook her head in confusion. "How did Tamar end up in Scotland?"

"You've heard the legend of Joseph of Arimathea taking the holy grail to Britain? If the grail is a metaphor for the bloodline, she's how it got there."

"So, your family tree splits off and then rejoins a few hundred years later?" Sarah gave him a side-eyed look.

James's cheeks turned slightly pink. "Closer to a thousand. We're not the Hapsburgs."

"Let me make sure I understand this." Sarah held a hand in the air above the family tree. "Jesus and Mary Magdalene had three children." He nodded. "And you are descended from two of them who married into the leading houses of Europe."

"Boy, when y'all say, 'divine right of kings' you really mean it." Sarah was beginning to get a clearer picture of why the Stuarts believed so strongly about the prophecy. "So, Sarah and Tamar are the vessels or the bloodline. The womb is the vessel, like a vase, or a bowl, which in Europe gets conflated with the Celtic cauldron of plenty."

"And the legend of the Holy Grail is born." James finished.

Including elements like the Fisher King, and the powers of the grail to heal and give food that were reminiscent of her own people's legend. Sarah now saw the thread connecting the Stuarts with her people, or at least one of them. She wondered how early this connection had been established. Was it with the ancient king 'lost in the mist' from "The River

Maiden"? And who was he; Arthur, Kenneth MacAlpin, or someone they hadn't even touched on? "This is a lot to digest."

"I understand. Knowledge of the bloodline has been whispered about through the last two thousand years, but usually people who teach or talk about it face repercussions or ridicule. The Cathars in the thirteenth century were eradicated by the church. A French politician wrote about it in the nineteenth century and was dismissed. Other writers have written about it, but nothing has ever made it into mainstream thought. And in spite of hints of Jesus's marriage in the Gnostic gospels and the Dead Sea Scrolls, most scholars are unwilling to accept it."

"And that doesn't tell you that maybe it's not true?" She asked playing devils advocate.

"It tells me that talking about it publicly risks embarrassing the family and losing credibility or attracting the attention of zealots who might mean us harm."

"Don't we already have their attention?" Sarah asked. "I'm pretty sure those are the guys trying to kill me."

"This is why it's in our best interests to keep this information within the family." James held a hand over the royal Stuart family tree. "We have been balanced on a knife's edge for two thousand years. As the church's power and Christian fanaticism grew, the benefits and risks of exposing the bloodline have also grown. There may be people who would embrace it and willingly follow me because of it."

"But there are also people who would call you a heretic or crazy for calling the accepted story into question." Sarah finished his thought for him. "So, you're left in limbo, but with a sense of entitlement of biblical proportions."

His laugh was low and the look he gave her self-deprecating. "I suppose you could say that, or you could say it leaves me with a sense of responsibility of biblical proportions."

He looked sincere. Poor James, she had known he felt a lot of pressure from his family, but this was a whole other level. She laid her hand over his where it rested on the wooden arm of the chair. "That's a lot of pressure for one person."

He turned over his hand and threaded his fingers with hers. His gaze lifted to hers searching. "Which is one reason why I'm so glad I'm not alone anymore."

"James," She started to warn him off, but found it hard to finish what she was going to say.

He patted her hand with this other hand and turned back to the table clearing his throat. "That is our history, how we got where we are."

James closed the folios and wrapped their leather covers around them, returning the documents to the room behind the bookcase. "I hope it helps you understand why we are so sure of our mission, and why we are so careful about security."

"Is it really so important that it's kept secret anymore?" Sarah asked.

James looked horrified. "I don't even want to think about what would happen if it became common knowledge."

Sarah looked at the books on the table thinking. "I don't actually think it would matter. I mean this book." She picked up one of the books she'd read that contained the bloodline theory and flipped to the copyright page. "Came out in 1982. It was a bestseller if the dust jacket is to be believed. It hasn't made much difference to people's perception. I mean I don't pay a lot of attention to it, but I haven't seen believers running around with their hair on fire."

"Well, this book is only speculation. There is no actual proof." He waved a hand at the book she was holding.

"I don't think proof matters anymore." Sarah took a step closer to him, laying the book on the table in front of him. "People believe what they want to believe, and they've been believing a certain version of events for so long. I don't think hearing another version would shake them. I don't think it matters anymore."

"Oh, it matters to some." He held up two fingers. "The Invigilare and the Circle care enough to send assassins after us."

"But they're zealots. I'm talking about the run of the mill, Sunday school going, Christmas caroling, Easter bonnet wearing Christians. I don't think they would care."

"Listen," Sarah leaned against the table. "As Christianity expanded beyond Israel and encountered other religions, it didn't obliterate them, it absorbed them adopting aspects of each one. It's why we have yule logs and Christmas trees. It's by All Saints Day coincides with the Celtic New Year, why some saints' days happen on the solstice or equinoxes. Every new bit of information gets absorbed and blended with what people already believed." She shrugged. "It's how folklore works. Every time someone retells a story, a new layer and new perspective gets added. If the holy bloodline were to come out in a way that made more of a blip than this book." She waved at the book. "It would either be ignored or absorbed, and folks would just move on."

James looked at the book, his brows knit together in consternation. "Well, when you put it like that, none of it seems to matter very much, does it?"

'No,' she thought. 'It doesn't!' And yet her life had been turned upside down because of it. She would be angry if she wasn't afraid of those zealots who believed all this mattered.

Sarah watched James as he turned her point over in his mind. She was reminded of Willie Cross and his reaction when their people's cauldron had started working again, causing him to question his beliefs. He hadn't been able to process what he had so fervently believed was wrong. In a sense it had broken him. He had become dangerous, setting Aunt Eilidh's cottage on fire and nearly killing her mother. Sarah hoped her theory didn't have the same effect on James. "I'm sorry if it feels like that. I'm not saying what you do as a leader doesn't matter. I don't think your family's history is as big a part of it as you might think."

***

James's mind whirred in fifty different directions. He tried to think of anything he could which might refute what Sarah was saying, something which would make the secret his family had been trying to keep for generations feel like it was worth the effort. But he couldn't. For all he'd been fed his family lore his entire life, as a modern man, he couldn't see how it mattered. Church rolls were shrinking, fewer and fewer people believed, and among those who did there was increasing flexibility in how they viewed their faith. The Catholic church's power was waning. The only people left who would be bothered by such a revelation were zealots like the Circle.

He picked up the book in front of him looking at the 'New York Times Bestseller' emblazoned on the cover. It had come out when he was a child. He remembered Walter bringing it with him to the house, angry these people had stumbled onto their secret. His father had read it and pointed out the many holes in the argument made in the book. They had decided to stay silent about it and see if the book's argument was refuted. When no one with any scholarly reputation gave it any credence, they simply waited for the furor to die down. And it did. James started to wonder what else of his family lore was less significant than he thought.

"One question." Sarah's voice broke through his rapidly spinning thoughts. He stopped ruminating. She looked as confused as he felt and seemed to struggle with how to phrase her question. "If Sara's descendants married into various royal houses and spread all over Europe, what makes the Stuarts special? Why doesn't every royal house in Europe have someone claiming to be the prince of..." She waved her hands around in an equivocal gesture. "...Everything?"

She still didn't seem to understand how important she was. "You haven't figured it out yet?"

She shook her head in confusion.

He shoved the books out of the way and sat down next to her. "It's you, darling. Your people are older than all the royal houses, older than Christianity. Your people hold the key to whatever it is that will bring about the revolution and put us back into our role as world leaders. You're the proverbial sword in the stone. You have something we don't have."

Sarah eyed him, her face incredulous. "What? I don't know why you would need us."

He sighed, "I'm afraid I don't know the specifics either. I only know the prophecy foretold our marriage and our heir would be the future king."

She sighed and slumped back into her chair. "Yeah, I heard that too."

James took her hand again. "Whatever our individual family stories have told us, and whether it's fact or folklore, it brought us together, and I can't regret that."

Her hand was warm in his. A hundred thoughts flitted behind her eyes. He waited for her to list her regrets, Dermot chief among them, but she didn't. Perhaps she had given up on regrets or given up fighting the expectations of their families and their enemies. Instead, she changed the subject. "What are we going to do tomorrow?"

"I thought we would go to Aix-en-Provence. Maybe we could visit the Musée Granet and do some shopping." He hoped shopping might have the same cheering effect on her it did on most women. She might not be as materialistic, but perhaps he could tempt her with some French finery.

"Is it safe? It sounds awfully public."

"As long as we have a security team with us, we'll be fine." He hoped she would agree; that the paparazzi hadn't scared her so much she was afraid to go out in public.

She stood. "Sounds good. I'd like to see Aix-en-Provence. I've heard wonderful things about it." Sarah looked around the table littered with books and letters. "I should put this stuff away."

"I'll take care of it. You look tired." She was beautiful, but he could tell she had some thinking to do. She needed to process everything he'd told her, and if he was honest, he needed to process some things she'd said to him.

Sarah put a hand to her cheek as if suddenly self-conscious about her appearance, which she rarely was. He wanted to take his comment back, but she said, "I am a bit tired."

He stepped out of her way. As she brushed past him, he stopped her and kissed her cheek. "Goodnight, my love."

"Goodnight."

He closed the door behind her, shutting himself in the library with his thoughts. He occupied himself with putting away the books Sarah had been reading. They ranged from academic analyses to literary works to sensational conspiracy theories. He wondered how she had managed to read so much in one day, but then she was a professional at research.

As he closed a volume on early church history, He tried to tell himself Sarah's words meant nothing, but that was a lie. The truth was he didn't think she was wrong about his family's secret. After two millennia, people would believe what they believed. He didn't think one family saying they were descended from Jesus would make a difference. It was arrogant of his family to think the bloodline even mattered anymore.

If the holy bloodline didn't matter, then what did the Stuart bloodline matter? Why on earth would anyone care. None of the European monarchies had any real power anymore. They had devolved into little more than state sponsored celebrities. What was the point?

He climbed the ladder with an armful of books to return to the high shelf. With each rung, he remembered whatever the holy bloodline meant or didn't mean, Scotland still wasn't free. Whether he was entitled to rule or not, he was sure

Sarah, and her people held the key to gaining independence. He was equally sure his dedication to that cause didn't depend on whether he ruled Scotland in the end. As the leader of one of the country's biggest commercial enterprises he was still best placed to use whatever power Sarah's people had to help make independence a reality. Sarah might be right about the holy bloodline, but on a practical level it didn't mean they would change course.

James finished putting the books away, and turned out the light in the library feeling somewhat better than he had when Sarah left. It was an interesting academic exercise to debate the relevance of the holy bloodline but changed very little on the ground.

CHAPTER TWELVE

Aix-en-Provence was like a dream world. When people rhapsodized about France, it was what Sarah imagined; sidewalk cafes, sculptural fountains, art museums, and couturiers. It was hard to remember she was in the wrong place with the wrong man when their surroundings were so beautiful. Everyone seemed to take their time. With everything Sarah had learned the day before, it was nice to take a break and enjoy the day.

She had meant what she told James. She didn't think the world would care about the bloodline, but she was painfully aware of people who did care, people who meant to kill her. And then there was Walter. She thought his hubris was off the charts before, now she wondered how she would ever defeat someone who believe he was the literal spawn of Jesus. Instead, she focused on building a bond with James and trying to enjoy the day.

They'd been at the Musée Granet for two hours. Sarah had noticed one woman sitting in front of the same Cezanne for the entire time. Sarah wondered if she'd fallen asleep but seeing her from another angle told her the woman was wrapped up in experiencing the painting. Sarah could see why. There was a richness, a fullness to Cezanne, which Sarah liked. She probably could have looked at his paintings for the rest of the afternoon herself, but James prompted her to move along.

He took her hand and drew her to another room. Sarah marveled at his enthusiasm to show her his favorite pieces in the museum. She thought, not for the first time if he had brought her to a museum like this one on a date before Dermot, she could easily be wooed by James. When they left the trappings of their lives behind, she liked James. He was charming, and intelligent, and from what she could tell honorable, which when he spent so much time around Walter, was an achievement. He even had a sense of humor sometimes.

He turned to her with sparkling eyes. "I think you're going to be very interested in this next room."

The room was less art and more archaeology. There was a mix of carved stones and plaques explaining them. Sarah stopped in front of one of the plaques. "Are these Roman?"

James stood close to her as she read the information provided. The stones were in fact Roman, and dated back to the first century, around the time when Mary Magdalene would have been in the area. Sarah took a moment to imagine what it must have been like. She thought of the woman she'd seen in the cave three days ago.

"This is actually not what I brought you in here to see." James said quietly.

His tone was light, but Sarah could tell he was impatient to show her something else. "Okay. Show me."

He drew her further into the exhibit hall past more Roman artifacts to a wall which included a diorama as well as a mural and stone carvings. James stood behind her. Resting his hands on her shoulders he said, "This is the Oppidum d'Entremont, or a model of it. It's located to the north of town and was one of the Celtic settlements. Archaeologists have dated it to around 200 B.C.E. Does anything look familiar?"

She did see some similarities in the symbols which had been carved in some of the stones. The diorama was an artist's interpretation of what the fortified settlement would have looked like with houses, communal cooking fires and even what appeared to be a place of worship. Next to the altar stood a figure wearing a headdress complete with antlers. It reminded Sarah of the figure her mother had seen in Làrachd an Fhamhair, a figure Sarah now believed had been Lyall Green, Dermot's mysterious grandfather.

"Some believe that is the Celtic god, Cernunnos." She felt James's breath on her ear, and in spite of herself she felt attracted. She fought against it, but another part of her knew if they consummated their marriage, she would increase James's attachment to her, and maybe weaken Walter's influence on him. She didn't want to use sex to build such a bond, but she wasn't sure how many options she had or how much time. And she had agreed to give him an heir.

"He was the god of—" She turned to look at him, and his eyes fastened on her lips. Oh God, was he going to kiss her? She felt frozen. She wasn't ready.

"Fertility." He finished. His breath feathering across her lips. His gaze flicked up to meet hers and held there.

"Sarah?" A familiar voice cut through the rising tension.

She was flooded with relief, which was why it took her a second to recognize the voice, one she had never expected to hear again. She whipped around in surprise. "Jon?"

James muttered something under his breath.

"Wow! You look…amazing." Jon Samuels gave his head a shake as if he was trying to grasp her presence in this new context.

James, who still stood at her shoulder cleared his throat, and Jon's eyes shot up to look at him and narrowed.

Sarah jumped in to save them from what she thought might be an awkward moment. "Jon, let me introduce you to James Stuart."

"We've met, remember?" Jon's face hardened as the memory of the night in Chapel Hill came back. Jon had meant to surprise Sarah with an apology, and he'd been tackled by James's security guard for his trouble.

Sarah laughed nervously. "Right. I guess a lot has happened since then."

"It seems strangely fitting we should see you. You were there for our first date, and now you're here for our honeymoon." James dropped that information into the conversation with the weight of a bomb.

Jon's eyebrows climbed up his forehead. "Well, I can't say I'm surprised. Although it seems a little fast for the Sarah I knew."

'I'm a long way from that girl.' Sarah thought to herself.

James grasped her hand. "When you know it's right, it doesn't make sense to wait."

Sarah looked at James, and she could see the tension in the way he held his head, as if daring Jon to challenge their relationship. He must have felt as unsure about their marriage as she did. To Jon she said. "What are you doing here? I thought you were trying to go to New Mexico with Dr. Johnson this summer."

"I was, but then I got offered a fellowship to come and study the Celto-Ligurian settlements all over Southern France. It's not my specialty, but I'm making some connections I hope will help me when I want to put together my own team to go back to Guatemala." He easily slipped right back into their old pace of conversations. Sarah was glad he didn't seem bitter about how they had split up. It had been a little acrimonious at the time, but they were adults. There was no reason to carry a grudge.

"That's great. I know it's what you really want to do." She smiled at him. Jon had never been a bad guy; he simply wasn't the guy for her.

"So, are you here studying the Oppidum d'Entrement?" James asked.

Jon glanced at the display before looking back at Sarah. "I've only been there for a week. I was at Bouches du Rhone in Marseilles earlier in the summer. I brought some new finds back to the university this morning to be catalogued. And I thought I would stop by here to look at the exhibit while I was in town.

"And what do you think of the exhibit?" Sarah asked.

Jon made a face looking askance at the model. "These things are always oversimplified, and sometimes people's preconceived notions of what's expected get grafted onto sites where they don't really apply."

"Such as?" James looked puzzled.

Jon waved a hand at the man with the antler headdress. "Well, for example, there isn't any evidence they worshipped Cernunnos. A figure like that has been found in settlements in Belgium and Germany, but never this far south. But he's a known Celtic figure, so I'm sure the artist added him to fit this settlement into what people imagine a Celtic settlement to look like."

James looked skeptically at him. "Isn't this kind of display about telling the story visually? I imagine artists need those sorts of visual cues to help people make the connections they want them to make."

"Sure," Jon stepped a little closer to the display case turning toward James as if squaring up. "But it can give the wrong impression too. That might be all right for telling stories, but we scientists like facts."

Sarah stepped in to diffuse the rising tension between them. "This is a longstanding debate Jon and I have had many times. Physical evidence versus folkloric evidence. When societies are as old as this one, and their materials might not have been as durable as later societies, there isn't always physical evidence of what they believed. Or if there is, it tells an incomplete story. We have to rely on disciplines like comparative folklore to fill in the gaps. By attempting to trace stories back to their original sources we can learn more about what a society like this told stories about and what they believed."

Jon looked smug. "And there are those of us who think thousands of years of the telephone game makes finding the origins of those stories impossible."

"And yet there are archetypes which persist for thousands of years and across cultures in the stories people tell like the Deluge, or deals with the devil, or Sleeping Beauty." Sarah countered.

"Sleeping Beauty?" James asked in surprise.

Sarah explained. "By tracing these archetypes across multiple cultures and paying attention to the migration patterns of ancient peoples, we can find out where some of these stories came from. Believe it or not, Sleeping Beauty, or a form of it may have migrated to Europe from India five thousand years ago."

James pulled back in surprise. "And here I thought it was from Bavaria."

"That's the version the Grimm brothers wrote down." Sarah told him. "Which relates to what we were talking about yesterday."

James cut his gaze to Jon in an unspoken warning Sarah shouldn't reveal too much. She gave him a smile telling him she wouldn't reveal any family secrets. To Jon she said. "We were talking about Christianity absorbing the traditions of each new culture it met as it spread across Europe."

James looked back and forth between Jon and Sarah. She could almost see the thoughts swirling around in his head. She hoped again these revelations wouldn't send him into a tailspin. It wasn't easy challenging things he'd been told his whole life. "Jon and I could go on all day debating fact and folklore, but I'm sure he has work to do, and I believe you and I were going to lunch."

"Yes, we were." James agreed easily. He was obviously relieved she was changing the subject.

"Oh, maybe you'd like to come and see the dig while you're here." Jon offered suddenly. "I'd love to show you around."

"That would be great, actually." Sarah would love the opportunity to see a dig up close.

Jon looked at James who nodded although Sarah could sense his reluctance. "Whatever my bride wants."

"I can arrange it. Maybe in a couple of days?" Jon added. "How can I get in touch with you?"

James pulled a card from his pocket and wrote a phone number on it. "Our number. If we're not there, the staff can take a message."

"Right. I'll give you a call." Jon looked excited as he turned toward a door marked for staff only.

James pulled Sarah toward the exit. It wasn't until she turned around that she noticed one of their bodyguards by the doorway. "Looks like Jon almost had a repeat of the last time he surprised us."

"It was a near thing." James said dryly.

CHAPTER THIRTEEN

He'd been about to kiss her when that blasted man had interrupted them. Ten months and an ocean away from the last time he'd seen Jon Samuels and once again the man was throwing a wrench in his plans. Still, Sarah had been happy to see him. He had hoped a day in the beautiful old town which had inspired artists for centuries would have drawn her out of her well of grief, but he should have known nothing would be as effective at distracting her from her grief than rehashing a long-standing academic argument.

Their lunch was a leisurely affair of wine, fresh-baked bread, local cheese, and salad niçoise. They talked about their conversation with Jon and how much Sarah would like to see the dig at the Oppidum d'Entremont. It was the most animated James had seen her since they'd come to France. He felt both hopeful and jealous at the same time. She was almost like her old self, and it had taken running into her old boyfriend to bring back the light in her eyes.

Folklore truly was the way to her heart. No wonder she'd fallen for Dermot. They already had a shared passion when they met. How was he ever going to compete? He would have to make sure he was there whenever she got to visit that part of her life. Perhaps they could make some more donations to academic programs she found worthy. Maybe he should start a foundation in her name. It would be a way for her to stay involved in the things she loved. He would have to watch for Jon's call, and make sure they kept the appointment.

"Are you sure you don't want to visit any couturiers?" He asked her as he signed the check at the café.

Sarah shook her head, relaxed by the wine and conversation. "You know I'm not into those things."

"You are so different from the women I'm used to." He smiled at her, challenged by her differences. "It's one of the things I love most about you."

Was she blushing or was it the wine? She looked down and folded her napkin, placing it carefully on the table obviously still uncomfortable with his compliments. "If you don't want to shop for clothes, what would you enjoy?"

Sarah looked around the plaza where they were sitting scanning the shops. "Those fashion shops we can find in Paris or Milan. I think I would rather see something unique to this area. Something that could only be in Aix-en-Provence."

He thought through some of the local places he liked. "I think I have exactly the place. They won't be open for another twenty minutes. Why don't we have a walk through the old town on our way?"

"Sounds great." Sarah rose from her chair. "I'd love to soak in more of the atmosphere here. It's really wonderful."

He rose with her and when he extended his hand to her, she took it. For the moment, she was his. She didn't seem to be wishing she was anywhere else. His heart was full.

***

"This is one of my mother's favorite shops." James told her. She must have made a face at the mention of his mother, because he rushed on to say. "But I think you're going to love it too."

The shop looked interesting enough from the outside. Its wooden façade boasted a broad curved front window which was etched with a swirling art nouveau border, and the words Parfumerie Cardell. The shop was dark beyond the window display of ornate perfume bottles in various colors. "Are you sure they're open?"

James checked his watch. "Yes, they keep it dark inside much of the time. Something about the sunlight affecting the potency of the oils."

He pushed open the ornate door and a bell above it tinkled. A young woman in an apron approached from the back of the shop looking only slightly bothered. "Can I help you?"

James spoke to her in French while Sarah took in the shop which was part retail and part workshop. The front area was lined with shelves holding apothecary style glass bottles with numbered glass stoppers filled with liquids in an array of colors from translucent blue and purple to warm amber.

Sarah didn't follow the conversation James was having with the woman. She was fascinated by the work area behind the counter. There were tools for extracting oils and essences from various materials. She recognized a small still, and a couple of presses, and cases containing non-liquid ingredients like myrrh, cedar, and what she thought might be ambergris. Sarah was curious about all the processes which went into getting the scent from these items into liquid form. The work area reminded her of Lyall Green's still room with its many glass vessels and tools.

"Sarah?" James called to her from a display near the front of the shop. The young lady who worked there was holding an ornate bottle of colored glass. "Would you like to try some scents?"

Sarah joined them to have a look, or a sniff. "Sorry, I'm fascinated by all the equipment, and the processes that must go into making this.

The young woman put the bottle onto the counter and pulled a slip of cardstock from a glass cup nearby. She pulled the stopper out of the bottle, a drop of perfume hung from the end of the glass dipper. She caught the drop on the piece of paper and then waved the paper through the air explaining in a heavily accented but honey-smooth voice. "Give it a moment to dry, and it will mellow. This is one of my favorites. It is a light and clean fragrance which reminds me of a garden in springtime."

She held the paper up and Sarah leaned forward to smell it. The shop girl was right. It did smell like a garden in springtime. It was softly floral and herbal, light like daffodils and honeysuckle. "It's nice."

Sarah straightened and gave James a chance to smell it. "It's very pleasant." He looked at Sarah, assessing her. "But I think it's a bit timid for my bride. Do you have something with more spice to it?"

Sarah had never thought of herself as spicy, but she let James lead the way. The young woman pushed a cup filled with coffee beans in their direction. James picked it up and held it out to her. "To cleanse your nose of the last scent."

Sarah took the cup and sniffed. The coffee overpowered any lingering floral notes. She took a second whiff because she liked it.

"*Princep!*" A voice boomed from the back of the shop. Sarah followed the sound to find a man she estimated to be in his early sixties. He was tall and thin; his manner was relaxed and self-assured. He looked weathered, as if he'd been baked in the sun and then left out in the strong mistral winds which swept through Provence. He wore white linen from head to toe, and his sleeves were rolled up. "It has been too long since I have seen you. You have grown so tall."

"Monsieur Cardell." James met the man as he approached them and greeted him like an old friend with busses on each cheek. "It's good to see you. How have you been?"

The older man made a distinctly French moue and said, "*Comme ci, comme ça.* These bones are old, but they keep going. But what are you doing in my little shop?"

"Ah, I had hoped to find a scent for my wife." James told him, shooting a smile over his shoulder at Sarah.

Monsieur Cardell's gaze lit on Sarah. He glanced back at James in surprise. "Wife! My boy, you must introduce us."

James led Cardell to her. "Sarah, this is an old family friend, Monsieur Daniel Cardell."

Monsieur Cardell eyed Sarah for a few seconds before holding out his rough and calloused hand with a slight bow. "*Donzella, enchanté.*"

"It's nice to meet you." With a glance at James, Sarah put her hand in Cardell's and he kissed it like a courtier from another time.

Sarah expected him to release her hand, but instead he held it in front of his prodigious nose and inhaled deeply. His dark eyes lifted to hers. He waved a dismissive hand at the shelves of finished scents. "None of these scents are for you, donzella! These are for tourists. You are far too enchanting." He gave

116 · MEREDITH R. STODDARD

her a rakish smile as he enclosed her hand in both of his. "I will make a fragrance only for you."

Cardell studied Sarah for several seconds. "I think you are very intelligent, but with a warm heart. No?"

He glanced at James for confirmation before turning back to Sarah. His eyes found hers again and his angular face softened. "You have incredible strength, donzella. It will be an honor to make a fragrance for you."

He released her hand before turning back to his work behind the counter. Sarah glanced at James unsure whether she should follow. James for his part was grinning. "This is a great honor. His bespoke perfumes are very sought after. He does not do them for everyone. My mother has a standing order for hers."

Cardell scanned the racks of bottles. He pulled one bottle from a shelf and removed the stopper. Waving the bottle under his nose he contemplated the scent. After several seconds he shook his head. "No, too innocent."

He glanced back at Sarah. "You lived on a mountain. Yes?"

Sarah wondered how on earth he could tell by looking at her. "Yes."

He tapped the side of his nose with a knotted finger before turning back to the shelves. He went through many more scents, asked many more questions, and made more observations which were eerily spot on.

When Cardell had collected nearly a dozen bottles of scents, he spread his hands out on the counter and looked at them. "I will work on this tonight. You must allow me to make it a wedding gift for you."

"That's too generous." Sarah protested.

"*Non!* The prince and I are old friends, and I am overjoyed he has found you." His words were effusive, but his demeanor was calm, as if simple joy was boring. He shifted his gaze to James. "You must come to the house tomorrow night. We will have dinner and you can collect your perfume."

"Will Celia make her aioli?" James grinned.

"For you? Of course, she will." Cardell matched James's smile.

"Then we will be there." James put his arm around Sarah and ushered her back outside. She turned at the door and looked back over her shoulder to find Cardell watching her with speculation.

CHAPTER FOURTEEN

James had been excited about visiting Monsieur Cardell's house all day. They had followed their developing pattern; Sarah swimming in the mornings, then spending the afternoon in the library while James worked in the study. If it seemed a strange way to spend one's honeymoon, no one said anything to him about it.

At the very least, he had managed to distract her from her grief. She spent less time in the pool and more time in the library. He'd found her there late in the afternoon. She sat at the table piled high with a new set of books, and a notebook where she was taking notes.

"I'm sorry to say you won't be able to take those notes out of here." He told her, looking over her shoulder.

She waved him off. "No problem. Writing them down helps me remember. Sometimes I need to draw out the connections to make sense of them. You can burn these when I'm done if you like."

He didn't. "I rather like the idea of adding your work to the family collection. I can put it in the vault with the other documents."

"My scribbled notes are hardly the same as source documents. And these are more about my family than yours." Sarah looked back at the book on the table. One amber curl fell in front of her eye.

His fingers itched to brush the curl back, maybe tuck it behind her ear as he'd seen her do countless times. Instead, he cleared his throat and asked. "Your family, really?"

"Well, I was curious about the Celto-Ligurian settlements Jon was talking about. It reminded me of something from an old legend my grandmother told me. So, I was looking for some kind of correlation."

"Did you find one?"

"No, I didn't." Her eyebrows drew together in consternation. "I can find bits and pieces like my people. But according to legend we've been toting around the cauldron for thousands of years. I have already connected the migration part of the legend with Doggerland which was flooded six thousand years ago. But the cauldron is iron, and the earliest known iron artifacts are only around four thousand years old. And there aren't any iron artifacts from Europe until 500 B.C.E."

"What does that mean for your people?" James tried to follow her logic.

"Well, if I'm interpreting the legend correctly, it means our cauldron is the oldest piece of forged iron in the world." She said with all the weight such a statement would entail "If my people didn't migrate over Doggerland from the continent as I originally thought--"

"Or the cauldron isn't as old as the legend led you to believe." He offered.

A low laugh bubbled up from her throat. "Also, entirely possible. 'the time before time' isn't exactly a specific date."

He laughed. "Is that what made you think they came from the continent?"

"Not only that. There are parts about migration, and boats made from roofs that suggested it. But the legend usually starts with those words." Sarah looked at a stack of books on the table. "Actually…I wonder what evidence there might be for those boats."

She reached for a large book in the middle of the stack, but he intercepted her hand. "It will have to wait for tomorrow. Now, we need to get ready for dinner at Cardell's."

"Right. Of course." She let him pull her away from her work toward the door. "Can we tell Martine not to disturb these books? I'd like to get back to this tomorrow."

"I'll lock the library, so they won't be disturbed."

***

"What was it he called you yesterday, *princep*?" Sarah asked James as they passed Aix-en-Provence.

He chuckled. "It's just a nickname. He's always called me that. I think it's Catalan for prince."

"Catalan, not Provencal?" Sarah had only heard a little of the native language there in Provence. Much like English in Britain, French had grown to dominate the regional Indigenous languages in France.

James shook his head. "No, Cardell is from Spain. Montserrat, I think. He settled here ages ago."

"And donzella?" She thought of the name Cardell had called her. She supposed it was some honorific or endearment.

"Probably also Catalan." James shrugged. "I think it means lady or miss."

Sarah returned to watching the fields and trees roll by. It wasn't Scotland, but it was nice. She could easily see how so many artists had been influenced by this region. The landscape was full of drama with rolling hills and ridges. The sun-bleached colors of late August were occasionally punctuated by bright blooms, or red tiled rooves.

Sarah wondered if they were ever going to get there when they rounded a hill and came upon a field of lavender. Although most of the blooms were gone, a few straggling stalks of purple flowers stuck out above the fronds of curling green-gray leaves. Sarah rolled down the window and drew in a long breath which she released with a sigh. "It's amazing."

"Wait until you see Cardell's greenhouses. He has every fragrant flower you can think of."

"Is this field his?" Sarah asked.

"It is. I'm told lavender was how he got started in perfume. Then he expanded out to other flowers which grow well in this climate." James explained. "Now, he grows all the flowers for his perfumes in climate-controlled greenhouses. Its rather extraordinary."

"Wow. I would think it would be easier and less expensive to buy the flowers he can't grow here."

"You'll have to ask him. We're nearly at the house."

They turned down a gravel drive. The car rumbled through a seemingly endless lavender field. Sarah could see some other fields, a low one with pink blooms which looked like thyme, and some towering sunflowers in the distance. Eventually they reached a modest stone house with a blue front door.

"My young friends!" Cardell came out the door to greet them, his arms opened wide. He had traded his white linen suit for some sturdy olive-green trousers and a faded blue cotton shirt. He looked as if he had walked out of some impressionist painting of a provincial farmer.

"Monsieur Cardell." James greeted him with a kiss on each cheek, and Sarah did the same.

Cardell tucked Sarah's hand in the crook of his arm and walked toward the house. "Celia is still cooking our dinner. So, I will show you around. I think you will like it here, donzella."

"I have been enjoying the lavender as we drove in." Sarah let him escort her into the house.

Cardell led them straight through and out the back door onto a covered veranda not unlike the one behind the Stuarts' chateau. However, the view from Cardell's veranda was of two large greenhouses extending from behind the house. There were also sheds, and outbuildings Sarah thought must contain the massive amounts of equipment it took to maintain a farm like this.

Everywhere there were flowers. Jasmine, and bougainvillea climbed the pergola covering the veranda, and the walls of some of the buildings. There were pots of lavender and other herbs, as well as dwarf citrus trees in large planters around the courtyard. "Wow!"

Cardell's laugh was a low rumble of satisfaction. "Oh, donzella, this is only the courtyard. The real excitement is this way."

He ushered her toward one of the greenhouses and opened a glass door. The weather stripping across the bottom of the door brushed the stone threshold. Inside the temperature didn't change but the climate was much more humid. Rivulets of condensation traced their way down the glass walls.

"This section simulates a tropical climate." Cardell told her as she looked around the space. The interior was about thirty feet wide, with the ceiling high enough to allow for small trees. The courtyard was full of plants suited to the climate in Provence, this room was packed to the gills with tropical plants. "We use this room to grow our frangipani, ylang ylang, and some varieties of jasmine among other things."

"It's amazing." Sarah leaned forward to sniff a frangipani flower, its five petals swirling together like a pinwheel. The fragrance was sweet and somewhat fruity, like a gardenia with a little kick.

They strolled through more sections of the enormous greenhouse. There was a room full of varieties of fragrant roses, and another which captured the climate of Britain where Cardell was growing peonies, sweet Williams, and peppery nasturtiums. "How do you manage this?" Sarah asked. "It seems like it would be more expense than it's worth. You could buy these from growers in their own climate."

"I could. But here I can guarantee their freshness. I can cultivate the most fragrant varietals, and I like to have a large selection available when I'm creating." Cardell strolled along beside her as James trailed behind them. "Like an artist with his palette. No?"

"Makes sense." Sarah followed him out of the far end of the first greenhouse and across the courtyard to the other. "But these have to be expensive to maintain."

He tapped a finger to his temple. "You are very smart, donzella. But so am I. I have a partnership with the university. Their students help me maintain the greenhouses and I allow them to do experiments in them. There is even a hydroponics laboratory in this building. We work together to share the expense."

"And how do you maintain all these different environments?" She asked.

"We use a combination of heating and cooling, humidifiers and so on." He pointed a finger at the ceiling. "We also have a sophisticated system of shades overhead. We can control the degree of shade and sun to take some of the weight of controlling the temperature. If we did not, these greenhouses would feel like saunas this time of year."

"I can imagine." The next door led them into the hydroponics lab. There a wide array of plants grew in baskets of soilless growing medium. There was everything from lettuce to melons. Sarah spotted tall stalks and blade-like leaves. "Is that corn?"

"Si." Cardell followed Sarah to the rows of corn.

"Ah." Sarah felt a wave of nostalgia for Granny's kitchen garden. "We used to grow corn. We would pick it, shuck it, and eat it all in the same day. It was so good."

"You grew corn?" James came up behind them.

"We grew everything; corn, tomatoes, peppers, onions, okra, garlic…" She chuckled. "Barley. We foraged for the rest. Granny didn't like buying what she could make or grow herself, and anyway we didn't have a lot of money."

Cardell studied her for a moment. "She was a wise woman, your grandmother."

His eyes held a speculative glint. Did wise woman mean the same thing here that it did in Kettle Holler? They meant she was a healer, which she had been to some extent. Sarah smiled softly, remembering how Granny navigated the fine line in the mountains between being someone people trusted to heal them and someone they suspected of being a witch. "She was the wisest I've known."

Cardell took her hand again and returned it to the crook of his arm leading her through the lab to the next room. "I'm sure she taught you well. I think you will like this next area."

They walked through another door into a room Sarah could have sworn was on a mountainside in the Blue Ridge. The familiar aromas made her homesick. The light was dappled shade like a forest. Rhododendrons lined walls with their big bundles of blooms in shades of pink and red. Mountain laurels were there too, no longer in bloom, but Sarah would know those leaves anywhere. Asters grew in clumps near the ground and there were even bright orange sprays of orchids. A hollow space of nostalgia opened in her chest as she imagined herself back in the forest, she'd grown up in. She could almost hear the creak of trees swaying and the buzz of summer bugs.

"You miss your home, no?" Cardell asked softly.

"Only this part. The forest was my best friend." She whispered. "I don't know how you did it, but this is exactly like my home."

"I like this room too." He gave her a fatherly smile before taking a step back. "Perhaps you would like to show your husband your favorites."

Sarah turned to find James watching from a few feet away. She pointed out the various plants to him, telling him stories about how they had been important to her as a little girl growing up in the mountains. She told him the uses for the coneflowers she found in a sunnier area next to some day lilies. He asked questions, genuinely curious about how Sarah had grown up.

She wasn't sure how long they spent walking through the garden of her memory. It felt like minutes and hours at the same time. A bell sounded somewhere in the distance, and Cardell appeared around a camelia bush. "That will be the dinner bell. We should not keep Celia waiting."

"Of course not." James agreed, offering Sarah his hand.

She looked around one more time wishing she could stay longer. "Right. Thank you for sharing the greenhouses with us."

"It has been my pleasure, donzella." Cardell bowed his head and smiled.

Celia was Cardell's housekeeper and all-around girl Friday, although he did not talk to her as if she was a servant. He treated her with deference, and she seemed to treat him with tolerance. She was a small, stocky woman of indeterminate age. Her gray hair suggested she might be in her fifties at least, but she bustled around the table on the veranda with an energy which made her seem younger than she looked. As Cardell explained it. "She takes care of everything in this house so I can focus on the greenhouses."

And take care she did. Although the house was full of rustic charm, it was impeccably clean. Their dinner was the best Sarah had tasted since their arrival. The Stuarts' chef was brilliant, but Celia was a virtuoso when it came to local cuisine. She joined them at the table, and the four of them enjoyed a comfortable dinner with a local wine and Celia's incomparable aioli with fish, vegetables, and fresh-baked bread.

They talked and laughed and had a wonderful time. The sun sank behind the trees and lights came on while they continued chatting about what Sarah and James had seen on their trip, and what their plans were. Cardell told stories about some of his more famous clients, and fragrances he had designed for the fashion houses in Paris. Sarah felt more relaxed than she had in months. She almost forgot her grief.

By the time the moon rose over the hills, their driver appeared near the back door and gave James the nod Sarah had come to recognize was the signal to leave. James leaned forward setting his glass on the table. "I'm afraid we must be going. But we had a wonderful time. Celia, you outdid yourself. Dinner was divine."

"Ah! But I have something for you." Cardell jumped up from his seat and disappeared into the house.

Celia graciously rose and saw them to the door. "Good night, my dears, it has been lovely."

Sarah kissed her cheeks feeling sorry the evening was ending. She would much rather stay here in the parfumier's enchanted garden. "Thank you so much for having us."

James stepped outside following the driver. Sarah was about to follow him when Cardell reappeared carrying a small, glossy red box. "This is for you. A fragrance all your own."

Sarah took the box blushing. "You are too kind. You really didn't need to."

"Ah, but I love to do this. It is my calling, donzella." He grinned, his bright white teeth contrasting his tanned face.

"What does that mean? Donzella." Sarah had to ask before she left.

"Oh." He waved a hand and shrugged. "It is a young lady, like mademoiselle."

That was puzzling. "But I'm married."

He tilted his head and his eyebrows knit together. Leaning in he whispered. "Perhaps not yet in your heart."

Sarah froze. How could he know? Was it obvious?

"Good night, my dear." Cardell patted her hand which still rested on top of the box.

"Sarah?" James called from outside.

With one last confused look at Cardell who smiled blithely, she followed James to the car, red box in hand.

"Is that your fragrance?" James asked as the car pulled onto the road.

"Yes." Sarah looked at the box she had almost forgotten she was holding. She opened the front panel to reveal an ornate bottle of red and clear glass. "Oh."

"Striking bottle." James said. "Well? I'm dying to know what it smells like."

Sarah lifted the bottle out of the box and held it upright. It was held closed by a stopper with a gasket around the base. Sarah pulled out the stopper and waved it under her nose. It was a complex blend of herbal and floral notes. She caught whiffs of heather, something smokey, and was that honeysuckle? It somehow invoked memories of both North Carolina and the Highlands. And there was something else, a soft note of spice Sarah couldn't quite place which lingered after the floral notes faded. It was like her story told in scent.

James leaned closer and inhaled. "That's heavenly."

It was incredible. Sarah put the stopper back into the bottle. "Monsieur Cardell was right. This is definitely his calling."

CHAPTER FIFTEEN

Edinburgh, Scotland
August 31, 1996

"Dermot?" Jujhar looked surprised when he opened the door of Lyall Green's stone cottage tucked neatly down a little side street in Dean Village. Dermot had never been to his grandfather's house before. If he weren't so bitter about Green's hands-off approach to the lives of his daughter and grandson, Dermot might have found the place charming.

"Is he in?" He asked without exchanging niceties with his friend. There was no need to explain who 'he' was.

Jujhar stepped back from the doorway to let Dermot enter. "In the conservatory. I'll show you the way."

The tiny foyer was dim, with no windows and minimal light filtering in from the next room. Like his grandfather, the house seemed to be out of another time.

Jujhar walked Dermot through a library lined with dusty volumes appearing to range in age from the latest bestsellers to leather bound folios predating the printing press. Dermot wondered if Green had amassed this collection himself or if he had inherited it from his predecessors, assuming he was telling the truth about his age and his role as a guardian of the prophecy. Even after all he'd seen, Dermot still didn't want to believe it.

"How have you been?" Jujhar asked as they crossed the library to the hall beyond.

"How d'ye think?" Dermot muttered grimly.

"I'm sorry." Jujhar said with sympathy. "We tried, mate."

They exchanged a look recalling their ill-fated attempt to help Sarah escape before her wedding day. Jujhar had been one of only a handful of people who had been willing to help him. Fortunately, Jujhar had survived. Dermot's old friend, Dez, hadn't been so lucky. He patted Jujhar's back. "Aye. We did. Maybe one day we'll succeed."

"Have you heard from them?" Dermot assumed he was asking about Sarah and James.

"Nah. I doubt they'll be calling me on their honeymoon." He grumbled.

"Of course, sorry." Jujhar hurried up the short flight of stairs. He knocked twice on the door before opening.

The conservatory was jammed to the rafters with plants competing for every inch of sunlight. There were worktables and shelves along one wall. His grandfather sat in the far corner on a stool in front of a rack of jars full of mysterious substances, none of which were labeled. He was grinding something with a mortar and pestle and mumbling to himself. He was so focused on what he was doing he didn't hear Dermot and Jujhar approach.

Jujhar stopped a few feet away and cleared his throat. "Sir, you have a visitor."

"Hmm?" The old man looked over his shoulder at his apprentice. When he noticed Dermot behind Jujhar, he sat up straighter and put on his glasses which had been resting on the table. He blinked in surprise. "Mr. Sinclair, I did not expect to see you here."

"Mmph." The old man elicited so many feelings in Dermot. Apart from his mother, Lyall Green was the only relative he knew of, but he barely knew the man. On top of their tense family relationship, Green had refused to help Dermot and Jujhar's ill-fated plan to save Sarah from being forced to marry James Stuart, something Dermot didn't think he would ever forgive him for. "Did ye visit my mother?"

"I'm sorry?" Green looked confused. "Please, sit down. Would you like a cup of tea?"

Dermot waved off the offer. "This isna a social call. A man visited my mother. He said something to her. It scared her so much; she won't go outside anymore. Was it you?"

"No, I haven't been to see her." Green changed his tone to the soft self-assured one he used when acting as a solicitor with a difficult client. His whole demeanor became confident and calm. "What do you know about this man?"

"Ye know what her memory is like." Dermot ran his fingers through his hair. He was getting frustrated thinking about it. "Gray hair, wore a suit. That's all she could tell me."

"That could be anyone." Jujhar said.

"Aye. But I know at least three men who might be interested in talking with her. This was my first stop." He sighed. "I reckon I would rather it was ye than one of the other two."

"What did the staff at the home say?" Green leaned an elbow on his worktable.

"They say it's more likely to be a hallucination, or paranoia." Dermot shook his head. "I know her disease will cause both, but it hasna before, at least not that I know of. And she was so scared."

Green looked thoughtful. "I assume the other men you suspect are Henry and Walter Stuart."

"I canna think of anyone else who would want to visit her." Dermot started to pace. "They did say a couple of doctors there might fit the description."

"There is one more person who it could be." Green said. "Your father."

Dermot looked at him sharply. "Are ye saying ye know who my father is?"

"And it might not be Henry Stuart?" Jujhar added.

Green held up his hands shaking his head. "I don't know any more than you do. But he would be the person with the most compelling reason to visit her."

"It's never compelled him to visit before." Dermot was skeptical.

"True, but you've never been this close to discovering who he is before." Green explained. "The matching ceremony proved you are as viable an heir as James. If your father knows about that, then he might have a reason to visit your mother."

"To warn her against telling me." Dermot finished for him.

Green cocked his head in confirmation. "Or to see if her disease has progressed enough that she can't tell you who he is."

"It's still got to be a Stuart. Who else would know about the matching ceremony?" Dermot thought through both scenarios. "If he was warning her off, he might have scared her. If he was trying to see what she remembers, he might have dredged up something which scared her. And he might be satisfied she doesna remember who he is."

"In which case, you shouldn't need to worry about him again." Jujhar put in. "In the first case, he might come back to make sure she remembers his warning."

Dermot growled in irritation. "I chose that care home because it had nice grounds, and now she won't even go outside."

"Meaning if he comes back, he'll have to come inside." Jujhar sat down on another stool at the workbench looking thoughtful. "Does the care home have security cameras?"

Dermot nodded, thinking about the cameras he'd been shown when he had chosen the home for Seonag. They covered all the doors and the common rooms. "Aye, they do. But I doubt they'd show me the footage."

"They might make it available to your solicitor." Green shifted some papers and jars around on the table until he found a notepad and pencil. "Who should I talk to when I pay them a visit?"

Dermot gave him Patricia's information and felt relieved Green agreed to help him for once. He was surprised it had been so easy. He left Green's house feeling hopeful he might find an answer to both questions; who was terrorizing his mother and who was his father. That didn't mean he was going to stop searching on his own in the meantime.

***

His grandfather had been easy to track down. Henry Stuart was more of a challenge. As Henry was no longer under the Alba Security umbrella, it was more than a matter of simply checking with the office to locate him. He had tried the yacht club, and the health club, before finally finding him at his golf club.

He spotted Henry coming out of the locker room talking with some friends. "Sir."

A genuine smile spread across Henry's face. "Dermot! It's good to see you."

"D'ye have a moment?" Dermot wasn't sure why he was suddenly nervous. He hadn't spoken with Henry very much since their confrontation at Taigh na Damh, Lyall Green's house in the Highlands. Dermot hadn't thought there was anything left for them to say.

Henry turned to his friends who were chatting away behind him. "Go ahead. I'll catch up."

The others went on their way to the dining room. Henry approached Dermot walking him out of the clubhouse to the patio overlooking the eighteenth green. "Is everything all right? Have you heard from James?"

"No. I mean, I havena heard from James, which likely means everything is fine." He didn't reckon James was likely to call and give him an update on how his honeymoon was going, but he was sure he would have heard at the office if something had gone wrong. At least he hoped he would. "It's about my mother."

"Ah. Henry's lips pressed into a grim line. Henry was usually easy to read, but he always seemed to shutter himself off where Seonag was concerned.

"Have ye been to visit her?"

Henry looked confused. "My boy, I don't even know where she is. I heard you had her moved to a new care home."

"I did." Dermot didn't know whether to be relieved it wasn't Henry who had terrorized his mother, or angry Henry hadn't tried to visit his old friend. "I thought it was a secret, but she says she was visited by a gray-haired man in a suit who frightened her."

"And the home doesn't know who it might have been?" Henry asked.

Dermot shook his head, deflated. "They're not even sure he was real."

Henry looked off at the city skyline rising above the golf course. Arthur's Seat towered over the surrounding land. "I can't imagine how difficult this is for you."

Dermot scoffed. "Not nearly as difficult as it is for her. Ye remember what she was like."

"Mmm." Henry watched the city, but his voice sounded like he was lost in memories. "Mind like a steel trap, your mother. It must be awful."

Dermot had been prepared to be angry with Henry. He frequently was. He'd also looked up to this man when he was a boy, dreamed of having a father like Henry. Now, in his early retirement, the former Lord Caledon seemed so feckless, and unmoored. It was as if when he turned his business over to James and Walter, he had not only abdicated his business responsibilities, but all other responsibilities as well. Now confronting him, Dermot realized Henry was probably the only person in the world who remembered and loved the woman his mother used to be. "It's like every time she turns around, there's another..." His throat clenched and tears pooled in his eyes. "...hole where her memories used to be. She blinks and the world shifts, and everything and everyone around her is unfamiliar and she's terrified."

Henry put a hand on his shoulder. His own voice cracked. "Oh, son."

Dermot shook off the hand and sniffed. "I've asked ye not to call me that."

Henry's jaw firmed. "I'm not going to stop. Not anymore."

Every muscle in Dermot's body went still. "What are ye saying?"

"I have loved your mother from the first moment I saw her. We were in a history lecture at St. Andrew's and she was peppering the lecturer with questions, good ones. She was so interested, and so passionate about the subject, which I think was the Fenian Cycle of Irish mythology or some such thing. She didn't care a jot about how it looked or that it wasn't polite to ask so many questions. She was curious, and she was determined to satisfy her curiosity."

He laughed softly. "All my friends thought I was mad for wanting to get to know her. Of course, they were all like me; spoiled, trust fund babies who were there as a rite of passage before taking on whatever the family business was. They didn't see what I saw. I wanted to get close to her. I wanted to understand what made her so passionate about old legends. And she told me. She talked about what she was researching and told me what had so fascinated her. I was in awe of her mind."

"Did ye ever...?" Dermot wasn't quite sure how to finish that question.

Henry sighed heavily. "I wish I could say we were in love. I have no idea how your mother felt then. I think she was too busy studying for romantic thoughts. But I let my friends and my brother convince me she was beneath us. No one knew who her family was. She hadn't gone to boarding schools like we did. In short, she wasn't of our class, and we were still an insular society then."

"Ye're a might insular now." Dermot had to point out. Henry and James's set might have loosened their collars, but they weren't likely to stoop to marrying people of the lower classes without something to gain from it. "Did ye know then who her father is?"

"Is?" Henry looked sharply at Dermot. "I thought he was dead."

Dermot studied Henry trying to gauge if he truly didn't know. If not, should he tell him? In the end he decided not to open that can of worms. "Aye, sorry. Was."

"I knew he was a clerk or something. I think he worked in insurance. At least that's what Seonag told me." He looked back at the city. The morning haze was lifting, and the skyline came into sharper focus. "I let them stop me from pursuing a relationship with your mother, and I have never regretted anything in my life more."

"Why then, were we always with you? Why treat us like family?" Dermot still didn't quite understand.

"For my part, I only wanted her and eventually you in my life. A couple of years after I finished school and married Anne, your mother sought me out. She came to me with the story of the prophecy. She'd been researching legends on Skye and came across one of a branch of the MacLeods who left the island and disappeared somewhere. Sarah's people. That led her to the prophecy and some connections no one else made. She wanted to see if we had anything in our family's records confirming it. I let her search everything we have and she found a record of the prophecy in our family documents. She took on the role of family historian."

"It was so hard having her around." Henry went on after a moment's pause. "When it became apparent Anne cared more about status and power than me, I wanted so badly to turn to your mother. But by then she was focused on her work and the prophecy she wouldn't hear of it. Please believe me, I have never been with your mother. And it's not for lack of trying. I have loved her for so long."

He turned to Dermot. "If I thought there was a possibility of you being my son, I would shout it from the top of that crag." He indicated the direction of Arthur's Seat. "I have loved you too. I have taken pride in every success you have had and fretted over every problem as much as I have with James. You are the son of my heart if not my blood."

Dermot shook his head with a sigh. "Much good it's done me."

Henry sniffed. "I know. I've not been a good father to either of you these last few years. I spent so long working at a job I didn't enjoy, married to a woman I barely like, but keeping up appearances for the sake of the family and company. I suppose I thought once you lads were grown you didn't need me anymore. I took off to Spain to escape."

"Meanwhile, she fell apart." Dermot spat out bitterly.

"You cannot possibly know how sorry I am I wasn't here to help you." Henry's voice grew thick with tears. "I have no excuse for not coming back. I was a coward, and I am sorry for it. If there is anything I can do now, for her, for you, you only have to ask."

Dermot let out a heavy sigh. "There's nothing to be done now. She probably wouldn't know ye. She barely knows who I am. Her mind is gone."

"I can visit." Henry offered dashing a tear from his cheek.

"It would probably only upset her. She gets upset if she thinks she's not recognized someone." Dermot thought of the last time he had tried to ask her about his father.

Henry bowed his head. "I'm so very sorry."

There wasn't anything left to say. Henry had made his choices, and it was too late to change course now. His mother was lost to them. Maybe the man was a hallucination or a doctor. The only other possible explanation was Walter Stuart.

CHAPTER SIXTEEN

Aix-en-Provence, France

Sarah waited eagerly as their car climbed to the top of the plateau. The sun gave Jon's light brown hair a momentary golden glow as he stepped out from beside a building at the top of the drive. He directed them around the building to a grass parking lot. James tensed at the sight of Jon. "How long were you involved with this man?"

'Too long.' She thought. Nudging James playfully with an elbow. She felt surprisingly light, as if some of the weight she had been carrying had been lifted. She wasn't sure what made the change. Maybe it was their dinner at Cardell's, or the excitement of seeing the dig site. "He was off at various digs for much of the time, and I learned he wasn't for me when he was at home."

"And yet, he keeps turning up like a bad penny." James muttered, keeping a wary eye on the anthropologist as if he was going to jump up and snatch Sarah away.

"It is a little strange that he's here. It's not his usual field of study, but he's still early in his career and sometimes you have to go where the funding takes you." Sarah tied her hair back into a ponytail. Jon had called the house the day before to arrange a tour of the site for them and recommended they arrive early to avoid the hottest part of the day.

"Mmm." James still sounded suspicious. Sarah was becoming accustomed to the Stuart tendency to be on guard, although she couldn't imagine Jon being a threat. That would require a level of passion Sarah wasn't sure Jon had for anything but his work.

Before Sarah put on her sunglasses, she gave James a look which said both 'relax' and 'behave.' James took her hand in his and they walked back around the building to where Jon waited for them. Calum, who was acting as their bodyguard today took his place a few feet behind them.

"Good morning." Jon said, stepping forward as they rounded the building. "You're in luck today. The site is closed to the public."

"Well, thank you." James shook Jon's offered hand. "I appreciate you making an exception for us."

Jon's smile was fleeting. "When I told the site director you'd be visiting, he insisted. I suspect he'll be hitting you up for a donation before you leave."

James looked toward the largest of the few buildings which seemed to house a sort of visitor's center and chuckled. "That's not unexpected. I don't mind."

"Great." Jon huffed in relief. "Let me show you around."

"Thank you. I'm excited to see everything." Sarah was excited, for the first time in weeks.

"We can start right here. In the second century B.C.E. this part of France was a frontier between the early tribes of southern France and Greek colonizers in Marseilles. There were some regular incursions back and forth until the Celto-Ligurian tribes around here formed a confederation. This location is strategic being near the river and also because of its natural elevation." Jon lifted an arm to point toward the tree line on the other side of the drive leading back to the road. "The edge of the plateau at one time was fortified with stone ramparts protecting the village up here. You probably saw some of the stone wall when you came up the drive."

Sarah had noticed. "Is the tree line a good indicator of where the walls would have been?"

"Yes, exactly. There were two periods of development for the town, and we'll see some of the ramparts from the second stage as we walk around. The first stage is mainly indicated by the tree line. Many of the stones were removed and reused elsewhere, but you'll see we have a lot of foundations left. If you'll walk this way."

He led them around another row of trees and into the ruins of the village where foundations of ancient row houses stretched like a grid on either side of a central lane. "As you can see, there has been extensive excavation. Archaeologists have been studying this site since the early nineteenth century. Most of what we do now is preserve and educate."

"So, this really was a fortified town." The foundations of the houses looked impossibly small, but Sarah knew there would likely have been whole families living in them.

"Exactly," Jon agreed. "Over here, you'll see Habitat One. This is what we believe to be the older of the two sections. The foundations are small, all opening into the street."

"Do you know how tall the houses were?" Sarah asked, stepping closer to examine one of the chambers. The foundations rose no further than a few feet above the ground.

"Sadly, no." Jon stayed where he was on the path. "On the other side of the street there is Habitat Two. This was built decades later to accommodate the growing population. We also believe this represents a class divide. These houses are larger with multiple rooms."

The 'street' Jon spoke of was really a gravel lane running down the center of the site and was wider than the narrow alleys. Where the grid of foundations in Habitat One was simple and relatively uniform, the foundations on the other side showed houses divided into rooms with a little more variation in shape and more elaborate stonework.

"If you'll walk this way, I'll show you some other spots of interest on the plateau." Jon walked backward along the street. James took Sarah's hand as they followed along. Jon showed them some other foundations outside the grid, the newer ramparts he had mentioned, and a small plaza bordered on three sides by the houses of Habitat Two.

They were exploring the plaza when Jon explained some of the history of the excavation. "For centuries, local people borrowed stones from the site to build roads and foundations or walls in their houses. In 1817, a professor at the university noticed some carved stones in a shed wall nearby and asked about them. He was led here to what was little more than a pile of rubble after centuries of practical predation by locals. Excavations occurred off and on over the next hundred years. A few more carved stones were found, but very little to show how these people lived. There were a couple of competing theories the settlement was Roman or Salyen. It wasn't until the Nazis excavated the site during the occupation that they found statues. This sparked more serious academic excavations after the war ended."

Sarah had been examining the stonework on a low archway, captivated by the way the narrow stones fit together to form the arch which had lasted two thousand years, but what Jon said caught her attention. "Nazis?"

"Surely, you know about the Nazi interest in archeology. You've seen the Indiana Jones movies."

"Yeah, of course, but that's Hollywood." She gave him a skeptical look. "They're not exactly known for historical accuracy."

"True, but they weren't entirely wrong. The Nazis went on a quest for ancient objects of significance. Historians think it was an effort to give them legitimacy. If they could claim to have the Holy Grail, the Ark of the Covenant, or the Spear of Destiny, it would give them authority similar to the church with some European Christians. There are also some who think the Nazis believed those objects had supernatural power which they could tap into."

Sarah glanced at James who was listening from a polite distance. She thought about the Magdalene connection with Provence and asked pointing to the ground. "So, they were here searching for the Holy Grail?"

Jon tilted his head as if unsure. "It's possible. But this settlement most likely collapsed before the first century."

Jon took a step closer to her, his tone changing to a conspiratorial one. "I think they were looking for something else. Have you heard of the Vril Society."

"I don't think so." Sarah shook her head. Lyall Green hadn't mentioned Vril when telling her about the Nazi interest in her people.

Jon started when James stepped closer to Sarah, no longer pretending not to listen. Sarah wasn't sure if James had responded to the topic or to Jon leaning in closer to talk. Jon went on looking past Sarah to include James. "This English writer, Edward Bulwer-Lytton."

"He was a politician as well." James added.

"I think so, yeah." Jon said.

Sarah thought she had heard the name in another context. "Wait. Wasn't he the 'It was a dark and stormy night' guy?"

Jon smirked "Yeah, and this has more to do with his questionable novels than his political career. His books were actually pretty successful. He was also interested in the occult. Spiritualism was all the rage in the late nineteenth century, and horror and science fiction were becoming popular. So, he wrote this book, Vril: The Power of the Coming Race."

"Oh." Sarah groaned. "That title suggests a lot of problems."

Jon agreed. "Unless you were a racist. The book was about a man who basically fell down a deep hole and ended up in an underground civilization made up of a matriarchal society called the Vril-ya. They were an ancient race which retreated to their underground world from the deluge. They used this magical energy called Vril to do everything from healing to telepathy."

"Huh." Well, that was disturbingly familiar. Sarah thought about her mother's description of the hidden village of Làrachd an Fhamhair, where their people lived in houses cut into the hills, with turf roofs, and used their cauldron for food and healing. If the Nazis had been looking for these fictional people, her people would have been good candidates. "I can see how the Nazis would have been attracted to the idea."

"Right." Jon went on. "It wasn't just the Nazis. The spiritualists and theosophists of Bulwer-Lytton's day went a crazy about it too. It didn't matter to them that it was total fiction. It spawned the Hollow Earth Theory, tons of snake oil cures claiming to be made with Vril, and all kinds of occultists became convinced Vril, and the race of people who were able to tap into it, were real. Decades later some of the Nazi occultists were still operating under the belief in Vril, and the Aryans as the Nazis defined them were the inheritors of Bulwer-Lytton's 'Coming Race'."

"So, you think they were looking for evidence of the ancient underground race?" Sarah asked.

Jon shrugged. "I think it's a possibility. France, especially the southern regions have some of the oldest evidence of people in Europe. There are caves all over southwestern France. This site is one of the oldest human settlements above ground. If they were trying to track the Vril-ya in their underground lair, this could be a link in the chain."

"So, they were casting about everywhere looking for evidence of these supposed ancient people?" Sarah's grandmother had been forced to leave Làrachd an Fhamhair for Canada in the late 1930's when a Nazi had found his way to the village, then disappeared. Her people had known he might bring back more, so the remaining two sisters in the village had been forced to go to Nova Scotia where the MacKenzie branch was already living. Maggie had never returned to Làrachd an Fhamhair to keep the sisters separate for their own protection.

"Very likely. I mean they were chasing a fiction. It wasn't like they had solid scientific grounds for what they were searching for." Jon said with a little laugh, oblivious to how close he was to her reality.

They finished their tour near the building serving as the on-site museum. A short man with unkempt salt and pepper hair and crooked glasses came bustling out of the door and strode toward them. James held up a hand letting Calum know the man was not a threat. Sarah couldn't imagine anyone thinking this man could hurt them. He peered up at James through Coke bottle thick glasses, and grinned. Extending a work-worn hand. "Monsieur Stuart. I am Dr. Desrosiers, the site director here. Thank you for visiting us today."

"Of course. It's nice to meet you." James shook his hand before turning toward Sarah. "This is my wife, Lady Sarah Stuart."

"*Enchanté, madame.*" He offered Sarah his hand.

Sarah cast a sharp look at James. He didn't usually introduce her in such a formal way, title, and all. She shook Desrosiers's hand, smiling. "Thank you for letting us visit on such a quiet day. We've very much enjoyed the tour."

"I am so glad, madame. Won't you both come inside out of the heat. I can show you some of the work we do today." The doctor gestured toward the building behind him.

"I should like to see that." James took a step in his direction. Desrosiers walked beside him leaving Sarah and Jon to follow.

"Lady Sarah?" Jon asked under his breath emphasis on the lady.

Sarah sighed. "That might have been for your benefit. He rarely uses his title."

"Sounds like your title now too." Jon muttered as they slowly made their way inside.

"I suppose it is."

"You don't sound too excited." He said. "Trouble in paradise already?"

Sarah shook her head. "I didn't marry him for his title or his money. They come with the package."

"You married him awfully fast if it wasn't for the money." His tone turned bitter. "I mean I never pegged you for one to use that particular asset to get ahead."

Sarah inhaled sharply, absorbing the sting his comment brought on. Any remaining good feelings she had toward Jon Samuels evaporated. Sarah stared him down, one perfectly shaped eyebrow raised. She felt like she was back in the basement anthropology lab where she had realized almost a year ago that he wasn't worth any more of her time or energy.

She took a step closer to him. When she spoke, her voice was deadly quiet. "You feel better?" She waited until his eyes met hers for half a second before shifting away uncomfortably. "You know, I refused to even date James when we first met because I knew what people would think. He wore me down and I went on one date with him and got photographed by a paparazzo. As soon as that image was published, my academic career was over whether I was involved with James or not. Didn't matter. So, you can tell yourself whatever you like. I know why I married him."

She didn't wait for his response. Jon's opinion didn't matter to her anymore, but it was hard to think about the people she had worked with before her marriage. How many of them were thinking the same thing? How many whispers and sidelong looks were being exchanged by colleagues when her name was mentioned? How much of her work, solid academic work was being viewed through a jaundiced eye now? The hollow feeling in her chest bloomed again.

CHAPTER SEVENTEEN

James shook the doctor's hand on the agreement to have his office send a donation. He approached Sarah who stood in front of a map of the site, she was distracted, not noticing his approach. "Are you ready, darling?"

She wouldn't meet his eyes. He wondered at the sudden change in her mood. Calum opened the door, and James ushered Sarah out. Samuels was nowhere to be seen.

"Are you alright?" He asked her quietly.

"Mm?" She sketched a fake smile. "Yeah, I'm okay."

He doubted it. She seemed to be lost in her own thoughts. "Did Samuels say something to you?"

Sarah looked off toward the tree line where the ramparts once were. Her tone was flat, emotionless. "Nothing I didn't expect, just a hit dog hollering."

It had upset her. She didn't often revert to her country colloquialisms. She had told him once what people in academic circles would think if she was in a romantic relationship with him. She had warned him people would assume the worst of her. He looked back toward the buildings as they neared the car and saw Samuels hovering near the shed next to the car park. James felt his blood boil. He took a step toward the man.

Sarah stopped him by taking his hand. "Don't. We already gave him all the time he's worth."

"He upset you." James rarely felt the impulse to hit anyone, but seeing the look on Sarah's face had his fist clenching. He would gladly plant one in the man's face.

Sarah shook her head. "You can't fight all my battles for me. And that one isn't worth fighting. There's no sense in trying to rescue a career that's over."

She might as well have kicked him. Samuels didn't bother her. It was the loss of her reputation, the idea of her former colleagues questioning her integrity. He and his family had caused it and talking with Samuels had only reminded her of it.

He stopped her beside the car and cupped her cheek. "Listen, I know what marrying me has cost you. But there are ways you can use our connection for good. You may not be able to do your work in the same way, but you can still find a way to be involved. We can fund any project you want. We can start scholarships. Say the word, and I will make it happen."

This time her smile was tentative, but genuine. Her eyes sparkled with unshed tears. "I'll think about it."

"I don't want to be the cause of your unhappiness." He rested his forehead against hers, enjoying the closeness she was allowing.

She sighed. "I know."

He hoped that was true. It was one thing to talk about prophecies and destiny, but another to see its effect on her life. This responsibility his family and hers had dropped in her lap had destroyed everything she had planned for herself. He was beginning to understand no amount of money or comfort, or security could make up for the loss of her freedom.

They drove back through Aix-en-Provence and were in the hills north of Belcodene when Calum spoke up, "Sir, I think we're being followed."

Adrenaline surged through James's system. "Where?"

"Silver sedan three cars back. They've been with us turn for turn for the last ten minutes." Calum watching the car in the rear-view mirror.

Beside James, Sarah who had been looking out the window and ruminating since they left the dig site, sat up straight. They both looked out the rear window to see the silver sedan. "It looks like the paparazzi figured out we aren't in Lake Como."

"Great." Sarah muttered.

Calum asked. "Should I try to lose them?"

The traffic wasn't heavy, but there were enough drivers on the road to make evasive maneuvers difficult. "That would be dangerous. Don't go back to the chateau until we lose them. But if all they want is a photo, I say let them have it."

"And be careful. You'd be amazed the extent some of them will go to for a photo." Sarah added. She was no doubt thinking about the all-out invasion of paparazzi which had shut down her research trip last spring.

He reached for her hand. "Sometimes it's safer to give them a little of what they want, than to make them chase it."

"Let's hope you're right." She said.

The car followed them for a few more minutes before taking the opportunity to pass. They approached in the next lane. Sarah sat rigidly looking forward, her hand was balled into a white-knuckled fist on her knee.

He wished he could make this easier on her. He bumped her elbow. "Want to give them a show?"

She looked incredulous. "Are you kidding?"

"The better the pic, the more they'll leave us alone." He gave her an exaggerated leer.

"Or the hungrier they'll be for more." Sarah looked beyond him to where the car had pulled up beside them. Her eyes went wide. "That's not a camera!"

James turned to look and saw the barrel of a rifle low in the open window of the silver sedan. "Gun!"

He threw himself between Sarah and the gun. Calum punched the accelerator. Their car surged forward pulling ahead of the sedan. He and Sarah crouched low in the back seat. Calum changed lanes weaving through traffic to get away from their pursuers, who still followed though not as aggressively. "We're not going to lose them on the highway."

"Get off when you can." James ordered. He peeked up over the door to see if he could spot the car. He muttered. "I'm going to ruin him."

"Who?" Sarah asked.

"Samuels." James snapped.

"What does he have to do with this?" She braced herself against the back of the seat in front of her as Calum made another quick lane change.

"Who else would have told these people where we'd be?"

"They could have followed us there." Sarah told him. "Maybe they know where the chateau is."

"We'll investigate it when we're done trying not to get shot."

Calum took the first opportunity to get off the motorway onto the roads winding through the hills. After several turns, they pulled to the side of the road next to a house, looking like they belonged there. The three of them stayed crouched down waiting to see if they'd lost the assassins. Calum reached into the center console for the car phone. He punched in a number and waited for an answer. "Thistle and Lion pinned down." He listened for a second and gave their location. "They're on their way."

"Good." James bit out.

A few minutes later a white van pulled up beside the car. The side door slid open, and Fleming Sinclair and another bodyguard jumped out. They stood on either side of the car door making a sort of protected path between the car and the van. Fleming pulled the door open and offered Sarah his hand. Staying in a crouch, she climbed out of the car and crossed the few steps to the van quickly. James was right behind her. Within seconds, the bodyguards joined them, and the van pulled away, leaving Calum in their car.

"You got here fast." Sarah said.

"They're never far away." James looked out the window to see if the silver sedan had followed them. When he was satisfied, they had lost them. "Thank you for coming so quickly."

"They follow us all the time?" Sarah asked.

"I thought Shaw was crazy for suggesting it." James sank back into his seat as the adrenaline drained from his system. "We use this protocol in places where ransom is a growth industry. I've never worried about this sort of thing in Europe before."

"What about Calum?" Sarah asked.

"He'll drive the car around for a while making sure no one follows him back to the chateau." He told her.

"Couldn't they figure out your family owns the chateau?" She asked.

"Not likely. A shell company owns it. Our name isn't on the property records." His uncle had suggested the change years ago to protect their privacy. Sarah, probably suffering from the same adrenaline drain he was, shook her head before leaning it back against the seat and closing her eyes.

The rest of the drive was quiet with the guards on high alert and James and Sarah's energy ebbing. When they arrived at the chateau Sarah went up to her room. In his study, James poured himself a drink. The burn of the whiskey reignited his temper. He picked up the phone and dialed the number for Mark Shaw, their head of security.

"I've already been briefed." Shaw said in his usual brusk manner.

"Good." James's tone was short, but he didn't care. "Your staff handled it perfectly, but I want to know why it happened. Either we have an internal leak or someone else who knew about our plans today told them where we would be."

"I hope it's the latter." Shaw said. "But I will find out."

"Look into an anthropologist named Jon Samuels." James gripped his glass. Not only had Samuels upset Sarah but James would wager it was Samuels who had told the assassins where they would be. "He arranged this outing, and he said something to Sarah about a surprise job offer here in France when Latin America is his usual area of interest. Something seems off."

Shaw understood how serious James was about this. "If there is anything to find, I'll find it."

CHAPTER EIGHTEEN

Edinburgh, Scotland

Dermot took his post outside James's office suite at Alba Petroleum. His conversation with Henry still weighed on him even the next day. It was hard not to spend the night dwelling on the years of missed opportunities and unhappiness of Henry's relationship with him and his mother.

He couldn't help imagining what their lives might have been like if Henry and Seonag hadn't been so caught up in the prophecy. They might have managed a life together. Dermot might have had a father, one he respected and cared for. Dwelling on what ifs was useless and would only make him more miserable.

At least his meeting with Henry had narrowed down the possibilities of his mother's mysterious visitor. There was only one other suspect. His grandfather had been able to get a look at the security footage from the care home, but none of it had shown him anything. Dermot could confront Walter about it, but he doubted he would be satisfied by the answer. Walter would deny it or knowing him he would admit visiting Seonag and dare Dermot to do anything about it.

Dermot glared in the direction of the old man's office only twenty-five feet away. It was too much temptation being so close to Walter. James had asked Dermot to keep an eye on his office while he was away because he suspected someone had been in without his authorization. He had pulled Dermot aside the day before the wedding. "Someone has been in my office and moved some things about. I think they were searching for something."

"Doesn't Miss Lennox move things about in your office. It was probably her." It was the day after his ill-fated attempt to escape with Sarah, so he hadn't been in the mood for AP intrigue.

"No, she's very precise about where she puts things." James said. "Whoever did this was shuffling things around as if they were looking for something."

"What sort of information would they have found that isn't already available to AP executives?"

James gave him a significant look. "None, except for certain test results, you are aware of. I'm afraid they might arrive while I'm gone so I told the lab to send the results to Miss Lennox."

"At the office?"

Dermot couldn't believe James would have taken such a risk. "Ye could have had it sent to me."

James looked embarrassed. "Sorry. Habit, I suppose. In any case, I don't want anyone rummaging about in my office. Will you keep an eye on things while I'm away?"

Dermot supposed it was good to have a job, however boring it might be. James could have simply told Miss Lennox to hide the results when they arrived. But maybe he hadn't told her the contents of the package he was expecting. Either way, it gave Dermot something to do other than sit around his flat imagining what might be going on with Sarah and James.

Instead, he was standing in the hallway letting his imagination run away with him. The dark paneled walls of the A.P. executive floor felt even more confining than usual.

Miss Lennox walked by carrying her valise and greeted him. He'd gotten used to James's buttoned up executive assistant over the last couple of weeks with her prim suits and dark hair wound into a neat bun at the nape of her neck. Today she had added the uncharacteristic flourish of a loose bow tied at the high collar of her off-white blouse.

She was a bit of a cipher, usually content to blend into the background. At first glance, Audra Lennox might seem a quietly capable person who was happy doing tedious tasks James couldn't be bothered to do himself. But after a few days of observation, Dermot had decided Miss Lennox's capabilities went deeper. She was a keen observer of the comings and goings in the executive offices and was regularly visited by the assistants of the other A.P. executives for quiet chats. Dermot had no doubt there was little going on in the A.P. leadership that Audra Lennox was unaware of.

It was a quiet morning, and Dermot had to fight to stay awake. He was grateful when Brendan Clark, one of the lads from downstairs arrived to spell him for lunch.

After a barely edible cheese and pickle sandwich from the vending machine in the security team's lounge on the ground floor, he returned to his post expecting several more hours of mind-numbing boredom. As he approached, he noticed the door was closed and gave Clark a questioning look.

"Mr. Stuart is in there talking with herself." Clark told him.

Around the offices, Mr. Stuart was Walter. All but the top executives referred to James by his title, a custom James thought was incredibly outdated. But there had to be some way of distinguishing the Stuart CEO from the Stuart COO, and Walter had insisted this was best.

"Right. Cheers." Dermot dismissed Clark. He wondered what Walter and Miss Lennox could be doing behind the door that warranted shutting anyone else out. He also wondered if Walter might not be the one looking through James's office.

Dermot kept an eye on the hallway but listened closely. Muffled voices came through the door, but he couldn't tell what was being said. He gripped the doorknob, planning open the door a crack without being noticed when he heard a clatter and a whimper sounding like distress.

Without further debate he opened the door to find Miss Lennox leaning back against the desk looking shocked and Walter Stuart standing too close to her for comfort. Several files and papers were strewn about on the floor beside the desk.

"Is everything alright?" Dermot pitched his voice a little deeper, his eyes focused on the scant distance between Walter and Miss Lennox.

Walter stepped back bristling in his usual haughty way. "Everything's fine. You should know better than to simply open doors. I know your mother taught you to knock."

"And ye know by now never to mention my mother to me." Dermot's tone was deadly, but softened when he turned his attention to Miss Lennox. "Miss Lennox, are ye alright?"

Her face was quickly turning a shade of just-caught red, but she lifted a hand to smooth her hair back while she gained her footing. Her voice only shook a little. "Perfectly fine, Mr. Sinclair. Mr. Stuart was just leaving."

Walter narrowed his eyes at her in an unspoken threat. Dermot had seen the same look directed his own way often enough. The old man tugged on the hem of his fine merino jacket. "Right enough. So, I was." He took a few steps toward the door before turning back to Miss Lennox. "I'll expect those signed documents as soon as the courier brings them."

She gave a tight smile. "Of course, sir."

Dermot held the door for Walter but closed it behind them once they were in the hall. Walter was about to walk away without another word, as if Dermot was nothing more than furniture. Dermot wasn't going to have it. He stepped in front of Walter. "I hope ye were not bothering her."

Icy blue eyes blazing blazed up at him. "Are you her guardian now, as well? You are a busy lad."

"I'm here to protect James's interests." Dermot took a step closer, invading Walter's space. "If that includes protecting his assistant, or protecting him from her, then so be it."

Fury flashed across Walter's face. "For once, I see you're doing your duty. I thought you had thrown James over for a woman."

Dermot drew himself up. "I have. But now their interests are aligned thanks to you."

A predatory grin spread across Walter's face. "That was me wasn't it. I'd be careful if I were you. You don't want to end up like your friend, Mr. Thompson."

Dermot's blood boiled at the reminder of his old pal Des who had paid for his role in Sarah's failed escape with his life. Des, who was the scion of a prominent organized crime family. "I do wonder what the Thompsons might do if they found out how Des really died."

"You think I haven't already bought the Thompsons?" Walter's laugh was dry and humorless. "Please. Everyone has a price."

He shouldn't be surprised, but he was. Of course, Walter would have immediately gone to the Thompsons to cover his own arse. He wondered how much it had cost him. What was the value of a son, and a master forger? Dermot's gut churned.

"And what was the price of a guard at my mother's care home? That's how ye got in, isn't it?" Dermot asked. He watched Walter's reaction closely. It was a gamble to come right out and accuse the man of harassing his mother, but maybe if he caught Walter off guard, he'd get close to the truth.

There was the slightest hesitation, no more than half a second before Walter's eyebrows drew together in a fairly convincing look of confusion. "I don't know what you're talking about. I haven't seen your mother since before you removed her from the home I selected. I have no idea where she is."

Dermot wanted to wring the monster's neck. He breathed and counted to ten hoping to calm his temper. His eyes never left Walter's as he enunciated every word carefully. "Stay away from my mother."

Walter smiled smugly, his laugh was low and raspy. "That pawn is already off the board, lad. I have no more use for your mother, which you would do well to remember. After your betrayal with Sarah, there is nothing else we need from you."

It was Dermot's turn to grin even though he was seething inside. "Are ye sure? You might want to ask James..."

Walter laughed again, lowering his voice further. "Don't overestimate the power James has around here or underestimate the power I have over him."

Walter turned and practically strutted down the hall. Dermot strangely found himself wishing James was back to put Walter in his place. He wondered how James would feel if he heard what Walter said. The old man might have a point that James wasn't as powerful as his uncle, but it didn't mean he didn't have leverage.

CHAPTER NINETEEN

Riboux, France

The attack on the highway had put an end to their outings for the past week. Sarah and James had kept themselves, or more accurately the security team had kept them confined to the chateau while they searched in vain for their attackers. Rather than let Sarah retreat to the pool and the library, James had tried to draw her out. She had spent her afternoons in the library, reading whatever she could about Mary Magdalene, the early church, and the bloodline. But in the evenings James had come up with things they could do together. They watched movies and played board games. He had even asked the chef to let them cook dessert one night, which she had reluctantly agreed to. They had laughed their way through making brownies, and Sarah had told him stories about baking midnight brownies with Amy. They were solidifying their friendship if nothing more. Sarah really didn't mind spending time with James. She liked him. He simply wasn't Dermot. Although there were times, when the light was low and the evening was growing late, for a second, she thought she was with Dermot rather than James.

That evening she was at a small table in the shade of the pergola looking at the horizon and enjoying a drink before dinner. Provence really was beautiful, and she hated they hadn't been able to explore it more. Still, she supposed there were worse places to be in hiding. She fingered the shawl collar of the soft cotton shirt she'd put on and enjoyed the swing of her buff-colored linen slacks. They were the finest quality of course and had been picked for her by someone. She suspected Gillian, the stylist Felicia Banks employed. Everything around her was the finest available.

Sarah wondered what the twelve-year-old girl who ran through the woods in Kettle Holler or searched for crawfish in the creek with Buddy Corbett would think about where she was now. What would the Sarah who used the proceeds from selling Granny's farm to go to grad school think? Those versions of herself seemed too far away to contemplate.

A part of her would happily trade the fine clothes, and posh houses to travel back to the holler fishing or foraging for her supper. Sure, she would rather be doing fieldwork or in the library listening to recordings of fieldwork, but even Kettle Holler would be preferable to being chased by assassins. A breeze brushed past lifting the scent of Cardell's perfume to her nose reminding her even more of home while also making her feel extremely spoiled. What other girl from the hills would have her own bespoke perfume. How had he known what scents would go straight to her memories?

She reached for her glass again wondering where James was. He was usually waiting for her by this hour. She looked around, making sure she was alone. Then she settled into her chair.

She hadn't used her gift since they'd come to France, but then she hadn't felt much need to. With a deep breath she relaxed her body and mind. Another breath, and she focused her mind on James. She breathed again, letting her co-walker take the lead. Her focus pulled her co-walker inside the house and down the hall to James's study.

***

"You need to call off your dog." Walter barked over the phone. He hadn't expected a call from the office today.

"I'm sorry?" James thought he knew what his uncle meant, but he would feign confusion to make Walter explain in more reasonable terms.

"You know what I mean." Walter refused to be cowed.

"I would prefer you not call him that." James kept his tone even. He'd heard his mother refer to Dermot as if he were a separate breed of person all his life. Whether the DNA results proved it or not, James thought of Dermot as family, and he wasn't going to let them treat him like less anymore. "Dermot is the person I trust most in the world."

There was a pause on the line, as if Walter was absorbing what he had said. "He tried to steal her from you."

James took a breath hoping to level out his tone. "She is not a prize to be stolen. She is a whole person. I will not have you talking about her as if she's an object."

Silence. Perhaps he finally understood James was not going to escalate the conversation. The clock on the library shelf ticked through seconds. Walter breathed loudly on the other end of the phone. "Of course. I beg your pardon. I take it you have done your duty then."

James knew what was meant by 'his duty'. Walter had used much cruder words before to ask, encourage, insist he consummate his marriage. James wasn't about to do that without Sarah's enthusiastic agreement. He'd told his uncle he wasn't a rapist and he meant it. Through gritted teeth James said, "My duty, is to care for and protect my wife which I am doing. Given your perpetual bachelor state, I don't think I need you to tell me how to go about it."

"I am only thinking of what's best for you and for Scotland." Walter's voice softened.

"If I cannot take care of my wife, then I shouldn't be trusted with a country." James matched his uncle's tone. There was no need to make this an argument, but he also wasn't going to give in to such pressure. Sarah had reminded him leadership was about setting an example. He was determined to be the leader she thought he could be.

"That is a fair point." Walter conceded. "However, caring for someone also sometimes means doing the hard things, some of which are best for them even if they don't understand that yet. She will come around."

"Not if you and mother continue to interfere in our marriage. Sarah has a will of her own." He thought they were at least finding their way to friendship again, but he worried she would never love him, not the way he wanted her to. He shouldn't voice such doubt, but he found himself saying. "I'm beginning to wonder if she'll ever view me as anything but the man who took her career away from her. Even if it wasn't my choice."

"She'll get used to it, to you." Walter sounded far more confident than James felt. "I've seen you charm tougher women than her."

"I'm not sure anyone is as tough as Sarah." He sighed. "She's not like other women I've known. Charm and gifts only get a man so far. She's something else entirely. Worth the effort, but I don't know what would win her."

"I'm sure you'll figure it out. You are the Stuart heir. Stop asking yourself if you're worthy of her." Walter told him. "Start expecting her to be worthy of you."

James's laugh sounded bitter to his own ears. "Fine speech, I'm not sure I believe it."

"Never doubt it. Our family has been building an empire, while hers has been hiding in huts and caves for countless generations. What have they been preserving while we've been the vanguard? They need us as much as we need them."

"I'm not sure Sarah has the same agenda as the rest of her family." James knew she didn't. She had told them as much. She wasn't alone. The only person in her family who seemed to care about fulfilling the prophecy was her great aunt, Eilidh MacLeod, and Sarah's relationship with Eilidh was contentious at best.

"Well, you must do your best to make our agenda her agenda as well." Walter pressed him. "I know you can."

"Mmm…" Again, James wished he had his uncle's confidence. "Will you transfer me to Mark Shaw? He should have a report for me by now."

***

"Aperitif?" James's hand appeared by Sarah's shoulder holding a tall glass of something which looked like lemonade. She'd been deep in thought about his conversation with Walter. She had drifted back from casting out after he'd been transferred to Mark Shaw. She'd heard enough. Walter was skilled at manipulation. He had made James angry but turned it around within a few minutes. She would have to keep that in mind in the future.

And she would have to think hard about consummating her marriage. She hated to think about trading her body for James's loyalty, it felt cheap and manipulative. But she was in a desperate situation. James wasn't going to wait forever.

Sarah took the drink and sniffed at it. It smelled of lemon and something else. "Thank you." She said before taking a sip. "Licorice?"

James took the seat opposite her and turned his chair to match hers facing the horizon. "Anise. It's called pastis, a local specialty. It's mixed with lemon syrup and water."

Sarah took a bigger sip and let the cold; tartness slide down her throat. "It's very refreshing."

James sniffed subtly. "Is that the fragrance Cardell gave you?"

"Yes," Sarah lifted her wrist to her nose. "It's very pleasant. Makes me think of home."

"It is lovely." James agreed, and they shared a contented smile. He leaned back in his chair, his face shadowed. He shifted his shoulders the same way Dermot did. Yearning pulled at her. Sarah had to blink to dispel the image.

They sat there quietly for several minutes watching the sun dip low in the sky. Sipping her drink and watching the sunset, Sarah almost felt content. It wasn't a feeling she recognized easily.

"I think this is the first day in a week I haven't had to drag you out of the library."

After hearing his conversation with Walter, she realized while her curiosity had distracted her from her grief, it had also distracted her from the real problem. She'd taken her eye off the ball. "I thought I would give the research a rest."

He turned to face her. "I have to tell you something unpleasant."

Sarah's blood chilled. She turned to him. Don't let it be Dermot. Don't say something has happened to Dermot. "Has something happened?"

"Nothing new." James assured her. "It's about the attack last week."

"Ah." It wasn't Dermot. She could handle anything else. "Okay, what about it?"

"Jon Samuels, and Professor Desrosiers were the only people who knew we were visiting the dig site the other day. I wanted to know how those assassins found us and who sent them." James rested his hands on the table, fingertips touching in a careful gesture. "I asked our security director to investigate it. Jon told you he received a surprise offer for the position here."

"Right." She said. "He usually works in Latin America, but he's not very good at interviews. I'm not surprised he didn't get his preferred position."

"Well, the position he did get was funded by a donation from a shell company we traced back to the Circle."

Sarah leaned away from the table; her shoulders slumped. The Circle was a group of American zealots who had their fingers in politics, and industry. They were suspected of being the ones who sent Ryan Cumberland, the first man who had tried to kill her, as well as a man who was found living in a car on her street in Edinburgh. "And you think Jon tipped them off about our location so they could kill us?"

"I hope he wasn't aware of what they intended." James's tone was grim. "I suspect he thought he was tipping off paparazzi. He also received a deposit of five thousand dollars the day before we visited the site."

Sarah's breath caught. Five thousand dollars to betray her. She shouldn't have expected any kind of loyalty from Jon, but this was another stark reminder of the world she lived in now. Even if he only thought he was tipping off photographers, he'd sold her out so easily. A chill ran down her spine. "How would they have known they needed to send someone to France though? I thought you made a decoy reservation."

"We don't know that yet." James tilted his head to the side acknowledging her point. "Shaw will be conducting an internal investigation to make sure there wasn't a leak. It could be they knew of the chateau and thought there was a chance we'd be here."

"Or someone leaked it." She said.

James appeared resigned. "As tight a ship as Shaw runs, it is still a large crew, and it's hard to always guarantee everyone's loyalty."

Sarah took a deep breath. Even with all their millions, the Stuarts couldn't guarantee their safety. Still, their personal team had done their jobs. "I don't know how you live with this anxiety all the time. I've lost count of how many times people have come after me. I thought I was paranoid before, but this is madness."

"We are doing everything we can to keep you safe." He reached across the table to take her hand. "I promise I won't let anything happen to you."

She wasn't sure that was a promise he could keep, but he was sincere about it. "I guess Jon really was still bitter about how we broke up."

"Or he needed money and wasn't particular where it came from." James offered.

"That's probably the more likely answer." Sarah acknowledged. "Jon seems to continually disappoint."

"I'm sorry if he hurt you, but I can't say I'm sorry you broke up." James smiled wryly.

Sarah sighed. "I'm more bothered by the idea of everyone thinking I married you for money."

"If they only knew how hard it was to convince you." He laughed.

"Not that it would matter."

"Why do you care what they think?" He asked with a shake of his head as if to say other people didn't matter.

"Good question." She took a sip from her drink and savored the cool feeling of it running down her throat. She chose her words carefully. "Kettle Holler was a small town. In fact, calling it a town is generous. It's more of a dip in the road with a store and a post office. Everyone knew everyone's business and with the exception of the Mackeys, the richest family in town, my family was the one folks talked about the most. Whether it was my granny's moonshine business, or my lack of a father, we were ridiculed, pitied, judged all my life." She paused, watching the track of a bird flying over the field behind the garden. "When I went away to school, I was in a new place where no one knew about any of that. I got to find out who I was free from all the baggage. I built my own life, and my own reputation. I've never had much, but that was mine," She hated the crack in her voice. She cleared her throat. "And I don't like losing it."

Sarah could feel his eyes on her, studying her from across the table. She focused on the setting sun in front of them. Her fingers drew a circle in the condensation collecting at the base of her glass.

"You are still you. You have the same integrity, the same honesty today as when I met you. It doesn't matter what anyone else thinks. You know it. I know it. Everyone who really knows you knows it. No one else matters."

Sarah breathed deeply, trying to believe his words. They were the right ones, and while they didn't immediately change how she felt, she appreciated his support. She smiled. They sank into silence again, each with their own thoughts sipping their drinks as the sun sank lower.

A maid came to tell them dinner was ready, and James rose. "Shall we?"

Sarah stood and took his hand. It was time she worked on cementing her relationship with James. He was a good man who couldn't help the situation they found themselves in. If she was going to battle Walter Stuart for his soul, she was going to have to use every weapon she had.

"I think tomorrow we might venture out." He led her to the dining room.

"Are you sure it's safe?" She fought the surge of anxiety at the thought of going out.

"It is if we take a small team and don't tell anyone but them where we are going." James explained. "Remember the element of surprise is our friend."

"If you're sure." She wasn't.

"I've been living this way a long time." He assured her. "What would you like to do?"

"Something relaxing and fun." She said. "I've been in the library enough."

A smile spread across his face. "I think I know just the thing. Do you get seasick?"

"I don't know." Sarah waited beside her chair as he pulled it out for her. "I haven't been on a lot of boats."

James gave her shoulder a gentle squeeze before taking his own seat. "Well, we will have to remedy that."

CHAPTER TWENTY

Sarah woke early to a note from James saying she should dress for boating. Naturally, her professionally selected wardrobe contained exactly the things she needed. A comfortable pair of boat shoes, capri pants, and boat necked top as well as a charming navy blue and white one-piece bathing suit. She dressed, pulled her hair back and applied her new fragrance enjoying the comfortable scents of home it brought her.

She stepped outside promptly at eight o'clock. As James turned to greet her, the bright sun behind him obscured his features, and his dark silhouette was so familiar it almost made her forget who she was there with. Dermot was slightly broader than James, but they were the same height and with his head tilted just so, it was hard to tell them apart.

James stepped closer, coming into focus. His blue eyes twinkled with excitement, and his smile rivaled the sun in brightness. He didn't notice her momentary confusion. "Good morning."

"Morning."

"I think you're going to enjoy this." He led her to the car where Calum stood holding the door.

His excitement was contagious. "Okay, where are we going?"

"To see the calanques." James's shoulder rested firmly against hers as he took his place beside her in the back seat. "They're something unique to this coast, and they are breathtaking."

"And we're going to see them by boat?" Sarah's stomach fluttered at his proximity, a new sensation for her. They'd ridden in the car together many times, and she hadn't been this nervous. Maybe it was nerves after the attack the last time they went out.

"It's the best way, and the safest for us." James explained, patting her knee. "I'm not going to let anything happen to you."

Sarah breathed deeply, trying to relax. The longer they spent in the car, the easier she felt. They chatted amiably about the weather and things they saw along the road.

Outside Cassis they turned into a boatyard harboring more boats than Sarah thought she had ever seen. The long narrow inlet was crammed cheek by jowl with yachts of all types and sizes. James and Sarah were escorted to a boat toward the mouth of the inlet where the water was deeper. "I know less than nothing about boats. What kind is this?"

"This is a forty-foot sloop." James explained. "You can tell it's a sloop by the single mast, and two sails fore and aft."

Sarah looked at the bare mast and sails which were wrapped up and hoped she wasn't going to be expected to know how to sail.

James must have read her mind. With a chuckle he led her up the gangplank. "Don't worry. We've got a small crew, all vetted through security, who will take care of the sailing. And Calum will be with us. All we have to do is enjoy the scenery."

They were welcomed aboard by the captain and crew and given a tour of the salon, galley, and cabin. They waited inside until the boat had pulled away from the dock and cleared the yacht club. Once they were out of the inlet, James drew Sarah outside.

"This is a calanque." He explained, waving a hand at the steep rocky walls of the inlet. "We'll see more, but this is one of the largest. This part of the coast is made up of many of these narrow inlets surrounded by cliffs.

"They're like small fjords." The cliffs of white limestone with orange striations rose high around them. They were dotted with green scrubby trees. The water was a brilliant turquoise. James explained the yacht club was in the Calanque de Port-Miou. Around them the crew cut the engines and hoisted the sails.

Sarah felt exhilarated when they caught the wind. The resonant snap of the sail suddenly filling, the creak of the rigging, and the rhythmic whoosh as the boat cut through wave after wave. They were off, cruising through one calanque after another. Each time Sarah marveled at the drama of the steep white cliffs, green trees, and bright water.

Some of the calanques were large enough for boats to sail into them and drop anchor. Others sported beaches people hiked to for the day. James told her this part of the coast was a national park, and there were many trails allowing people to view the inlets from above, or bravely climb down to the shingle-like beaches.

When they arrived at one of the larger calanques, James surprised Sarah by pulling his shirt over his head. She couldn't help admiring his physique. She could see why so many women went mad for him. "Come on. There's a beach over there. It's completely deserted. Let's swim."

Sarah looked toward the inlet. This calanque didn't cut quite as deeply into the land as the others, which might be why there weren't any other boats around. Still, she wasn't sure of its safety or her swimming abilities. "I don't know."

"I know you swim." James coaxed. "You've been swimming every day since we arrived."

Sarah wasn't sure she could call what she'd been doing swimming, but she couldn't exactly explain that to him. Nor did she want to go into her complicated relationship with water. "In a pool."

"Don't worry. The current here isn't bad." He persisted.

Reluctantly she agreed and stripped to her bathing suit. James's eyes ate her up despite her suit being relatively modest.

At his instruction, the captain took the boat as close to the shore as they dared, but the beach James promised was still hidden by a rocky outcrop. They climbed down to the platform at the stern. Before diving into the water, he reassured her. "Don't rush. We'll take our time and have a leisurely swim. The beach is around that rock."

Sarah took a deep breath, tamping down her nerves and dove into the water. She had taken swimming lessons. Learning to swim was a requirement at Carolina. She had not, however, used the skill much. She was surprised to find swimming in open water was less scary than taking baths. Something about being able to move her limbs and stretch out gave her some reassurance that she wouldn't be trapped underwater. And James had a point. She'd been practicing in the pool for weeks now.

It took her a few strokes to find her rhythm, but eventually she established a comfortable breaststroke moving through the water easily. James stayed within an arm's length of her in case she had any trouble.

She could see clear to the rocky bottom and spotted some small silver fish flashing in the sunlight. Fortunately, there didn't seem to be any large fish swimming around them. They made it to the small, hidden stretch of rocky beach. Fifty feet of white tumbled stones and coarse sand was enclosed on three sides by cliffs.

As they climbed out of the water Sarah couldn't even see their boat on the other side of the rock. It was quiet, only the sound of the soft waves lapping against the rocks, and the occasional chirp of small birds. Sarah hadn't felt peace like this since quiet mornings on Granny's farm. "Wow."

James grinned. "Incredible, isn't it?"

He found a flat spot on the beach and laid down, lounging back on one elbow. "Come sit. Enjoy the quiet."

Sarah sat down next to him. She couldn't stop looking around at the hills. There was so much to see. A bird with long brown wings and a white belly soared past and disappeared inside a cliff. "That was a large bird."

"Probably a Bonelli's Eagle." James had lain back resting with his hands behind his head. "They build their nests in the cliffs. There are also caves in some cliffs. I have occasionally seen large bats flying out of them in the evenings."

"You've been here before." She observed.

"Many times." James said without lifting his head. His voice sounded distracted as if his thoughts had turned inward. "I can be alone here. It doesn't matter who I am or what I do. I can simply be."

Sarah laid back beside him and listened to the waves and wind. The sun warmed her skin, and her limbs grew languid. Like James, she enjoyed the feeling of solitude. No one was demanding or expecting anything from her. There were no dragons, or scheming in-laws to fight. It would seem even James didn't expect anything from her here. He was beside her, but he didn't try to make conversation. He seemed content with his own thoughts. They were alone, but he didn't push her for anything more than she was willing to give. "This place is special to you."

He didn't look at her. "Yes."

Sarah turned to him and leaned in to kiss his cheek. 'Thank you for sharing it with me."

***

She'd fallen asleep. They both had, but Sarah had turned to him and curled around his side. He woke to find her head resting on his shoulder, and his arm curled around her. He was afraid to move, afraid to wake her and break the spell, because he knew what would happen. She'd pull away, like she always did, guilt flashing on her face before she thought to hide it.

He didn't want to see it, not here. This place was special, a hideout from the pressures of the world. He'd first come here while sailing with his father one spring when he was fourteen. It had been only the two of them on a small boat, and they spent the day fishing and swimming, where no one knew them. No one followed them. They didn't have to worry who was watching.

There had been no pressure from his mother or his uncle, no schoolwork to be done. His father had wanted him to have a day away from all the expectations. It had become a springtime ritual for them when he was a teenager, one he had kept up whenever he was able to spend time here.

His skin felt tight and hot from the sun and dried saltwater. As much as he didn't want to move, they would have to or get sunburnt. He brushed Sarah's damp hair behind her ear. "Darling."

He expected her to start and pull away. Instead, her eyelashes fluttered before lifting to reveal her light green eyes. For once, she didn't retreat, didn't leap away from him. Her eyes met his and held there. They stopped, locked in an unprecedented moment of intimacy, he thought he could see the thoughts flashing in her mind.

'He was the wrong man. She was in the wrong place. And yet, she was attracted to him. She cared for him.' He felt it. She showed it when she listened to him talk about his family history, when she let him take her hand, or kiss her cheek. He wanted so much to turn that into something more. He could build on this friendship they had. It would take patience, but he was sure he could do it.

He didn't try to kiss her though he was sorely tempted. He would wait. He'd wait forever for her. That was what she didn't understand. She thought he loved an idea, a myth he'd been told, a fairy princess who would make his dreams come true. But she was wrong.

He saw how conflicted she was with their shared destiny, with her feelings for him and for Dermot. He saw her plain honesty, her humility, her rejection of the trappings of the life others were pushing on her, and he loved her for it. He loved her integrity, and her generosity. He loved her intelligence, and her temper.

Sarah was the one to break their frozen moment of honesty by pushing herself up. She cleared her throat and nervously brushed her hair back from her face. "Wow. That swim must have worn me out."

"We should get out of the sun."

"Yes." She rose to her feet brushing the sand from her arms and legs.

"Are you ready to swim back?" He asked. There wasn't much shade to be had there, only a few scrubby bushes not far off the beach.

Sarah looked back in the direction of the boat. "Yeah. Sure."

"Right." He rose too, walking toward the water.

Sarah joined him at the water's edge. "James, this is really beautiful. Thank you again for bringing me here."

He hoped sharing this with her might make her realize how much he loved her. "It's my pleasure."

CHAPTER TWENTY-ONE

Even in the hot afternoon, Marseilles bustled around the old port as they sailed into a berth. Boats came and went. Vendors under canopies sold everything from the morning's catch to T-shirts, and tourists wandered through it all. Queues of people waited for tour boats and ferries. Sarah stood on the deck taking it all in; sun, salt-sea air, and the bustle of France's second largest city. She wished she could be a regular tourist and explore the city too. But she knew that was a dangerous proposition.

After swimming back to the yacht, Sarah and James had rinsed the salt water off and enjoyed a relaxed lunch. The crew hugged the coastline exploring more of the calanques between Marseilles and Cassis. Sarah allowed herself to enjoy the company, James's company. Their conversation had been easy, and it had reminded Sarah why she liked James.

She had asked him several times where they were going, but he would only say, Marseilles, although he clearly had a plan. He'd only come up with the idea for this little side trip the night before and made a phone call. Today, everything had gone without a hitch. The yacht and crew were ready, the galley had been stocked with refreshments. Now, they were met at the dock by another bodyguard and a driver.

As soon as they disembarked, they were escorted to a waiting car, which whisked them off to a hotel. To call it a hotel hardly captured where they were taken. Uphill from the old port, the imposing façade rose above the harbor like a fortress. It was near enough to the port to enjoy sweeping views of the coastline but perched above the city's noise.

The car did not pull up to the front of the hotel but swung around to what looked like a service entrance. Although, when they entered the building, it wasn't the utilitarian hallway Sarah expected to see, but a well-appointed miniature lobby. James, Sarah, and Fleming were met there by a very solicitous concierge who informed them everything had been prepared and their bags had arrived earlier.

He then led them to the presidential suite and after asking several times if there was anything more they required, left. Fleming immediately checked the suite and terrace for both security and privacy including a sweep for any possible listening devices. Sarah loitered in the sitting room while he saw to their safety.

A bottle of champagne chilled in a bucket of ice near the door. Remembering the alias James had admitted to using when he traveled, she said. "They sure rolled out the red carpet for Alan Young."

He half-shrugged and reached for the champagne. "They know me here, and Alan Young."

"All clear, sir." Fleming returned to the room. "We'll be right next door, should ye need us."

"Thank you, Mr. Sinclair." James gripped the top of the cork and gave it a slow and practiced twist until it popped. "I'm sure we'll be fine."

With a quick nod, Fleming left. James poured the champagne into a pair of flutes and tilted his head in invitation toward the terrace. "You really must see the view, it's one of the best in the city."

Sarah followed him onto the terrace accepting the glass. Marseille spread out before them from the hotel's courtyard to the Old Port, and across to the basilica atop the peak. "What is that church over there?"

"That is Notre Dame de la Garde. La Garde being the name of the peak it sits on." James stood close to her at the railing. "The church you see now is nineteenth century, but there's been a church there since 1218. In the sixteenth century, the king decided the city needed more protection, and the most strategic point for a fort was..." He tilted his head toward the church.

"La Garde." Sarah finished. "I see your passion for history extends beyond your family's exploits."

A blush spread across his cheeks. He took a sip of champagne and turned back to the city skyline. "They built a fort around the church. In times of peace, the chapel was open to the public, then in times of war, the primary purpose became one of protection."

"So, the church and the army working hand in hand." It fit what Sarah knew of the Catholic church at the time.

"It's certainly not a first. There was a time when the church had its own armies, and fighting orders like the Templars, Hospitallers, Order of the Dragon."

"The Invigilare?" Sarah offered.

"The Catholic church of today would disavow all knowledge of The Invigilare." The look he gave her showed disbelief of the church's company line. "They are a fringe group of zealots who have no connection to the Church."

"Right." She had seen the danger posed by the group firsthand on more than one occasion. She had little doubt the people who attacked them on the road the week before were

Invigilare. Previously, an assassin had chased her through the Highlands, and days later through Edinburgh's Old Town.

"Of course, they pose a greater threat to you than they do to me. I'm of no consequence without you." James gave her a knowing smile before his gaze drifted to her mouth.

Sarah looked at the glass in her hand. "I think we both know that's not true."

"Enough. We've had a wonderful day, and I don't want to ruin it with talk of our enemies." James glowed with excitement. "We have dinner reservations. It's a Michelin starred restaurant. Should be exceptionally good. Your clothes are in the bedroom closet. Let's get dressed and enjoy what the town has to offer."

She looked doubtful, but he ran a comforting hand down her arm and gave her hand a squeeze. "It's under an alias, with a private table. Security will be with us. I've got it all in hand. I'm your husband. I won't let anything happen to you."

Husband. Yes, he was. And she needed them to be a team before they went back to Edinburgh if she was going to get his help dealing with Walter. Fortunately, they had another week left of their honeymoon.

Today had helped her feel closer to him. He had shared something meaningful and shown his vulnerability. They'd been two people, James, and Sarah. He hadn't pressured her. Funny, this was the most honeymoon-like day they'd had so far. While she hadn't felt romantic toward James, she had enjoyed herself. Whether it was lingering relaxation from the day they'd had or the knowledge she needed to get James on her side, she decided to let him lead the way for the evening.

"Okay. I'll go get dressed." Sarah took her champagne with her to the bedroom. Her clothes were thoughtfully picked out and hung in the closet; an elegant dress, an outfit for the next day, and a nightgown. She went to the bathroom to find her skincare products, perfume, and cosmetics were arrayed on the counter next to the sink. James's things were on the other side.

Catching her reflection in the mirror, she almost didn't recognize herself. The Mediterranean sun had pinkened her cheeks and lightened her hair. She had lost the haunted, exhausted look she'd had for the past two weeks. It reminded her of a vacation she'd spent once with Amy's family at the beach back in North Carolina when the sun and salt had baked away the tension of graduate school.

Sarah turned on the shower, her limbs still relaxed and languid from swimming and napping in the sun. She got in and stepped under the spray. As the misgivings about her marriage and thoughts of her situation started to creep back in, she let the water wash them away.

When Sarah had showered, she put on the dress she found hanging in the closet and applied the makeup the way Tony had shown her, and tried not to think about the situation she was caught up in. She was merely Sarah going to dinner with her friend James. She dabbed Cardell's perfume on her neck and pulse points, and was instantly hit with the scents of home, and something more. She inhaled and a sense of calm settled over her.

Stepping out into the bedroom, she found James already dressed. He faced the window, his broad shoulders and dark hair for a brief second reminded her of Dermot, not the outright confusion of this morning, but still an uncanny resemblance. Then he turned, and she was struck once again by how handsome he was. He gave her that grin, the one that made a person feel like they were the only two people in the world.

With the scents of home surrounding her and James's eyes looking so much like Dermot's, Sarah felt a sense of belonging which was so entirely new to her it almost knocked her over. She had to reach a hand out to the wall for support.

James jumped to her aid quickly, and the feeling only grew. Sarah tried to laugh it off. "I'll never get used to wearing heels."

***

The restaurant didn't disappoint. The food was exquisite. The wine was a perfect accompaniment. Their table was in a private alcove where they weren't disturbed by other patrons. Sarah looked beautiful, not in the dramatic way of some other women he'd been with. Sarah's beauty was a quiet, steady sort, the kind of classic beauty that wouldn't fade as she got older but merely evolve.

Their dinner conversation had been light, aided by plenty of good wine and fine food. James was starting to feel some hope Sarah might be breaking free from her grief. She seemed more relaxed and present. He found himself wanting to linger over dessert.

When they left, he didn't want the evening to end with them returning to their suite only to sleep in separate rooms. To his surprise, it was Sarah who suggested they extend the evening. "Can we take a walk? I feel like I need to walk off the wine."

"I don't think the security team would agree to a walk. We shouldn't be out in the open." He hated to say it. The idea of a romantic stroll through the port would be a dream.

Sarah sighed. "Yeah. I guess not."

"How about coffee back in the suite?" He suggested. If she wanted to keep talking, he was going to enjoy it while he could.

"Make it decaf and you're on."

He placed the order for coffee before they went up to their suite. He didn't want to give her time to change her mind. While they waited, he and Sarah looked at the city lights from the terrace.

"Tell me more about Marseilles." She said looking out at the ocean.

James didn't mind playing tour guide if it kept her talking. "It was founded around six hundred B.C.E. by the Greeks, but of course there have been people here for much longer. In the 1980's a man named Cosquer discovered a cave in the calanque park with paintings on the walls as much as thirty thousand years old."

"Wow, that old?"

"I've no idea how he found the cave, or why people might have painted the walls there. Now, it's only accessible by diving through an underwater cave to get to the painted chamber. It seems a long way to go to paint a mural."

"Maybe it was holy to them." Sarah suggested making him think of the cave carved under Lyall Green's house in the Highlands where they'd tested her people's cauldron and its unusual powers.

He tightened his hand into a fist remembering the slash of the knife across his palm. It had tingled. The sensation of cells knitting back together when they poured water from the cauldron over it. He glanced at Sarah wondering if there was some cave in the Highlands where her people had painted their story on the walls.

Fleming Sinclair entered the suite with their coffee. He and Sarah went inside. He poured and added sugar and cream to hers as he had seen her do. She took the cup gratefully and sat on the couch while he poured some for himself.

Before joining her, he dimmed the lights. By the time he sat next to her, he could tell her attention was turning inward as if often did. Not wanting to lose their companionship to her dark thoughts, he asked. "Would it help if you told me about your father?"

CHAPTER TWENTY-TWO

His question surprised her, although it shouldn't have. For all James knew it had been simple grief overwhelming her the past couple of weeks. He didn't know she had tried to escape two days before their wedding. He didn't know his uncle had threatened everyone she cared about and killed her father to prove he meant it. He thought she was mourning for a man she'd only just met who had drunkenly fallen down some stairs.

She spoke softly and James leaned closer to listen. "I know it seems odd. I only met him when we were in Lochinver on our research trip, but I felt like I already knew him."

James hmm'd sympathetically but didn't interrupt. Sarah thought for a moment about whether she should tell him about her family and how much she should tell. He had trusted her today with his hidden beach and his memories. Still, she hesitated to trust him with all of her secrets. She decided to tell him what she thought she could without revealing her gift or her sister, Oona's.

Setting her coffee on the table in front of them, she turned to face him. Nervous, she fidgeted with her skirt, twisting the fabric around her fingers. The breeze coming in from the open doors to the terrace carried a new whiff of her perfume to her nose, adding a sense of comfort and calm.

He scooted closer to listen, and in the low light, she had another flash of familiarity like the one she'd had on the terrace earlier in the evening. It was as if Dermot flashed into James's place for a fraction of a second. She shook it off looking down at her hands where they rested in her lap.

"My mother's death wasn't an accident." She blurted out. He had asked about her father, but it was impossible to understand Sarah's feelings about Rab without knowing more about Molly. James didn't say anything. He reached across the back of the couch and gave her shoulder a comforting squeeze.

Sarah took a deep breath before diving into the story. She told him about her mother's memoir, and her parents' affair. She told him about meeting her father in Lochinver. "He was drunk when I met him. He'd been living for decades with the guilt of abandoning my mother and me. It permeated his whole life. But when he died, he was getting it together or trying to. He'd been in rehab, and for all I knew he still was when they found him dead the day before the wedding."

"Do you think he was trying to come to the wedding?" James tenderly brushed a stray curl over her shoulder.

Sarah shook her head and sighed. She twisted the fabric of her skirt with her fingers nervously. This was the tricky part. The truth was Rab hadn't been planning to attend the wedding. He had been taken from his rehab facility and brought to Edinburgh by Walter. But she didn't dare tell James that. Walter had warned her what would happen if she did, and she'd seen firsthand what he was capable of. She'd held her father while he died. "I don't know." Her voice sounded small even to her. "Maybe. He wanted to be a part of my life. But I'm surprised he would risk his sobriety."

"He probably didn't realize how big a risk it was. I don't know a lot about alcoholism, but I don't think relapses are uncommon." James's voice was soft, his tone gentle.

"I'm sure they're not. I feel so guilty about it. I mean he wasn't fully present for Ruaraidh and Oona. Then I show up and he goes to rehab and dies trying to go to my wedding." This part was entirely true. "It doesn't seem fair to them."

He rested a warm hand on her bare shoulder. "None of it seems fair."

"No, it really doesn't." This prophecy hadn't only destroyed her life. It had upended Dermot's and James's as well. It had caused Bridget's murder and held Oona's life in limbo until Sarah showed up. It had ruined her mother's and father's lives and robbed Grant MacDuff of a life of his own and her mother's love. It had torn Amy's life apart. "There seems to be a lot of collateral damage on the way to this future king."

Sarah let go where she'd been gripping her skirt and smoothed the fabric down over her knee. She felt his gaze on her. She hadn't meant to condemn him or his family, merely to lament the situation they found themselves in. After a moment, James cleared his throat. "You still haven't explained how your mother died."

"Right." She had gotten lost in the backstory. "My mother never really got over what happened to her in Scotland. I'm not sure if it was being rejected by her people, or beaten nearly to death, or Rab's betrayal, or just..." She waved her hand in front of her to encompass everything. "...all of it. She always had a sadness about her. Then one summer, she snapped. I think she realized the same thing was going to happen to me. And she couldn't bear it. She slit her wrists." Sarah paused for a beat. "I found her."

He grunted, short and sharp, his head shaking back and forth. It reminded Sarah so much of Dermot's personal language, she almost leaned into him. "How old were you?"

"I was six." She didn't need to mention the message Molly had left smeared on the wall in her own blood. 'Run.'

"God, Sarah." He groaned. "Have you ever had an easy time of it?"

She gave a low fatalistic laugh. "I'm not sure what easy is. Graduate school felt comfortable. I didn't have much money, but I had a plan. Something to look forward to, and something I could control on my own. I liked that feeling."

"And I took it from you." He sounded deflated.

She shook her head. "You didn't do it alone." She stroked her hand over the soft fabric of her skirt, assigning a name to each wrinkle she smoothed. Walter Stuart, Eilidh MacLeod, Ryan Cumberland, the Invigilare... "I'm starting to realize between your family, my family, and groups like the Circle and the Invigilare. I would never have been allowed to live in peace."

"If I could change that I would.' He sounded sincere, but of course it didn't mean he was going to give her up. After a pause, he asked. "Why did you abide by the Nine's decision to choose me?"

This was a loaded question. She had relied on James believing she was forced into the marriage to hold him at arm's length. Maybe it was time to pull him a little closer. "Actually, that was my decision."

"I thought..." His brows drew together in confusion.

"I broke the tie." It was true, she didn't need to tell him the real reason she'd made the choice. "It was my choice to marry you."

James eyed her warily, as if he was trying to fit this new information into everything he knew. "Why? I mean, I've seen you over the past few months. You haven't behaved like a woman who chose this."

She closed her eyes unable to face him. She hadn't been a blushing bride, at least not when they weren't in front of cameras. "I know. It wasn't an easy decision for me to make. But I realized I couldn't do anything else. You and I are both trapped by the same prophecy. Neither one of us has much choice in what we do. The same people would be after me. Your enemies would still be after you. If I had chosen Dermot, he never would have understood. I don't think there is anyone else in the world who could understand what we are facing. I chose you because I think you're the best person to face it with."

His hand came up to caress her cheek. "Ye canna imagine how much I've wanted to hear ye say that. We are going to make a formidable team."

Sarah's eyes flew open in surprise. Those had been James's words, but said with Dermot's voice and accent, the deep rumble and burr was the music of her heart. She watched him in alarm.

He leaned closer and touched his lips to hers. It was tentative, not the practiced kiss he'd given her before. He was unsure of himself. Sarah was unsure of everything. Had she had too much wine? Was she hallucinating?

Once again, the breeze carried the scent of Cardell's perfume, and with it a sense of calm which felt unnatural.

Sarah's mind still questioned what she'd heard and whose lips were kissing her, but the pulse-jumping confusion and anxiety eased. Her muscles began to relax. James moved closer, deepening the kiss. It was James, right?

His arm wrapped around her pulling her closer. The strength of it felt like Dermot, Sarah's muscle memory recognized him, yearned for him. God, she missed him. Without thought, she slid her hand to the back of his neck pulling him to her. His hand found her breast and he groaned in appreciation. The sound of Dermot's desire made her blood sing.

He kissed his way across her jaw and down to where her neck and shoulder met. Sarah leaned her head away expecting the graze of his teeth on his favorite spot. Instead, James whispered. "We should take this to the bedroom."

Sarah blinked, momentarily disoriented. He pulled away and rose from the couch. She looked up to see James standing in front of her, with his hand out. But a second ago, it hadn't been James. It was Dermot's voice she had heard, Dermot's lips she had felt, his hands, his arms. She looked at the hand he held out to her. It was smooth, the nails short, manicured. Dermot's hands were rough from the training he did for his security job.

Her gaze snapped back up to his face, and it was him, Dermot. Relief swept through her, and she gladly slid her hand into his. In the back of her mind, she thought this back and forth should alarm her, but for some reason she couldn't understand, it didn't. Maybe she had drunk too much wine, but this strange confusion had started before dinner.

The bedroom was dark but for a sliver of light coming from the nearly closed bathroom door. In the dark Sarah couldn't tell who she was with any more than she had in the light. But she longed so much for Dermot she couldn't stop, couldn't miss the next flash of him. James slid the straps of her dress off her shoulders and turned her around. Dermot unzipped the back of her dress and bit down on that spot he loved. Sarah whimpered with the need it sparked.

James turned her and kissed her deeply, backing her toward the bed. Dermot crowded her until she fell back onto it. He descended on her, finding her nipple with his mouth as he shifted them both further onto the bed. James settled himself between her legs and took her mouth. Dermot entered her. James Dermot. James. Dermot...

CHAPTER TWENTY-THREE

James. Only James. Sarah blinked into awareness as the morning sun shone through the windows, illuminating the sharp plane of his cheek and the cut of his jaw. Even with sleep-tousled hair, James was somehow neater, more polished than Dermot, as if he'd been buffed to a shine. Sarah closed her eyes against the sight of him, but there was no escaping the knowledge of what they'd done.

She breathed in, his scent was different. His arms were slightly thinner. The legs tangled with hers under the sheets were more lithe, less muscular than Dermot's. Last night she'd been fooled and for a moment she wished herself back; back to when she thought he was Dermot, back to when she had yearned enough for him to grab at whatever glimpses she could get. She didn't know how it had happened, and last night she hadn't really cared. What trick of her mind had made her see him, feel him, the night before? She had definitely seen him, heard him, felt him.

But in the warm morning sunlight examining last night's experience, she couldn't understand how she'd been fooled. She slid quietly, slowly, from James's arms trying not to wake him. Swinging her legs over the edge of the bed she sat up, bracing herself with her arms and trying to think rationally.

Well, that was it. Marriage consummated. Check one off the beat Walter Stuart to do list. It was a hurdle she had known she would have to get over but that didn't wipe away the guilt. She felt sick and satisfied at the same time.

Memories of the event flashed in her mind. Every breath feathering across her skin had come with whispered words of love, gratitude, and devotion whether it was James or the illusion of Dermot who uttered them. The two blended together in her mind, and her nerves fizzed with alarm. What if she forgot Dermot, what it was like to be in his arms, to make love to him? She didn't want them blending together. She didn't want any of this.

James shifted in his sleep. Sarah glanced over her shoulder at him. He looked completely at peace. He deserved better. They all did, and the strange experience of the night before filled her with fury.

Sarah faced forward, putting James behind her. She would give herself a few minutes to be alone with her thoughts, to be Sarah before Lady Sarah had to face the day. She breathed in and out, focusing on her heart. Yep, it was still beating; bruised, cracked, not completely broken. Her mother had described a broken heart; punched through, and dragging behind catching on stones and picking up debris. Sarah had certainly had her moments in the last few months, but she wasn't quite there yet.

What was Dermot doing right then? Would her gift let her see him from this far away? Desperate to see the real Dermot, she took another deep breath and exhaled. With another breath she could see herself sitting on the bed with James sprawled asleep behind her. Another breath had her floating above the hotel. Another gave her a bird's eye view of the city. She focused her thoughts on Dermot and felt the pull to the north.

But then another pull had her coming back down. It felt like draining from the sky back into her body. James's chest was against her back and his arms were around her. He kissed the back of her neck. "Good morning, my love."

It took a second for Sarah to settle into her own body. "Morning."

"Are you feeling alright?" He asked with all the awkwardness and care the situation called for. At least it would have called for if they were a normal couple and this had been their first time.

She leaned back into him, giving her best performance of a woman who didn't regret what they'd done. "I'm fine."

He kissed a path up the side of her neck to her ear. "I can't express how good it feels to wake up next to you. I've been dreaming of this since the day we met."

She didn't have any response, and it didn't matter. James took her earlobe between his teeth and bit down just enough. He did know his way around a woman's body. In any other circumstance, this would have been arousing, but Sarah's hitched breath wasn't one of pleasure, but of shock.

Oblivious to her rising panic, his hand came up to cup her breast. Sarah thought about saying no, she needed time to settle into this new intimacy. She was saved by a knock at the bedroom door.

James stopped resting his forehead against the back of her neck. He raised his voice to be heard through the door. "Leave the breakfast out there."

"It's not breakfast, sir." Fleming's voice came from the other side of the door sounding grim.

James groaned.

"You'd better get it." She told him.

He placed a lingering kiss on her neck. "Don't move."

Climbing around her and out of bed, he tied his robe closed before opening the door a crack. "Someone had better be dead or in the hospital."

Fleming's voice was hushed. "Actually, I think several people are dead and several more in hospital."

"What?" James snapped.

"There was an explosion on one of our oil rigs in the North Sea." Fleming said.

"Right." James's demeanor changed entirely. In a blink he was all business, and in charge. "Give me five minutes."

He closed the door and turned back to get dressed. "I'm sorry, darling, but I have to deal with this."

"Of course." She said as he rushed into the bathroom to brush his teeth.

Sarah got up as well and started getting dressed. This explosion sounded bad, but she was grateful for the space it would give her. She was still processing the events of the night before. Although the ice had clearly been broken on her marriage bed, she wasn't ready for the kind of intimacy James wanted.

"Please don't get up for me. You should rest." he said as he paused beside her on his way to the door.

Sarah gave him a smile which was braver than she felt. "Nope. We're a team now, right?"

He gave her a quick kiss. "We're a team."

CHAPTER TWENTY-FOUR

September 13, 1996
Edinburgh, Scotland

They were well into their descent to the private airfield. The Scottish weather was such a sharp contrast from the hot sun they'd left in Marseille. James shifted restlessly in the seat next to hers, eager to hit the ground running.

"Thank you for stepping up this morning." He said for the dozenth time since they'd taken off.

"Of course," She patted his hand on the arm of the seat. "This is part of the job, right? You'll get through this."

"There's going to be some fallout. Two deaths, half a dozen more in hospital with injuries." He leaned forward to look out the window as if seeing the ground might get them to it faster. "All of our safety measures will be scrutinized closely. There was a terrible explosion on a rig eight years ago. One hundred sixty-seven men died, and they found it was because of poor maintenance. It wasn't one of our rigs, but it resulted in a lot of new regulations and Health and Safety breathing down the necks of every oil company that so much as launched a dinghy in the North Sea."

"Do you think this could be poor maintenance?" She asked.

"It had better not be." His tone was fierce. "In the last couple of years, we've completely overhauled our equipment and procedures to meet the new standards. If I find out someone has been cutting corners..." He trailed off as their wheels bounced on the runway.

Sarah cast a look out the window as the jet came to a stop. Dermot stood next to the sedan waiting for them. To anyone else, his broad shoulders would look intimidating in his black suit jacket paired with dark sunglasses. To Sarah, he looked like home.

"Ready?" James asked from above her. He had already risen and was pulling on his own jacket.

His voice threw cold water on any warm feeling she had at seeing Dermot again, reminding her exactly what they'd done the night before. This was her life now. Lady Sarah. This was who she had to be, at least for now.

***

The plane came to a stop a safe distance from the waiting car. Dermot eyed the door, willing it to open so he could clap eyes on her. The seconds seemed to stretch for hours before the door cracked open and swung downward, revealing the stairs. Dermot held his breath.

Fleming Sinclair, a distant cousin, and fellow Alba Petroleum bodyguard was the first to emerge. After scanning the area and giving Dermot a nod, he descended the stairs and turned to wait for James and Sarah. James came next, his shoulders filling the doorway. His dark brown hair was burnished by the sun, and his cheeks were slightly bronzed. At the bottom of the stairs he turned to offer his hand to his bride.

Sarah stepped out of the plane and took James's hand as she descended the handful of steps to the ground. Dermot's heart flipped. She looked like a soft breeze blowing in from the Mediterranean. Her cheeks were sun-kissed and the dress she wore flowed around her calves like waves on the shore. He was equal parts relieved she appeared to be alright, and insanely jealous as James tucked her hand into his elbow.

'Look at me.' He thought. He needed to see her eyes to know she was all right. 'Look at me.'

***

'Don't look.' Sarah thought. 'He'll see what happened. And anyone who sees us looking at each other will see how we feel.' Betraying her feelings for Dermot could be dangerous to him. If anyone else noticed how they looked at each other and commented on it, it would get back to Walter, or to James. As understanding as James was, as much as he cared about both of them, Sarah wasn't sure he would tolerate his wife being in love with his…whatever Dermot was.

***

They strode toward the car with an easy grace contrasting the muscles bunching in Dermot's shoulders. He should be doing his job, making sure there was no one approaching them, no one trying to sneak a photo from outside the chain link fence, but all he could do was watch James and Sarah as they approached the car. James said something to make her smile, and she leaned into his arm looking up at her husband with what looked like adoration.

'Look at me.' Dermot fairly screamed in his head. As they got closer, he opened the door to the limousine, trying not to show how affected he was by the sight of them looking like a couple returning from their honeymoon.

***

'Don't look.' Sarah thought as she surreptitiously did exactly that. He was whole. He looked healthy. She couldn't see behind his sunglasses, but she hoped his eyes were bright, and not red-rimmed or tired. She was relieved she couldn't see them, and afraid he could see hers.

She shuddered to think what Dermot would feel or do if he saw what had happened between her and James. He was so adept at reading her mind. Surely, he would figure it out. A part of her knew he had to expect it, but expectation and reality are two very different things. He didn't need to see the guilt reflected in her eyes. And she certainly didn't think she could take the sadness in his. 'Don't look.'

***

"Alright, mate?" James clapped him on the shoulder as they arrived at the car.

"Aye, alright." Dermot hoped he was convincing.

"My love?" James stepped back allowing Sarah to get into the car first.

She stepped between them brushing a hand down James's arm as she lowered herself onto the seat. She hadn't spared Dermot a glance. His heart ached, and his throat tightened with each breath. He looked back up and met James's eyes.

They were the same blue as his own, but James's were filled with sympathy, and a question. 'Would he be able to do this?'

Dermot drew in a breath and pulled his shoulder's back. He lifted his chin giving every appearance of being in control and dispassionate. His eyes never left those of his childhood friend, his employer, and maybe relative. He would have to do this. He didn't have a choice.

CHAPTER TWENTY-FIVE

They settled into a limousine taking them home from the airport, all of them pretending the situation wasn't awkward. James and Sarah took the forward-facing seat, while Dermot took a position facing them, but trained his attention carefully out the window. Sarah supposed this was going to be the new normal. Dermot was James's personal bodyguard after all. Whenever she was out with James, Dermot would no doubt be nearby. It was a horrible tease to have him so close while having to pretend there was nothing between them, or at least pretend she wouldn't rather grab him by the hand and run until there wasn't anyone left to run from. But she knew the Stuarts' reach was farther than she and Dermot could ever run.

She looked out the window, trying not to get caught staring at him, although she wanted to examine every inch of him to be sure he'd made it through the last three weeks unscathed. Had she? On the surface, France had been lovely. She and James had deepened their friendship. Sarah thought she understood more about their situation, and the Stuarts' belief they were entitled to the throne. She felt a little more confident she would figure out a way to navigate their schemes. Still, she couldn't shake the feeling that something was off, especially after the previous night.

"We'll drop ye at the house. I'll need to go to the office." Dermot's voice came from beside her. Sarah turned away from the window in alarm. Dermot wasn't sitting beside her; he was in front of her. James was beside her. He must have seen confusion on her face. "Are you alright, darling?"

Sarah tried to put on a confident front. She must be tired, or the acoustics in the car created an illusion. She gave him a reassuring smile. "Of course, just a bit of jet lag. You were saying?"

"I was saying I'll have to go into the office, and I'm not sure when I'll be home." She watched him closely as he spoke. He sounded like himself, poised, precise, patrician, nothing like Dermot. He looked like James. He sounded like James.

Her mind must be playing tricks on her. No doubt because she wanted to hear Dermot's voice. "I understand. Don't worry about me. I'll be fine. Please let me know if there is anything I can do to help."

"Miss Banks has scheduled a press conference, and there'll be a meeting with Health and Safety." Dermot said, keeping a carefully bland expression on his face.

"Good." James turned back to Sarah. "I'm afraid I'll probably have to go to Aberdeen tomorrow to oversee things more closely. I hate to leave you so soon after arriving home."

"I'll go with you." Sarah said.

"There's no need, darling." He squeezed her knee, giving her a loving look. Dermot averted his gaze.

'How were they going to get through this strange proximity?' Sarah thought. To James, she said. "Of course, there's a need. We're a team. You do the business part; I'll do the human part. There are injured workers and families who will need reassurance. We can't let them think A.P. doesn't care about its workers."

Dermot turned to look at her in surprise. She suspected Alba Petroleum didn't usually give such attention to its employees. It likely didn't expect the wife of the CEO to care about them either. Sarah tried to imagine Lady Anne going to visit workers in a hospital. She had to stop herself from smirking at the image.

James took her hand and kissed the back of it, his face glowing in approval. "You are so thoughtful. I think that will be a help."

They pulled into the drive at Polwarth Terrace. As soon as the car stopped, the front door opened, and Lady Anne and Henry Stuart came out to greet them.

'Speak of the devil.' Sarah thought while trying not to look annoyed. Of course, Lady Anne would be waiting to greet them. James had barely gotten out of the car to greet his mother before he got back in to go to the office.

Lady Anne greeted Sarah with performative cheek kisses and a disingenuous welcome home. "I'm so sorry your honeymoon was cut short, my dear. How did you like the chateau?"

"It was lovely. Thank you for letting us use it. Martine sends her best." Sarah had talked briefly with Martine while arranging to have their things sent back to Edinburgh. The housekeeper had expressed her disappointment they were leaving and wished Sarah and James would come back soon.

"Ah yes, Martine is so efficient at keeping things in order." Anne's perfectly coiffed hair didn't move an inch as she shook her head. "I do wish we could go there more often. I understand you met a friend of mine, Monsieur Cardell."

"Yes, he was kind enough to invite us to his farm for dinner."

Anne looped an arm through Sarah's and drew her into the parlor, as if they were old friends ready to sit down for a natter. Lady Anne never mentioned the rig accident. "Did he take you on a tour of the greenhouses, aren't they marvelous?"

Henry was subdued. Sarah was a little surprised he wasn't engaged in any of the business discussions. He might not be CEO anymore, but he was still chairman of the board and he was responsible for building the company. Even in retirement, he had a stake in how well the company did, but he seemed to have ceded all responsibility to James and Walter.

After a reasonably appropriate time, Sarah excused herself to lie down. Her things, minus the giant portrait her sister, Oona, had given her as a wedding gift had been moved to the master suite. Sarah thought it was a good thing the marital ice had been broken, or this homecoming would have been even more awkward than it already was.

She unpacked her things and considered whether she should brave Lady Anne's passive aggressive prodding for information. Sarah was absolutely not going to talk to her mother-in-law about the state of her marriage. In the end she decided she would claim jet lag and stay in her room. Truthfully, she was a bit tired. It had been quite a day, and tomorrow would be even more eventful.

Sarah decided it would be best to get rest while she could. Closing the blackout curtains against the early evening sun, she put on her most comfortable pajamas and went to bed.

***

James arrived at the Alba Petroleum offices to find the place hopping. Even the executive floor was abuzz with activity. Miss Lennox was on the phone, but she relaxed a fraction when she saw him. He had to admit he felt more relaxed with her on the case as well. There was no one more capable than Audra Lennox, who even amid the madness of this emergency, was poised and put together. She was unflappable.

She ended her phone call and got straight to the point in her usual fashion. "The fire is out, or at least the one on the oil rig is."

"Well, thank heaven for that." James, Lennox, and Dermot went into his office. "Tell me where we are."

Miss Lennox handed him a sheet of paper. "Miss Banks wrote up some talking points for the press conference. As of now, all personnel have been evacuated, the fire is out, and Mr. Shaw and the investigators are on their way to the rig to discover how it started."

"Any leakage?" Next to the lives on the rig, potential environmental damage was their most immediate concern.

"Minimal. The explosion happened away from the well head. They believe it was a problem with the generator, which according to the newer regulations was separated from the production equipment."

James breathed a sigh of relief. "So, the narrative is our compliance with the new regulations prevented a much bigger disaster."

Miss Lennox flashed a smile. "I'll let Miss Banks fill you in on the narrative, but that's fairly accurate."

James thought about Sarah's concern for the employees. "And our people? What is the situation with the staff?"

"The names of the deceased are in the talking points. Their families have already been informed so we should be able to release names and photos. The injured are in the Royal Infirmary in Aberdeen. The rest of the staff are being debriefed at our offices there."

"Excellent." He found himself asking what Sarah would do for these people. "Do we have counselors available for the survivors and their families?"

Miss Lennox paused before giving him a look of approval. "We have one talking with the families of the deceased and those injured, but we can bring in more for the others."

"Please do."

She made a note in her agenda. "I have already arranged travel for us to Aberdeen for the rest of the week."

"Yes. Make sure you add my wife to those arrangements. Also, can you make arrangements for us to visit with the families of the dead and injured?"

This time she blinked at him looking puzzled. Miss Lennox rarely missed a beat, but this was clearly unexpected. Sarah was right in her instinct. He would have to do better. "Is there a problem?"

"No, sir." Her cheeks turned pink. "I hadn't expected your wife to take such an active role. That's all."

"She reminded me today; we have a duty of care for the people we employ beyond only meeting the minimum safety requirements."

"I suspect your uncle will balk at the added cost of counseling for all of the evacuees." She warned him.

She was likely right. "I'll deal with my uncle. Where is he, by the way?"

"Already in Aberdeen. He went up this morning."

"Ah, well. I'm sure we'll see him soon enough."

A mere hour later, James was in their largest meeting room answering every question he could at the time. They still didn't know the cause of the explosion, but it appeared the damage could have been much worse than it was. Now, he had to hope this emergency didn't cause damage to his fragile marriage when it had barely gotten started.

***

Sarah woke to an arm snaking around her waist and a body pressing against her back. She inhaled deeply, smelling the now familiar scents from home and the Highlands. The muscular chest pressed against her could only be Dermot's. She rolled over, reaching for him. "How?"

"Sh. Don't talk. I've been doing nothing but talking since I left ye." His hot breath against her throat sent her pulse racing. "I need ye."

"You have me." She sighed, as he kissed his way from her throat to her breasts. They made love slowly, wordlessly. Each of them exploring the other, finding new ways to please each other, releasing the tension of the day before falling into satisfied rest.

CHAPTER TWENTY-SIX

"Mr. Stuart should be arriving shortly." A woman in a navy-blue pants suit escorted them into a conference room at the Alba Petroleum offices in Aberdeen's city center. Unlike the staid and traditional offices on The Mound in Edinburgh, Aberdeen's office was all glass and steel, leaving the conference room visible to anyone who walked by.

Sarah was already on edge after waking up in bed next to James, and not Dermot, again. She'd been sure it was Dermot the night before when she was half asleep. Of course, rationally awake Sarah recognized that it wasn't possible. She wasn't sure what was going on with her, but the grin on James's face had told her he'd definitely been the one in their bed the night before.

Then she'd had to sit on a plane and in a car with both of them, trying not to look guilty for having sex with her husband or for thinking he was Dermot. At least today, they had the added presence of James's assistant, Audra Lennox as a buffer. Sarah had heard much about Miss Lennox's capabilities. She hadn't heard how pretty she was. Sure, it was a buttoned up, bookish sort of pretty, but Sarah had a feeling when Miss Lennox let her hair down, if she ever did, she'd be quite stunning. Sarah also got the sense from the way she behaved around James, Miss Lennox relished her role as James's girl Friday.

Felicia Banks and a couple of other people in suits. The woman escorting them opened the door, but Sarah balked. "Actually, I think I need a minute. Can you show me to the ladies' room?"

"Everything alright?" James turned back to her from the threshold.

"Fine. Just need to powder my nose. I'll be back in a minute." Sarah followed the woman to the ladies' room. She checked and rechecked her makeup, hair, teeth, making sure everything was in a fit state. She didn't look like a person who may or may not be having hallucinations. She also didn't look like a poor girl from the holler who wandered her way into the life of a princess.

She was sure she would be on camera at some point in the day, in her first official capacity as Lady Sarah/CEO's wife, and if it was going to be a success, she was going to have to keep it together. They needed it to be a success. So far James seemed to be heeding her advice on leadership. Today would be a test, and she needed her advice to work.

With a deep breath and one last glance in the mirror, she returned to the conference room to find everyone crowded under a monitor hanging in the corner of the room watching with rapt attention. No one noticed when she came in, except for Dermot who stood at his post near the door. She brushed his hand with the backs of her fingers as she passed him. His fingers jumped and flexed. It was the first time they had touched in reality since the wedding. Her fingers tingled where their skin met. She curled them into her palm savoring the memory of his skin. Glancing over her shoulder, their eyes met and her heart swelled.

For one frozen moment they stood caught in each other's eyes. Sarah's breath caught, remembering the illusion of the night before and every night when it had really been Dermot. She hoped he also was thinking of their time together, of the time before Walter Stuart's threats. 'Wait.' She tried to send him the thought with her eyes. Her heart was still his.

Dermot blinked and gave the slightest nod, as if he'd read her mind the way he so often did.

A noise behind her caught their attention as someone pointed out something on the screen. The grainy footage that was holding everyone's attention appeared to be from an infrared camera. It showed the corner of a platform. The edge of a building stood on the left side of the screen. A faint light bobbed on the horizon between the dark green and the inky black sea approaching the rig.

A moment later, something new appeared much closer to the camera. A silhouette of a person climbed over the edge of the platform. They crouched on the surface and pulled something up from below, before scurrying around the corner of the building. The figure returned a moment later and climbed back over the edge of the platform and disappeared. The faint light reappeared on the horizon and faded into the distance.

The man standing closest to the monitor hit the pause button and turned to the room. His expression and voice were grim. "Exactly four minutes later, the explosion destroyed our generator and started the fire."

"And we have no idea who this person might be?" James asked.

"Not the man himself." The man who must be Mark Shaw, head of security, turned to James. "This isn't in the press yet, but I'm sure it will be soon. A group calling themselves the Sea Maidens has claimed responsibility. We've been tracking several of these eco-terrorist organizations, but that one has not been on our radar before now."

"*An Mhaighdean Mhara.*" Sarah said without thinking. All eyes turned to her.

Shaw was the one who answered her with narrowed eyes. "Are you familiar with them?"

Sarah shook her head. "No, but it's a Scottish folktale about a mermaid who offers to trade a fisherman a series of things in exchange for one of his three sons. He refuses, but eventually after the sons have grown up she claims two of them through magical means then the third kills her and revives his brothers."

"What symbolism does that have for an eco-terrorist?" Walter asked clearly annoyed.

"Well, it is primarily a story about unfair exchange and retribution." Sarah gave Walter a significant look. "But I suspect it's also a reference to The War of the Maidens." Shifting her focus to Shaw, she explained. "It was a conflict in France around eighteen thirty where peasants dressed in women's clothes led armed battles against forest guards and charcoal-makers in protest of new forest codes. It's considered by historians to be the first eco-terrorist action."

"I don't think we need history or folklore lessons to tell us how we should deal with these people." Walter said sourly. "Our agents should be working on infiltrating these Sea Maidens immediately. We cannot let them use this as a springboard to raise their profile."

"I'll put my best people on it today." Shaw answered.

Sarah could tell Walter's blood was boiling, although his demeanor was outwardly calm. "I want them found and prosecuted."

Murmurs of agreement rose around the room. Shaw put the remote control on the table. "I've already given the tape to the appropriate authorities. They'll be pursuing prosecution. Naturally, we'll help them as much as we can."

Felicia stepped into the pause in conversation. "I'll draft a press release stating that A.P. has been cleared of any wrongdoing or negligence and reminding groups who think to do this sort of thing that our workers don't deserve to be attacked for simply doing their jobs."

James turned to the room at large. "Good. Let's push back the press conference until the statement is ready. Make sure we verify those claims with Health and Safety."

"We've got it." Shaw put in. "They did the inspection while I was examining the security footage."

"Excellent. In the meantime, Sarah and I are going to visit with the families of the victims." James gave her a smile, and everyone turned her way again. Sarah tried to tamp down the rising panic. She could do this. It wasn't her first time in the public eye.

***

Two children without a father, one mother whose son would never come home, four men with severe burns, one with a broken arm and two with concussions. They'd spoken to every injured man and their families at the hospital. James had come away with a mile-long list for Miss Lennox to be sure the families got things they needed to aid the men's recoveries. Then they had gone to the homes of the two dead men.

Sarah was a wonder. She had jumped right in and comforted them. She'd held Connor Murchison's infant son on one shoulder while letting Sophie, his widow, weep on the other. She had enlisted him as well, asking him to make tea for them. Him. He couldn't think of a time when someone had asked him to make tea. He barely knew how, but he'd done it in the cramped kitchen of the Murchison's second floor flat.

While James had talked with Mrs. Murchison about how Alba Petroleum would help her, Sarah had played dolls with the Murchison's little girl, Charlotte. The little girl, whose hair was tangled and whose shirt had a jam stain on it, handed her a stuffed tiger. "My daddy took us to the zoo. We saw monkeys and…and snakes, and he bought me this tiger."

Sarah looked at the tiger which was nearly bald on the back of its head. "He seems nice. Does he have a name?"

"Stripey." Charlotte said, wiping her nose on the back of her hand. "My daddy…" Her eyes began to fill with tears. "My daddy…"

Sarah rubbed the girl's back. "Did you know my mama died when I was only a little bit older than you?"

Distracted by this new information, Charlotte brushed away a tear. "She did?"

"She did." Sarah's voice was soft. "I have a memory of her that I like to hold in my mind when I miss her. We went out picking flowers on a spring morning. I made her a crown of flowers and we danced our way home. It was the happiest I ever saw her. Do you have a memory of your daddy when you were both happy?"

Charlotte nodded slowly. "We got ice cream at the zoo. I got some on my nose, and daddy was silly and put some on his nose too."

Sarah brushed a curl from in front of Charlotte's eyes. "Whenever you miss your daddy, you should think about that memory. Can you do that?"

At Effie Gordon's little cottage, Sarah had put on an apron and cleaned the woman's kitchen while James listened to her tell him about her son and all the plans he'd had for his future. Sarah had come in with tea when she was done, still wearing the apron. She promptly sat down in the lounge and began folding laundry. She seemed to know exactly what all these people needed, not material needs but emotional ones. Sarah connected with them in a way he found difficult, and he was grateful for it.

In the car on the way back to the offices, he took her hand and brought it to his lips. "I'm glad you insisted on coming. You sensed what these people needed better than I could."

"I'm glad you agreed. If people are still going to work out on those rigs, they need to know A.P. cares about them." She gave his hand a squeeze.

"I don't know that I ever thought about it before today." He looked out the window at the busy city center, embarrassed it had taken her to show him. "You've taught me so much."

"I'm sure you would have learned it eventually." She leaned back in her seat resting her head.

"You must be tired. I should have them drop you at the house so you can rest." He offered.

Sarah shook her head. "No, I'll be fine until you're done."

"You don't have to be there for the press conference."

"I know." She said. "But wither thou goest and all."

"You're a marvel."

The press conference went off without a hitch. The narrative was put out that Alba Petroleum followed all the appropriate safety precautions and attacking hard working citizens was not an acceptable form of political discourse. The press's questions were satisfied except for the one who in poor taste asked about ending his honeymoon early.

"That's of no consequence when you think about what these families are going through. It's not even a question worth answering."

Later they were gathered in the lounge of the house the company kept in town for when executives visited. James, Walter, Shaw, and Miss Banks were having a nightcap.

"Did Sarah go to bed?" Miss Banks asked stretching her legs out in front of her.

"Yes." James answered. "She did a lot of work with the families today. I think she was a bit drained."

"I don't know why you bothered." His uncle said from the wing-backed chair in front of the empty fireplace. "They'll be taken care of with insurance."

James studied Walter not knowing how to answer in a way that might change his uncle's mind. In the end, he didn't have to. A report about the oil rig fire came on the news. Shaw turned up the volume.

After covering the basic information about the explosion and The Sea Maidens, the report shifted gears to show James and Sarah visiting the hospital. They had even managed to get footage of Sarah in the hallway embracing some of the families of the injured. It looked personal, as if they were extended family. Sarah spoke with everyone, but more importantly she listened.

"That is why they did it." Miss Banks gestured toward the television with her crystal whiskey glass. "That's Diana-hugging-a-child-with-AIDS good. Stood up against terrorists planting a bomb, we'll come out of this smelling like roses thanks to her."

"We'll come out smelling like roses thanks to the clear Health and Safety investigation." Walter argued.

Miss Banks took a sip of whiskey and brushed her hair back over her shoulder. "The report may keep us out of hot water, but the average person only cares about Health and Safety when something goes wrong. The sight of Lady Sarah putting her arms around our workers' families; that's gold. The public will care far more about that than they will about our safety record. We should see about getting her to do more public appearances."

"She'll need an admin. I can't ask her to manage everything herself. I'll talk with her about hiring someone to help her with the tedious bits."

"I'm sure we can find someone from the company." Walter suggested. "Ask HR to send someone."

A moment ago, Walter had been skeptical of Sarah's talents. Now, he was endorsing an assistant for her. "I suspect she might want to choose the person herself. Maybe we can send her a pool of candidates to choose from."

Walter shrugged and looked back at the television, but the news had shifted to a story about a teacher at a local primary school winning some award. James watched Walter turn away from the screen and focus on his drink. He knew his uncle well enough to imagine the disgruntled monologue running through his head. The old man seemed to be losing his touch, or perhaps Sarah had opened his eyes to some of Walter's faults.

CHAPTER TWENTY-SEVEN

Dermot was relieved to be back in Edinburgh even if he was still glued to James's side. They'd returned from Aberdeen the day before, after clearing up the media circus resulting from the explosion. He had loved and hated the trip. Being forced to spend so much time with James and Sarah together was torture. She was so close, but out of reach. He was forced to settle for the occasional knowing glance or brush of their fingers. Meanwhile, James was constantly touching her, holding her hand, resting his hand on the small of her back or her knee. It was almost too much.

At least now, he and James would be spending their days at the office without Sarah. That morning, he'd arrived to accompany James to work, and they'd gone off to the office without seeing Sarah at all. The comings and goings of the executive suites might have been mind-numbing, but they didn't make him feel as though his heart had been ripped out.

He was ready to be done with the day when he and James got into the car at five o'clock. But James had other ideas. "Come in with me. We need to talk."

"Right." Dermot said through gritted teeth.

They went inside, and James directed him to the study. Dermot stood on the rug in front of the desk, waiting. James glanced at him and shook his head before turning to the decanters on the bar cart. "Don't be ridiculous. You and I have never been so formal. Drink?"

"Alright." Dermot relaxed his stance and unbuttoned his jacket. "Whiskey."

James handed him a tumbler. Dermot took a small sip. The whiskey burned as it went down.

James came around the desk and leaned back on it. He swirled his drink in his glass. "I'm afraid in all the fuss, we haven't had a chance to talk about what I asked you to do while I was away."

Right, his assignment. "Aye, well. I'm afraid there isna much to report. The only person who went in or out of your office was Miss Lennox."

"No one else?" James's brows knit in frustration.

Dermot took a thoughtful sip. "There was something odd, with Walter. I came back from lunch the other day and the door was closed. I took my post and a moment later heard something that sounded like a scuffle. I opened the door to find Miss Lennox and Walter standing over a mess of folders on the floor."

"A scuffle?"

Dermot nodded. "I've no idea what happened to cause the sound or the folders to fall. I only know Miss Lennox looked upset."

"Did she say why she was upset?"

"No, she seemed to brush it all off. Said everything was fine, but it didna look fine. And as soon as I opened the door, your uncle was ready to leave. Does Miss Lennox have any connection to him?"

James considered it. "I don't know. She was assigned to me when I first came on. I don't know who she worked with before, if anyone. She's about our age, so I can't imagine she worked too long with anyone else."

"Our age, but they made her assistant to the CEO when ye came on?" That didn't make sense. "I would think they would have given ye someone with more experience right out of the gate."

James studied the amber liquid in his glass. "I've never thought much about it, but you make a good point. I suppose we relied on Walter to show me the ropes."

"Hmm." Dermot sipped his whiskey. "I dinna want to cast aspersions. Miss Lennox is certainly capable and seems to do a fine job. I wonder if it's really you she's working for."

James sighed. "I must admit I'll be supremely disappointed if she's not who I think she is. I don't know what I would do without her."

Dermot raised his hands in an equivocal gesture. "I may have misread the situation, but that was the oddest thing I saw while ye were away."

James was lost in thought. "I'll have a look at her personnel file, perhaps have Shaw run a background check. I'm sure they did it when she was hired, but I haven't seen it."

"I would make it a check on all of the clerical staff for the executives, so they won't know ye've singled her out."

"Excellent point. I'm still concerned someone internal leaked our location in France." James said. He pushed away from the desk and walked around to his valise. He pulled out a large envelope. "Our report from the lab came back while I was away. Are you ready to see this?"

A ball of ice formed in Dermot's stomach, in spite of the whiskey. He set his glass down on the desk and came to stand next to James. "Ready as I'll ever be."

***

"My dear, we simply must talk with the stylist about your dresses. The weather will start getting cool soon, and you're not an ingénue anymore. We must decide on your clothes for the next season." Lady Anne simpered as they gathered in the parlor for pre-dinner drinks.

After what Anne called Sarah's triumph in Aberdeen, her mother-in-law had taken a different tone with her. Where before, Lady Anne had insisted Sarah follow her dictates, now she was attempting to be Sarah's friend, albeit an overbearing one. "I have spoken with Gillian. She and my personal shopper are working on some options. We've got it all in hand."

Lady Anne was biting her tongue. "Perhaps I can go with you when you review them."

"Maybe. I'll be—"

"Ye lied to me!" Dermot shouted from the doorway. His face was red with rage. He crossed the room to Henry in two steps. Henry backed against the wall. He was clearly as shocked as the rest of them. "Ye told me ye were never with my mother!"

"What impertinence is this?" Lady Anne rose from her place beside Sarah on the couch. "How dare you!"

"Oh. I'm about to get seriously fucking impertinent." Dermot threw the comment over his shoulder, not taking his eyes off of Henry. "Ye told me—"

"I did not lie to you." Henry struggled to remain calm himself. "I don't know what you are talking about."

"Dermot and I had our DNA tested." James stood near the door tension made his voice tight. "We are brothers."

"That's impossible!" Anne cried in outrage.

"I'm sorry mother." James turned to her holding out a sheet of paper. "Half-brothers."

Lady Anne snatched the letter and read it. Without another word, she sank back down, face white as a sheet. Whatever indignation she had been feeling drained out of her.

Sarah took the letter from Anne's loose fingers. She skimmed the paragraphs about alleles and chromosomes but got the gist of the conclusion. James and Dermot were in fact half-brothers. Sarah's blood went cold and boiled at the same time. She felt shocked and angry. Dermot still had Henry cornered. He hadn't moved, but he vibrated with rage.

Henry's gaze was equally as intent on Dermot's. "What I told you was the absolute truth. Much to my shame, I have never been with your mother."

Dermot growled, clearly fighting the urge to pummel Henry.

"If that is true, then..." James eyed his mother who was slumped against the arm of the couch, her head in her hand. "Mother?"

Anne slowly shook her head back and forth. "No one was ever to know."

Every eye in the room turned to her. Henry leaned around Dermot to look at his wife. "What are you saying?"

A tear trickled down Anne's cheek, she looked at Henry. "We'd been trying for over a year with no luck. Adopting was out of the question. The prophecy...We did what needed to be done."

Shock swept over Henry's face. "You...and my brother?"

"No!" Dermot barked.

"We had to do something." The words rushed out of Anne now. "We hadn't been able to conceive, but we had to carry on the line, even your precious Seonag said so. We had to."

"No, no, no, no, no, no, no, no." Dermot gripped the back of a chair for support. "My mother would never."

Lady Anne snapped. "I have no idea what your mother would and would not do, but there are only two men I slept with that year."

"What on Earth is everyone in such an uproar about?" Walter Stuart came into the room as if they'd conjured him.

"Speak of the actual devil." Sarah muttered.

"You and my mother?" James narrowed his eyes at his uncle, well father.

Walter did a fairly good imitation of bewilderment until Anne said. "I've told them."

"Good God, why?" For all the anger, surprise, and shame swirling around in the room, Walter was cool as a cucumber.

"Because we've had a DNA test done." James took the paper from Sarah and handed it to him.

Walter tossed the paper down onto the coffee table without a glance as if it meant nothing. "Then you know all there is to know."

"I don't." Dermot snapped. "What did ye do to my mother?"

"I would have thought you'd have learned that by now." Walter arched an eyebrow significantly.

Dermot went for his father. James stepped in front of him. "Don't let him goad you. You're better than him."

Walter sighed as if clinging to his patience. He gestured toward Henry. "You needed an heir, and you weren't doing the job, old man. Someone had to step into the breach, and it had to be someone from the Stuart line. Anne and I agreed you never needed to know."

"And what am I, the spare?" Dermot seethed, still blocked by James.

To Sarah's astonishment, Walter's face softened when he looked at Dermot. "I realize this may be difficult to believe, but your mother and I had a passionate relationship. We argued passionately about most things, but that summer our passions found a new outlet."

"I dinna believe it." Dermot scoffed, his face growing red.

"Nor do I." Henry's fury almost matched Dermot's.

Walter dismissed their doubts. "You can believe what you like. The fact remains a problem needed solving, and I solved it as I often do."

Henry turned to Anne. "Was this his idea or yours?"

Anne still leaned on the arm of the couch in defeat. "Does it matter? And why are you so angry? It's not as if you've been a model of fidelity."

"I haven't had a child with any of them." Henry snapped. "The only one I truly cared about apparently had a child with my brother too."

"It was my idea." Walter stepped between Henry and Anne. "Anne told me several times about how worried she was that you hadn't conceived. She was distraught, she feared you would divorce her if she couldn't give you an heir."

Henry looked at Anne. "Did I ever once suggest to you that I was impatient for a child? Why would you think that?"

"No, no you didn't." Anne blew out a breath. "I was the one worried about an heir, and about the prophecy. I wondered if you even cared about it at all. You seemed content to go about our lives as if we weren't destined for something more."

Henry exploded. "How is building the largest oil company in an oil rich country not enough for you? Why does there have to be this grand prophecy about kings and princes. Good God!" He gestured to the antique-filled room which could easily have been in an actual palace. "We live like royalty already. What more can you all want?"

"An independent nation to rule." Walter countered his frustration showing on his face. "How can you be satisfied when you know it was stolen from us?"

"That was generations ago!" Henry cried. "You're talking about a country that doesn't exist anymore."

The room fell silent. Sarah glanced at James who gaped at Henry. She wondered if Henry had ever admitted before that he wasn't completely committed to their cause.

"Why then were James and I treated so differently growing up?" Dermot asked. "Why was he the heir and I the steward?"

Walter shifted his attention to Dermot. "Simple. He is the son of Lady Caledon. You are the son of a professor, the orphaned daughter of a lorry driver."

To the surprise of everyone, Dermot started to laugh. It escalated from a low, fatalistic chuckle to a full-on belly laugh.

"What on Earth is so funny?" James looked at Dermot as if he'd gone mad. Sarah wondered to herself if the Stuarts had finally broken him.

"Sinclair was her stepfather." He said, still laughing. "Her father is Lyall Green."

"How is that even possible?" Henry sputtered.

"Ye believe a prophecy thousands of years old supported by swirling runes in a mud puddle told her to marry him, but ye canna believe a man who looks yer age could be my grandfather. Ye're all mad."

With a dismissive wave he stormed out of the room. Sarah leapt up from the couch to follow him. "*A'Dhiarmaid?*"

He stopped on the verge of opening the front door but didn't turn around. She stood frozen there in the hallway. Sarah was terrified he might walk out and never come back. He had finally had all of the Stuarts he could take. He might leave her in this hell with these people. She should run right out the door with him. But she couldn't seem to move forward. It was like some invisible tether was holding her back.

As if he'd read her mind, he stalked to where she stood. He threaded his fingers into the hair at the nape of her neck and held her head in place as he rested his forehead against hers. She wanted to lift her face to his, to be absorbed by his kiss, enveloped by his arms the way they used to. But he held her in place, their bodies inches apart sharing nothing but an inch of skin and their breath. "I love ye. I'll be back but I need time."

"Sarah?" James's voice came from behind her sounding lost and uncertain. And the invisible tether Sarah was feeling seemed to pull tighter drawing her backwards. Dermot seemed to feel the division within her. He planted a kiss on her forehead and turned away. She couldn't move. Her heart drew her forward, but something she couldn't put her finger on also drew her back to James. An ache bloomed in her chest as she watched Dermot slip out the front door.

The sound of the door latch clicking into place released a torrent of fury inside her. Sarah turned on her heel and marched right past James back into the drawing room. Before anyone had a chance to stop her, she slapped Walter Stuart's face so hard her hand stung, and her wrist hurt. "You knew! All this time! All their lives you knew that either of them could be the heir and you said nothing! You played God, deciding which one got everything and which one had to fend for himself while you sat smug in your place at the top of the pile. But there's going to come a time when you're not going to be able to control them anymore."

"Careful, my lady." He leaned hard on the honorific to emphasize he'd already won by forcing her to marry James. His tone turned threatening. "You wouldn't want to let slip anything that might have serious consequences."

Sarah took a breath, remembering that Walter had no problem killing to get his way. Her eyes still shot fury at him. "One day, you son of a bitch, it's all going to come out, and there won't be anything you can do to stop it."

"Your people won't thank you for that." His threat was almost whispered, but Sarah was sure the others heard it. Whether they understood his meaning was another story.

Sarah drew herself up straight. "One thing about my people, is they taught me the value of a good curse."

Her red handprint spread under his skin and confusion flickered on his face, she did something she hadn't done since she was a child. She used her Gaelic to scare someone.

If these people thought she was magical, then she would use it to her advantage. Her eyes blazed at Walter as she intoned each word carefully. *"A mhic an uilc, bathadh air muir is losgach airtir. An-aghaigh ort!"* (Son of hell, may you drown at sea and burn on land. May you suffer shame.)

"What's she saying?" Lady Anne cried. Sarah noted how anxious she sounded. Good. She didn't mind striking fear in Anne's heart as well.

"Nonsense." Walter spat.

Sarah gave him her most enigmatic smile. "We'll see."

With one last withering look at Walter, she left. She needed to get away from them before her brave face crumbled and her fear for Dermot took over. When her feet hit the hallway rug, she broke into a run and didn't stop until the door to the bedroom was locked behind her.

CHAPTER TWENTY-EIGHT

"Sarah?" James knocked softly on the door to the room they now shared. She had been hiding out there for the last two hours crying, pacing, trying to figure out what this new information meant for her. Eventually, she had decided she wasn't going to answer those questions that night, and what she did was going to depend on what Dermot did.

Realizing she couldn't hide in there forever, she started to get ready for dinner. She wasn't about to behave as if she'd done anything wrong. The act of getting ready felt like putting on armor; lingerie, clothes, foundation, makeup, fragrance. Each layer made her feel a little less feral, a little more confident, a little more safe. Dabbing Cardell's familiar scent with its notes of home on her pulse points made her feel able to leave the room, even happy at the prospect of facing James.

She was putting on her shoes when James knocked at the door. She opened it to find him in the hallway balancing a tray with a light dinner for two on it. He gave her a tentative smile. "I thought I would spare you coming down to the dining room. Do you mind if I join you?"

He looked so hopeful, but also a bit guilty. She couldn't take this out on James or blame him. He had been as shocked by the day's revelations as anyone else. She suddenly felt selfish for locking him out of his room when he'd just found out his uncle was actually his father. She stepped back inviting him in. "Of course. It's your room too. Sorry I locked you out. I needed some time alone."

"I understand." He set the tray on a table and hovered over it not looking at her. "I've got a salad, prawn cocktail, and for dessert a chocolate almond mousse."

"Sounds fine." She said. James still wouldn't look at her. Guilt swamped Sarah. He'd had a bombshell dropped on him and she and Dermot hadn't even considered how he felt. Sarah took his hand and pulled him to the chaise which stood between the doors to his and hers closets. "How are you doing?"

James perched on the edge next to her as if he might spring to his feet at any time. He gripped her hand and took a deep if shaky breath. "I hardly know. It's a lot to process."

"For all of us." She agreed, hoping to encourage him to talk. "I'm sorry you had to find out this way."

"So am I. I had absolutely no idea there was ever anything between my mother and uncle. There was always tension between my father," He paused giving his head a brief shake. "I mean Henry and my...Walter."

Sarah squeezed his hand. "Henry is still your father. He's the one who raised you. He's the one who loved you the way a father should all these years. This news doesn't change that."

"The thing is, Walter helped raise me too. He was there for every event, every birthday, and football match. He was always part of my life, and since I took over the business, he's been an invaluable mentor. Looking back, it's like I've had two fathers all along. Henry was always there for me on an emotional level, while Walter always encouraged me to push myself and achieve more."

"Walter always knew you were his son." Sarah pointed out. She hoped this revelation didn't bring James and Walter closer. "It was all built on a lie."

The muscles in his jaw jumped as he gritted his teeth. "Yes. The last six months have taught me Walter has been more active than I originally thought in guiding the events in my life. I'm still not sure how to feel about it."

There was a lot more to say on the matter of Walter's machinations, but telling James would put her family at risk. And James was already hurting from this. She could see it in his slumped shoulders.

"And then there is my mother. I don't know what to think of what she did." He looked down at their joined hands, his head shaking. "I know she has always been ambitious, but to deceive my father all this time. It's unconscionable."

Sarah hated to think about her own deceptions. "Some women get into desperate situations and go to extremes. I think she didn't see a lot of options for herself."

He grunted in affirmation, reminding Sarah of Dermot. "That's true. What's frustrating is my mother's ambitions for me are always in line with Walter's, or they're for her benefit. She's never asked me what I want. She has always told me what I should want. I'm not a person to her. I'm a vehicle."

'Welcome to the club.' Sarah thought. That was a remarkably clear-eyed assessment of lady Anne's relationship with her son, even if it was depressing. Sarah gripped James's hand in both of hers offering silent comfort.

"I feel so disappointed in all of them. In my mother and Walter for lying all this time, and my father for being in love with Seonag. I think that's obvious now, and it made him blind to what was going on right under his nose. But I—" His voice cracked. "I have a brother. Dermot and I were close as children and he's so good. I am happy he's more to me than a friend or a cousin. Though it doesn't seem to matter because they've always held him at arm's length, and I'm afraid he'll never see me as his brother because of everything that's come between us."

"Because of me." Sarah said softly.

He closed his eyes for a second, and his grip on her hand tightened. When he opened them, his gaze sought hers. They were the same blue as Dermot's, and Sarah supposed, Walter's. "Are you going to leave me?"

Sarah didn't know how to answer. "James…"

"I wouldn't blame you. I…Dermot could be the heir as easily as I could. We're the same age. We're Stuarts. It's why the matching ceremony didn't show a difference between us. You were right."

Sarah couldn't speak. She had been right months ago. She could be with Dermot like she wanted to without the Stuarts pushing back about the prophecy. James had given her an opening. She could tell him, now. She looked away not wanting him to see her indecision. In a flash, she was kneeling on the stone floor of an underground vault in a pool of her father's blood, only it wasn't Rab. The face and body in front of her gasping its last changed and changed and changed again; Dermot, Duff, Oona, Amy, Barrett, her. Faces and bodies flashed from one to another, all bleeding, all dying.

When she spoke, her voice was flat. "I'm afraid that ship has sailed. I made my choice. And the reasons for it still stand."

"You're sure?"

"It's hard to be sure of anything. But I don't see that changing anytime soon." She was sure it wasn't the profession of love he wanted to hear, but at least it was true.

"You're right. It is hard to be sure of anything."

"Let's eat." She stood and went to the tray he'd brought in. "I've had more than my share of days like today, and I can tell you the best strategy is to keep doing what needs to be done; eat, sleep, work. Focus on those, and eventually with enough distance and time, you'll be able to examine the hard things."

They ate. They changed and got ready for bed. When Sarah came out of the bathroom, she found James standing beside the bed wringing his hands. He asked her haltingly. "Do you think...Do you think I might hold you?"

'Poor man,' She thought. He must feel so unmoored. "Of course."

***

He was going to lose her, and there was precious little he could do about it. Oh, she might say she wasn't going to leave him, but he knew what they had was tenuous at best. He should have let her go before. He should have let her go with Dermot after the matching ceremony.

But lying there with the weight of her in his arms and her curls tickling his nose, he couldn't imagine living his life without her. He had tasted her now, had known what it was to have her for a partner. In a few short weeks, she had taught him so much. She had listened to him and cared about him as a person, not an opportunity. She treated him like James, not Lord Caledon, or a CEO, or a playboy. He couldn't bear to give her up.

Sarah shifted slightly, reminding him of the proximity of her breast to his hand and her glorious arse to his cock. He willed his arousal away. That was one thing he would not ask of her tonight, not when the memory of her fury over Walter's treatment of Dermot was fresh in their minds.

He felt her muscles relax as her breathing slowed. At least one of them could find sleep tonight. It reminded him of what she'd said. 'Keep doing the things that need to be done.' Her strength amazed him. She was right earlier. She had been through so much, and her experience tonight had helped him. He needed her strength. He needed the wisdom her trials had given her. The things she had been through, even before they met would have destroyed him.

He could say the same thing about Dermot; his mother, the injury that ended his army career, losing Sarah. How could he have thought she would want him when he'd had everything in his life handed to him? He hadn't earned any of it. He hadn't earned her. James wished he had an ounce of the strength Sarah and Dermot had. He had a feeling in the coming months and years he was going to need it.

***

He was there again, warm, and solid against her back. She knew it wasn't Dermot. It had to be James. He had even asked to hold her. After the evening's events she shouldn't be confused about which of them she was with. But when the lights were out, when she closed her eyes, her body only felt Dermot or the memory of Dermot. She still wasn't sure.

In her mind she knew it was an illusion, and she knew she should care. But for some reason, she didn't. It was as if no amount of rational thinking could make her pull away. She only wanted to relax in his arms. She only wanted to shut him out and feel the man she loved even if he wasn't the man she was with. It was so strange, but the almost supernatural calm she felt wouldn't let her be alarmed by it.

His arms tightened around her, and her muscles relaxed. She breathed in the mix of their scents and sank further into sleep.

***

Dermot went to visit his mother as soon as the facility opened the next day. If he had any hope of talking to her about Walter, he needed her as lucid as possible, and that was more likely early in the day. He signed in at the front desk and made his way to his mother's room.

He found her in the lounge sitting in front of a window looking out onto the garden. He pulled up a chair to sit next to her. "Good morning, mum."

"Oh, hello." She looked at him as if he was familiar, but she couldn't place him. "It's a lovely day."

He hmm'd in agreement. "No knitting today?"

"Och. I have more important things to do than knitting." She said. "I'm writing an article for the Journal of British Folklore."

"Really? What's the article about?" This was a new wrinkle in her memory. She'd written many articles for the Journal, but she hadn't said anything about her work in the last couple of years.

"It's a comparative study of tree symbolism between Irish and Norse cycles." She said matter-of-factly.

250 · MEREDITH R. STODDARD

Dermot tried to remember if that was an actual article she had written, or if this was new. "Sounds interesting. Are ye tying Yggdrasil to the oak?"

"Not only the oak, all the guardian trees. Yggdrasil and the guardian trees all come from something older. The prevalence of trees in multiple traditions speaks to their importance in general. But in northern Europe in particular trees are both the source of life and the source of knowledge."

Dermot couldn't help smiling. She sounded almost like her old self. He couldn't remember if she had written this article, but he had no doubt it would have been a great one. "I'd like to read this article when ye finish it."

She grinned at him. "What have ye been working on, young man."

"I'm working on a project for the Stuarts." He watched her closely gaging her reactions to the mention of the name.

"The Alba Petroleum Stuarts?" Her brows creased in question.

"Ye know them?" He asked.

"Aye, of course I do. I attended Saint Andrews with Henry Stuart. We've been friends for years." She smiled, and he could almost see her laughing with Henry on one of their summer holidays. "How is Henry? I havena seen him in a while."

"He's alright." He didn't want to give too much current information in case it made her anxious. Gaps in time or in her memory frequently upset her. "What about Walter Stuart? Do ye know him?"

"Och." She sighed and shook her head. "Walter, always lurking about the edges. He has a head for business, but he isna good with people. Aye?"

"Were ye friends with Walter?" Dermot asked, almost afraid of the answer.

His mother wrinkled her nose in distaste. "Is anyone? We tolerate each other for Henry's sake."

"That's all? Never more than that?" How could that be?

"No. Walter has associates and employees, but not really friends and certainly not me."

"It doesna sound like ye have a very good opinion of Walter."

She shrugged. "As I said, we tolerate each other."

Dermot wondered how Walter had managed to father a child with a woman who merely tolerated him. Sure, babies could be conceived under worse circumstances. Still, he didn't like the idea of his mother with Walter. Was her animosity toward Walter the aftermath of a failed relationship?

"Did Dermot know the Stuarts?" He asked her, assuming she didn't realize he was Dermot. It had been some time since she had recognized him as anything other than the nice young man who visited her on occasion.

"Of course. Dermot and wee James are great friends. A nice young man, that James."

"Yes, he is." Dermot agreed.

"A mite spoiled, mind ye. His mum thinks he's the second coming and treats him accordingly."

Dermot laughed. It seemed a fair assessment of the way Anne had treated James growing up. He got his way in all things as long as he submitted to her overbearing attention to his schooling and who his friends were. Dermot couldn't help thinking Anne would have treated them much differently if she'd known Dermot was James's half-brother. She'd likely have banished Seonag and Dermot from their lives for good.

Did Walter ever take an interest in Dermot?" He wondered if she knew about Walter's visits to him at school.

Seonag took a moment to think about it, as if searching her memory. "Sometimes, although no more than Henry did."

He braced for her reaction to his next question. "And what of Dermot's father?"

"What father?" Seonag asked, her expression turned sour. "Henry is more father to Dermot than anyone else."

He couldn't help asking. "Was there ever a time you wished Henry was Dermot's father?"

"Aye, sure." A secret smile grew on her face. She started to say something else then sighed.

"What were ye about to say just now?"

"Och, nothing ye need to worry about." She scoffed.

He wanted to push it. But he didn't dare upset her or the conversation would be over. Did she mean before an affair with Walter, before she told them about the prophecy, before she apprenticed for her father? He didn't understand how Walter could be his father while she gave no indication they had ever been lovers.

He thought they had exhausted the subject of the Stuarts. Changing the subject, "Have ye had any more unwelcome visitors?"

"What unwelcome visitor?" Surprise was evident on her face, as if she had never mentioned a mysterious man who had terrorized her in the garden.

CHAPTER TWENTY-NINE

A week later no one had heard from Dermot. He hadn't shown up to work the day after what Sarah had come to think of as the Great Revelation, nor had he called to say he was taking time off, or to even let them know he was alive. Sarah was worried sick.

He'd gone dark on them before, after the matching ceremony. This time, she didn't wait for him to contact her, or give him privacy. She used her gift to check on him every day. She had watched him sleep, eat meals, exercise. He was doing the basic things needed to keep himself alive and healthy. He even went to visit his mother. He was simply staying away from the Stuarts, and she couldn't blame him.

She took a moment while James was in the shower to use her gift to check on Dermot. He was running through the early morning mist. She thought she recognized Queen's Drive which skirted around the Salisbury Crags. He turned off the road and up a trail into the hills. Satisfied that he was safe and taking care of himself, Sarah returned to herself in time to hear James cut off the water.

She sat up in bed and slipped on her robe. She wasn't usually shy in relationships, but she felt that way in the mornings around James. When every night her brain was somehow turning him into Dermot, every morning was like an ice bath.

They had found their way back to the marriage bed a couple of days after the revelations of the week before. Sarah suspected it was a result of her strange delusion. In the dark, James became Dermot or at least that's what her senses told her. She missed Dermot so much. And as much as the unexplainable confusion disturbed her, she still craved his touch, Dermot's touch.

Still, the intimacy of waking up and getting dressed in the same space with him felt wrong. She would often wait until he left for the office to take a shower and get ready for her day. Today, however, she had to get up.

James emerged from the bathroom scrubbing his hair dry with a towel, another towel wrapped around his waist. He went into his enormous closet. At some point in its history the house had been renovated and the smaller bedroom next to the master bedroom had been divided into his and hers closets. Sarah got up to brush her teeth.

"Your assistant starts today, doesn't he?" A fully-dressed James poked his head into the bathroom as she was rinsing the cleanser off her face.

Sarah dabbed her face dry with a towel. "Yep. I'm relieved. Since Aberdeen, your mother has been trying to recruit me to her charity events. Now, whenever she asks, I can refer her to my assistant."

James leaned against the door frame watching her in the mirror as she applied moisturizer. "She does mean well."

Sarah no longer had any interest in making nice with Lady Anne. She would avoid fights for James's sake, but she wasn't about to get drawn into the society charities holding endless fundraisers that didn't actually help anyone. "Most of those charities raise money to put toward their next gala fundraiser or to paying their boards than to the actually helping the causes they're supposed to help. I would like to do more, and my new assistant can help me vet which charities I want to work with."

James straightened, looking a little uncomfortable. "I suppose I hadn't thought about it that deeply. I'm sure you'll make an impact. He kissed the top of her head. "I'll look forward to hearing about your plans this evening." He started to leave but turned back. "I think it's time to have your contraceptive implants removed. Perhaps, you could have your assistant schedule an appointment for you."

Sarah kept her face still, but her nerves sizzled. They hadn't talked more about the impact of learning about James's parentage on their plans. Sarah knew it had been weighing on James. He'd been pensive for the last few days still trying to sort through his own emotions and whether it would affect their plans. She supposed this was him telling her he had made a decision.

"Right. I'll tell him." She smiled sweetly, trying not to betray her feelings. "Have a good day."

Sarah decided she didn't need to put on makeup yet. No amount of powder or blush would cover up the misery she was feeling. She pulled the stopper out of her perfume bottle and applied the scent along her pulse points and between her breasts. She breathed in the fragrance and with it the sense of calm it usually brought her.

***

"Ma'am." Conley, the butler cleared his throat and spoke from the doorway. Sarah was in her sitting room. It was a lovely room next to the master suite. She had decided it was the best place for her personal 'office.' She didn't want to share the study with James and Lady Anne was likely to walk into any of the other common rooms at any moment. The sitting room was equipped with a writing desk, couch, and chairs. Sarah added a credenza and bookcase, all of the finest quality. She would have been content with particle board and laminate, but that wasn't good enough for Lady Caledon.

"Mr. Gurudat is here." Conley said, his nose firmly in the air. Sarah had come to appreciate Conley's lofty standards, but she knew he also had a heart. She was still getting used to having a butler but was determined to be on good terms with Conley. So far, her efforts seemed to be working.

"Excellent." She stood. "Please send him in."

Conley stepped into the hall and ushered Jujhar into the room. "I'll have a pot of tea sent up."

"That would be perfect. Thank you." Sarah smiled warmly.

When Conley had gone, Jujhar's face lit up and he held out his arms to her. "It's so good to see you."

Sarah hugged her friend. It had been too long since she'd seen a face she thought she could trust. They'd met in January when they had worked on the Preservation Scotland research team that brought Sarah to Scotland and quickly became friends. A linguist by training, Jujhar had a fascination with esoteric subjects and had been secretly looking for Sarah's people and their hidden glen, Làrachd an Fhamhair. "I am so glad you're here."

"I rather like this idea, and it gives me a break from Mr. Green." He took a seat on the couch as Sarah indicated, his brown eyes sparkled with mirth.

"How is it going? I'm surprised you had time for this between graduate school and our mutual friend." Sarah sat down next to him on the couch.

"Ah, well." He shifted uncomfortably. "I've put my dissertation on hold for now. My time had been given over to learning my way around our friend's library and still room. Which reminds me, I have some tea for you." He reached for his satchel and pulled out a small jar of dried leaves of some kind.

"What kind of tea?" Sarah took the jar he offered and opened it sniffing the contents.

Jujhar chuckled. "I can't say I blame you for being suspicious, but I made this one myself. It's for stress relief; a little lemon balm, mint, and valerian."

"Then I'll take it." She put the cap back on the jar and set it on the coffee table. "In fact, I might order some up for James and Dermot, if he ever comes back."

"Things still tense between them?"

"You don't know the half of it." A quick knock at the door preceded Conley entering with the tea tray, including some finger sandwiches. He set the tray on the coffee table in front of the couch and discreetly left after Sarah thanked him. "We've had some news."

She filled Jujhar in on the revelations of the DNA test and the fall out. He listened carefully, and she had no doubt he would be recounting the situation for Lyall Green the next time he visited the watcher's house in Dean Village. When she was done, he asked. "And Dermot hasn't been back here since?"

"Nope. No call, no show." Sarah took a sip of her tea. "I've used my gift to check on him every day. I think he'll be okay. He's taking care of himself; doing what he needs to do, but he's doing it all alone. That has me worried."

"I understand. Maybe I'll check on him. Does he know I'll be working with you?"

"I don't know. I didn't have much of a chance to talk to him before all of this hit the fan." Sarah sighed. "Unless James told him, probably not."

"I'm sure Mr. Green would want to know this too."

"I'm a little surprised he doesn't know this or that he didn't know about Walter and Seonag." Sarah had wondered what Seonag's father might have to say about his daughter having an affair with a Stuart. That was the very opposite of the hands-off role the old wizard liked to maintain.

"I am too." Jujhar looked puzzled. "He might not take a direct hand in Dermot and Seonag's lives, but I know he keeps track of them. I can't believe he would condone such a relationship."

"It's not as if a lack of his approval has stopped Seonag before." Sarah thought about what Dermot had told her about his mother's role in bringing knowledge of the prophecy to Henry and Walter.

"Mmm. True." Jujhar agreed, setting his teacup on the table and pulling a notepad from his satchel. "Now, let's talk about what you need from your assistant."

Sarah couldn't help smiling at the thought that he would be there to help her. "It's pretty simple actually. I need you to have my back, be my sounding board, and run interference between me and Lady Anne. I've been alone here for weeks, and I need someone in my corner."

He grinned. "I can do all of those things. What did you have in mind first?"

She took a deep breath. "First, I have been reminded I need to find a doctor to remove my contraceptive implants."

"Already?" He looked surprised.

"Already." She looked at the plate of elegantly cut crustless sandwiches. "After everything with Walter and Dermot, James is worried I'm going to leave him. I think he wants to get on with things before I have a chance to."

Jujhar watched her closely. "How do you feel about that?"

She picked up an egg salad sandwich and took a bite, chewing while she thought about it. "I think if giving James an heir gets me out of this situation faster, I should be trying to do it. Putting it off only prolongs things."

"But do you want to be a parent?" Jujhar looked at her in concern.

"No, but I think we've proven what I want has very little to do with it." She put her sandwich down on a plate and brushed the crumbs off her fingers. "I have to pick my battles, and I'm afraid that's one I will always lose."

"Right. I'll find someone."

Sarah shook her head and inhaled, rising from the couch. "Enough marriage talk. Let's do some good." She retrieved a folder from the desk. "After the good press I got in Aberdeen, James and Felicia Banks, (You met her. She's the head of PR at Alba Petroleum.) are after me to take a more public role. They want me to do some charity work. Felicia gave me this list of suggested charities to focus on."

He took the folder from her and scanned the list. "Have you chosen one?"

"That's what I'd like your help with." Sarah returned to her seat and took up her teacup again. "I want to make sure I choose charities who actually do good, not merely the appearance of good, and I'd like to pick more than one."

"More than one? Do you have enough time?" Jujhar's brows creased as he looked at the list.

Sarah waved a hand around the posh sitting room. "It's not like I'm doing anything else."

He gave her a sympathetic look. "It's hard for you not to work, isn't it?"

"You have no idea." She laughed. "I've never not worked.'

"Alright. What are you looking for in a charity?"

Sarah leaned forward, eager for this conversation. If she was going to have access to the Stuarts' money and influence, she was determined to do some good with it. "First the charities have to give back some of what an oil company takes. So, I'm thinking we need at least one environmental charity. I'd also like one which focuses on cancer clusters around oil producing communities. Lastly, and this one we might need to start ourselves; I want a charity for the employees and families who are injured working at Alba Petroleum facilities."

"Does the company not take care of those families?" Jujhar asked.

"Only as far as insurance payments." Sarah shook her head. "I'm looking to do more. I saw those families in Aberdeen, and I'm sure they aren't the only ones. They'll need support probably for years while they're recovering, and not only monetary support. I don't want them thinking A.P. forgot about them."

Jujhar grinned in approval. "I'm afraid I don't know the first thing about starting a charity."

Sarah returned his smile. "Then we'll have to learn together."

CHAPTER THIRTY

"I would think you would want to support the museum. It seems like precisely the kind of charity you should be supporting." Lady Anne continued to push the subject as they moved back to the parlor after an excruciating dinner. Anne had lain low for days after the revelations about her relationship with Walter avoiding both James and Henry until it became apparent neither was going to send her away.

Sarah didn't quite understand why James and Henry were ignoring Anne's transgression. She had asked James about it, and he had mumbled something about avoiding scandal, and the offense happening decades ago. He was sure his father had done worse since then.

Lady Anne seemed to think Sarah was going to be her ally and way back into her son's good graces and had been trying to ingratiate herself with her daughter-in-law. Sarah had no idea what gave Anne the impression that she would help her, but in the interest of harmony, she was trying to tolerate the woman. After a few days, Anne had tentatively resumed "advising" Sarah on small things; hair styles, conventions of etiquette, and which invitations she should accept. By the next week she was back to nagging Sarah into getting involved with Anne's token charities.

That evening Sarah's patience was limited. She'd spent the morning getting her implants removed. Jujhar had found her the perfect OBGYN. Dr. Perez was friendly, confident, and didn't talk down to her patients, which Sarah valued. After explaining the procedure to Sarah, Dr. Perez warned her to use some other contraceptive for the first week or so to allow the hormones from the implant to get out of her system. Then she should have no trouble conceiving.

The procedure had been simple enough. They had numbed the inside of her arm and made a small incision and pulled the implants out. She hadn't even needed a stitch to close the incision, only a bandage and a warning to keep it clean. The inside of her arm was still a little numb. She'd had a headache for the rest of the day, which she suspected was more from anxiety over what removing the implant meant than from the procedure itself. She was still lost in her thoughts while Lady Anne droned on about her charity.

"Oh, Henry, please don't go." Anne interrupted her diatribe to Sarah reaching out to stop her husband.

Henry had developed the habit of retreating to the privacy of his own room after dinner if he came to dinner at all. It was clear Henry wasn't interested in being anywhere Anne was. "I'm really quite tired."

"I'm sure." Anne's tone was acidic, as if she doubted he had worn himself out on the golf course. "Please, spend a little time with us."

They eyed each other for several seconds before Henry shrugged and walked to the decanter and poured himself a drink. He turned back to face the room, taking a sip of amber liquid. "I think it is about time for me to return to Spain." He glanced at James, who was reading the paper on the couch beside Sarah. "You don't need me here now that the wedding is done and you two are settling in."

"I think I'd like to stay a while longer. Sarah needs help." Anne seemed flustered.

"I'm sure I'll manage." Sarah tried not to betray her excitement at the prospect of Lady Anne's departure.

But her comment was lost when Henry spoke over her. "Stay. Go. To be honest, I don't care anymore. You'll do what you want anyway. You always have."

If anything was likely to draw Sarah out of her funk, an argument between Henry and Anne would do it. James put down his paper and watched his parents.

Anne refused to take Henry's bait. She seemed determined to be as pleasant as possible. "I know the last week or so has been tense, but I really feel we should be working to get things back to normal."

"What can be normal about this situation?" Henry was incredulous.

"Mother, I think we are all still processing the new information." James sounded tired.

"Mr. Stuart is here, ma'am." Conley said from the doorway.

"Thank you, Conley." Anne replied. Conley didn't move. Anne looked sharply at him.

It took a moment for Sarah to realize he was waiting for her acknowledgement, reminding Sarah that this was her house. She outranked Anne. "Oh. Thank you, Conley."

"Ma'am." Conley left and was replaced in the doorway by Walter Stuart.

Already a tense environment, everyone instantly bristled. James was the first to speak. "What are you doing here?"

Anne stood. "I invited him."

Henry turned to her. "Why would you do that?"

"Because we are still a family, and we should behave like a family." Anne pleaded. "Nothing needs to change in the way we live."

"Maybe for you." Henry tossed back the remainder of his drink and set the glass down on the bar cart with a clink. "But I'm done pretending this marriage isn't over. I'm going to Spain. You can do what you like." He turned to his brother, "And as for you, it's all yours. You always wanted it anyway."

"Don't pout, Henry." Walter's tone was one only siblings get with each other, a sort of derision born from decades of irritation. Walter opened his mouth to say something else, but they were interrupted by voices in the hallway.

"Mr. Si—" Conley said in a placating tone.

"Dinna bother. I need her." The hair stood up on Sarah's arms. It was Dermot.

He got past Conley and strode into the parlor and made straight for Sarah. His eyes were wild, and his hair stood up in all directions as if he'd been running his fingers through it repeatedly. Through panting breaths, he said. "I need yer help."

His desperate eyes met hers, and everyone else in the room disappeared. Sarah forgot all about James and his arguing parents and Walter. There was only Dermot and his obvious need. "What is it?"

"My mother is missing. She left the care home and we canna find her."

Sarah's blood went cold. Seonag wasn't able to take care of herself. She could so easily become disoriented and lost. "How long has she been missing?"

"It's been an hour since they told me. I don't know how long it was before that. No one signed her out." The words tumbled out of his mouth in a flood.

"Okay, I'll—"

"We'll get A.P. Security right on it." James cut in. Sarah had forgotten they had an audience. She had been about to say she would use her gift to find Seonag, the gift she had so far kept from the Stuarts. She hadn't even told James about her ability. She was afraid they would try to use it for their own gain. And now she was going to have to use it in front of all of them. Even if she went to another room, they would all demand to know how she found Seonag so quickly.

Dermot also noticed the others in the room for the first time. He looked from James to Henry and Anne before settling on Walter.

With an animal growl, Dermot was on his feet and across the room in a flash. He pinned Walter to the wall with a forearm across his throat and spitting fury. "This is yer doing. Just like last time. Just like Rab."

"Careful, lad." Walter warned coldly.

***

Everything Dermot saw was tinged red. His pulse throbbed in his ears. He pressed his arm into Walter Stuart's throat cutting off the last of the man's air before he could say another word. Walter's face reddened, and he pushed against Dermot's chest, his hands fumbling. Dermot enjoyed the growing alarm he saw on Walter's face.

"Dermot." A voice said next to his ear. "Dermot!"

Someone tried to work an arm between him and Walter, but Dermot shoved them off.

"Dermot!" Sarah. He blinked. Her arms were around his waist. The red haze cleared like clouds after a storm. "That won't help us find her."

She slid under his arm and pushed between his body and Walter's. "He's not worth it. And it won't help us."

Walter slid down the wall coughing and wheezing.

A breath shuddered through Dermot, the rage prickling out through his skin, and the fear for his mother expanding again in his chest. Mum. They had to find Mum.

Sarah put a hand on his cheek and pulled his gaze down to her. "I'll help you. We'll find her."

"I'll call Shaw." James put in.

"Come sit with me." Sarah pulled Dermot toward the now empty couch. He glanced around the room. Henry and Anne were standing alert near the door as if they feared Dermot would come after them next. Walter still huddled on the floor coughing. James went for the phone.

"Don't worry about them." Sarah kept her tone even and held his hand in her lap. "We don't need them. I'll find her."

She would. He knew she would. That was why he had come here, but he hadn't thought through what it might cost her. He suddenly started to rethink his request.

"Look at me." Sarah said sharply. His attention swung to her. He didn't need to tell her what he was thinking. "They're not important. She is. I'll do whatever you need."

All he could do was nod. The fear for his mother and for Sarah blocking any words from his mind. She kicked off her shoes and sat cross-legged as if about to meditate.

"Keep them quiet." Sarah told him.

He shot warning looks around the room as Sarah closed her eyes and inhaled. The Stuarts stood around with puzzled looks on their faces. The red was fading from Walter's face, but he still massaged his throat. James stood in a corner with his hand on the telephone, but he focused on Sarah.

She exhaled, and he felt her sway ever so slightly. He had seen her do this before, but that was in a car while they were hiding from an assassin. He'd never seen her use her gift in a quiet setting like this. With another breath her hand relaxed in his. Another and her head fell against the back of the couch. Her breath was so quiet, she was so still. If he hadn't known better, he would have thought she was dead. He could tell she was gone, or her co-walker was.

"What is she doing?" Lady Anne's whisper was full of urgency.

Dermot shushed her sharply. Walter used the wall to push himself up from his knees. Dermot shot him a look warning he'd find himself back against the wall if he dared to speak. James silently came closer and sat on the coffee table staring at his wife.

It felt like she was gone for an eternity. Everyone in the room waited silently watching Sarah's limp form on the couch.

"How long does this usually take?" James whispered.

"As long as it takes." Dermot whispered back. "I think it depends on how far she has to go. I've only ever seen her do it when a person was within a mile."

As the minutes stretched on James whispered again. "At what point should we worry?"

"I think we need to keep her body safe while she does it."

Any further discussion was cut off when Sarah inhaled deeply. She leaned forward and opened her eyes. "She's at the university, the Old Medical School building."

Dermot sighed. "It's where her office was."

Sarah gripped his hand. "We need to get over there. The building is closed now and she's outside worried about losing her keys."

"Right." Dermot shot to his feet. "Let's go."

James and Sarah rose to join him. They wasted no time getting to the door. Dermot never let go of Sarah's hand. James followed behind them shouting orders to Conley.

"Call campus security. Tell them there is a vulnerable woman near the Old Medical School. They need to make sure she's safe and wait for her family to get there."

CHAPTER THIRTY-ONE

Sarah's tension didn't ease until they saw Seonag pacing by the door of the building. A security officer stood nearby trying to talk with her. Dressed only in her house coat Seonag paced back and forth, her agitation clear. As they approached, Sarah could hear her arguing. "I dinna understand the problem. I work here. I've simply lost my keys."

"Mum?" Dermot's voice was weak, no doubt he was unsure if she would recognize him in her current state of mind.

Seonag turned their way and took in the three of them, her eyes passing from one to another before they settled on Sarah. *"A bhana-phrionnsa?"*

Sarah stepped forward forcing a smile. *"Halo, mo charaid. Ciamar a tha thu?"* (Hello, my friend. How are you?)

Seonag looked back and forth between Sarah and the security officer then at her surroundings. She took in the people, most of whom felt like strangers to her. Her bottom lip began to tremble. *"Tha mo cheann briste."* (My head is broken.)

Sarah smiled warmly. Tears pricked her own eyes in response. She held out an arm to Seonag. "Come with me. We'll figure things out."

Dermot's mother stepped into Sarah's arms, and she hugged Seonag cooing Gaelic endearments to her. Sarah knew

Seonag's mind had been sharp once. She could only imagine how shocking the confusion of losing her memories was.

She looked over Seonag' s bowed head to see James talking with the security officer, no doubt identifying them as Seonag's friends and family and ensuring the incident was kept private. Dermot stood next to them; his fists clenched as if he was trying desperately to hold on to control around his mother.

***

James had no idea it was that bad. They'd gotten Seonag into the car. Sarah offered her a bottle of water and kept a comforting arm around her while Dermot drove them back to the care home. He looked out the window at the city in twilight listening to Sarah speak softly in lilting Gaelic which he couldn't understand and wondered when he had lost track of the people who had once meant so much to him.

Seonag didn't even recognize her own son much less him. He remembered her from summers at Tweedholm, playing with them, laughing at his father's jokes, or reading in the library, always taking notes. She had taught him to read that way one summer after he'd been struggling in school, writing down the key points of whatever book he was reading. She'd always had time for her boys then, time his mother was rarely willing to spare.

Once again, he felt like he'd been missing something without realizing it. He'd been so focused on meeting the expectations his mother and Walter had put on him he'd forgotten about relationships that should have meant more. He'd been so involved in fitting into the mold of people he thought cared about him and his future. But if the revelation of their parents' perfidy had taught him anything, it was that they cared more about their political goals than they did about him or Dermot.

Seonag had never made him feel like he was a means to an end. She had always shown genuine interest in both him and Dermot as boys. And he had repaid her by ignoring her after she'd become ill. He hadn't even visited her after he went to university. Come to think of it, he hadn't paid much attention to Dermot either, beyond what Dermot had been able to do for him as an employee. He'd been neglecting his true family for the one he was born into. Worse, he had robbed Dermot of Sarah and the careers they'd wanted.

The care home where Seonag had been living was nice enough. They were met at the door by medical staff eager to check her over and ensure she hadn't been injured in the hours she'd been missing. Dermot had allowed them to lead his mother and Sarah away, with a bleak look before turning his attention back to her case manager.

His brother was seething. "I see ye were working hard to find her. Have ye figured out how she escaped?"

The short middle-aged woman looked apologetic. "A new staff member left a door propped open because of the heat. I'm afraid I don't have a good answer for how she got out of the gate. We are still interviewing our security staff about it."

"And where were ye looking for her?" He barked. "We found her at the university. That's miles away from here."

Surprise registered on the woman's face. "We searched the immediate area. I'm shocked she got so far away."

"Aye, well. It seems to be a day for shocks." Dermot's voice dripped with disdain."

"I cannot apologize enough, Mr. Sinclair. I can assure you this won't happen again." The woman tried to reassure him.

"Oh, and what are ye doing to ensure that?" Dermot sounded doubtful.

The woman fidgeted with a pen, struggling for something to say.

"If I may," James spoke for the first time. Her eyes widened in recognition. James went on before she could say anything. "We have a security staff accustomed to securing facilities from offices to oil rigs. I would be happy to send someone to perform an audit of your security measures and recommend some ways to tighten things up."

"Oh, my." The woman patted her hair obviously flustered. "That's very generous, but I'm not sure a security overhaul is in our budget."

James gave her his million-dollar smile. "I would be more than happy to donate the funds required if it means keeping my friend's mother safe."

The woman looked at Dermot with new recognition. Clearly, she hadn't known that he had such illustrious friends.

Dermot's attention had turned back in the direction they had taken his mother and Sarah. James took the woman's elbow and steered her back toward what he thought were the offices. "Why don't you and I discuss that while Dermot checks on his mother?"

A blush crept into the woman's cheeks. "Yes, of course. My name is Patricia Bascomb."

"It's nice to meet you, Patricia." He led her away from Dermot. "Please, call me James."

They went to Patricia's office to discuss when a security consultant would be sent and where to send the bill for the upgrades. This was familiar territory for James. He was frequently asked for donations, and although he usually referred people to Miss Lennox, he sometimes managed things himself.

When he was finished with Patricia, she showed him to Seonag's room. Sarah sat in a chair next to the bed while Dermot stood looking down at his mother who was fast asleep. James knocked on the door as he stepped inside the darkened room.

Sarah rose and came to him whispering. "She's sedated. They said it's not unusual when people elope for them to return to their family homes or places they used to know. Tomorrow she probably won't remember any of this."

"I don't think any of us are likely to forget it." James muttered.

Sarah hmm'd in agreement looking back at Dermot with a heavy sigh.

"Will he be alright?"

"I don't know. He's barely said a word."

As if he knew they were talking about him, Dermot glanced up at them before walking out of the room. Sarah and James followed.

In the hallway, Dermot stopped with his back to them. His head was bowed, but the muscles in his shoulders were tightly coiled.

"Can you find us a private room?" Sarah asked before stepping closer to Dermot.

James stood rooted to the spot as he watched her lift her hand. She touched Dermot's back and his brother made a sound like a wounded animal. His shoulders began to shake.

Shit. She'd asked him to find a room. James jumped into action and a few doors down, found a vacant patient's room. "Here."

Sarah's grip on Dermot tightened and she pulled him to where James stood in the doorway. "Give us a few minutes." She said as they brushed past him.

James watched Sarah take a seat on the empty bed. "It's okay." She told him. "It's safe here."

He watched Dermot crumble into a million pieces, and his wife caught them as they fell. Dermot, who he'd known all his life, who was full of fire and strength, sank to the bed and wrapped his arms around Sarah's waist. He turned his face to her stomach and quietly sobbed. James shook himself and stepped into the hallway, closing the door on the sound of his brother weeping.

***

"Thank you for being so patient." Sarah looked over at James who hadn't said a word since their driver had dropped Dermot off at his flat after returning Seonag to the care home.

"I would never get between you offering a friend comfort." His voice was low, and it was hard to get a read on his mood after the evening's events. She couldn't tell if he was struck by the change in Seonag, or jealous of the bond she had with Dermot. "I hope you know that."

Sarah reached across the seat where his hand rested between them. "Still, given everything, I know it couldn't have been easy. Thank you."

"He's my brother. I don't like seeing him in pain." The words sounded right, but his tone was flat. Clearly something else was on his mind.

"Me neither."

James turned his hand over and gripped hers. "I had no idea Seonag's condition had deteriorated so much. She's so changed."

Sarah hadn't known Seonag before, not the way James had, but Dermot had told her how different his mother was now. The extreme anxiety induced by her condition had changed her.

"He's been dealing with this all on his own." James looked down, his bowed head dark against the motion of the city lights outside the car. "I'm ashamed I didn't know. I took his word he was dealing with it. I've missed so much that was right in front of me."

"He's also not very good at asking for help." Sarah noted.

James let out a short, mirthless laugh. "You're not wrong. Still, I should have asked more. We were a family once. I need to do better."

Sarah felt a little excited. James planned to pay more attention to what went on outside of the Alba Petroleum offices, like the things Walter did in his name.

James turned to look at her, his eyes stormy with emotion searched hers in the dim light. He asked with enough steel in his voice to let her know she'd better answer truthfully. "Can you explain how you found her?"

Sarah's stomach sank. She'd known when she used her gift in the presence of James and Walter that they would ask questions. She had hoped she might have time to come up with a story they would accept, one which kept them from attempting to use her gift for their gain. But she found she didn't want to lie to James. She wasn't ready to ruin the team they were becoming.

"It's hard to explain. Lyall Green calls it a co-walker, it's like a spiritual self I can send out to find people or things."

"Lyall Green knows about this skill of yours." Bitterness crept into his voice.

"There is very little Lyall Green doesn't know." Sarah warned him. "My mother and grandmother had this ability too."

"What about the other sisters, do they have this ability?" He asked, his tone curt.

"No." Sarah wasn't about to tell him about the gifts they did have. She didn't want to think about how the Stuarts would take advantage of Rona's precognition or Oona's ability to see the truth. Even Ruaraidh's ability to tell if someone was lying would be too useful for the Stuarts to ignore.

"Hmm." He went back to staring out the window. Sarah couldn't tell what he was thinking. After they'd ridden a few more blocks and were nearing Polwarth Terrace he asked. "Were you ever planning to tell me about it?"

Sarah studied him. He hadn't turned to look at her, but she could see the tension in the way he held his head. She was tempted to say yes, for the sake of harmony. She knew she would lose his trust if she said no. She had told him many of her secrets. So far, he had not used them to hurt her. She didn't think he would intentionally. "I don't know."

"Well, I suppose that's honest." His tone was acidic.

"I trust you, James." It was true. She hadn't realized it until she said it. But she thought she had come to understand

James over the last few weeks. "But I don't trust the people around you. I was afraid if your uncle found out what I can do, he would want me to use it for his ends, and I don't want that."

"Even though his ends often benefit us as well." He snapped.

"Us, or Alba Petroleum?"

"We are Alba Petroleum." His tone grew sharper.

"No," She shook her head emphatically. "We are individual people with our own lives and hopes and dreams. Alba Petroleum is an enterprise. You might run it now, and it might be made up of people who depend on it for their livelihood, but it's only a business. People have to be more important."

"Of course, they are."

Sarah cocked her head at him. "Are they? Or is that what Felicia tells you to say?"

He pressed his lips together as if he could keep harsh words inside. The car stopped in front of the house. He turned to her. "I have tried my best to balance my duty with my respect for your autonomy." He pulled his hand from hers a second before the driver opened his door. "I thought we were a team."

He got out of the car, heading for the door and upstairs to their room. In an unexpected show of rudeness, he didn't help her out of the car or wait for her. Sarah closed the bedroom door behind her and leaned on it watching him as he unbuttoned his shirt and pulled it from the waist of his trousers. "Of course, we're a team. We became a team as soon as I agreed to marry you."

"And yet he knew." James showed more temper than Sarah had ever seen from him. He pulled his undershirt over his head and tossed it toward the hamper as he paced back and forth. "Dermot knew what you're capable of and I didn't."

Ah, now she saw the problem. "Dermot knew because I had to use it to find the assassin who was chasing us in the Highlands. I don't go around advertising it."

But James was beyond logic. He spun toward her and gripped her arms pressing her back into the door. Sarah winced as his grip pressed on the wound where her implants had been removed. "He knew! Just like he knew if he came to you for help you wouldn't hesitate. You would drop everything."

"Would you have done any differently?" Never one to back down, Sarah leaned closer.

"No!" He punctuated it with a shake, thumping Sarah's shoulders into the door behind her. Pain shot through her arm, and she cried out.

James turned away from her, running his hand through his hair. "He came to you, and you did what you should have done. But he didn't come to us, his family. He didn't come to me."

Sarah stepped around him to see his face, holding her sore arm. "Are you jealous that he knew I could help, or that he asked me rather than you?"

"I don't know. Both. And ashamed that I didn't know how bad it was." James sighed and his shoulders slumped. "Why are you holding your arm?"

"Because it hurts, asshole. I think the wound opened up when you grabbed me." She pulled her arm from inside her shirt to look at it.

"What wound? Jesus, you're bleeding!" James exclaimed when he saw the bandage. Blood was seeping through. "What happened to you?"

"I had my implants removed this morning." She snapped at him. "You know, like you asked me to."

His temper dissipated like a cloud of smoke. James took her hand. "Come here."

She pulled her hand back. "No, thanks."

"Please. I'm sorry. At least let me tend it." He pleaded, gesturing toward the bathroom.

Sarah grudgingly went into the bathroom. The room was spotless and smelled of her perfume. Sarah took a seat on the stool by her vanity table. All of the fury she'd felt only a minute ago drained out of her.

"May I?" James gestured to her arm.

Sarah gave him a look saying, 'You might as well.'

He took her elbow and wrist and positioned her arm on a towel on the vanity. He unwound the bandage and lifted the gauze away from the wound. A purple bruise marred the inside of her arm. The small incision was closed with butterfly bandages, but one of them was twisted away from its position, and blood seeped from the incision. James looked away from her shaking his head. His voice was soft. "I'm so very sorry."

"That can't happen again." She knew he hadn't meant to hurt her, but she wouldn't excuse it.

"You're right." He looked thoroughly contrite, avoiding her eyes. "It's inexcusable."

Sarah stared at him for several heartbeats. Lyall Green had warned the Stuarts that if she wasn't treated with respect, she could leave. But he didn't know about Walter's threats. That was before Rab's murder, before the wedding, before they had consummated their marriage. They'd even taken her passport when they went to France. She had never felt so trapped. She would have to smooth things over until she could think of what to do. "I think there is a first aid kit under the sink. It should have what I need."

James retrieved the first aid kit and found another bandage and roll of gauze. He set it on the vanity beside her and opened the gauze pad. She winced as he pressed it to the wound. James carefully applied enough pressure to stop the bleeding, without causing pain.

Sarah looked away. "It wasn't so long ago that Dermot and I were together. Our situation may have changed, but we can't stop loving each other overnight. Neither of us is wired that way."

Satisfied the bleeding had stopped, James wrapped the rolled gauze around Sarah's arm. "I know. I wouldn't love you if you were the kind of person who forgot someone so easily. It's only," He struggled to find the words, so he focused on taping the gauze. "When I saw the two of you together in a crisis. I felt like the outsider."

Sarah watched his hands. "And that's not something you're used to feeling."

"Not when I love both of you." James whispered. "I thought we had turned a corner. I thought the jealousy was past us."

"Ask Dermot if he's past it. I'm not sure it will ever be gone."

"God! We're as bad as my parents." He picked up the wrappers from the first aid supplies and flung them into the trash bin.

"Not yet." Sarah pulled her newly bandaged arm back into her sleeve. "We don't have to be."

"No more secrets?" He asked.

Sarah saw her father struggling with his last breath, and remembered Walter's threats to her family, her friends, Dermot. "No more secrets."

CHAPTER THIRTY-TWO

He had put his hands on Sarah in anger, something he would regret for the rest of his life. The previous night had shown him plenty of things he should be ashamed of, but none was greater than that. He had never physically hurt a woman before, and he told himself he would never do it again. He hadn't even been able to face her this morning. He'd gotten up early and left for work before she woke up.

Something else bothered him. Sarah had been angry at first but hadn't chucked him out of the room immediately. She hadn't left. She had let him tend her wound, and then gone to bed allowing him to sleep right beside her. The Sarah he knew, the one who challenged him at every turn wouldn't have tolerated his behavior. The Sarah he'd fallen in love with wouldn't have given him the chance to do it again. He didn't understand.

His thoughts were interrupted by voices arguing outside his door. Opening his office door to find his uncle (strike that) father looming over Miss Lennox's desk speaking sharply. "I didn't ask when he had time to talk with me. I asked if he's in. I think you're forg—"

James interrupted by clearing his throat.

Walter shifted his focus. "You're in early this morning."

"I had work to do." James kept his tone flat, as was his habit now when dealing with his...Walter. He was civil for the sake of the company, but they were no longer inseparable as they had been when James first stepped into his role.

Walter turned with a sneer. "I trust everything was resolved last night."

James gave Walter a warning look. "We found Seonag Sinclair if that's what you mean by resolved. She was right where Sarah thought she would be."

"That's what I wanted to talk with you about." Walter cast a sidelong look at Miss Lennox. "Shall we talk in your office?"

James knew this conversation was coming. He still wasn't sure what to do with the knowledge of Sarah's ability. He had no doubt Walter had already thought through a dozen ways her particular talent could help them.

He held out a hand toward his office door in invitation. When Walter had entered the office, James looked to Miss Lennox.

"I'll call for tea." She read his mind as usual. Her expression was pinched rather than her usual calm. Serenely competent was how he always thought of Lennox. She was unflappable, but this morning she seemed nervous.

"Thank you." James gave her a reassuring smile. "You always know the right thing."

He nodded a greeting to his bodyguard who had accompanied him from the house to the office and was now taking his position by the door. Brady, he thought the man's name was. He was having trouble remembering it, probably because he would rather it was Dermot watching his back.

He followed Walter into his office and closed the door. His uncle/father stood by the window looking over the Princes

Street Gardens with the air of a man who controlled everything he surveyed.

James took a seat at the conference table. "Well, go ahead. Ask your questions."

Walter couldn't hide his enthusiasm. "You must have asked her about it. How did she do it?"

James sighed. He had been having this debate with himself since Sarah had explained her ability. He didn't want to abuse her skills or what little goodwill she had left for him, but he couldn't deny it could help them. In the past, he would have taken all the details to his uncle, and they would have gamed out different scenarios determining which was the best path to take. Now, taking in Walter's calculating look he wasn't so sure Walter had been giving him the best advice. "It's a kind of astral projection. She can send her mind out to see things."

"How does she find the things she needs to see?" Walter asked.

"I don't know exactly. I didn't ask her for that level of detail." James tapped his pen on the table in irritation.

"We need to find out what her capabilities are." Walter strolled in front of the window as he thought. "We have to figure out how they can be applied."

"We must remember Sarah is not only a person, but also my wife. She's not a new piece of technology for you to play with." James shook his head in disappointment. Within minutes, Walter proved Sarah right.

Walter gave him a condescending look. He was about to say something which James was sure would set his temper to boil, but they were interrupted by Miss Lennox's knock at the door.

"Come in." James called.

The door was opened by Brady. Miss Lennox entered and deposited the tray of tea and biscuits on the conference table. She faced James, studiously ignoring Walter. "Can I get you anything else?"

"No, thank you, Miss Lennox." James sketched a smile.

She left them to return to their conversation. James poured them both cups of tea. Walter sat down at the table taking one of the cups. "Have you ever heard of a CIA project called Stargate?"

"I can't say I have had much need to pay attention to CIA projects." James blew across the top of his tea wondering what the point of this tangent was.

"You really should. Some of the most advanced technology comes from secret government projects, many of them American. The internet everyone is going mad about these days was a government project." Walter took a sip of his tea. 'Project Stargate was a remote viewing experiment, very much like what Sarah did last night. The idea was they could spy on the Soviets using a team of people who could watch them remotely. I'm told they used some of these people to watch hostages in Iran in '79."

James gaped at him. "How do you know this?"

"They declassified it last year. But I have known about it for longer." Walter tilted his head to the side with a smug smile. "I have my ways."

James was sure he did. "Well, Sarah is neither an employee, nor is she the subject of an experiment. So, don't get ideas we're going to build our own Stargate project around her."

"My dear boy, don't you see? We must." Walter leaned forward. "This is why she's so important to us."

She was important to James for many other reasons. "What are you talking about? The prophecy says she's the mother of the king."

"Any woman can bear you a child." Walter waved a hand in dismissal. "The prophecy demanded you marry this one so she would bring her unique skill to the equation, a skill I have no doubt her people have cultivated for generations. Can others from her clan do this?"

"She says not." James looked wary.

Walter raised a skeptical eyebrow. "Do you believe her?"

James narrowed his eyes at Walter. "I believe her over the man who's lied to me for my entire life."

Walter seethed. James could almost hear him mentally counting down from ten to calm himself, a trick Walter had taught him for maintaining his poker face in business meetings. Walter's voice was calm when he asked. "Have I ever steered you in the wrong direction?"

"Have I ever asked to be steered at all?" James countered. "I have asked for your advice, yes, when I was green and needed help. But I have listened to your advice and made my own choices."

The calculation was apparent on Walter's face. "Of course, you have. I only meant to ask if my advice had ever been bad."

"Not usually, at least not when it comes to business." James agreed. "It's the things you do when I'm not looking that worry me. Like the business with Seonag and the care home. What other manipulations are you enacting behind my back."

"My boy," Walter started.

"Nola." James snapped. "Biology means nothing where we're concerned. I'll wager my brother feels even stronger about it than I do."

"I don't doubt he does." Walter looked down at his teacup. "I won't make excuses for what I've done. Everything I have done has been for us and for Scotland. I may have gone about things badly, but I did it with the best of intentions."

"What else don't I know about?" James doubted he would get an honest answer.

Walter leaned back in his chair thinking. When he spoke, his tone was sincere, and he looked directly at James. "I'm sure there are hundreds of small things I have done which I didn't think merited your attention. I couldn't even begin to categorize them all. But you already know of all the things that matter."

James held Walter's gaze for several seconds, searching for the truth behind his words. He doubted he would ever know the extent of Walter's schemes. Worse, he knew he might not want to. In that instant, James knew he wasn't as strong as Sarah thought he was. He might not like what Walter did in his name, but given what they had learned so far, he was afraid to examine it too closely. He was a coward.

"I can promise you all of that stops now." Walter added, appearing sincere.

James chose to believe him, because he wouldn't even know how to go about untangling Walter's web of lies. He felt sick. "Make sure it does. I would hate for you to fall back into bad habits."

"I will." By all outward appearances, he meant it. "Which is why I want to keep all discussion of Sarah's ability in the open. Please think about it. There are so many ways her talents could be used to help us, not only with public relations."

"She is exceptionally good for public relations. We can't allow any other work she does to interfere."

Walter gave him a significant look. "Nor with providing us an heir."

James's stomach turned. He had no intention of discussing his sex life with Walter, and after last night he would be surprised if Sarah ever wanted to sleep with him again. "That is between Sarah and me."

"Of course," His uncle rose placing his teacup back on the tray. "I'll let you get to work. But think about what I said. She could help us with so many things."

James watched Walter walk out the door. He had treated him as an ally for so long, but James now wondered what Walter's aims were. He was going to have to pay much closer attention to every conversation they had going forward."

Miss Lennox came in with her agenda, closing the door behind her.

James looked at her. "Does my uncle often come to bother you before I get in in the mornings?"

Her face retained its usual calm, but her cheeks turned pink. "I don't know what you mean, sir."

"Does my uncle pester you when I'm not here?"

Her demeanor didn't change, but her fingers fidgeted with the corner of the day's page in her agenda. "He stops by to ask questions when he has them."

"And you answer those questions?" She shifted her weight to her heels without changing her posture. He had to give her credit, if he hadn't spent the last couple of years working so closely with her, he wouldn't have noticed the change.

"When his questions relate to business." Her voice wavered only slightly.

James came to stand in front of her, watching her reactions closely. "Good. I would hate to think anything I told you in confidence was making its way to my uncle's ears."

"Of course, sir." She swallowed, and his eyes zeroed in on the pulse thrumming in her throat.

His gaze sought hers. "I have to know I can trust you."

"You can trust me completely." She said unequivocally.

He could trust her, he thought. Not because he chose to turn a blind eye, as he'd done with his uncle, but because she was loyal to him. He could see it in her look, in her spine, like an extra bit of steel. That was the difference. His uncle was flexible, in everything from his loyalty to his relationship with the truth. Miss Lennox was steadfast. "Excellent. What do we have on today?"

She went over the schedule for the day. As usual it was full of meetings; the refinery acquisitions, internal review of the oil rig explosion, more of the same. All needed his attention, but he doubted he'd be able to focus after the previous night. All he could think about was how he had failed; failed Sarah, failed Dermot, failed Seonag.

He was deep in thought and didn't notice when Miss Lennox stopped talking. She was watching him; a questioning look on her face. "Do you have any changes to the schedule?"

"No, it's fine. Leave me a copy and I'll be in all the correct places at the correct times. I have a project for you."

She handed him a copy of the day's schedule and closed her portfolio with a snap. James put the schedule on his desk on his way to the credenza beside it. Among the books he kept in his office was something he'd bought shortly after he met

Sarah. Dermot had told him she was having an article published in the American Folkways Journal. He'd had Miss Lennox call the journal to order copies of the issue before they were printed. There was another copy in his study at home, and another in the library at Tweedholm.

Picking up this copy, he thumbed through it until he found the correct page. He tore a corner off of a paper on his desk and used it to mark the page before handing the magazine to Miss Lennox. "I need this article framed, today. I don't care how much it costs."

She opened the magazine and glanced at the article. "Any specifics about the framing; color, finish, anything else?"

"Make it look good." He said. "I trust your taste."

***

The framed article was waiting for him when he arrived home. Once again, Miss Lennox proved to be invaluable. Conley informed him as he was taking his jacket off that the package was in his study. James unwrapped it to make sure he was satisfied with the work. The article complete with images and a brief biography of Sarah was arranged in a long frame with a precisely cut mat around each page.

There was a note from Miss Lennox informing him she'd had to borrow the copy from his study as well for the pages printed on both sides. She had also thoughtfully ordered replacement copies of the issue from the publisher. He knew he could count on Lennox. She was always thorough. Now, the question was, would Sarah like it or would she see it as a reminder of the career she lost.

James found Sarah in her sitting room talking with her assistant. He knocked on the open door. "My love, do you have a moment?"

"Sure." She stood up and smoothed her skirt.

Mr. Gurudat rose as well and gathered the papers from the coffee table in front of them. "I'll put these reports on your desk."

"Thanks. I'll try to read through them, and we can discuss tomorrow." Sarah said.

When Gurudat had left he said. "How was your day?"

"Fine. I think we're making progress on picking charities." She walked behind her desk. It wasn't lost on him how she'd put the desk between them. She fidgeted with the folder, moving it to the corner of the desk. "How was yours?"

"Miserable." He came closer but kept the desk between them. "I have to apologize again for the way I treated you last night. It was unforgivable."

She watched him, listening. But didn't give any indication of what she was thinking.

"How is your arm?" He asked.

"Sore." She said stiffly. Looking at the frame he was holding with one hand. "What do you have there?"

He lifted it up and held it out to her over the desk. "Ah. I had this framed for you. I am proud of the work you're doing now, but I also want you to know how proud I am of the work you did before."

Sarah took the framed article from him. She scanned the pages, blinking in surprise. "You had a copy?"

"I ordered several copies when I heard you were having an article published." He confessed.

Her green eyes narrowed at him. "We had barely met when this was published."

"I wanted to know you better. I thought reading your work would help." He bit his lip nervously, not sure how she would take his gift.

"That's very thoughtful." She looked back down to the article. "I appreciate it. I'll have to hang it in here."

"Would you like to go out for dinner?" He felt like he was asking her out on their first date again. She was almost more distant than she had been then. "We could avoid having dinner with my parents."

Apparently, avoiding his parents was enough of a sweetener. "Okay. I don't feel like dealing with your mother today."

He laughed. "I can't say I blame you. I'll let you change while I make arrangements."

"Okay." She flashed an awkward smile.

He left her to find Conley to get help with a reservation, daring to hope they would recover from this.

***

Sarah had wanted nothing more than to run when she woke up that morning. She had fooled herself these past few weeks into thinking James was in her corner. For all his professions of love, and talk of teamwork, the way he'd manhandled her had proved it all a lie. All his reserve and mild-mannered behavior had lulled her into a false sense of security. She had been so shocked she hadn't even fought back. All of Duff's training had flown right out of her head.

The DNA test had proven that Dermot was an alternative. Green had warned them. Still, as long as Walter Stuart had his resources, it wasn't safe to enlist Green to get her out of her marriage. She had no doubt Walter would make good on his threats to her family. She didn't dare tell anyone, not even Jujhar. If it got back to Dermot, she knew his reaction would only put him in more danger.

Sarah had spent all day mentally gaming out every scenario she could think of to get out of this before something worse than the previous night happened. She'd lived with unpredictable physical violence before when her mother was at her worst. She had no desire to stay in another volatile situation. Even the hint of it, which was really all she'd gotten the night before, was enough to make her want to run for the hills. But there was no getting past the memory of what had happened the last time she tried. She was trapped.

All her ruminations during the day had faded by the time they went to bed. After James's thoughtful gift, Sarah had put on her Lady Sarah armor and gone to dinner. Something happened when she put on her Lady Sarah clothes and her Lady Sarah makeup. Something about the act of putting on that armor soothed the sharp edges of anxiety buzzing below the surface all day to a low hum tickling the back of her mind. She became detached from her physical body.

Lady Sarah had taken James's hand and let him escort her to the car. She'd let him caress the small of her back as they were led to their private table off the dining room of some posh restaurant whose name she hadn't caught. Lady Sarah had engaged in polite conversation, nothing significant, merely small talk.

Meanwhile Sarah's mind relived a memory from what she thought of as her mother's ghost year, the last year her mother had been alive. Sarah was once again the little girl sitting across the table from the shell of a woman who had destroyed the painting wee Sarah had made at school.

Lady Sarah was served a plate of Monkfish in a lemon butter sauce.

Wee Sarah had a plate of catfish fried in a cornmeal batter.

Lady Sarah ate quietly chatting with James about anything and nothing.

Wee Sarah stuck out her chin and stared her mother down, refusing to show fear.

But wee Sarah had Granny and Duff to defend her when her mother's demons got the best of her, and Molly had lunged at her across the table. Lady Sarah had no one, no one but herself.

She wished she could find the courage of defiant wee Sarah. She wondered where that little girl was, and when she'd lost the ability to stare down her tormentor and take another bite. Had it been when Ryan Cumberland told her Dermot had been lying to her, when Dermot had tried to tell her they couldn't be together, when she'd finally understood the last verse of "The River Maiden", or when she'd watched her father die?

Lady Sarah took another sip of wine.

Wee Sarah continued munching her catfish while Granny and Duff wrestled her mother out the door.

A woman trapped in a life she didn't choose.

A little girl trapped in a hostile home.

Lady Sarah excused herself to the ladies' room, waiting in the hall while her bodyguard cleared the room first. Fleming was adept at protecting her from outside threats, but useless on the threats in her own house, her own mind.

In the bathroom Lady Sarah checked her makeup and reapplied her lipstick catching the scent of her perfume on her wrist. She returned the lipstick to her bag and glanced at the mirror and gasped. The woman from the grotto was there, her face full of worry. Lady Sarah took a stumbling step back staring in disbelief. She looked around as if to ask if anyone else was seeing this, and she found wee Sarah standing beside her looking equally as perplexed.

The woman, Sarah had come to think of her as Mary, extended a hand. The two Sarahs watched in horror as the woman's hand reached out from the mirror, a fold of her saffron colored robe draping out of the frame.

At the woman's encouraging look, the two Sarahs looked at each other, questioning. Both of them reached to take Mary's offered hand. Lady Sarah laid hers on top of wee Sarah's. The child's hand was enveloped by the two larger hands. Mary pulled them closer. Lady Sarah half expected her to pull them through the looking glass. When Lady Sarah's forehead was close to touching the mirror, the woman looked in her eyes, but the voice coming from her was Granny's. "If ye canna get out, ye mun go through."

In a flash, Sarah was once again standing alone in front of the sink with her clutch in her hands. It was as if nothing had happened, but her heart raced. Putting her head in her hands she breathed deeply, the calming scents of home soothing her. It took several deep breaths before she felt calm enough to exit the restroom.

She made her way back to the table outwardly calm, but inwardly confused. James had ordered her favorite dessert, but she found it hard to enjoy. After a few bites for the sake of politeness, she told him she was tired.

At home, when she had taken the evening off, Sarah slid between the sheets prepared to go to sleep, hoping that the next day would make sense.

James came out of his closet. He paused before turning off the lamp. Into the darkness he said. "Please tell me what I can do."

It wasn't James's voice. Once again it was Dermot's. Once again in the dark, when she couldn't see him, they were indistinguishable. And after the day and evening she'd had she didn't care. "Come here."

Whether he actually said it, or she wanted to hear it so much she imagined it, she couldn't be sure. But she heard Dermot's voice say, "I'll be there in a tic."

The words in her grandmother's voice ran through her mind again. 'If ye canna get out, ye mun go through.'

"Will you come to the study with me? James poked his head into Sarah's sitting room, asked his question, and left without waiting to hear her answer.

Puzzled, Sarah put down the report on an environmental charity Jujhar had put together for her. James had been in a good mood that morning, which shouldn't be surprising. He no doubt thought he'd been forgiven. Just because Sarah had allowed things to go back to normal, didn't mean she forgave or forgot. It only meant she saw no way of changing her situation yet. So, she followed James downstairs to the study where she found him waiting with Dermot.

Dermot looked equally surprised to see her. He stood in front of the fireplace, as if ready to bolt at any second. He looked like he had managed to get some rest in the three days since the last time she'd seen him.

"Thank you, darling." James held out a hand to her, "I wanted us all to have this conversation together."

Sarah walked hesitantly over to James. "What is this about?"

"Please, let's sit." James waved to the couch behind him.

Sarah sat and James took the seat next to her close enough to emphasize they were a unit. He might be feeling insecure in their relationship, but he wasn't about to let Dermot see. She looked up at Dermot who, by the flexing of the muscles in his jaw, didn't seem to miss James's signal.

He took the chair across from them with a look of impatience. "What's this about, James?"

"I've been thinking about your mother and her situation." James began. "I've had an idea."

"Are ye going to cure Alzheimer's now?" Dermot's reaction was barely short of eye rolling. Sarah wondered how James had gotten Dermot to come to the house.

"Of course not." James said patiently. "I think I have a solution to the care home problem." He glanced at Sarah before looking back to Dermot. "We'd like to offer to house your mother at Tweedholm."

Dermot shook his head and started to rise.

"Hear us out, will you? We will cover private round-the-clock nursing and medical care. There is already security there, but we can increase it to make sure no one bothers her, and she doesn't elope again. She'll get personalized care in a familiar environment, and she'll never have to move again."

"Provided I come back to work, aye?" Dermot's tone dripped with cynicism.

"I'll admit I want you to come back to work, but whether you come back as my personal security or something else entirely is up to you." James kept his tone even. "But my offer stands for your mother whether you come back or not. There are no strings."

"What d'ye mean 'something else'?" Dermot asked.

"You are as entitled to an executive position at the company as I am. You could come back to work with us in an executive capacity. We'll find a role for you, and Walter will retire someday. Imagine the two of us running the company together."

"I've no interest in working at Alba Petroleum. Security is one thing, but I'm not made for business. That's why I was going to school for folklore." Dermot shook his head. "Did he put ye up to this?"

They all knew 'he' meant Walter.

James looked at him squarely. "He doesn't even know we're speaking. I've learned to pay closer attention to Walter's motives."

"Finally." Dermot muttered.

James nodded seriously. "I know. It's taken me too long. I hope you understand that I'm not him. I'm offering to help your mother because I care about you both. You're family as far as I'm concerned, and you should never have had to struggle with her care by yourself."

Whatever Sarah had thought when James called them into the room, she hadn't expected this. She looked between her husband and Dermot hopefully. She'd worried James might move closer to Walter after he learned she'd been keeping her gift a secret, or her emotional distance after their confrontation might have driven him closer to Walter. This may be another gesture to get back in her good graces, but she would take it if it helped Dermot.

Although James hadn't told her about this plan, he pitched it to Dermot as if they were united in this scheme. This was their offer, not his, and it was a signal to Dermot that they were together despite the new revelations. James might be questioning Walter's motives these days, but his methods were another story. Giving with one hand while taking with another was certainly a move he'd learned from Walter.

Dermot was thinking about it. Sarah could see his wheels turning. "And Walter, are ye willing to keep him away from her?"

"If that's what you prefer." James agreed. "I'm no more excited to spend time with him than you are. And Tweedholm belongs to me now. My father signed it over along with everything else when he retired."

"A nurse around the clock, ye say?" Dermot gave him a speculative look.

A hint of a smile teased at the corners of James's mouth. "I've already had Miss Lennox contact a private agency to make sure it could be done.

Dermot sighed. "It would be nice to know she's safe and familiar surroundings might help slow the memory loss."

"I wish I had thought of it sooner." James was sincere.

Dermot shifted his gaze to her. "Was this yer idea?"

She shook her head looking at James. "No, it was all James, but if it helps you and Seonag, I'm all for it."

Dermot gave James a long look, as if he was trying to figure out whether there was a catch coming. 'Thank ye."

He stood preparing to leave. James and Sarah both stood. James said. "You'll think about joining the company?"

"I'll think about it. I'm no businessman." He bowed his head to Sarah before slipping out the door.

"That was a very nice offer." She said to James after Dermot had left.

James was still looking at the door. "It was too late. I've been blind to so much."

"It's only too late when they're gone." She said.

James took her hand. "I hope you mean that."

***

The next morning James lowered the boom, or so it felt. Sarah was getting ready for a meeting with the family's solicitors about the foundation she wanted to establish. She was seated at her vanity table in the bathroom when he leaned against the doorway watching her in the mirror. "How is your arm?"

"Getting better." Sarah picked up her angled brush and started applying contour to her cheeks. "You look like there's something on your mind."

He smiled. "I was thinking about your special skill."

Sarah was immediately wary. She had known this conversation was coming. "What about it?"

James came to sit on a stool behind her. "It strikes me that your ability could be applied to a number of things."

Alarm bells went off in her mind. "Like what things."

"Well, you could view our competitors, or political rivals to give us an advantage.' He said carefully.

Sarah gave him a side-eyed look. "Are you asking me to commit corporate espionage?"

"How would you ever get caught?" He arched an eyebrow at her.

"So, if you can't be caught, then anything is fair game?" She countered. "Good to know."

James looked affronted. "I can guarantee you if any of them had someone with your abilities, they wouldn't hesitate to use them for the same purpose. We're not playing games here."

Sarah fumed. "What happened to all those boarding school ethics classes you told me about?"

"It's easy to stand on ethics when you're talking about personal interactions. A.P. operates on a much larger scale and there is too much at stake not to do everything we can to gain an advantage. You've used it to save your own life, but you won't use it to preserve the livelihoods of thousands of people."

"Wow. Those are some impressive ethical gymnastics." She tipped the makeup brush at him like a wand. "I can see the apple doesn't fall too far from the tree."

He drew in a sharp breath as if she had surprised him. 'Walter may be devious, but that doesn't make him wrong. There is a lot you could do to help us."

"You've discussed my gift with Walter. I guess I should have known you would." She turned back to the mirror and went back to applying her makeup.

"How could I not have? You did whatever you do right in front of him." James eyed her in the mirror, clearly irritated this conversation wasn't going the way he had hoped.

Sarah watched his hands closely; ready should he make any sudden moves. "So, you'll take care of Seonag if I use my gift to spy for you. Right?"

"I never said that." He bit out. "I plan to take care of Seonag as long as Dermot agrees to it. One has nothing to do with the other."

"Except you are asking me to use my gift right after telling Dermot about it. The timing seems a little too convenient." She leaned into the mirror and applied eye shadow.

"Is that what you think of me?" His eyebrows drew together. Sarah worried she might have pushed him too far.

"That sounds like exactly the kind of deal Walter would propose." Sarah worried she might be pushing him too far, but using her gift for Alba Petroleum seemed like a slippery slope she didn't want to start down. "I won't use it to break the law. My ancestors didn't preserve this gift for thousands of years so you could spy on other oil companies or the Tories."

"Really?" He stood, looking over her. His voice was biting and determined. Sarah's nerves sizzled.

She watched his hands. "And here I was thinking we had reached a point where I was a person to you and not a means to an end."

"That's not fair." James snapped. "And you chose this when you chose to marry me."

He lifted his hand and pointed a finger down in a jabbing motion. It wasn't a threatening move, but it was sudden enough to make Sarah flinch.

James stopped, taking a step back. Shock and shame showed on his face. He suddenly didn't know what to do with his hands. He closed them, then opened then, clasped them, then put them in his pockets. He took a deep breath. "Forgive me. I didn't mean to scare you."

Sarah was frozen, sure she wouldn't move again until he was gone. Her voice was quiet, but steely. "I won't break the law for Alba Petroleum."

He paused, thinking. "Could your gift be used to find oil deposits? That shouldn't break any laws."

Sarah thought about it. She wasn't crazy about the idea of using her gift to find fossil fuels either, but it was better than spying. "I've never used it to search for something other than people. I'm not sure it would work."

"Are you willing to try?"

If that was what it took to get him to leave. "I'll think about it. I'll need to get familiar with what I'd be looking for."

"I'll see what I can set up with our research and development department. They can show you what to look for." He said stiffly.

"When you have a plan, have Miss Lennox set something up with Jujhar." Sarah wanted this conversation to end. She wanted him gone so she could relax. She couldn't help feeling like this whole exchange was a win for Walter Stuart.

"Sarah, I…" He struggled for words. "I told you I would never put my hands on you in anger again, and I meant it."

She had no answer. There were any number of things she could say. 'Saying and doing are two different things.', 'Never is a long time.' 'I don't believe you.' In the end she simply said. "Okay."

"I'll see you this evening." He slunk out the door, closing it softly. Sarah let out a breath and relaxed her shoulders for the first time since the conversation started. She dropped the makeup brush she'd been holding so tightly she'd nearly snapped it in two. Damn Walter Stuart, and damn James for listening to him. She had known as soon as they learned about her gift, they would turn it into some advantage for themselves. She had hoped it would take longer for Walter to convince James to exploit Sarah's ability. She had hoped her influence on James would have protected her from Walter's scheming. But then she hadn't expected this tension with James.

She was so angry and scared her hands were shaking. She would wait until she calmed down to finish her makeup. She sprang up from the stool and whirled around ready to stomp her way into the closet. Her robe must have swung out when she spun around. The fabric swept across the dressing table knocking off several bottles and brushes.

Immediately, the fragrance of her perfume surged up from the floor strong enough to make her gag. Looking down she saw the bottle on its side spilling its contents onto the floor. With an irritated sigh, Sarah bent down to clean up the mess, and she was swamped with such a wave of longing for James, for Dermot, for home that she had to grip the table for support. Her head ached from the strength of the scent, which was pleasant enough in small doses, but this was too much.

The longing became desire. Images of their lovemaking sprang to her mind, and her body craved a man's touch. Sarah couldn't understand how it was possible after the conversation she'd had with James. She looked down at the puddle of perfume on the floor, thinking. She walked out of the bathroom, closing the door on the mess and went to a window. Opening the window, she took several deep breaths of clean fresh air.

When the scent was out of her nostrils and the pain in her head began to clear, Sarah looked back toward the bathroom. It was possible the intensity of the spilled perfume had caused the headache and nausea, but it didn't explain the weird wave of desire. Testing a theory, she walked back toward the spill.

With every step, the same sense of longing grew. She tried to tamp it down, tried to remember her anger at him, but it was like her mind was at war with itself. She switched from anger to arousal so quickly, like a strobe light with hot images floating through her mind.

Holding her breath, Sarah dashed past the bathroom door to her closet and grabbed a scarf. She held the scarf in front of her nose and mouth and approached the spill. With the scarf as a filter, she found it slightly easier to resist the effects of the scent. With careful fingers, she picked up the bottle trying not to get any of the perfume on her hands. She set the bottle upright on the table and retrieved the stopper from the floor putting it back in the bottle.

She ran back to the window to breathe for a minute before returning to the bathroom to hunt down a plastic bag, which was a bit of a stretch. In the end she had to run down to the kitchen. On the way, she ran into Conley and asked him to send someone up to clean the spill in her bathroom. She was going to need the scent eradicated before she could be in the room again.

***

After the meeting about the charitable foundation, Sarah and Jujhar returned to work in her sitting room.

"I will get on the next steps they mentioned." Jujhar opened the agenda where he kept track of all Sarah's appointments. He was turning out to be an efficient and reliable if grossly overqualified assistant, although Sarah had been more interested in having a friend around when she'd offered him the job. She also had the ulterior motive of wanting to stay on friendly terms with Lyall Green's eventual replacement as Merlin, or watcher, or facilitator, or whatever they chose to call themselves in this century. "In the meantime, you have a meeting with Gillian."

"Okay." Sarah went to the door adjoining the bedroom. "Wait here. I need to get something."

Sarah went to the bathroom, relieved most of the fragrance from the perfume spill had been cleaned up. She noticed they had left the exhaust fan on in the hopes of circulating more air. She reached under the sink where she had stashed the perfume bottle zipped into a plastic bag and retrieved it.

Returning to her sitting room she closed the bedroom door. Jujhar was at the desk looking through some papers. He looked up when she came back in.

Sarah held a finger in front of her lips to warn him to be quiet. She didn't want to risk anyone overhearing their conversation. She hoped the Stuarts hadn't thought to bug her sitting room. Although she wouldn't put it past them. "I have something I'd like our mutual friend to take a look at."

"Oh?" Jujhar looked confused.

Sarah grabbed a notepad off the desk. 'Better safe than sorry.' She thought. She wrote Jujhar a note.

Put this in your bag.

And handed him the bag with the perfume bottle. Without so much as a glance at the contents, he took the bottle and put it in his satchel.

"I think I could use some fresh air. Why don't we take a walk in the garden, and we can talk through those next steps for the foundation." She suggested.

When they were safely in the garden and closer to the canal than the house, Jujhar asked. "Is it safe to talk now?"

"I think so." Sarah looked back toward the house to make sure they were alone in the garden. "I don't know if my sitting room is bugged, but where Walter Stuart is involved, we can't trust anything. And it seems like wherever James is, Walter is involved."

"Right." Jujhar indicated they should sit on the bench overlooking the canal. "What was that in the bag? It looked like a perfume bottle."

"It is." Sarah took a seat on the bench. He sat next to her, and she bent her head close so she could talk quietly. "It's a gift I received on our honeymoon, but I suspect it's something more. I'd like you or Mr. Green to analyze it and see exactly what it is."

His dark brown eyes narrowed at her. "What do you think it is?"

"I'd rather you did the analysis first." Sarah didn't want to influence the result with her theories. "I have my suspicions, but I'd rather hear your thoughts first. It could all be in my head."

He inclined his head. "Your instincts are usually good, but we'll have a look."

"Thanks." Sarah hoped she could count on Jujhar. He had kept his interest in her people a secret from her when they first met, but he had never lied to her. It seemed like everyone else around her these days had at one time or another.

CHAPTER THIRTY-FOUR

The rolling green hills of the border region undulated as far as she could see. Sarah was finally going to Tweedholm, the Stuarts' country house. She'd heard stories about it from James and Dermot for so long, she was excited to see it even in difficult circumstances.

Seonag sat beside her in the back seat of the car. Dermot sat in the passenger's seat while James followed in another car, much to Sarah's relief. In the days since their conversation about her gift, things between them had been tense. They had been cautiously polite, even scrupulously pleasant with each other, but both had held back anything significant. They had not trusted each other or themselves to speak about anything in any depth without upsetting the other.

They had not made love since the perfume spill. Jujhar had not provided an answer about the perfume, but she had also not had the same hallucinations she'd been having before. James was still James when the lights were out. She didn't hear Dermot's voice in the dark anymore. More importantly, she didn't have the detached feeling between what her brain thought, and her body felt anymore. She did miss the fragrances of home that had made her like the perfume from the start, but she was relieved to feel more like herself. She had begun to worry about her neurological health, could that have been how things started for Seonag?

As was often the case, Seonag didn't recognize Dermot as her son. In Seonag's mind, her Dermot was an adolescent boy, and she found it stressful trying to reconcile her memory of her son with the grown man who visited her regularly. She had a similar issue when they had introduced her to James at the care home while picking her up.

Sarah on the other hand was someone she had met recently, which made Sarah easier for Seonag to remember from one visit to the next. Sarah was the nice young lady who liked to talk about legends and myths. Sarah was her friend who didn't expect anything from Seonag but conversation. Although Sarah was still puzzled, Seonag seemed to know she was the one from the prophecy. She frequently referred to Sarah as *'a bhana phrionnsa'*, princess.

When they turned into a gated drive. Seonag sat up straight her voice full of nostalgia. "Are we going to Tweedholm?"

"We are." Sarah noted the wonder on Seonag's face. "I've never been here. Is it nice?"

"Och. It's grand. The gardens sweep down to the Tweed and there are ruins in the forest. It's lovely."

Dermot turned and watched his mother's face light up as they drove through the hills toward the house.

"Did ye know they say Merlin is buried along the banks of the Tweed?" Seonag gave Sarah a mischievous look.

"Really?" Sara immediately thought of Seonag's father, Lyall Green. Of course, he'd told them Merlin was more of a title than a name, so it could have been a Merlin buried near the Tweed.

"Aye." Seonag leaned closer. "After the battle of Arderydd, Merlin was devastated and took to the forests. He lived rough among the animals and spoke to no man for ages.

Then Saint Mungo happened upon him, and Merlin told him of his guilt. He blamed himself for Arderydd and he couldna bear it." Her voice took on the dreamy quality it often did when she told old stories. 'That's what Geoffrey of Monmouth wrote."

"What do you think?" Sarah asked.

Seonag's expression changed as she seemed to get lost in a memory. Sarah hoped this wouldn't upset her. Seonag's memory was a tricky thing. "My father says ye canna trust Monmouth. It's all Welsh Christian propaganda."

Sarah laughed. Seonag's father would know better than anyone she supposed. "Does he know what happened?"

"Och. He doesna ken. They dinna pass those sorts of things down. Some stories say Merlin was set upon by shepherds who stoned him and beat him. Then he fell onto a stake and drowned in the river."

"Sounds like Rasputin." Sarah asked thinking of the tale of the many things which should have killed the Russian priest and mystic who was poisoned, shot, and thrown in a river before dying of exposure.

Seonag cocked her head. "I'd never made the connection before, but aye. I wonder if…" Her voice trailed off. "We'll likely never know how that Merlin died, but dinna trust Monmouth."

"I'll keep it in mind." Sarah noted. "Didn't I hear Merlin predicted the Union of Scotland and England on the banks of the Tweed?"

"Bollocks." Seonag scoffed.

***

His mother could remember a fourteen-hundred-year-old legend about one of Lyall Green's predecessors, but she couldn't remember her own son was a grown man now. He tried not to be bitter when she wanted to talk with Sarah more than him, or when she treated him like a recent acquaintance rather than the man she'd raised. It wasn't her fault. Still the familiar surroundings of Tweedholm House seemed to lift her spirits.

The gravel drive and stone front were much the same as he remembered them. He hadn't returned to the country house since his army days, but little seemed to have changed.

Buff-colored sandstone stood stark against the bright blue of the early autumn sky. Sharp points of the corner turrets and gables reached for the heavens in the ornate baronial style. Dermot glanced up at the window above the front door where he and James had loved to sit as children recalling simpler times.

Dermot was opening his mother's door when Henry Stuart appeared at his shoulder. "Let me, lad."

"What are ye doing here?" Dermot asked.

"Righting a wrong." Henry's attention fixed on Seonag through the window.

"She won't know ye. In her mind ye're a young man." Dermot warned.

"I know." Henry gave him a look telling him it didn't matter. "I won't trouble her with my memories. I simply want to be near her, and to help you."

Dermot opened his mother's car door, and Henry offered his hand to Seonag. "Welcome to Tweedholm House."

Seonag's eyes met Henry's and she tilted her head as if she was trying to place him. For a second Dermot, Sarah and

Henry all held their breath waiting to see if she would recognize him. "Have we met?"

Henry choked back tears. "I am Henry. I take care of the place."

She looked confused, and Dermot worried she might be upset. "Not Henry Stuart. He's much younger. Are ye a relative then?"

Henry cleared his throat and gave her a welcoming smile. "I am."

Seonag placed her hand in his and rose carefully from the car. "Och, I've been here many times. My Dermot and I spend summers here. I'm surprised we've never met before."

"I've heard much about you, Ms. Sinclair." Henry tucked Seonag's hand into his elbow. "Won't you come inside and join me for tea?"

"Thank you. I'd like that." Was his mother blushing? He wasn't sure if having Henry about would be good for her or make things worse. He would have to have a talk with Henry about which things made her anxious and how her memory got spottier late in the day. He started to follow them into the house, then he remembered Sarah was there.

He turned to speak to her, but the car James and the security staff were riding in pulled up behind theirs. Sarah glanced at the car then back at him with a look that said, 'later.' But he didn't know when later might be.

He turned back to the house to follow Henry and his mother. The car door opened behind him, and James asked. "How was the drive?"

"Fine." Sarah sounded cheerful. "We talked about legends of Merlin along the Tweed."

James chuckled. "Seonag was always handy with local legends. I can see why you get along."

He heard a quick kiss, then Sarah's low voice. "Henry is here."

The rest was lost as the door closed behind Dermot and he stood in the chilly stone foyer of the manor house. He drew in a breath noting the fragrance of stone, old drapes, and furniture polish. It was the scent of childhood holidays. If it had still been summer, he would have smelled the fresh flowers Mrs. Miller always arranged in the front hall.

As if he'd conjured her with his thoughts, Mrs. Miller came out of the parlor. The years hadn't slowed her down, though she looked grayer and softer than he remembered. When she saw him standing in the foyer, her face lit up and she came toward him with open arms. "Dermot, lad. I'm glad to see you again."

"Mrs. Miller, the place wouldna be the same without ye." He hugged her and bussed her cheek.

"I've just brought tea to yer mother and Mr. Stuart in the parlor. Go and have yourself a cuppa." She jerked a thumb over her shoulder toward the parlor. "I'll see to the lord and lady."

No one in the city referred to them as lord and lady. James preferred not to use the title when possible. He was sure Sarah did too, but Mrs. Miller would stand on formality. It seemed hard not to think of their titles when they were in the grand country house. "Are your ginger biscuits on the tea tray?"

She gave him a secret smile reminding him of the many times she had slipped him an extra ginger biscuit when he was a lad. "I made a fresh batch this morning."

"Ye're a treasure, Mrs. Miller." He gave her another quick kiss on the cheek.

"Go on with you." She waved a hand at him, grinning.

***

"No!" The sharp cry came from the next room. It took a second for the fog of sleep to lift enough for Dermot to recognize the cry as his mother's. Her voice changed to a whimper. "I don't want this!"

In an instant he was out of bed and at her door, thankful they'd put him in the room next to hers rather than his old childhood room. He burst into her room terrified of what he might find. Lit only by the moonlight coming through the windows, his mother struggled alone in the bed. She was sobbing and pushing against something invisible.

He gripped her arms. "Mum! Mum!"

She pushed against his chest and twisted away from him; her eyes still closed. "No! Stop!"

"Seonag!" He shouted, trying whatever he could to wake her from her nightmare.

Her eyes flew open looking wildly around the room. They settled on him, and her eyebrows drew together. "Who are ye? What d'ye want?"

"It's alright." He tried to sound calm, but his heart was racing. "Ye were having a bad dream."

She pushed away from him and scrambled backward. Her voice came out in ragged sobs. "Not again. Not again. Not again."

Dermot backed away from the bed, holding his hands in the air. "It's all right, Seonag. I'm not going to hurt ye."

"Not again."

Sarah and James appeared in the hallway. Dermot looked at them helpless to explain what was happening. Sarah pushed into the room and took in the scene.

"Not again." Seonag chanted from her place huddled against the headboard.

"What happened?" Sarah asked.

Dermot's heart thumped and electricity skittered along his nerves. "She was having a dream, but when I woke her, she didna recognize me. I scared her."

"Right. Leave us alone." Sarah commanded. He fought the impulse to insist on staying but doubted his mother would calm down with him in the room. Sarah went around the bed to where Seonag was huddled. "Go."

He stepped out into the hallway. James and Henry hovered there looking as impotent as he felt. None of them said a word, listening to Sarah's attempts to sooth his mother.

Sarah spoke to Seonag in Gaelic and English, trying whatever she thought would help. After a minute, his mother's chanting of 'not again' turned into weak sobs. Sarah cooed soothing words to her.

"What's all this then?" Mrs. Miller arrived hastily dressed in her usual tweed skirt and white blouse.

"Seonag's had a nightmare." James told her.

"The poor dear." Mrs. Miller shook her head in sympathy and hustled past them to peek into Seonag's room. "What can I do to help, my lady?"

Sarah maintained her soothing tone. "I think a glass of water and perhaps a sedative would be good."

"Right away, ma'am." Mrs. Miller looked to Dermot who went to his room to retrieve the sleeping pills Seonag's doctor had given him 'just in case.'

Mrs. Miller returned with a glass of water and Dermot handed her a pill. He wished he could see his mother, but he was afraid to peek in the door. He didn't want to set her off again. Mrs. Miller came out a moment later. She gave Dermot a pat on the shoulder. "Come along, lads. I'll put the kettle on."

"I might need something stronger than tea." Dermot muttered.

"I've got that too, love." She made her way down the hall. For lack of anything more useful to do the three men trailed in her wake. As they descended the stairs, Dermot heard Sarah softly singing a Gaelic lullaby.

In the kitchen, Mrs. Miller made tea. Henry stopped by the study to retrieve a decanter of whiskey. He poured a shot each into four tumblers, then added an extra one for Dermot. Dermot barely tasted the first sip of what he was sure was an exceptionally fine single malt. By the third sip warmth started to spread in his chest, and the adrenaline surge drained away.

"Does this happen often?" Henry asked.

"Not that I know of." Dermot swirled the whiskey in his glass. "I havena lived with her for a couple of years. The care home never said anything about nightmares or night terrors."

"The nurses should be here tomorrow to tend her. We'll want to make sure the night nurse knows about this possibility." James sat at the kitchen table.

Mrs. Miller placed a teapot on the table. "Here you are, lads. A pot of chamomile tea if the whiskey doesn't help the nerves."

322 · MEREDITH R. STODDARD

"Thank you, Mrs. Miller." Said James.

***

Sarah brushed Seonag's hair back from her forehead and continued humming the tune of *"Cagaran Gaolach"*. A faint memory of her mother singing that song to her flitted through her mind. She wondered if there was a Gaelic lullaby Seonag had sung to Dermot when he was little.

"Tha oran snog." (Nice song.) Seonag said softly, "My mother sang it to me when I was very young."

"Ye miss yer mother." Seonag sat up. She was calmer now, and her tears had stopped.

"Lately, I've been missing her more and more." Guilt flickered as it often didn't when Sarah thought about her mother. She was still processing what she had learned about Molly's experience and what she had done thinking to protect her daughter, but also remembering the unpredictability of her mother's mental illness. "But I didn't always."

"Oh?"

"Here, this should help you sleep without having another nightmare." Sarah handed Seonag the glass of water and the sleeping pill. Sarah watched her take the medication. She wouldn't normally have suggested it, but if it gave Seonag some peace then she wouldn't hesitate.

After she took the pill, Seonag put the glass on the night table. "You were going to explain why you didn't miss your mother."

"Can't get anything by you, can I?" Sarah hadn't been ready to tell that story.

Seonag's face clouded with worry. "I wish that were true."

Sarah took her hand. "Lie down, and I'll tell you the story, but I don't want to upset you."

Seonag smirked and positioned herself in the bed. "It might do me good to be reminded mine isna the only sad story."

"Misery loves company, eh?" Sarah settled on the edge of the bed as if she was about to tell Seonag a bedtime story. "I'll tell you about the dream that wakes me up at night. I don't remember a time when my mother was happy. She laughed and played and celebrated things, but there was always a sadness about her. It was like a shadow always followed her. Some days, it was so close it seemed like a second skin, like it controlled her. I felt sometimes like I was fighting the shadow for my mama."

"One day, when I was six years old, the shadow won. We had been out in the woods picking flowers and enjoying the first warm day of spring. We came inside laughing and dirty, and Mama was going to give me a bath. I thought she was happy. We'd been laughing and having a good time, but I knew the shadow was there. So, I thought I would tell Mama about something I'd seen in a dream, something I thought would make her happy. But it didn't."

"Whatever I said made her so sad and scared the shadow took over. She pushed me down in the bathtub. The flowers from my hair floated on top of the water, as she held me under until the shadow controlling her covered me too, and everything went black. My grandmother saved me. I never saw my mother after that day, only the shadow."

Seonag's hand gripped Sarah's. "Oh, lass."

She wondered if Seonag's 'not again' came from some trauma. "Sometimes I think when we keep that kind of pain bottled up like my mother did, it builds up pressure. Like a soda when you shake it, the bubbles get so excited when something breaks the seal, it comes bursting out. Do you know what that's like?"

Seonag's eyes filled with tears again.

"Oh, please don't' cry. I don't mean to upset you." Sarah pleaded.

Seonag shook her head. "Och, no. It's only, I dinna remember." She waved a hand toward her head. "I'm never sure what is memory and what isn't anymore. I canna tell what's real."

"I understand." Sarah assured her. "But whether it's real or not, it terrified you tonight. It might help to talk about it."

Seonag looked off toward the far corner of the room. "I canna tell ye much, only that I felt smothered, like someone was sitting on my chest."

"I'd be upset too. We could find you a different room if you think it would make things better." Sarah suggested.

"No. I've slept in this room every summer and holiday for years. I'll bide." Seonag yawned. "Thank ye, lass."

"Well, you let me know if there is anything else we can get for you."

"Aye. I will, lass." Seonag rolled away onto her side. Sarah pulled the blanket up to her shoulder. She waited a few more minutes until Seonag began to snore softly. Then she silently left hoping Seonag would sleep peacefully for the rest of the night.

CHAPTER THIRTY-FIVE

"And you're planning to stay here indefinitely?" James asked incredulously.

"I plan to be here as long as Seonag is here." Henry said firmly. It wasn't the first time he'd said it, but James needed to hear it more than once.

James cast a look at Mrs. Miller who was puttering about the kitchen before he leaned closer to Henry to whisper. "Are you and mother divorcing?"

Henry sighed. "I think you know that's not possible."

"But you'll live apart." James clarified.

"We've been living separate lives for years now. We only stayed under the same roof for appearances' sake." Henry told him. "The only difference now will be a matter of proximity."

Dermot had been listening to this back and forth without adding his two cents. He drank his tea and crumbled one of Mrs. Miller's biscuits on a plate. His mind was with Sarah and his mother upstairs. He was on the verge of getting up to check on them when Sarah appeared in the doorway. "Dermot."

Dermot, James, and Henry all sprang to their feet. She raised a hand to stave off their questions. She looked as tired as the rest of them, but even bleary-eyed she was beautiful. "She's sleeping. I think something in her room triggered an unpleasant memory. She seems fine for now."

"I'll go and keep watch." Henry stepped around the table.

Sarah stopped him with a hand on his arm. "You can listen at the door, but don't go into the room before she wakes up. It will scare her."

"Very well." Henry patted her hand and nodded at Dermot before leaving.

Sarah took a seat at the table, and Mrs. Miller put a cup of tea in front of her. Dermot slid the plate of biscuits her way. "Thank you."

"Did she say what it was that scared her?" He was desperate for anything he could do to help his mother, anything to make her life easier.

Sarah reached across the table and covered his hand with hers. "She doesn't know. She felt like she was being smothered. I asked if it was a memory, and she said she doesn't know anymore what is memory and what is hallucination."

He felt something in his chest snap like a guitar string. Maybe it was the last connection to his childhood with Seonag. They'd been a team. They'd traveled all over together, and she'd taught him so much. She'd been mother, father, and friend, but all he had wanted was a man in his life to give him the same guidance she had. When she'd been right there and now, she was all but gone. Tears stung his eyes, and he looked down at his plate full of crumbs.

***

On the advice of the private nurse who arrived the next day, they decided to move his mother to Tweedholm's guest house. The small cottage sat next to the caretaker's cottage on the other side of the wood from the main house. This meant they would have a nice country view, and Mrs. Miller next door for company when the family wasn't in residence. It also meant the nurse had fewer entrances and exits to manage if Seonag tried to leave.

Dermot had to admit, he felt a bit easier about his mother being in a smaller space free of triggers for the few memories that might make it through the fog. He much preferred the idea of her and her nurse in a cottage than his mother rattling around the empty grand house like some ghost out of a Bronte novel.

"I've got your knitting here." He held up his mother's brocade knitting bag as her nurse, Lottie got her settled into a chair in the lounge.

"Och, thank ye, lad." She gave him a polite smile.

"I'll put the kettle on." Lottie, who was a little younger than his mother with short salt and pepper hair, olive skin, and kind brown eyes patted his shoulder.

Lottie had moved their things in that morning while Dermot and Henry had stayed with Seonag at the great house. He thought James and Sarah had gone back to the city first thing that morning. It had been a day and a half since Seonag's nightmare, and she didn't seem to remember anything about it.

"Cheers." Dermot said to Lottie before turning back to his mother. "Well, what do ye think of yer new home?"

"Mine?" She looked around the room surprised. "It's a lovely cottage, but why am I here?"

Dermot sat on the ottoman in front of her chair. "I know ye werena happy at the last care home. And I wanted to make sure ye're in a place where ye'll be comfortable. Here, ye'll have the garden out front and Mrs. Miller and yer new friend, Henry can visit ye."

"And Sarah?" She looked hopeful.

Dermot cleared his throat. "And Sarah when she can."

"Good," She said, reaching for her knitting. "It's better this way."

The tension he'd been holding since they left the city released. "Now, there will be a night nurse and another on weekends, but I'm assured they're all professionals."

She eased back into the chair relaxing for the first time since they'd left the care home. He hoped this would prove to be the best thing for her.

His mother began to knit. It was a strange patchwork of blocks in different colors and textures. It looked as if each time she started a new color, Seonag forgot what she was making and went off in a new direction with a new stitch pattern. Her current block was made with a fuzzy yarn in an amber color. He had stopped asking her what she was making. The answer varied with the yarn she was using. Dermot picked up a corner of the piece and fingered a soft blue block.

Lottie came back in with the tea tray. He heard the tea pouring into cups, and one was set on the table next to him. He didn't look up from the knitted piece, but said, "Cheers."

"What are you working on there, Seonag?" A familiar accented voice sounded behind him.

He whipped around to find Sarah holding a cup of tea for his mother. His breath caught in his chest. She gave him a tentative smile as if she was afraid she had startled him.

"I thought ye had gone back to Edinburgh with James." He said.

"I wanted to make sure y'all got settled in here." She put the cup on the table next to Seonag. "Milk, no sugar. Right, Seonag?"

"Aye, that's right, dear." His mother grinned at Sarah. "How nice of ye to visit."

"Of course." Sarah said. "How do you like the cottage?"

"It's lovely. Although, I'm not sure what I've done to deserve it."

Sarah patted her arm and met Dermot's eyes. "I can think of a few things."

God! He couldn't stand being near her and not being able to touch her. It was bad enough he'd spent the last two nights under the same roof without being alone with her. The temptation had been nearly unbearable.

James, Sarah, Henry, and Dermot had formed an alliance to take care of his mother. He'd been taking care of her all on his own for so long he was relieved to have others to carry some of the load. Was this what having a family was like?

He had agreed the night before to go back to Alba Petroleum in the guise of James's bodyguard, but with the purpose of learning all he could about the business. Henry and James had the idea to give him stock in the company, so even if he didn't take an active role in the business, he would benefit financially.

The three of them had their tea and talked about the cottage, knitting, and the weather. They pretended to be easy friends for Seonag's sake. After an hour of listening to Sarah and his mother chat with occasional interjections from him, Sarah rose and kissed his mother on the cheek. "I'll let you settle in and get some rest."

"Thank ye, dearie. I am a bit tired."

"Well, you take it easy." Sarah admonished. "I'll be by tomorrow to check on you."

"Tioraidh, a'nighean." (Bye, lass.) His mother said.

Not wanting this little bit of time with Sarah to end, he jumped up. "I'll walk ye back."

He kissed his mother on the cheek and told her he'd see her in the morning. After thanking Lottie, he was relieved to find Sarah waiting for him in the front garden.

The autumn sun caught the gold streaks in her hair. It was pulled back into a knot at the back of her neck, but a few curls had escaped as they often did. He missed the tangle of her curls around his fingers as if even they didn't want to let him go. It was months since they'd lived together, but he still found curly hairs clinging to a jumper or jacket. Every time it happened; a crack opened up in his heart.

She looked the part of the lady of the manor in a serviceable brown skirt, blouse, and tweed jacket. The only thing missing was a pair of wellies. Instead, she wore classic loafers he was sure had been styled for her by Felicia's girl. She looked like Lady Sarah.

"Ye shouldna be walking around the estate alone, even here." He warned her. "Where's Fleming?"

She took a couple of steps down the path leading toward the house casting a shy look over her shoulder. "I sent him back to the house when I knew you were here."

With a shake of his head, he caught up with her. "D'ye think that's a good idea?"

"Probably not." At least she was honest about it.

"How will James feel about it?" He looked up and down the path as if anyone might come along and see them.

"I'm not sure I care." She walked on.

"Trouble in paradise?"

Her laugh was short and bitter.

"Ye looked thick as thieves in Aberdeen." He'd been surprised by the united front they'd presented. He thought Walter had been surprised as well.

"We were for a while. I thought I was making progress, but," She waggled her head back and forth. "It's a fine line. I've been working on pulling Walter's mental hooks out of James. I thought I had him on the side of good and then he learned I'd been hiding my gift from them. He didn't take it well. Now, he wants me to use my gift to help Alba Petroleum."

His heart sank. "I'm sorry. This is my fault."

She shook her head. "I would do it again in a heartbeat to find your mother. You have nothing to be sorry about."

He looked back to the cottage. "This isna part of some deal ye worked out with James, is it?"

"He says it isn't, and I think in his head he believes that. But he also asked me to use my gift the morning after he made you this offer. I find the timing suspect." She paused. "I want to think better of him. I think he's been playing Walter's games for so long; he doesn't even recognize when he's doing it anymore."

"What does he want ye to do for A.P.?"

"He originally wanted me to spy on competitors. I told him I wouldn't break the law. Instead, I agreed to consider helping them look for oil. I figure it's not much different than dowsing."

He made a grunt of agreement. He supposed she was right. He didn't think A.P. employed dowsers to find oil, but he remembered a time when they'd hired one there at

332 · MEREDITH R. STODDARD

Tweedholm to help them decide where to sink a new well to provide water to the house. "I reckon that's reasonable. Are ye going to do it?"

"I don't feel great about it. You know I've never felt right about the oil money. I think the last thing we need is more fossil fuels, but I'm not sure I can get away with not doing it." She kicked a rock down the path. "I may have to give a little to get something."

"Aye." He agreed. "That's often how it works. What about the other thing?"

She gave him a questioning look, to which he raised an eyebrow and cocked his head in an unspoken, 'you know.' Understanding dawned on her face. "You mean the heir."

"Mmmph." He didn't like to think of it, much less talk about it.

"Nothing yet. Though it's not for lack of trying. And there's no need to dance around it. Anne asks me almost daily."

He felt equal parts sick and angry so much of their future depended on her having another man's child. How was he ever going to survive this? He wanted her to have a child, because maybe then James would let her go, but the thought of her in his brother's arms left him simmering with rage.

They were coming close to the forest which separated the lawns of the great house from the guest and caretaker's cottages. The forest spread in a wedge down to the river. It was the forest he and James had played in as boys.

Sarah must have been thinking about that as well. She stopped and looked at the trees. "Show me the ruins."

"I dinna think it's a good idea." His brain buzzed with all the reasons why it was a bad idea to take her there. The ruins were crumbling the last time he'd seen them and that was years ago. Any number of things could happen to her while walking off the path into the woods, to say nothing of the temptation of being alone with her in the quiet of the forest away from the world.

"Come on." She gave him a pleasing look. "I've heard so many stories about you boys playing at the ruins. I want to see them."

The mischief he saw in her expression was hard to resist. He shook his head no. She gave him a taunting look. "You're not afraid, are you?"

She took a step backward off the path, and he followed her. She pulled at him like gravity. Another couple of steps and she was behind the tree line. Against his better judgement, he followed her into the forest.

CHAPTER THIRTY-SIX

Sarah looked up and up at the stone wall looming over them. The forest was doing its best to reclaim the ruins. There were tree roots twisting and creeping across the fallen stones, more stones the size of a person's head littered the forest floor. Only a couple of walls still stood, but they stretched into the upper branches of the trees.

"I dinna think any of the forest was here when they built it. It would have commanded a view of the river and the land on the English side." Dermot said. Since they left the path, he'd been doing his best impression of a tour guide telling her about the history of the area's border skirmishes all while keeping a polite distance between them. She would find it sweet if it weren't so sad.

She pointed to the wall in front of her. "Is this where you saved James's life when you were twelve?"

He cleared his throat awkwardly. "On the other side. There's a partially collapsed wall. We used to climb on it."

Sarah skirted around the outer wall to view what was once the inside of the tower. One wall was entirely missing, and another had collapsed enough she could almost imagine little Dermot and little James climbing the tumbled stone raising stick-swords above their heads and shouting war cries. Behind her, Dermot came around the wall into the inner part of the tower.

She spun in a slow circle looking up at the walls. "Let me guess. James was always the king, and you were his knight."

He gave her that half-smile she loved so much. "We traded off. Although to be fair, James was king a bit more often than I was. He always said he needed the practice." His thoughts turned inward. "It wasn't until we were older that I understood what he meant."

Sarah stepped up onto a large stone. Dermot watched her feet looking slightly alarmed, which she thought was funny. She liked that he was worried. "How old were you when he told you that you were meant to be James's second or whatever you want to call it?"

He thought about it as he came closer. She saw him battling the urge to offer her a hand down from the rock she stood on, but he was reluctant to touch her. It reminded her of the tension between them when they'd first met, and he had convinced himself she wasn't for him. A part of her missed those days when she could tease him and tempt him. She wanted so badly to flirt and tease, but she was sure it would hurt them both in the end.

"It's hard to say," His hand fidgeted at his side. "Walter started grooming me for the role when I was twelve or thirteen. He would visit me at school and tell me about the Stuarts and the Sinclairs and how our families were tied together. Looking back now, it sickens me how he was always making me into this..." He waved a hand as if trying to think of the word. "Appendage when all along he knew I was his son."

Sarah hopped down from the stone and went to him. "Don't." She wanted to touch him, to put her arms around him. But she kept her hands to herself and settled for standing as close to him as she dared and meeting his eyes. "You are the best man I know in spite of him, in spite of all of them."

His fists clenched and unclenched at his sides. His desire to touch her was a tangible thing between them, the same desire fizzed along her skin like static electricity. They were never going to get past the pull they had on each other.

"God, I've missed ye." He breathed; focused on the temptation of her lips.

"You have no idea. I've wanted to talk to you a thousand times a day. You're always there. Your voice is a constant whisper in my brain."

"I canna see ye without itching to touch ye, and when I dinna see ye it's like the world has gone a dull gray." He inched closer. "I ken we said we'd wait until ye gave him an heir, but this is killing me."

"It's killing me too. I watch for the merest glimpse of you when he gets home. These last couple of weeks have been torture."

"I had to stay away. I couldna stand seeing ye and knowing I have as much right to be with ye as he does." He said through gritted teeth.

"I've been watching you." She confessed. She lifted a hand to him, and he leaned back, shying away from her. "I was worried, so I spied on you with my gift. I had to see if you were okay."

"It's alright." He leaned closer. There was barely an inch of air between his chest and her hand. "Ye do what ye have to do."

She wasn't sure if he was giving her a pass for using her gift or permission to touch him. But she would take them both.

She let her fingers bend forward until the tips touched him. He inhaled deeply. Sarah flattened her hand against his muscled chest and savored the feel of him. She stepped closer and leaned her ear against his sternum. She needed to hear his heart beating, a reminder of the time they'd had before the matching ceremony before all the madness. Those nights when she'd slept draped across him listening to the proof he was alive, and he was hers.

His chest heaved against her as she pressed herself to him. She could feel him fighting the urge to put his arms around her. Even after all they'd been through, all that had been taken from them, he didn't want to betray James. But how many other chances would they get to steal a moment together?

Sarah wrapped her arms around his waist, spreading her hands across his back and pulling him closer. He stood frozen and Sarah began to doubt herself. Then she felt it, the moment his control broke. His hands seized her arms and pushed her back. James pushing her against the door flashed in her mind, but instead of anger, there was only desire in Dermot's eyes. She barely had time to register that before his lips came crashing down on hers. He walked her backwards, but she tripped on a stone, falling. He caught her and, in an instant, she was off her feet and in his arms.

He carried her away from the ruins where the scattered stones created hazards. Walking around the remaining walls of the tower and down a low rise toward the river. He stopped beside an overgrown mound and set Sarah on her feet.

Vines covered the entrance, and Dermot pulled them back to reveal an opening. He held out a hand to her. The look on his face said everything. He knew what he was asking her. He knew what he was doing. It was a risk, a betrayal for both of them, but it wouldn't stop him anymore. Sarah had to make the same decision. Could she betray James, or had she already been betraying Dermot? What were marriage vows when they were coerced? When had she had a choice in any of this? She grabbed onto his hand and the only choice that mattered anymore, the choice to love this man.

He drew her into the dark chamber. They were surrounded by stone. She couldn't tell if it was placed there by people or carved out of the ground. The roof of the chamber was a combination of old timber joists, tree roots and moss with a few beams of dappled sunshine making it through to partially illuminate the chamber. In the center was a large rectangular stone about waist height.

Before she had a chance to speak, Dermot speared his fingers into her hair at the nape of her neck and pulled her to him. Where their kiss before had been full of pent-up desire and urgency, this one they savored, exploring every inch of their connection. Tongues dueled, hands explored, and breath was exchanged. He lifted her and set her on the stone without breaking contact.

They both pulled her skirt up as if they were in a race to see how fast he could get himself inside her. Sarah leaned back like a sacrifice on a stone altar as Dermot freed himself. In one swift stroke, he was home.

Sarah relished the familiar fullness of him. She had missed this. She needed this. He pulled her close and set a driving rhythm, one as familiar to her as her own heartbeat. She wrapped her arm around his shoulder and hung on.

A sound like a gasp came from behind Dermot. Sarah froze thinking they'd been caught. Dermot was lost to anything around them, lost in her. Sarah tried to look over his shoulder, but there was no one in the entrance to the chamber. Dermot shifted his angle of attack and hit a spot deep inside her, sending her spiraling toward ecstasy. She leaned back basking in the sensation.

Then Sarah saw her. Through half-closed lids she caught a glimpse of herself. It wasn't a reflection. It was her, a look of utter shock on her face. Then it registered what she was seeing. Behind the other Sarah, she didn't see the walls of the chamber. She saw trees, and a couple of moss-covered stones, and moonlight. She remembered the vision she'd seen over a year ago that night on Grandfather Mountain. The vision her mother had shown her of herself and a man making love on a stone exactly like the one under her.

Sarah's gaze shifted to Dermot, the man she loved, the one who had found her that night after her mother's vision had broken her, the man who had kissed her the very next night. Maybe her vision hadn't been a warning so much as preparation. Dermot's rhythm picked up, and his breaths came shorter. All thought about her vision, or her mother stopped, and Sarah's attention focused on him and the inch of flesh inside her that he touched now with every thrust. In a few more strokes, Sarah felt herself come apart as he spilled himself inside her. She was overcome with the rightness of what they'd done.

***

He never wanted to let her go again, and he knew he would have to. Resting his head against her breast, he tried to catch his breath. He wished they could go to the river and escape in a coracle like Teneu, Saint Mungo's mother. They'd drift away in each other's arms and make a life wherever they landed.

He licked the salt from her skin, imprinting her taste in his mind. Who knew when they'd be together like this again, if they'd be together like this again. He was greedy and selfish, taking her on a cold stone. He was ashamed he hadn't even spared a thought for her comfort.

Straightening, he said. "I'm sorry, I—"

"Do not dare apologize for that." She crooned, stretching herself luxuriously across the stone. "That was amazing."

He chuckled and felt his cheeks turning red. "Ye're the only woman I've ever met who wouldna complain about being taken on a cold stone in an ancient ruin."

She sat forward and pushed her skirt down over her knees. She gave him a sassy smile. "Are you kidding? You've met my people. Ancient ruins are our natural habitat."

This time he laughed out loud. He'd missed her humor. For a second, he forgot who they were. He forgot people waited for them; they would likely send a search party if they didn't arrive at the big house soon. He only knew he loved her.

"What is this place?" She asked, hopping down from the stone.

He set about putting himself to rights. "It's a bit like a souterrain I suppose. I've no idea how long it's been here, but the roots suggest longer than the tower. I found it when I was a kid."

"It's not a tomb, is it? She looked around checking all the shadowed spots as if she might find bones.

He reached for her hand. "Believe me, if there were any bones in here, I'd have found them back then. I had to dig a lot of brush and muck out of here."

"Did you and James play here?" She asked, running a curious hand over the surface of the stone. There was a faint semicircular indentation making it look a little like a seat. "This almost looks like…" She shook her head as if rejecting the thought that crossed her mind.

"What?"

"Nothing, it reminded me of a legend from my people about a giant's footprint being chipped away until there was nothing left but a toe print." She seemed to lose herself in thought, her gaze fixed on the stone. "It's silly. There's no evidence for that."

"We'd better get back before Fleming calls the cavalry."

"Right." She followed him out the door.

"In answer to yer question, no I never told him about it." He pulled the greenery back in front of the opening. "I've always kept it to myself."

CHAPTER THIRTY-SEVEN

"You're looking rather bright and cheerful." Jujhar said with surprise when he arrived for work the morning after she returned to Edinburgh. "Did you get Ms. Sinclair settled in alright?"

"Eventually." Seonag was comfortable in the guest cottage. Over the past three days, she and the nurses had established a comfortable routine with walks around the grounds, naps, and daily visits from Henry. Seonag seemed at peace in her new home and with the people who were caring for her. "It was touch and go for the first couple of days, but I think she'll be comfortable there."

"I understand Mr. Stuart has also taken up residence there." Jujhar took his agenda from his satchel.

"He has. I get the impression he is ready for a quiet life in the country." Seeing to Seonag's needs firsthand while Dermot worked in the city was Henry's new mission. She appreciated that. Although, she couldn't help feeling sad because he had waited until she was too sick to recognize him to do it. Sarah worried she and Dermot would get caught in a similar triangle with her married to James and Dermot waiting until she could be free. "I was surprised to find Lady Anne still here when I got back. I thought she would have gone back to France or Spain or anywhere else."

"Thought or wished?" He asked softly, giving her an arch look.

Sarah let her head wobble back and forth as if to say, 'six of one, half a dozen of another'. "She hasn't been bothering you, has she?"

"Only with daily inquiries about your schedule." He joined her on the couch to discuss their plans for the rest of the week.

"I suppose we'll have to tolerate her for the time being." Sarah mused. They planned meetings and analyzed charity reports. They discussed next steps for the foundation Sarah wanted to start in support of the families of oil workers.

When they had finished reviewing the status of their projects, Jujhar set aside his agenda and spoke softly. "I have an answer for you about the other task you gave me."

"Ah." Sarah braced herself. She had a feeling she knew what was coming. "Can you tell me while I put on my makeup?"

"Sure." He took a box roughly the size of the one Cardell had given her from his satchel.

Sarah led Jujhar to the bathroom and turned on the tap before taking a seat with her back to her makeup mirror.

Jujhar set the box on the vanity table. and leaned against the wall. "Yes, it is a perfume, but there is another element to it. It's a fascinating concoction really."

Sarah gave him a warning look. "Maybe if you're not the target."

"It works on multiple levels like a perfume should. Smell is the sense most connected to our memories. The scents that remind you of home are meant to put you at ease."

"That part isn't the problem. I kind of like it." Sarah acknowledged.

"Yes, but this has an amplifier of sorts with additional calming effects, almost like an anti-anxiety drug."

Goosebumps started to rise on her arms. "Right. I'm not happy about that, but it seems pretty innocuous."

"There is more." He paused, thinking. "Have you ever heard of witch's salve or floating salve?"

Sarah tried to remember. Despite Granny's best efforts, folk remedies weren't really her area of expertise. "Was it the salve European witches were supposed to have used to fly to commune with the devil?" She didn't believe any of that. "Haven't we all decided the witch scares were a collective hysteria caused by a fungus in wheat?"

"To some extent, yes. But as you know, there is usually some seed of truth, and there were people who practiced herbal remedies, and some who made concoctions to do other things. Witch's salve was a hallucinogenic ointment which made users feel like they were flying. ``

"Okay." She didn't like where this was going.

"This perfume uses some of those same herbs, in the nightshade family. They can be absorbed through the skin. It can cause hallucinations. And combined as they are here," He tilted his head toward the box. "With a powerful aphrodisiac, they could potentially make your mind see the person you desire most."

Sarah went from goosebumps on her arms to every inch of her skin tingling with fury. "Let me get this straight. I have been tricked for weeks into applying a mind-altering substance to my skin."

Jujhar sighed. His dark eyes held hers. "That certainly seems to be the case."

"Anything else in there I should know about?" She watched the box as if it were a bomb.

"I think psychoactive scents, topical hallucinogens, and aphrodisiacs are enough." He said. "Mr. Green recognized the maker straight away."

"I'll bet he did." She muttered.

"It seems the proprietor of Parfumerie Cardell is his counterpart on the continent." Jujhar gave her a sheepish smile.

"Of course, he is." Sarah thought back to Cardell's shop and the glass vessels and instruments which looked so much like the ones she'd seen in Lyall Green's work room, and Cardell's marvelous greenhouses supporting climates that hardly seemed possible in the south of France. She shook her head. "How did I not see it before? Wait. Counterpart?"

Jujhar nodded. "There are watchers, like Green, in strategic locations around the world; here, the continent, a couple in North America. I have learned that one of my gurus in India is one. That's where my curiosity about your people started."

"Do they talk to each other?" Sarah wasn't happy about the prospect of a cabal of old wizards plotting her life out for her. "So, did Green put him up to this?"

"He says not." Jujhar appeared to believe that. "He thinks Cardell must have realized that you hadn't consummated the marriage yet and thought he would help things along."

"Heaven save us from busybody wizards. I should know by now I can never let my guard down." She tsked with disgust. "Will you have my personal shopper line up some commercial fragrances for me to choose from? Something floral, but not cloying."

He gave her a side-eyed look. "So, you won't continue using Cardell's perfume? There is some left in there, and I'm sure we could make more."

"Why on earth would I?"

"Hear me out." He held out a hand to hold off her objections. "You are in a difficult position, married to someone you did not choose. It's important you at least appear to be in love, and this marriage works long enough to produce an heir. The potion might make that easier to tolerate going forward."

She pressed her lips together. "You have no idea what I've been going through. I went to bed every night for weeks thinking it was Dermot reaching for me in the dark, making love to me, only to wake up and find myself in bed with James. I knew." Her voice cracked and she shook her head in disbelief. "My brain knew I was with James, but I felt like my body was out of my control. Even though I knew it wasn't really Dermot, I couldn't stop myself. I thought I was losing my mind."

"I can appreciate how disorienting that must be, but now you know what to expect. You're in control. You can choose when to use it and when not to. It's something you should consider." He left her to think.

Sarah turned the tap off and sank back down onto the stool, staring at the box on the table. Her mind reeled through the implications of everything he'd said. Jujhar had a point. She could use this to make things with James easier. Maybe they could get back some of the closeness they'd had before he'd learned about her gift. But at what cost? She wasn't sure she could handle the dissonance of her body doing one thing while her brain was repelled and told her something else.

She and James had reached an uneasy truce. She could tell he was still disappointed she'd kept her gift from him, and she was disappointed in him for asking her to use her gift in ways she wasn't comfortable with. But there was an alternating current of suspicion and longing between them. They had been a team, and they had both done things to damage that. But this, this deception was beyond anything she could have expected.

She was tired of getting manipulated. Tired of being under the thumb of people who didn't deserve her gift. It was time she took back some control. She was the chosen one after all. They needed her. It was time she acted like it. It was time she got something good out of it.

***

The elevator dinged and the door slid open. Sarah balanced on the two-inch heels she was coming to think of as her war boots. She'd spent the time since Jujhar had left her getting madder by the minute. The more she thought about the perfume manipulation, the angrier she got. James had planned the trip to Aix en Provence. He had taken her to Cardell's shop. He had gushed about how rare and coveted Cardell's bespoke perfumes were. The more she thought about it the more she wanted answers.

So, she had put herself together like a god damned princess in her sharpest suit. She pinned an Hermes scarf to her lapel with a Stuart crest brooch and slipped into her war boots. She walked off the elevator in the early afternoon looking like she ate idiots for breakfast, and she was still hungry.

The click of her heels resounded on the marble floors of the executive suite. Fleming strode in beside her, scanning the room. Sarah went straight for James's office. Miss Lennox rose to intercept her, but Sarah didn't break stride. Fleming stepped between them, stopping Miss Lennox from getting in Sarah's way. Sarah grabbed the knob and pushed the door open without even the ghost of a knock.

James was sitting at his desk with Dermot looking over his shoulder. She supposed James was showing Dermot the business as they had talked about. But that was going to have to wait. Miss Lennox bustled in behind Sarah making excuses for the intrusion, but Sarah paid her no mind. "Everybody out."

"My love?" James's years of poker face conditioning kept him from showing too much surprise.

"We need to talk, and we don't need an audience." Sarah stood several feet in front of his desk. She didn't even look at Dermot. She had to handle this herself.

James must have gotten the message because he turned to Miss Lennox and said. "Leave us."

Miss Lennox and Dermot left, closing the door softly behind them.

Sarah removed the perfume bottle from her purse and planted it in the center of his desk with a thunk. Her voice was knife-sharp when she asked. "Did you know?"

"Know what?" James looked back and forth between Sarah and the bottle in confusion.

Sarah wished Ruaraidh or Oona were there to tell her if he was lying. He seemed not to know what she was asking, but maybe he was a better liar than she thought. "Did you know it's a drug?"

"A drug?"

"An anti-anxiety drug, mixed with a hallucinogen and an aphrodisiac. It's basically a love potion." He looked at Sarah as if she'd lost her mind. He turned his attention to the bottle and sighed. "I told Cardell you were grieving; that your father had just died, and I thought you needed something to help you through your grief. I thought a custom perfume would be a thoughtful gift. I did not ask for a love potion or any kind of aid. That's a ridiculous notion. This isn't a fairy tale."

She cocked her head at him, her eyes shooting daggers. "Really? Rags to riches princess from magical tribe marries stealth prince to help him reclaim throne and birth the second coming of...whatever? Sure, sounds like a fairy tale to me. You draw the line at love potions?"

He walked around the desk to stand in front of her. Sarah resisted the urge to step back. She refused to be scared. "I didn't know. Since you agreed to marry me, I have only been honest with you. Can you say the same?"

Sarah breathed deeply. She believed him, but she wasn't wrong to keep her gift from the Stuarts. Some of her fury faded. "You know damned well why I didn't tell you about my ability."

"I do." He folded his arms across his chest. "I also know there is a reason your people preserved that ability, and there is a reason we were meant to be together."

She considered it. "I can't believe my people, some of whom lived rough for centuries, would preserve this gift to aid something that hurts the environment."

"What other reason is there?" James asked.

Sarah huffed. "You tell me you love me, and want me to be the mother of your child, and you don't know what value I bring to the table? This is why I didn't want to tell you. Even you, though you claim to care about me, can only see my gift now, only what I can do for you. You don't see the person you want to raise your child, share your life, share the responsibility of leadership with. All you see now, is what I can do for you."

He looked properly guilty, and started to speak, but Sarah cut him off. "I'll do it, but I have conditions."

He was shocked. He blinked several times trying to process what she said. "I expected you would."

"I don't think you're going to like them." She warned.

"Tell me and we'll see."

"I will help you find new places to drill if I can. But I want A.P. to establish a new division for renewable energy."

He took a step closer. "I have to admit that is not the kind of thing I was expecting you to ask for." His eyebrows drew together. "It's a big investment."

"You said so yourself, my gift can save you millions in research and development. Apply the savings to researching renewables. You know I've been ambivalent about how A.P. makes its money. Oil is finite, and it's damaging the planet. A.P. should be setting itself up for a future that doesn't include oil." Sarah's confidence in her argument grew as she spoke. If she was going to be pressured into helping A.P. She could at least do some good.

James watched her, speculation written on his face. "We'd have to change the name.

"Alba Energy sounds good to me." She had thought of the name on the drive over. She'd wanted to know James's role in the poisoning before she committed to doing anything for Alba Petroleum. But if she was going to get roped into helping them find oil, she was going to get something good out of it.

"Alba Energy." He repeated, thinking. "I like it."

"If we roll it out the right way, we can ride the wave of good press we got after Aberdeen."

"And it will appease the environmentalists." She could see him gaming out all the different ways a shift in focus would play out for the company and for them.

"I'm not merely looking for appeasement here." Sarah warned. "Alba Energy can be on the leading edge of change."

"Of course." James agreed. He eyed her approvingly. "This is very strategic thinking. Now we need to prove a business case for it."

"I'll leave that up to you."

James went to the door and opened it. "Would you get my uncle and Miss Banks? I have something I would like to discuss with them."

Closing the door again, he came to stand in front of Sarah. He was close enough she had to tip her head back. He ran his hands down her arms in an affectionate gesture. It was something he'd done a hundred times in the last few weeks, but without the perfume, it felt wrong. She tried not to show her reluctance. "I'm glad you came to me about the perfume, instead of assuming I was involved. I don't like thinking you're suspicious of me, but I can't blame you."

"I didn't want to believe it." As difficult as their relationship had gotten lately, she still liked James. If he had been in on the perfume deception, it would have meant she had grossly misjudged him, and she hadn't made as much progress with him as she thought.

"Darling, I…" He searched for the words. "I don't want to believe that what we have is dependent on some potion, or what you can do for the business. That's not what I want for us."

"I don't want that either." She needed him to care for her, and maybe even love her enough to eventually let her go. She feared if she cut the relationship off now, it would drive him right back into Walter's clutches. For the time being, they were going to have to go on as they had been before her gift and the perfume were exposed.

He sighed, relief evident on his face. "I'm sorry I pressured you to use your gift so soon after offering Tweedholm to Seonag. I truly didn't realize how the timing made it look."

She silently acknowledged his apology, cringing as she said. "I'm sorry I accused you of trying to bewitch me."

James laughed. He tipped her face up to his. "Ah, well. I'm afraid you bewitched me first."

He gave her a lingering kiss. Neither of them heard the door open, but they were interrupted when a throat was cleared behind them. Sarah glanced over her shoulder to see Dermot in the doorway looking disgruntled. "Himself is here."

James stepped away from her. Sarah dabbed a finger along the edge of her lips hoping her lipstick wasn't too smudged before facing the room.

CHAPTER THIRTY-EIGHT

Dermot ushered Walter Stuart into James's office and took his customary place by the door. He and James had decided to keep his new training in the company operations secret from Walter for the moment. So, Dermot was careful not to show how closely he was observing the conversation. Sarah had her back to them, setting herself to rights.

"You wanted to see me?" Walter was clearly annoyed at being summoned like an employee, which was after all what he was.

James leaned back on the desk as if perfectly comfortable. "Yes, you'll be happy to know Sarah has agreed to use her gift to help us find oil."

"That's it. Only to find oil?" Walter said. He carefully didn't look at Sarah while asking this.

"Yes." James's tone was flat. "I've decided your other proposal is a non-starter. We cannot be seen to be doing anything that might be considered illegal."

Dermot assumed the 'other proposal' James was talking about was Walter's idea of using Sarah's gift for espionage.

"Considered by whom?" Who will even know about it but us?" Walter scoffed.

James leveled an imperious look at him. "I would. I've spoken to you before about this. We are done with that sort of scheming. Alba Petroleum will not involve itself in illegality. My decision is final."

"It's a curious line to draw, son, when you've taken full advantage of it before." Walter puffed up his chest and looked down his nose at everyone else in the room.

"It is the line I am drawing now." James bit out.

"You're drawing it, or she is?" Walter tilted his head toward Sarah. His tone was as cool as ever. "I didn't think you were one to be led around by your cock."

The energy in the room was suddenly electric. Sarah arched an eyebrow but didn't speak up. James's eyes shot pure blue flames at Walter, and Dermot himself burned with rage at the old man's offensive comment.

"I'll remind you; Lady Caledon is my wife." James placed all the emphasis on her title. "A wife you wanted for me. You yourself said you believe her gift is essential to our cause. But she is a person whose moral code is important to her, as is mine to me. Sarah and I are united on this."

That hadn't been what Sarah told Dermot at Tweedholm, but he was glad James was standing with her on her refusal to break the law.

A knock at the door interrupted the tension he could have cut with a knife.

"Come." James barked.

Miss Lennox leaned into the room. "Miss Banks is here."

"Please send her in." James said. Everyone in the room took a breath, trying to ease the building tension.

Dermot caught Sarah's eye, and a ghost of a smile touched her lips. He could almost hear her say, 'small victories.'

Felicia strode into the room, a portfolio in her hand and her usual unflappable confidence. "Afternoon everyone. What's this about?"

"Miss Banks." James waved an arm at the small table in the corner. "Why don't we all sit at the conference table. There's an idea I would like us to game out together."

Felicia, Sarah, James, and Walter all sat at the round conference table. Dermot kept his place by the door, enjoying his fly on the wall status for once. If anyone objected to him being in the room, they never voiced it.

James laid out the idea of establishing a renewable energy division and changing the company's name to reflect that. Felicia eagerly jumped on the idea. She made some great points about how it could improve the company's image by showing both a consciousness of their impact on the environment and looking to the future as a smart business strategy.

Walter was not enthusiastic. He acknowledged it would be good public relations to show they at least heard the environmentalists. "This could certainly help the stock price recover from the hit it took after the rig explosion."

"It definitely can't hurt." Felicia agreed. "We can spin it to look more proactive than reactive."

"But I'm not sure we're ready for a whole division, or to change the name of the company." Walter continued as if Felicia hadn't spoken. "It's one thing to be willing to try other energy sources, but I think caving to environmentalists will make us look weak."

James shook his head. "I think it will make us look like good corporate citizens. Clinging to the past when we know our business is based on a finite resource makes us look weak. And as Miss Banks said, it looks proactive."

"Of course, all of this will need to be brought to the board. This is too big a decision to be made unilaterally." Walter leaned back and dropped his pen onto his portfolio as if to mark the end of discussion.

"Of course." James agreed. "A new division would obviously need their approval, but I see no reason why R. and D. can't get started researching now."

"This is good thinking, sir." Felicia grinned at him.

"Actually, it was Sarah's idea." James reached over to take Sarah's hand, giving her an approving look.

Dermot didn't miss the flash of disdain crossing over Walter's face only to be replaced with a pasted-on smile. "Lady Caledon's beauty is only surpassed by her intelligence."

Sarah cocked her head at him. Her accent was thick as treacle when she said. "Well, bless your heart. Aren't you sweet?"

Once Walter and Felicia cleared out, James finally looked Dermot's way. "What do you think?"

Dermot unbuttoned his jacket and took a seat at the table. "I think ye'll have to watch him. His support is tepid at best. He could be whispering poison in the ear of some board members, and if ye dinna convince them first, this idea might be dead before it ever makes it to a board meeting."

"You're probably right." James said. "We'll have to start pitching the idea to board members without him. Make sure they know we're serious."

"Telling him it was my idea might have been a bit like waving a red cape in front of a bull." Sarah leaned back in her chair relaxing for the first time since she'd arrived there.

"Maybe it was, but it was also strategic." James reached for her hand again and leaned close, catching her gaze. "I want him and everyone on the board to know we are a team and we're united. Your guidance was invaluable in Aberdeen. You're not the window dressing some people think you are, and I want it to be clear to everyone."

Sarah took in a deep breath. "What about Dermot? I thought he was going to be taking on a bigger role too."

"I am." He said. "But we're keeping that quiet for now."

"It enables Dermot to sit in on meetings without having to explain his presence or why the change." James explained.

"I'll start working board members on the new division idea, maybe we should plan some dinners at the house so we can convince them together." James suggested to Sarah. He stood, returning to his desk.

Dermot asked following James to the desk. "Have ye found out any more about the Miss Lennox issue I mentioned a few weeks ago?"

"Mmm." James pressed his lips together and exhaled before answering. He kept his voice low. "It seems she worked as Walter's assistant for a few months before I came on board, and she was assigned to me."

"So, she could be reporting yer movements to him." Dermot leaned closer to listen and matched James's tone.

"I certainly hope not." James muttered. "She knows my every move. It will be hard to set up meetings with board members without her knowing."

"Also, your mother is still at the house. She might tell Walter about any meetings we have with board members." Sarah threw another wrench in their plans.

James sighed in frustration. "He really does seem to have a finger in every pie. I'll find a way to deal with my mother."

"I can talk to Lyall Green. He might be able to help connect with other board members without going through Miss Lennox." Dermot suggested. He didn't relish asking his grandfather for help, but he expected the old wizard would like their plan.

James looked at him sharply. "Is it true, he's your grandfather?"

"Aye." He nodded. "My mother lived with him for a short time after her mother died. I only found out when we were at Taigh na Damh."

"Do you think he'll help us?" Sarah asked.

"It's hard to tell." Dermot remembered how his grandfather had refused to help them get away before the wedding. "He generally prefers not to intervene, but as you know there are times when he'll step in. It's difficult to predict."

"It's worth asking. At least we know he's not one of Walter's minions." Glancing at his watch, James rose effectively ended the conversation. "We can use all the help we can get."

A quick knock at the door preceded Miss Lennox coming in to remind James of an appointment.

Dermot returned to his place by the door, blending in with the background. He watched as Miss Lennox stepped forward to hand James a file. "They're waiting in the conference room."

"Thank you." James took the file and gathered a notepad and pen.

Miss Lennox's eyes lingered on him. As she turned to leave the office, her attention skimmed over Sarah with a look of such profound sadness it caught Dermot's attention, making him wonder what would cause it. He looked over at James who seemed oblivious.

***

Later that afternoon, Dermot went to talk with Green about gathering support from other board members. James found himself alone sitting at his desk, completely unable to focus on work. He couldn't stop thinking about Sarah's accusation. She had believed him capable of drugging her. Despite his efforts to build a relationship with her, she would have believed the worst of him.

He had told Walter countless times how important Sarah's consent was to him, but she thought he was capable of drugging her. He couldn't blame her. She'd been betrayed by so many people in her life. Her own mother had tried to drown her. Her grandmother had failed to warn her about the prophecy. They'd sent Dermot to spy on her in the guise of being a colleague. He had compounded her doubts with his show of temper. He was beginning to see how much Walter's methods of manipulation had tainted his view of things, and the people around them.

The perfume bottle still sat on his desk; the swirling blown glass was a work of art in itself. The golden liquid made him wonder about its effects. What had she said was in there? Anti-anxiety, and a hallucinogen. How had she known that?

He considered asking one of their laboratories to analyze it. He picked up the bottle and pulled out the stopper, sniffing.

It smelled much as he remembered; floral, and earthy, slightly smokey. But he didn't smell or feel anything unusual. He thought back to the time when Sarah had been wearing it regularly. He had thought she was reaching some kind of peace with the death of her father, but was she? Was it a reaction to the perfume?

Perhaps the drugs only affected the wearer. He tilted the bottle, so the remaining perfume touched the stopper. Then he drew it out again and applied a few drops to his wrist and neck. He might smell a bit feminine, but he needed to satisfy his curiosity. He waited for some effect but felt nothing. He went back to work thinking there must be something he was missing. Maybe it needed to build up over time.

Half an hour later, he'd read the same paragraph four times and still couldn't remember what it said. His head was throbbing. He closed the blinds and lowered the lights in his office. He would rest his eyes for a few minutes before getting back to it.

"Here, I brought you some water. Can I get you something for your head?" Sarah said. A grin spread over his face. He could never mistake that accent.

"I thought you went home." He'd been sure she had.

"Why would I go home? You're still here." Her drawl was music to his ears. He heard her open the medicine cabinet in his bathroom. "Here."

He opened his eyes to see her hand near his shoulder holding the pills. She stood behind his chair. He held out his palm and she dropped the pills into it. With his other hand he caught hers and pulled it to his lips. "Thank you, my love."

"Sir?" Sir? When had she ever called him sir? She pulled her hand away.

James turned around to find Miss Lennox behind him looking thoroughly shocked. Good God, he'd kissed her hand. "Miss Lennox."

"Sir." She blinked at him clearly confused.

"Please forgive me." He bowed his head, shocked himself by his mistake. He had sworn it was Sarah's voice he heard. "I mistook you for my wife for a moment."

"Of course." A thoroughly flustered Miss Lennox took several steps back. "I'll just…" She said nothing else, but quickly left the room as if the devil himself was on her heels.

How had he made such a mistake? They sounded nothing alike. But he'd been sure it was Sarah's voice he'd heard. He rested his sore head in this hand. He'd never made such a mistake before, even when he was exhausted, or drunk.

He spied the perfume bottle on his desk. Was this the effect of the hallucinogen? If it was, he could see why Sarah was so furious. It was incredibly disorienting. And if she'd been with him, he thought he knew exactly who she'd seen in her hallucinations. Suddenly he felt as betrayed as she did.

That night he wasted no time in speaking to his mother. She came into the study dressed for dinner. "Conley said you wanted to see me."

"Thank you, mother. Have a seat." He motioned to the sofa and took a seat beside her. He and his mother had spoken very little since learning of her deception. They maintained a strict cordiality, but they never talked about anything of consequence and certainly nothing about their relationship. He didn't particularly want to talk to her now, but this had to be done.

"Darling, I'm so glad. I've been wanting to talk with you about Sarah." She leaned closet and lowered her voice. "I'm worried about her."

"So am I. Although, I suspect we are worried for different reasons. Why don't you go first?"

"I fear she might be putting a foot wrong with some of the ladies at the art museum. I've asked her several times to meet with them about her attending our fundraising luncheon, and she declined the invitation. It's such an exclusive event. No one has ever declined. And she declined to donate to the garden society. I know these things seem minor, but she is offending some of the leading ladies in Edinburgh society. Ladies whose alliances can help you."

James eyed his mother in consternation. "Yes, but she has been working on establishing a foundation to help the families of injured workers and cancer patients. She simply prefers a different type of charity."

Disdain flashed across her face before she rearranged it to a look of conciliation. "I understand. But these charities aren't about helping people. They're about networking with the wives of other executives and politicians. Wives can change their husbands' minds and plant the seeds for deals which will benefit you. It's what I've been doing for the last thirty years to put us all on the right path."

"That may be, mother, but Sarah sees a different path. We're never going to reclaim anything without the support of the people of Scotland. Sarah is working on making a difference for people."

His mother waved a dismissive hand. "Yes, it's all very Diana of her, but you saw how that turned out. Divorced, and everyone's reputations in tatters. More people would have stood by Diana if she'd only played the game the way the rest of us do."

'Good Lord' He thought. 'How antiquated she sounds.' Had he thought like this before he got to know Sarah? "Mother, Sarah is here for a reason, and I happen to think this shift is very valuable to us. I have no interest in trying to change that. I'm afraid the museum ladies will simply have to do without her at their luncheon."

"But, darling—" His mother wanted to say more, but he held up a hand to silence her.

"Speaking of getting Sarah, did you ask Monsieur Cardell to make that perfume for her?" He gave her a pointed look.

"Good lord, no." Her face showed the same disdain she had for her personal shopper or their chef. His mother might be more polite than most to the people who worked for her, but she wasn't going to be friends with them. "I hadn't spoken to Cardell in ages before he called to say he'd had you and Sarah over for dinner." He believed her.

"Alright. Now, I wanted to talk with you about your plans. Are you going to return to France or Spain?" He intentionally did not include staying in Edinburgh or at Tweedholm as options.

She looked confused. "I wasn't planning on going anywhere. Why would I?"

James cleared his throat. "Mother, Sarah and I are trying to settle in to married life, and to be honest we find that difficult to do with you here. Sarah still feels like a guest, rather than the lady of the house."

"Well, perhaps if she would take some interest in running the house she might feel more at home." Anne said sourly.

James gave her a warning look. He was not going to tolerate any disparagement of Sarah. "You know very well Conley and Ratcliff between them keep things running quite nicely without any input. Sarah needs her own space. And after everything, I think it might be a good idea for you to have your own as well." She opened her mouth to say something, but he silenced her with a look. "You have done wonderful things for the family and the company. Why not take some time to reflect on what you would like to do next?"

"I would like to stay here and see this through." Her perfectly shaped eyebrows drew together. "I have worked my entire life setting you up for success and helping the independence movement. I'm not going to step away when we're on the verge of success."

"Independence is still years away." James kept his tone even, and his argument rational. "You have worked tirelessly." And by worked he meant whisper campaigns and surreptitious alliances. "Take some time away before the final push. By then Sarah will have found her feet and you can both work together."

"We could work together now, if she would simply follow my lead." She pleaded.

"Mother, I'm not sure you've been paying attention to current events, but Sarah is perfectly capable of taking the lead. She won many hearts in Aberdeen, more I'd say than you ever have. Sarah can get people on our side." James said. "She's taught me more about leadership in the last few weeks than anyone has in years."

Anne looked affronted, as if she had never considered the possibility he could learn anything from Sarah. She opened her mouth to say something but closed it again like a fish gasping for water.

"We can have Conley make your travel arrangements. Would you like to go to the chateaux or the beach house?" He asked confident of his victory.

Her face fell. "I suppose I'll go to France."

"I'll have Conley arrange it and call Martine to tell her you're on your way." There. It hadn't been so hard, and Sarah would definitely appreciate having his mother out of the house.

CHAPTER THIRTY-NINE

After a week-long crash course in what oil looks like when it's underground and where she might be likely to find it, Sarah hoped she was ready to do some viewing. Her head was swimming with geological terms like anticline, stratigraphic, and Pinchout and what all of them looked like. She had also been practicing on her own trying to find other geological formations, inanimate objects, and things at greater and greater distances.

She was getting surprisingly adept at 'casting out' as her mother called it. Jujhar had become her support person whenever she did it. She had started thinking of him as a boxing trainer, getting her whatever she needed to keep going between rounds.

The small team of geologists who were working with her hadn't believed at first that she could do what they said she could. On course, they had been respectful with their doubts, saying things like, 'You'll have to pardon my skepticism, Lady Sarah, but we are scientists.' She couldn't blame them. If she hadn't seen the gifts of the three sisters at work, she wouldn't have believed any of them either.

So, she spent the better part of the first day with them demonstrating her ability in small ways; finding someone's keys hidden by another person on the team or looking at a picture of one of the geologist's children and telling him which school they went to and even what they were wearing that day. Some of the team still doubted her abilities, thinking it was some parlor trick. With each experiment they looked for an alternate explanation. She didn't blame them. It seemed impossible to her too. Others quickly got excited about further testing her gift and asking her questions about it.

Now, Sarah was ready to try to find something underwater. The day before, they had shown her a large rock with the Scottish Flag painted on it. Then they dropped the rock into the ocean past the firth. Sarah's job today was to find the rock. This was the biggest test so far of whether or not she would be able to find oil.

"Are you ready?" Dr. Seto, the head of the research team asked her. He was a Japanese man whose reserved demeanor which was occasionally broken by a warm smile. Of everyone on the research team, he had been the least skeptical of Sarah's ability, saying there were still things science could not explain, and he was confident one day they would find an explanation for this too.

"Ready as I'll ever be." Sarah tried to sound confident. She wore her most comfortable clothes to avoid any sensory distractions, and she had been doing her best to stay relaxed all morning.

"I'm sure this will go as well as all the other tests." He told her with a comforting nod.

"So am I." James's voice came from behind Dr. Seto.

The doctor shifted revealing James and Dermot standing in the hallway outside of the room she used for viewing. "What are you doing here?"

"You seemed nervous about this test at breakfast, and Dermot worries more than a mother hen. I thought we would come and lend our support." James beamed at her and leaned in to kiss her cheek. He had been extra attentive in the past week since she had confronted him about the perfume. Sarah thought he was trying to woo her all over again without Cardell's mind-altering concoction. It certainly helped things that he had asked his mother to leave. Lady Anne had packed her bags and tearfully departed for France promising Sarah that she would return if she needed any help. Sarah was sure Anne was the last person she would turn to.

"Mmhmm. It wouldn't be because you're interested in the result?" Sarah teased him.

James chuckled, "I have every confidence in you, my love."

Sarah looked past him to Dermot who watched with concern but kept silent. He gave a look of encouragement which helped her nerves more than anyone else's words could have.

"Okay." With a deep breath, she looked to Jujhar who stood close by. "Let's get this show on the road."

She went into the viewing room, which was designed to minimize distractions and maximize comfort. An overstuffed chair sat opposite the door. Sarah found she preferred to sit while casting out. She had done it sitting and lying down, but lying down made her anxious. The room was equipped with a camera so the team could watch her while she was using her gift. So far, all they had seen was Sarah seeming to meditate and coming back with information. Still, she was glad for the safety measure.

Sarah pulled her legs up into the chair to sit cross-legged as if she was about to meditate. Resting her hands in her lap and relaxing her shoulders, she inhaled deeply. When she exhaled, she felt lighter. All the practice she'd been doing over the last week had given her more confidence casting out and made the ritual more consistent. With a few deep breaths, she was out and floating. She focused her mind on the image of the rock, and soon she was being pulled toward the coast. She soared out over the water of the firth and followed it out to sea.

Soon she was over open water. Sarah could feel where the rock was below her, but she didn't see any landmarks above the water which might mark the spot. She couldn't exactly carry a compass or give them the coordinates for the spot where something was underwater. They had decided to use landmarks on the ocean floor and compare them to topographical maps.

Sarah took a deep breath and let the rock pull her down under the waves. This was unfamiliar territory. She reminded herself that she was not really underwater. This was her co-walker. Her actual body was back in a windowless room in an industrial park on the outskirts of Edinburgh. It was a strange feeling. She could see the water and the light filtering past the waves as she sank down. The silence under the water was pierced occasionally by the sound of shifting currents, bubbles, or the squeal of a dolphin.

What she didn't feel was the change in temperature and pressure as she sank deeper into the ocean. The water grew darker. She worried if it got much deeper, she would not be able to see the bottom to find the rock. Then she saw the ocean floor. Rippling sand littered with small rocks stretched out below her as far as she could see.

Eventually, Sarah was able to make out the Saltire of St. Andrew on the large rock below her. There it was. She had found it even in the ocean. The trouble was she couldn't see any identifying feature to use as a reference. She had proven to herself she could find an object deep in the water but had no way of proving it to anyone else. She looked around for a ridge, trench, or a shelf, but saw nothing. It was flat sandy bottom as far as she could see.

Deciding she had exhausted all possibilities; she began to pull her co-walker back to her body. Looking toward what she thought was the surface, she was surprised to see a large shadow drift between her and the little bit of light she could see.

***

Dermot could have heard a pin drop in the room as they all directed their attention to the small TV screen showing Sarah sitting silently.

"Is this how it always is?" James asked.

"Usually, yes." Dr. Seto said. "She's quite remarkable. She goes quiet and then a few moments later gives an answer."

"Amazing." James marveled. Dermot shook his head. James still didn't understand what she was doing. Dermot barely understood it, but he had been worried this morning when James told him they were doing an underwater test. That's why he'd insisted on coming to see it.

Dermot couldn't take his attention off the screen. Sarah sat, legs folded crossways, eyes closed, her face peaceful. The light in the room was dim. She could have been meditating, and in a sense, he supposed she was.

Jujhar waited outside the door to the room watching the monitor from about ten feet away. Dermot asked him. "Does she usually take this long?"

"No, but she's never gone this far or underwater before." Jujhar said.

Dermot watched the screen. Sarah tilted her head back as if looking up. Her breathing changed, breaths becoming shorter. Dermot tensed.

"Give her a moment." Dr. Seto held out a hand indicating they should wait. "This happens sometimes, she usually re-regulates and is fine."

Dermot watched as her shoulders tensed, but her breathing seemed to regulate. At least they couldn't see her chest rising and falling as dramatically anymore. Then he wondered if her chest was rising and falling at all.

He began to count the seconds watching Sarah's chest and shoulders looking for any sign of movement. When a full minute had passed, he said. "She's not breathing."

"No. She's fine." James said. "She calmed down."

"No!" Dermot barked. "She's not breathing!"

As he said it, Sarah collapsed against the back of the chair, her body twisting as if she were trying to swim to the surface, but her arms didn't move.

"Shit!" Jujhar moved at the same time Dermot did. He jerked the door open and plunged into the room, grabbing Sarah by the arms, and calling her name.

Dermot was right behind him. He pushed Jujhar out of the way and gave her a hard shake. "Sarah!"

She didn't respond. Her head lolled around with no support. Her arms hung like a ragdoll's. Dermot laid her on the floor and tilted her head back. He held her nose closed and breathed into her mouth several times. Jujhar knelt by her head calling her name.

"Come on, love." Dermot urged. He thought he heard the others shouting behind him, but his sole focus was on Sarah. He breathed into her mouth again.

Her chest rose on its own as she drew a ragged breath. Her eyes fluttered open and met his. He rested his forehead on hers. "Ye gave us a scare."

"Yeah. Me too." She rasped.

"Is she alright?" James asked at his shoulder. Dermot lifted his head. Giving Sarah one last relieved look, he backed away and leaned against the wall next to the doorway. The adrenaline draining from him leaving him exhausted.

James took his place kneeling beside Sarah. He pulled her into his arms. "God! I thought I'd lost you."

"You're not the only one." She muttered as James fussed over her.

"There is a medic on the way." One of the researchers said.

"Good." James replied before turning back toward Sarah. "What happened?"

"A whale." Sarah pushed up to a sitting position leaning back against the chair. She looked past James, her gaze meeting Dermot's "Startled me, and I had some sort of flashback which triggered a panic attack, I guess. It's like I...forgot I wasn't actually underwater. I couldn't breathe."

"We're going to have to find another way to do this." James pulled her close again. "You're entirely too precious to me to put you at risk this way."

She was at risk every day, even more so now that the research team knew about her gift. How long was it before someone offered one of them more money than A.P. paid and her gift wasn't a secret anymore. If James didn't want to put her at risk, he shouldn't have asked her to do this. Of course, Dermot wasn't going to make that point now in front of everyone. So, he held his tongue, but he would have to talk with his brother later.

Sarah pushed away from James and started to rise. "We're going to have to find another way anyway. I found the rock, but I couldn't find a landmark to help me tell you where or to verify it. It was flat all around, and the water is so dark down there."

"We had planned to compare her observations to a topographical map of the sea floor." Dr. Seto told James.

"That only works if there are things to observe." Sarah got to her feet and took a deep breath. James kept a grip on her elbow for balance. "There was nothing where I was. I didn't see anything above the surface to serve as a landmark either."

Dr. Seto turned to one of the other researchers. "Do we have the coordinates of the rock?"

The woman left to find the coordinates.

"Can we get out of this room? It's a little bit close in here." Sarah said.

"Of course." James ushered her out of the viewing room and into the larger laboratory.

Sarah found a stool next to the table and sat down. "Can I get some water?"

Jujhar was there in an instant with a bottle of water. Sarah thanked him before taking a sip.

The researcher returned with a topographical map which she spread out across the table. "The coordinates the crew of the boat gave us place the rock here." She pointed a thin finger to a small plateau off the coast.

"Well," Dr. Seto looked between Sarah and the map. "That explains why it seemed so flat to you."

"Even if it was on a ridge, how would we know which ridge?" Sarah pointed out. "It's not going to work with me doing this from a viewing room on land."

"The alternative is doing it from a boat or from the air." Dr. Seto said. "Then we could note the coordinates where you see deposits."

"If I can even see deposits." Sarah took another sip of water. "If this is what happens when I try to view underwater, what's going to happen when I try viewing under the ground?"

James had to pull the plug on this. It was putting her in danger. Dermot elbowed him and gave him a look which should have said. 'Aren't you going to stop this?'

Instead, James asked. "Would it work from the air? How would we do that?"

"We have scout planes, but I think in this case a helicopter would be most effective." The doctor said.

"The medic is here." Jujhar interrupted. He was followed by a man in Alba Petroleum shirt carrying a red bag.

The man took in James, Sarah and the crew and said. "What's all this then?"

"I fainted, and maybe had a panic attack." Sarah told him. "I'm sure I'm fine now."

"Let's make sure, shall we?" James admonished.

The medic examined Sarah. James and Seto stepped away to discuss something while Dermot and Jujhar stayed with her. Dermot kept an eye on James, his frustration growing. James was seriously considering sending her out in a helicopter to look for oil even after this.

CHAPTER FORTY

"Ye canna be serious about this." Dermot said when he
and James were finally alone. It had been a long ride back to
James's office and they had barely uttered a word. Once the
medic had cleared Sarah, she had told them they should go
back to work. She was going home to rest. "She could have
died today!"

"Do you think I don't know that?" James snapped.

"She almost drowned once before." Dermot spat.

"I know. She told me about her mother." James looked
down at his feet.

"She told ye about her mother almost drowning her when
she was a child and ye asked her to do that? Is it so important
that she use her gift to find oil?" Dermot fought to keep his
voice down. "Would ye really trade her for more money?"

"I wouldn't trade her for anything?" James took a step
toward him. "I love her."

"Not enough to keep her from reliving her childhood
trauma." Dermot barked.

"I didn't think it would be dangerous. In France she swam
every day. She would stay under the water for…" He trailed
off, thinking.

Dermot had known Sarah was grieving, but he hadn't
expected her grief to take such a self-destructive form. Had
she meant to drown? Was she trying to be closer to her
mother? Was she wishing Molly had been successful all those

years ago? He watched as what he thought might be the same questions flash across James's expression.

"If ye love her, ye should let her out." Dermot didn't back away from James. He wasn't sure if he meant the project or their marriage. He would let James interpret his meaning.

James's eyes met his and Dermot watched his internal debate. He watched the uncertainty solidify into a decision. "Her clean energy initiative depends on the success of this project. We're to shift funds from exploration to the clean energy research."

"But is it worth risking her life?"

"Ask her." James's tone grew sharper. "Ask her if she wants to give up the clean energy project." He took a breath and spoke more calmly. "I can't get the board to agree to the clean energy division if I can't find those funds from somewhere else."

"Have ye tried?" Dermot asked.

"Clean energy is a big investment. The money must come from somewhere."

"Does it have to come from there?" Dermot pleaded. "I know that's the idea she pitched, but have ye tried to find the funds from anywhere else?"

James didn't have an answer. Dermot was sure it was because he hadn't thought of it. He scrubbed a hand through his hair trying to diffuse some of his own tension. "Look. I'm sure ye know plenty about this business, but most of your knowledge comes from Walter. I wouldna put it past him to keep things from ye. Information is power, and there is nothing he holds dearer than that."

James sighed. "He's a snake to be sure, but one thing I think he is right about is that Sarah's gift is why she is the one from the prophecy. It's why she is essential to our plans."

"And it couldna be because she's the best mother for the heir?" He didn't say James's heir. He didn't want to think about it. "It couldna be because she is the best person to teach him how to lead us to whatever has been promised?"

James thought about it. "That's about personality, not genetics. The events of her life, and the people in her life made her the woman we love. But how could anyone have known a thousand years ago she would be the person she is? They couldn't. But they could know, they could plan to maintain their gift. That's what the matching program among her people was all about, maintaining the gift, the gift will help her fulfill the prophecy."

Dermot wasn't so sure. "Yes, her gift was preserved, but their traditions and way of life were also preserved. Until her Aunt Eilidh broke that covenant. Sarah's personality and the way she was raised are all affected by the generations before her. It can't be only about her ability to find things."

"I think perhaps your feelings are clouding your view of the situation." James said without heat.

"And I'm wondering why yers aren't." He said he loved her. Surely, he loved her enough not to ask her to continue these experiments.

"Perhaps Walter taught me a bit too well."

***

382 · MEREDITH R. STODDARD

"Are you comfortable?" Jujhar asked as Sarah stretched her legs out on a chaise on the patio once they got home. "Are you sure you shouldn't take a nap?"

Sarah waved him off. "My mind is buzzing. There's no way I could go to sleep now. Have a seat."

He took the chair beside her. "And you're really feeling better?"

"Perfectly fine." She said. "Stop fussing."

"That is literally what you pay me for." He gave her a stern look, but she could see a hint of a smile lingering in the corners of his mouth.

"No, it's not." She told him. "I pay you to be my sounding board, and I'm thinking."

"Alright. Sound away." He sat back waiting.

Sarah looked around the patio to make sure no one was nearby. Lady Anne had left, but Sarah didn't know who on the staff might be loyal to Anne. "I'm starting to wonder if Walter Stuart isn't right about my gift. Maybe it is meant to help them find oil."

"Really?" Jujhar looked at her like she might be mad.

"I know. No one hates thinking he might be right more than I do." She leaned closer to him. "But it's about Bridget."

He looked confused for a second. "The sister who was murdered?"

"The sister who was a geologist being recruited by Alba Petroleum."

"Ah." Realization dawned on his face. "But you have always been the one. It didn't fall to you by default after Bridget was murdered."

"True, but maybe the three sisters working together was always the plan. Me using my gift, and Bridget using her knowledge."

"And what would Oona's role be in this situation?" He asked.

"It's a great question. My theory hasn't developed that far." She shrugged. "Human lie detector?"

"Hmm." Jujhar thought for a moment. "It's an interesting theory, but there is so much more to you than your ability. And I'll wager there was more to Bridget than her ability or her knowledge of geology."

"And we know there's more to Oona." Sarah acknowledged thinking of her half-sister, the artist who painted the truth as she saw it. "I hope you're right. I would hate to be reduced to an oil finding asset."

Jujhar chuckled. "I doubt there is much chance of that. Speaking of your sister, I heard the other day her paintings will be displayed at the Keen Eye Gallery all next month."

Sarah sat up. "No! She's supposed to be in London safely out of Walter Stuart's sight."

Jujhar shrugged. "I'm only the messenger. You'll have to take it up with her."

"I don't dare go see her." Sarah leaned back in the chaise. "I don't want to attract any of the Stuarts' attention to her."

"You could try to see her privately." He suggested. "Or I'm sure she would meet you somewhere."

"I'm not so sure." Sarah said. "Her father gave his life to save Duff because of me, and don't get me started on her childhood spent with him mourning my mother and me. I'd be surprised if Oona ever wants to see me again."

"I think maybe you should give her some credit. The portrait she painted of you suggests she sees more than simply the things happening around you."

"That was before Rab was killed." Sarah was afraid Oona would blame her for Rab's death.

"You won't know if you don't try." Jujhar said. "I'll see what can be arranged."

CHAPTER FORTY-ONE

Another week, another experiment. After the partial failure of the underwater viewing, the team decided helicopter viewing and pinpointing with a global positioning system was the best solution, which was how Sarah found herself at an industrial dock outside Aberdeen as Dr. Seto explained what they were about to do.

"Those boats over there are seismic vessels. They use sonar to comb the ocean floor for clues about where oil deposits might be found. They have already surveyed the area we're going to be viewing today. We are going to fly over, and you tell us where you see oil or possible trap locations."

"And we'll compare my results to theirs." Sarah filled in.

"Precisely." Dr. Seto grinned broadly. He waved over a pretty woman with wire-rimmed glasses and tightly bound black hair. "This is Dr. Melhotra. She'll be recording the locations of your sightings today."

"It's nice to meet you Dr. Melhotra." Sarah shook her hand as Dr. Seto stepped away to talk with someone on their team.

"Please call me Nishaa." Nishaa had a lovely smile making her deep brown eyes sparkle. "I'm excited to be joining the project.

"Well, I hope we won't disappoint." Sarah waved a hand to the men behind her. "Let me introduce my personal assistant, Jujhar Gurudat, and my bodyguard, Fleming Sinclair." Fleming, who only learned about Sarah's gift the day before, was new to the circle of people who knew what she could do. There had been some debate over whether to allow Fleming on the flight or send Dermot instead. James had argued he needed Dermot with him and won. Fleming had responded well when he was briefed about what they were doing. Of course, he was also given a supplemental nondisclosure agreement to sign.

"Gentlemen." Nishaa shook both of their hands. "Have you been in a helicopter before?"

"No, and I have to admit I'm more than a little nervous about it." Sarah had been dreading it. Flying didn't bother her so much, but a helicopter seemed somehow less safe.

"I'm not an expert, but I've done it plenty of times, and our pilot, Sorley is the best. Shall we?" She waved toward the helicopter.

Sarah was relieved to see it was a sturdy-looking machine and was fully enclosed, with windows along the sides. It could have easily taken tourists on sightseeing trips along the coast except for the A.P. logo on the side.

They approached the helicopter at the same time as their pilot, a lanky man with a salt and pepper beard and brown hair, which was slightly thinning on top. He looked old enough to have plenty of experience but fit enough to control the machine he was about to pilot over the ocean. His broad smile put Sarah immediately at ease.

"Morning, Sorley." Nishaa called as they approached.

"Morning, doc." He dropped a duffel bag near the steps going up into the helicopter and turned to greet them.

"Sorley, this is Lady Sarah Stuart, Jujhar Gurudat, and Fleming Sinclair." Nishaa indicated each of them.

Sorley shook the men's hands, saving Sarah for last. He shook her hand and bowed slightly, not releasing her. *"Madainn mhath, a phiuthair.* (Good morning, sister.)"

Sarah froze. Only her people would address her as sister. Sorley lifted his eyes to hers. His look showed her he knew he had surprised her. *"Madainn mhath. Co as a tha sibh?"* (Where are you from?)"

"Tha mi a Làrachd an Fhamhair." (I'm from Làrachd an Fhamhair.) He said as if the village weren't a secret. Although he was probably confident, she was the only person who understood him. Sarah glanced at Jujhar who was looking warily at Sorley. *"Bha mi na chairaid dha d' athair.* (I was a friend of your father's.) I'll make sure our flight goes smoothly today."

The sudden rush of emotions was part relief he didn't seem to have been sent there by Aunt Eilidh, and grief that Rab was protecting her even from the grave. Tears clogged her throat, and it took several seconds for her to squeeze Sorley's hand and say. "Then I am truly pleased to meet you."

"Is e urram a th' ann." (I am honored.) He bowed his head again, then straightened and spoke to the rest of the group. "Shall we?"

Sorley opened the door of the passenger compartment and held it as the rest of them climbed into the helicopter. Dr. Seto was the last to join them. He sat in the front with Sorley, while Sarah and Fleming sat behind them and Nishaa and Jujhar took the back row.

Sorley's words about her father had eased some of Sarah's jangling nerves. No one from her people would take unnecessary risks with her safety. She only had to worry about things like weather and mechanical errors. Any number of things could go wrong with a helicopter, and they were going to be over open water. She really would rather have stayed on land, or a boat, but for the distance they were covering, the helicopter offered the fastest and most agile method of pinpointing their location.

Once they were in the air, Dr. Seto turned around to speak with them. "We are some distance from the area we'll be examining, so we have about twenty minutes before we need to begin. How are you doing?"

"I'm glad I have a little time to relax. I'm nervous as a cat in a room full of rocking chairs right now." Sarah might as well be honest. Relaxation was key to doing what she did.

"I worried you might be. Would you like a sedative?" He offered.

"No, thank you. I think it's better if I'm not under the influence." Sarah tried to settle back into her seat. "I'll practice some deep breathing."

She cast a wary look at Fleming who gave her a reassuring nod. Leaning her head back against her seat, she closed her eyes. Jujhar and Nishaa struck up a low-voiced conversation in what Sarah thought was Punjabi. Their soft vowels and quick consonants combined with the whomp-whomp of the rotor blades worked like a hypnotic blanket steeling over her. By the time they reached the part of the North Sea where she would be viewing, Sarah was much more relaxed.

"We're here." Sorley announced.

Dr. Seto turned back to Sarah. "Alright. Are you ready? Is there anything you need?"

"I'm ready." She turned back to Nishaa only to find her with her notebook open and a pencil in her hand. "I guess you're ready too."

"Tell Sorley where to go, and he'll move us wherever you say." Nishaa explained. "I've got the GPS right here. Say 'here' when you find something, and I'll record the coordinates."

"I'll hold the GPS for you, so your hands are free." Jujhar offered.

"Sounds simple enough. Although, I don't usually talk when I'm casting out." She warned. "We'll see how this works."

She faced forward and leaned back in her seat, taking a deep breath. On the exhale she focused on relaxing every muscle and calming her mind. She continued what had become her casting out routine, and soon she was hovering above looking down at the helicopter. Its rotors were a translucent haze as they spun.

Sarah shifted her focus to the signs of oil deposits. She concentrated on images of crude oil, and the geological formations where it should be found. Keeping herself relaxed she waited for the pull, the little tug in her brain telling her which direction to go in. When it came it pointed her to the east-northeast. Ten o'clock from their current bearing.

Now, to tell Sorley. She had never tried to speak while casting out before. When she had done it on the run in the Highlands, she had drawn back to herself before telling Ruaraidh where their pursuer was. But she wasn't sure she'd be able to come back and cast out again as quickly as they would need for this method to work.

She thought about the connection between her mind and her body during the underwater experiment. The belief that she was drowning had stopped her breathing. Could the same connection be used to talk while her co-walker was viewing. There was only one way to find out.

It took a lot of concentration to keep part of her mind focused on the thread pulling her toward her destination, while turning another part to the sensation of speaking. She focused on pushing air out of her lungs and over her vocal chords. She visualized her lips, tongue, and teeth forming sounds. 'Ten o'clock.'

She couldn't hear or see what was going on inside the helicopter. She had no idea if she had actually spoken, or if it was only in her mind. But seconds later, the helicopter turned toward ten o'clock and flew slowly in that direction.

Sarah turned her attention back to the pull to see if there was any change in its direction. They were on the right course and flew for several minutes before there was a change. They needed to turn toward the south now, about one o'clock. Again, Sarah split her attention and focused on speaking. "One o'clock." The helicopter turned.

Soon they reached the point where the pull turned downward. Sarah said, "Here."

Sorley began circling the spot where she had said to stop. After the last experiment, Sarah knew she probably shouldn't view under the water, but she couldn't resist the temptation to confirm what she was sensing. Sarah decided to take the risk for a quick look under the surface.

She plunged down and down, until she reached the bottom. She stopped above a small him of sand like a dune. She couldn't see the oil under her, but she could feel its pull. Satisfied she had found something, she focused on returning to her body. Unlike the last time, she remembered not to look up, and not to be startled by the marine life around her. Within seconds she was back in her body drawing a deep breath.

When she opened her eyes, Dr. Seto was looking at her wide-eyed. She glanced around the cabin. Fleming looked stunned. He hadn't seen her do this before, and she could imagine it was a shock. She tried to reassure him. "I'm alright."

Then she turned back to Jujhar and Nishaa. Jujhar gave her a smile saying he knew she could do it. Nishaa was busy comparing the coordinates of the spot Sarah had indicated to the results of the seismic survey. She looked up, shock on her face. "This is incredible. The survey readings suggest there is a fault trap right there."

Sarah didn't know whether to be elated or alarmed. She'd done it. She wasn't crazy about helping them find oil, but she was excited about redirecting those funds to cleaner energy options. She tried not to think about the amount of time she was going to be spending in a helicopter casting out. With a sigh, she leaned back in her seat.

Sorley turned the helicopter toward land. Dr. Seto turned to him and said. "I suppose we'll be needing your services again."

"I wouldna miss it." Sorley glowed with approval.

The ride back to Aberdeen went by faster than the ride out. Sarah even dozed off at one point. Casting out always tired her, but this was a whole new kind of tired. It must have been from the tension of riding in the helicopter and not knowing what the result of the experiment would be.

When they landed, everyone went into the hangar to celebrate. Dr. Seto provided champagne which they drank out of paper cups. They made plans to start surveying further

392 · MEREDITH R. STODDARD

south than they had surveyed before. They would let Sarah search first, then follow with seismic vessels after she had told them where to look.

In the car at the end of the day, Sarah relaxed with Jujhar. "Nishaa seems nice. What were you two talking about earlier?"

"We were commiserating about our parents' matchmaking efforts." His expression was dour.

"Are they pressuring you?" Jujhar rarely talked about his family. His parents had pushed him to become a religious leader in their community, but he was more interested in academics and now his esoteric studies with Lyall Green.

"My younger sister got married last year and I have heard of little else since then." He looked out the window as they approached the airfield where a private plane waited to take them back to Edinburgh. "Nishaa hears much of the same pressure from her family. It's the perpetual clash of traditional parents and modern children."

"Nishaa would be a catch. She's very pretty and accomplished." Sarah watched for his reaction.

Jujhar studied her, ever perceptive. "I don't feel sexual attraction the way most people do. I am attracted to people's minds, their personalities, but physical relationships simply aren't something I have ever desired. That aspect of marriage would not be a good fit for me."

"Ah. Makes sense. That must make the pressure from your parents even harder."

"It does." He agreed. "It's hard for them to understand I don't want a traditional marriage." He was quiet for a moment. "On the other hand, it makes me perfectly suited to be our friend's apprentice. Ours is not a life that lends itself to romantic relationships."

"Mm. As Dermot's grandmother could confirm if she was still here." Sarah muttered. "You might be a better fit than Mr. Green is."

"We'll see." Jujhar looked out the window again. "There has been a time or two when my sense of justice and fairness have butted up against the drive to make events happen the way Green believes they should."

"Like helping me before the wedding." Sarah whispered.

"Exactly." He patted her hand, then changed the subject as if to close the book on it. "Did you mean to speak Gaelic when you were giving directions?"

"What?" She asked in confusion. "I didn't even know that I did. I only focused on making my body speak."

"It's lucky the pilot understood you."

"You did too, but I'm sure that made it easier." Sarah said. "It's funny. Granny used to call it the language of her heart. I guess it's mine too."

CHAPTER FORTY-TWO

Sarah waited until the last of the guests had left the gallery. She had arranged through the manager to come in through the back near the end of the night. Her stomach twisted with nervous nausea at seeing her sister again so soon after their father's death.

As she emerged from the office, she was struck by the size of the paintings. Many of the canvases were almost life-sized. And like the portrait Oona had sent her, all of them showed the truth of their subjects. The gallery was empty for the moment, giving Sarah the opportunity to wander around. She strolled through until she came to a painting that was the star of the show. It was no larger than the others but drew attention like a magnet.

Rab Ballantyne stared out from the canvas with the same ice green eyes he'd passed down to both of his daughters. Sarah was captivated. He stood inside a bottle with amber liquid coming up to his nose. Swirling around in the liquid, in subtle lines Sarah recognized all of Rab's regrets. There was her mother, belly rounded with pregnancy. There was a fiddle and a guitar. Sheila was there, her auburn hair swirling and mixing with the amber. The background was dark, but Sarah thought she could see the stone walls of the vault where Rab died. Of course, Oona would have been able to see past the public story of Rab's accidental death.

"He would be proud of ye, ye know. He was proud of ye." Sarah had been so focused on the painting she hadn't heard Oona approach.

"He'd be proud of you too." Sarah said. Oona looked much like she had the last time Sarah had seen her. Her hair was jet black and cut bluntly so it stood out at interesting angles. Her dark eyeliner made her light green eyes look almost unnatural. Her clothes were a little nicer than the jeans and torn T-shirt she'd been wearing before, but they were still edgy and interesting. They had both inherited much of their looks from Rab, but where Sarah was earthy and soft, Oona was all sharp angles and shadows. "I know it."

"It's good to see ye." Oona said with a soft smile.

The tension winding itself through Sarah's muscles released with a sigh. Her voice was thick with tears "I wasn't sure you'd feel that way. I thought you would hate me."

"After all ye've done? Never." Oona turned to face her looking at Sarah as if she'd lost her mind.

Tears filled Sarah's eyes. The words she'd been afraid to voice spilled from her mouth. Even though Oona could see whatever she was feeling, she had to say it. "It was my fault. I knew what Walter Stuart was. He told me what he would do if I didn't marry James, and I tried to run anyway. I should have stayed, I put you all in danger and Rab paid the price."

Oona wrapped her arms around Sarah and let her cry for a few minutes. She pushed Sarah back and wiped away her tears with the cuff of her shirt. "Ye're not to take responsibility for what that bastard did. He's the villain here. Not you. Never think any of us blames ye for Rab's death. We don't any more than we blamed ye for him being an alcoholic or an absent father. None of this is yer fault."

"I wish I could feel that way." Sarah sniffed. "You're too generous."

"I'm not really." Oona said flatly. "But I've seen the truth of enough people to ken what kind of person ye are. Ye're my sister."

Sarah smiled through tears. "Say what you will about Rab's parenting, but he and your mother raised some wonderful people."

"Eh. We have our own issues." Oona gave her a look suggesting there were plenty of things she didn't share. Sarah was sure it was true. Her half siblings were complicated people, but they had treated her like a sister from the start. Probably because they had known she existed long before she knew about them.

Deciding it was time to lighten the mood. Sarah looked around the room. "These paintings are amazing."

"They do the trick." Oona cast her own gaze around at some of the paintings.

"When are you planning to go back to London?"

"Anxious to be rid of me, are ye?" Oona laughed.

"I only want you to be safe." She loved seeing Oona but wanted her to leave Edinburgh before Walter Stuart found out she was there, assuming he didn't already know.

"Will ye let me worry about myself?" Oona bristled.

"What is a big sister for if not to nag you about staying safe?" Sarah gave Oona her best disapproving big sister look. "I don't want to have to make another call to Ruaraidh like the last one."

"Ye won't. Unlike our father, it's hard to surprise me." Oona reminded her. "And I'm here for a month. Now, tell me about life married to Prince Charming."

"Don't you want to get back to Rachel?" Sarah asked.

"Rachel can manage herself." Oona slipped her arm into Sarah's as they strolled around the gallery. "Besides, she's coming to visit in a couple of weeks."

"I was surprised to see you having a show here. I thought you were determined to stay away from Scotland." They walked into a room filled with Oona's portraits from London.

"I'm determined to stay away from Lochinver, or Lairg, or anywhere small. Cities are easier for me to be in because of the gift."

"I would have thought the fewer people the better." Sarah said.

"Nah." Oona thought about it. "All the people in the city give me variety. I see so many different stories, and when I'm not looking it's like white noise. I can tune it out easier. In the Highlands, it's silence and then every person I meet shouts their truths and innermost secrets at me. It's bloody awful."

"I suppose it would be." Sarah was once again glad truthseeing wasn't the gift she had inherited. She wasn't sure how Oona could stand it.

"But I want ye to tell me how I can help ye while I'm here." Oona offered.

"I don't want to ask you to do that." There was no need to embroil Oona any further into the Stuart mess.

"What are these gifts for it if it's not to help us?" Oona tugged her arm to get her attention.

"Sure, but help us do what? James and Walter have me using mine to find oil. I really don't want to believe that is what it's for." Sarah said. "And I don't want you to get pulled into using your gift for them either."

"Och well, ye can be sure I willna be helping Walter Stuart."

"Exactly. I have a hard time believing our people preserved these gifts for all this time for it to be used by the likes of Walter, or for such material purposes."

"Mmmph. I see what ye mean." Oona sounded thoughtful. "But we can use them to protect ourselves."

"I suppose you're right."

"Think about it. If there's a way to help. I will."

***

Sarah did think about Oona's offer. She genuinely liked Oona and wanted to spend more time with her. It was true Oona's gift could be incredibly useful. But she didn't have any desire to pull her sister further into the Stuarts' web. Meanwhile Sarah got pulled in more by the day.

Now on her third trip of the week over the North Sea in the helicopter, she was beginning to think she'd been too hasty offering to do this in exchange for the clean energy initiative. There had been very little movement on that front. James said he was meeting privately with board members, but Sarah hadn't heard of any renewable energy research being done yet.

"We're here." Sorely said through his headset. They had left Edinburgh and gone south hugging the coast for a while before turning to the east.

Sarah looked behind her to where Nishaa was ready to record the coordinates. Turning to face the front again, Sarah leaned back in her seat. She began the process of casting out. Soon she was above everything and waiting for the pull. Dr.

Seto and Nishaa had briefed her this morning on the type of trap formation they expected to see. Sarah focused on those images in her mind.

Unlike the prior trips, there was something else. When she tried to focus and feel the pull toward the oil formations, another feeling caught at her. Usually, the thing she was looking for would pull her like a thread attached to her mind. It might be as thin as spider silk, but it would draw her to the thing she was looking for.

This other feeling was different. It was like a soft tug on her attention, like when you are on your way to work, but can't remember if you turned the oven off. It was a niggling feeling of something she should have known but didn't; something familiar but hard to place. Whatever it was it kept distracting her from the pull of the oil.

Sarah refocused. The thread of the oil pulled her to the northwest, but as soon as she divided her attention to tell Sorley the direction, the distracting tug to the south started again. It was as if there was something there wanting her attention. When Sarah opened her mouth she said, "South."

Sorely turned the helicopter to the south, going slowly. Sarah felt the mysterious tug grow stronger. The further south they went, the feeling grew stronger. Sarah let herself leave the helicopter behind and cast further away. She soared over the ocean looking for the source of the feeling. When the tug took a downward turn, she let it pull her beneath the waves.

She never made it to the bottom. She let her senses stretch out to feel more of the item, drawing her to that spot. It was deep, deeper than the sea floor, deeper than the oil, and it was big. She could feel it extending out across the Earth's crust beneath her. It was a large deposit of something solid. It wasn't oil or shale. It was something else, something very dense. Whatever it was, it wasn't what Alba Petroleum was looking for, and something she couldn't quite explain told her she shouldn't tell them it was there.

The helicopter caught up with her. Sarah redirected her attention. It took a lot to refocus on the oil formations. Now that she knew the other deposit was there, she found it easier to tune it out even when she focused on telling Sorley she'd been mistaken. She told him to head northwest, and he followed her instructions.

The rest of the trip went exactly the way the other trips had gone. Sarah told them where to look for oil. They dispatched a seismic vessel to the area, and it searched for deposits. Where before, the seismic vessels would have been canvassing much larger areas, Sarah's advice was letting them be more calculated with their deployments. So far, she was identifying trap formations with one hundred percent accuracy.

Sarah's gift was on track to save A.P. millions. She was holding up her end of the bargain. She made a mental note on their way back to Edinburgh to remind James of his promise. And she tried to forget the mysterious deposit she felt under the sea floor.

***

The oak paneled walls and bottle green velvet drapes of the members' dining room at the Nor Loch Club reminded Dermot of the study at Tweedholm, but on a much larger scale. He'd accompanied James to the door of the private club many a time but had never been inside. It wasn't lost on him that the city's most exclusive club was named for the stagnant, open sewer they'd drained to make way for Waverley Station and Princes Street Gardens. Either the club's founders had meant it to be ironic or hoped to scare away social climbers by naming their club after the place where the city's sewers terminated.

The club was where the highest echelon of Edinburgh's businessmen and old money crossed paths while lunching, lounging, or attending the occasional event. That day, James had signed Dermot in as his guest, and they were hoping to 'run into' some of the Alba Petroleum board members. James scanned the dining room. "We're almost sure to see Monkton. He's here every Thursday."

"Stuart!" A man about their age with wind burned cheeks approached with his hand outstretched.

"Murray. How are you?" James shook the man's hand showing less enthusiasm than Murray did.

"I'm doing well. Just been stalking in The Trossachs. Took down a stag the size of an elephant. You really must join me some time. How's married life?" The man named Murray asked with more enthusiasm than Dermot thought was necessary.

"Bliss." James grinned. "Have you met my friend Dermot Sinclair?"

"Sinclair, eh?" Murray eyed Dermot closely, and for the first time he could remember, Dermot felt self-conscious about the quality of his suit. Murray offered his hand. "Graham Murray. Are you in oil as well?"

"He's working with me." James said.

"Right. Well, good to meet you." Murray offered his hand.

"Likewise." Dermot gave his hand a firm shake.

"Well, I'd best get back to the office." Murray clapped James on the shoulder. "We should have dinner sometime. Get the wives together."

Murray left, and James leaned closer to Dermot. "We were in the same class at Saint Andrews. He lives for hunting, and his wife would bore Sarah to tears. But he's old money and works in banking, so very few doors are closed to him."

"Right." Dermot thought if Walter had ever claimed him, he would likely have been a member of this very club rubbing elbows with the likes of Murray. He felt like he'd dodged a bullet.

"Ah. There's Monkton. Come on." James took off toward a table where a man sat alone with his back to the room.

"Bernard." James said as they rounded the table to face the man. He looked to be in his early forties, was still fighting fit, although his hairline was receding. He stood to shake hands with James and Dermot, who James introduced again as his friend.

"Join me. I've just ordered." Monkton took his seat again waving them to the other seats at the table. "You barely missed Murray. He's trying to get me to help sponsor that insufferable American for membership."

"We saw him on his way out. Which American?" James asked.

Monkton waved and rolled his eyes. "I don't remember the name, the obnoxious one with the ridiculous hair whose mother was from Lewis or somewhere. I told Murray I would resign my membership if they let him in."

"I think I know the one you mean. I don't think he's Nor Loch material." James agreed.

A waiter came and took their orders. They chatted about some mutual acquaintances, their wives, sports. Monkton was good company, even if he was a bit of a snob. They were halfway through their entrees when James turned the subject to business. "This sabotage on the oil rig has gotten me thinking."

"I should hope you're thinking about strengthening security on the rigs." Monkton said.

"Oh, we're already on it. No question." James leaned back in his chair looking thoughtful. "But I'm starting to think beyond oil. We have the apparatus established to continue drilling. We've expanded beyond the North Sea, so we'll keep going and making a profit without any trouble. Our natural gas business is growing. But those resources are finite, and I think we need to look at some other methods of generating energy beyond fossil fuels."

"Have the environmentalists gotten to you?" Monkton looked askance at him.

"Not the way you're thinking." James shook his head. "As I said, we're on the alert now for any kind of sabotage. But they have a point that oil isn't unlimited. Eventually, the whole world is going to have to find something else to power everything. And some predictions tell us it might be sooner than any of us thinks. Very few of the oil companies I've looked at have plans for after supplies start to decline."

"They're too busy finding cheap ways to extract it from tar sands." Monkton said.

"Right. What I'm proposing will position us for when those resources decline. Forget tar sands. We should be developing renewable energy sources. Wind, tidal, hydro, geothermal." Dermot had been doing the same reading James had done into renewable energy. He was surprised at James's enthusiasm, though. "There are so many possibilities other companies aren't investigating. That leaves a strategic gap and I want A.P. to fill it."

Monkton watched James thoughtfully. "It's an interesting idea. So, what are you proposing?"

"I want to start a renewable energy division. We have a couple of small projects already under R and D. Phase One, I want to expand those projects and divert some of the funds from researching oil to this new division. Once we have some promising research, we start investing in projects which will generate revenue. We keep growing from there."

"Aren't there already some companies doing these things?" Monkton asked.

"Small companies who are getting started." James said. "With our resources, we can invest more and control the market within a couple of years, or we can buy one of those smaller companies, add our resources and expand faster. By the time the other oil and gas companies decide to get into renewables, we'll control the market."

"Very strategic. What does Walter think of all this?" Monkton asked.

James let his head wobble. "He's still skeptical. He can see the business case, but I think he's more in favor of the status quo. As my wife might say, 'If it ain't broke, don't fix it.' Walter thinks it ain't broke. I think it will break, and I want us to be prepared."

"And you're going to propose this new division at the next board meeting?" Monkton asked.

"That is my plan." James said. "Can I count on your support?"

406 · MEREDITH R. STODDARD

"You make a good case." Monkton gave him a speculative look. "I'm going to have to think about it."

"I would expect nothing less." James grinned. "We'll leave you to enjoy your coffee and newspaper. Thank you for hearing me out."

"Nice meeting you." Dermot said as they rose to leave.

When they were a reasonable distance from the table, Dermot said quietly to James. "You really sold that."

"Selling is half the job, really. Selling the right ideas to the right people." James muttered.

They were near the foyer when James paused and hissed under his breath. He elbowed Dermot and jerked his head in the direction of the lounge.

Dermot turned in time to see Walter going in. He was talking with a rail thin man who looked to be in his sixties or seventies. As they walked into the lounge Walter gave the man a companionable pat on the back.

"That's Giles Tait." James muttered. "Also, on the board. I knew we'd never get his vote, but I see Walter is making sure of it."

***

Sarah stepped out of the car and put a hand on the door to steady herself as her stomach churned. Fleming took her elbow.

"Alright, hen?" He gave her a concerned look.

Sarah took a deep breath which seemed to help. "Yeah. I'll be okay. Still getting my land legs back."

"Right." He helped her shift to the side to let Jujhar out of the car. They both walked her to the door.

"I'll sit here for a minute." Sarah sank down onto a bench in the front hall. The sour feeling in her stomach intensified. "I'm sure I'll be fine in a sec."

"Can I get you some water?" Jujhar offered.

Sarah shook her head, which didn't help the feeling, but it was easier than talking. "Something fizzy maybe. Ginger ale?"

Meanwhile Fleming picked up the phone in the front hall and tapped a few numbers before saying, "Thistle is in the lion's den." That was code for 'Sarah is at the Polwarth Terrace house'. Sarah was usually amused by the security team's little code, but she barely noticed.

She leaned back breathing deeply and shutting the world out. She tried to focus on calming the churn in her stomach.

"Sarah?" James's voice came from the direction of his study. She didn't want to open her eyes, but she knew he would fuss over her if she didn't.

"I'm fine." She sat up straight and did her best impression of being fine.

"You're not." James knelt in front of her and placed the back of his hand against her forehead. "You're white as a sheet."

'I'll be okay. Just give me a minute. I think the helicopter messes with my equilibrium." She said through her teeth.

"When was the last time you ate?" He looked worried.

"I had a salad for lunch." She told him.

Jujhar returned with a glass of cold ginger ale and a small plate with crackers. "Mr. Ratcliff suggested crackers as well."

"Thank you." Sarah took a tiny sip of ginger ale. Jujhar put the plate beside her on the bench.

"We're pushing you too hard." James hovered over her.

"I'll be the first to admit almost daily helicopter rides might be a little too much." Sarah nibbled on a cracker. She looked past James to see Dermot standing in the hall, looking as concerned as James. She tried to give him a reassuring smile.

"We'll have to cut back on the scouting trips. I'll talk to Seto about modifying your schedule." James propped his hands on his hips looking every bit in control of the situation.

Sarah continued sipping and nibbling. She looked at the four men standing around staring at her. Suddenly, she wanted very badly to be alone. "I think I'd like to lie down. I'm sure I'll feel better in a few minutes."

She set her glass next to her plate of crackers and pushed herself to her feet. Her stomach churned and the room shifted. Before she knew it, Dermot had pushed James aside and swept her up in his arms.

"Can someone get the drink and crackers?" He said over his shoulder as he headed for the stairs.

"This really isn't necessary." She told Dermot, resting her head on his shoulder.

"Maybe not, but I'd rather ye didna fall down the stairs." He said before lowering his voice. "And I'll never pass up an excuse to touch ye."

"You're flying a bit close to the sun on this one." She warned keeping her voice low. "James is right behind you."

"I'm aware." His voice rumbled under her ear. "Should I be worried about ye?"

"I'll be fine in a bit." Sarah hoped she was right. "This happened after yesterday's ride too. I need to get used to solid ground again."

Dermot pushed into the master bedroom and carried Sarah to the bed. James followed a second later with the drink and crackers. As Dermot set Sarah down on the bed, James said. "Maybe you should stay home tomorrow."

"That's probably not a bad idea." Sarah agreed.

James inserted himself between Sarah and Dermot and deposited the plate and glass on the bedside table. "Are you sure you'll be alright?"

"I'm sure I'll be fine." She said. "I'll drink my ginger ale and lie down for half an hour, and I'll be good as new."

He looked doubtful. "I'll be checking on you in half an hour then. And you'll take tomorrow off."

She tried to ignore her churning stomach. A day off sounded like a good idea.

CHAPTER FORTY-THREE

In the end she took more than one day off. James suggested she spend the weekend in the country. Sarah had jumped at the idea and mentioned she might invite Oona and her girlfriend along for a girls' weekend. He had fully supported her plan and called Mrs. Miller to let her know they were coming, or more accurately he'd told Miss Lennox to call and arrange it.

With her usual efficiency, Miss Lennox arranged for a car to pick them up, along with Sarah's security team and deposit them safely on the gravel drive in front of the manor house on Friday evening. Sarah felt a little strange being there without James or Dermot, but Henry and Mrs. Miller welcomed them and made them feel right at home.

Rachel was stunning. Where everything about Oona's look was dark and spikey, Rachel's was softer, though no less interesting. Her light brown skin contrasted with short bleach blond curls and jade green eyes. A silver piercing in her septum provided the perfect ornament above her full lips which were often curled into a warm smile. Sarah could see she and Oona adored each other.

Sarah and Rachel had become fast friends on the ride down from Edinburgh, and by the time Oona and Rachel joined Sarah and Henry on the veranda for a glass of wine before dinner, the three of them were forming a comfortable camaraderie.

"This house is amazing." Rachel enthused, taking a cracker and slice of Irish cheddar from the cheese board Mrs. Miller had laid out.

Henry smiled with pride. "Thank you. My grandparents acquired it from the original owners when they returned to Scotland from the Continent."

"Growing up here must have sparked a wee lad's imagination." Oona studied Henry. Sarah wondered if Oona was using her gift on him.

"It did." He looked off toward the river, lost in memories. "It's hard to live this close to the border without having our heads filled with tales of conquest and succession. I used to imagine I could hold the English back single-handedly." He nodded toward Rachel. "Present company excluded of course."

"No bother to me. I'm Cornish." Rachel said with a smile.

"Single-handedly? Not you and Walter?" Sarah asked.

Henry gave his head a shake. "Walter was never much for make believe. He was more chess and strategy games, or books and studying. He's always been the serious one."

"Seriously something." Oona muttered.

Sarah bit back a laugh and changed the subject. "How is Seonag doing?"

Henry sighed, his face a mask of contentment touched with sorrow. "She has settled in nicely. We have a routine. I visit her in the mornings and evenings for a walk. She struggles to remember things in the evenings. She does remember me from day to day but doesn't recognize me from when we were younger."

Sarah reached over and gripped his hand. "I'm glad you're here with her. It's not easy, I know. But I think it helps."

He gave her hand a squeeze. "She'll be happy to see you if you can visit tomorrow."

"I plan to." She leaned her head back against the chair and propped her feet up on another one. "In the meantime, I think we should enjoy this wine and have a relaxing evening."

"Then I will leave you ladies to it." Henry rose from the table and kissed Sarah's cheek before making his way inside.

"He seems nice enough for a retired oil baron." Rachel said when Henry was out of earshot. She turned to Oona. "I thought you said he was a mess."

Oona's eyes followed Henry into the house. "He was a bit of a mess when I met him, like he was being pulled in too many directions. He seems more relaxed now, more settled."

"I think he let go." Sarah told them. "He had some disappointments and then realized Dermot needed help with Seonag. I think he's pulled away from all the things other people told him he should care about."

"I like this version of Henry." Oona turned back to them.

"Me too." Sarah picked up a slice of cheese and took a bite.

"Now," Oona rubbed her hands together. "What sort of mischief can we get into tonight?"

"Not much out here in the country." Sarah laughed. "I vote for eating ice cream and watching movies, or we do have some board games."

"What did I say?" Oona turned to Rachel. "That sister of mine is a wild woman."

**

"We have Lyall Green, Monkton, Bashar, and my father in our corner." James tapped a notepad with the end of his pen in agitation. They had less than a month until the quarterly board meeting where they would propose Sarah's clean energy initiative and rebranding, and he wasn't sure they would have the votes to overcome the expected pushback from Walter. He knew his uncle had attempted to court Monkton and Bashar as they'd seen him doing with Tait. Fortunately, they had both been a little spooked by the rig explosion. They hadn't taken too much convincing.

"What about Menzies?" Dermot reclined in the chair across from James. They had slowly shifted their working relationship from bodyguard to apprentice. Now, Dermot attended meetings with him rather than waiting outside of conference rooms. He rather liked having his brother along. He made a good sounding board in moments like this.

Dermot and his connection to Lyall Green had also been a good way of getting around Miss Lennox when setting up meetings with the board members. James still wasn't convinced Miss Lennox was spying on him, but he supposed they were better to be safe than sorry. "I'm golfing with him tomorrow morning."

"Who else is there?" Dermot leaned forward and glanced at the list on James's pad.

"Apart from Menzies, there are Sutherland, Tait, and my mother."

"How do you think she'll vote?" Dermot asked.

"By my father's proxy usually." James circled her name on his list. "Her position on the board is only nominal. She's never shown much interest in the running of things. She gives my father her vote, and now she's gone to France. I don't imagine that will change."

Dermot cleared his throat. "Of course, that was before your father retired to Tweedholm and ye asked her to leave yer house."

He had a point. James leaned back in his chair and looked out the window. "I'll call her and try to get a sense of what she will do. I suspect she won't be interested in coming back for the meeting, but it's better to be sure."

"And the other two?"

"Tait has voted lockstep with Walter for as long as I can remember. We may have to write him off as a loss." Giles Tait was an old school chum of Walter's from Gordonstoun. James wasn't sure if Tait actually shared Walter's opinions, or if he merely bowed to Walter's first-hand knowledge of the industry. Either way, they weren't likely to convince him.

"That leaves Sutherland." Dermot's voice broke through his thoughts.

"Sutherland we might be able to convince. Some of his land might be good for wind farming. He could stand to make a lot of money, but he's also conservative. He may take some convincing."

A knock at the door interrupted their conversation. "Yes?"

Miss Lennox stepped into the office. Even on a Friday evening, she looked poised and dependable. "I thought you would want to know Lady Sarah and her friends arrived safely at Tweedholm House."

"Excellent! Thank you." He hoped Sarah had a good time with her sister. He admired the portrait Oona Ballantyne had painted of Sarah, even if he didn't completely understand its meaning. "Have a good weekend, Miss Lennox."

She turned to leave but stopped. "Actually, might I have a word?"

James stood and waved to a chair in front of his desk. "Of course."

She approached the chair he indicated. Her gaze cut to Dermot who had also risen when she entered the room. "A private word?"

"Right. I'll be right out there." Dermot jerked his head toward the door before walking out."

"Please, sit." James began to take his seat again, stopping when he noticed she remained standing with her hands clasped together at her waist.

"Have I done something to upset you?" She kept her focus on the desk, and there was the slightest tremor in her voice.

"Why would you think that?"

Her fingers twisted together. "Mr. Menzies's assistant called this afternoon to confirm your tee time tomorrow, but I don't have a tee time on your calendar. You've left the office early several times over the last few weeks without telling me where you were going. I feel like there is something you're hiding from me." The last sentence came out in a rush.

James took a breath. He should have known he wouldn't be able to hide his activities from her forever. He walked around the desk to stand within her line of sight. He waited, taking control of the situation with his silence, a tactic his uncle had taught him.

Eventually, her eyes lifted to meet his. He could read the anxiety in her brown depths, and something else...pain. He kept his voice soft, but no less deadly. "Actually, Miss Lennox, I think perhaps you have been hiding something from me."

Her breath hitched, and she blinked quickly. He'd made a direct hit. Perhaps Dermot was right about her. She started to speak, her perfect lips with their understated lip color parted but no sound came out. He waited while watching a dozen thoughts and responses flick through her mind. In the end her shoulders sagged. Her voice was flat. "He put me here to spy on you. You know I was his admin for a few weeks before you joined the company. He had me moved to your office so he would know everything you did."

Fury sizzled across the back of his neck. "Why?"

She shook her head saying softly, "I don't know. I only know he wasn't sure if you would be as malleable as he wanted you to be. He's been a shadow CEO since your father's time, and he didn't want to change."

"Malleable. That sounds like him." He digested this latest information for a moment, pinning her with a speculative look. "What I don't understand is why you would go along with it."

A flush crept up from the collar of her blouse. Her pulse jumped in the elegant column of her throat. "I'd rather keep my reasons to myself, sir."

He cocked his head to the side. "Miss Lennox, you are very close to being dismissed from this company's employ. If you wish to keep your job, you will tell me, now."

She drew in a breath and firmed her jaw. "I don't see how you could possibly continue to employ me after today, so I would rather the reason remain private."

Whatever it was, it couldn't be good. He leaned back against the desk, affecting a casual pose. He made his tone as soothing as he could. "Miss Lennox, Audra, you are very good at what you do. You have become indispensable to me. I would rather keep someone of your skills and reliability in the company."

She closed her eyes, trying to shut out the conversation. He went on. "I have very few illusions left about who my uncle is. I doubt I will be surprised by anything you say."

"Maybe not about him." She blinked back tears. "But…" She shook her head and looked away.

"Why don't we sit." He took her hand and led her to the couch near the window thinking a more relaxed position might loosen her up. Her fingers fluttered nervously in his, but she followed him. She smoothed her skirt behind her and perched on the edge. James took a relaxed posture, stretching his arm across the back of the couch. On instinct he asked. "What does he have on you?"

Her eyes shot to his in surprise. "What do you know?"

"Only a bit about how he operates." He tried to look reassuring.

Miss Lennox seemed to come to a decision. She inhaled and looked straight ahead of her. "He knows my father through their club or something, and he hired me as a favor after I finished university." She sighed heavily. "At first, I worked with Mr. Shaw. It started not long after I came to work here. I was stupid, and he was this powerful man who complimented my work, even though I felt like I couldn't do anything right. He paid attention to me and took care of me. He had me moved from Mr. Shaw's desk to his. It made me feel special."

She rubbed her thumb over a ring she wore on her right hand. "I still can't believe what an idiot I was, but I fell for his lies, and he got me into a compromising position. Then you joined the company, and he shifted me to your office. He wanted me to keep him informed of everything you do."

"I told him I wasn't comfortable with that. I have gotten more and more uncomfortable with it over time. I hope you know I would never do anything I thought would hurt you. But he threatened me." She pressed her lips together as if she would do anything to keep the next words from coming out. "He said he would tell my father I'd thrown myself at him, I had tried to sleep my way up the ladder here. And I would be sacked. He…" She looked down at her lap and James had to lean closer to hear. "He has photos of me."

The back of his neck prickled. He knew his uncle could be ruthless, but he never expected him to extort a young woman. Audra Lennox wasn't a business rival. She wasn't involved in any of their schemes. She was simply an innocent young woman who Walter had ensnared for his own ends.

James leaned forward, taking her hand in his. "Listen to me. You are not to blame."

She kept her gaze down but made a sound like a sob. "But I've—"

"You've done what you thought you had to do. And that's an end to it." He couldn't hold any of this against her.

She brushed a tear from her cheek. "What now?"

James took out his pocket square and handed it to her. "That's a very good question."

He wondered what to do about it. His first instinct was to protect Miss Lennox from any further manipulation by Walter. But he would have to find her a position somewhere else. He had come to rely on her, and spying aside, she was imminently capable. He watched her as she worked to collect herself and found he didn't like the idea of sending her away.

She mistook his hesitation for dismissal. Pushing up from the couch, she said. "I'll clean out my desk."

"Don't go." He stood as well. "I don't want to lose you."

Her brown eyes were filled with hopelessness. "He's not going to leave me alone."

James felt strangely unsure of himself as he asked. "Do you want to leave me?"

She swallowed and shook her head slowly.

He was surprised at how relieved he was. "Good. I'd rather not do this without you."

"And what about Mr. Stuart?" She sniffed, dabbing under her eyes.

"I don't think there is much I can do about the photos, but I can protect you from the fallout." He took a step closer, resisting the temptation to take her hand again to reassure her.

Something dawned on her. "I could continue feeding him information, but only what you want him to know."

"I can't ask you to do that. It would make me as bad as him." He refused to be like Walter.

One side of her mouth ticked up in a smirk. "I hope you don't mind me saying you fight too clean, sir, especially if you want to fight him."

"You might be right, but I don't want to put you in a difficult position." He suddenly felt very protective of her.

"I've been in an untenable position for years now. This would be different because I'll be on the right side."

"I'm going to have to think about that. For now, keep what you tell him to a minimum."

"I can do that." She flashed a quick smile before turning toward the door.

"And Audra," When she turned around, he said, "Not a word about Menzies, eh?"

Her expression was serious. "Not a word."

***

"Does Rachel know about your gift?" Sarah's feet crunched on the gravel path from the manor house to the guest house the next morning. A small shopping bag full of yarn dangled from her fingers.

"I dinna like keeping secrets about myself. I see so much of other people's secrets." Oona walked beside her. "She knows what I can do, but not where the skill comes from. It's not for me to tell, aye?"

"I suppose that's true." Sarah understood. It was the same reason she hadn't told James about Oona's gift. "I appreciate you doing this. I wouldn't normally ask, but Seonag is a special case."

Oona eyed her. "She's Dermot's mother, right?"

"Yes, and she has Alzheimer's. So, her memory is unreliable. Something traumatic happened to her at the manor house many years ago." Sarah told her. "I'm afraid your gift may be the only way for us to really know what happened to her."

"She canna remember, or has she buried the memory?" Oona asked.

"Maybe both. It's difficult to tell what has been lost to her disease versus what she doesn't want to remember or examine. At this point, I don't think it matters. Her long-term memory only comes in pieces which often slip away again. She spent her first night here in the manor house and had a nightmare. I think it was a memory breaking through. But she couldn't talk about it. She barely remembers people from back then."

"Poor Dermot." Sympathy was thick in Oona's voice. "Da used to black out sometimes when he was drinking and then not remember things he'd done when he sobered up. That alone was hard enough."

Sarah gave her sister a sympathetic look. She had only seen their father a few times, and he'd been sober for most of them. "I can't imagine. My mother may have been difficult to live with when she was in the worst of her depression, but she never forgot who I was."

"God. We've all had it rough, haven't we?" Oona bumped Sarah's shoulder with her own.

Sarah smiled ruefully. "Yeah, I guess we have."

"No bother." Oona gave her arm a squeeze. "It's made us who we are."

They rounded the edge of the wood, and the guest house came into view. It was a good time to give Oona the rundown on Seonag. "You'll like her. She was a Celtic antiquities scholar before she got sick. And she speaks Gaelic as easily as English."

"Right." Oona said as they stepped through the gate into the small garden in front of the cottage. "Anything else?"

Sarah thought for a second, stopping with her hand on the doorknob. "Oh, she's Lyall Green's daughter and used to be his apprentice, if she says something about who or what we are, it's probably a flash of memory. She sometimes calls me princess."

"Och, I'm sure ye love that." Sarcasm dripped in Oona's tone.

Sarah chuckled and shook her head as she opened the door. Oona's quick wit reminded her more than a little of her friend, Amy. "Hello?"

"In here?" Lottie called from the kitchen. Sarah and Oona followed the sound of her voice. When they entered the kitchen, she said. "We're finishing up our breakfast. Aren't we, love?"

Seonag looked up from a bowl of porridge and her face lit up. *"Madainn mhath a bhana phrionnsa!"* (Good morning, princess.)

Sarah shot Oona a see-what-I-mean look before stepping around the table to give Seonag a hug. *"Madainn mhath, a Sheonag. Ciamar a tha sibh?"* (Good morning, Seonag. How are you?)

"Chan eil dona." (Not bad.) Seonag wobbled her head. She continued in Gaelic. "Who is with you?"

Sarah turned toward Oona who stepped forward. "This is my sister, Oona."

"You have a sister!" Seonag grinned up at Oona and stretched out her hand. "I am pleased to meet you."

"Likewise." Oona replied slipping easily into Gaelic and shaking Seonag's hand. "Sarah has told me so much about ye."

"Och, she's a sweet lass." Seonag patted Sarah's hand where it rested on her shoulder. They shared a smile.

"Yes, she is definitely the sweet one." She gave Seonag a mischievous look. "I'm the salty sister."

Seonag laughed. "Ye'll do."

"Don't you usually take a walk this time of the morning?" Sarah asked. "Why don't we take a turn around the garden? You can show me what's still growing this late in the year."

"Alright." Seonag rose from the table. She was still only in her early fifties and relatively fit physically. Sarah was glad being at Tweedholm gave her more opportunity to spend time outside and get more exercise than the care homes had given her.

They walked around the garden chatting about the heather and the last of the year's roses. The leaves had started to turn, and most of the flowering shrubs were now sporting berries instead of flowers. As Sarah and Seonag walked, Oona followed them. She didn't say much beyond general pleasantries.

Sarah continued her visit as normal, trusting Oona was doing her thing. She had no idea what that looked like. Did she need to talk with the person or simply observe them? Sarah hoped Oona would speak up if she needed any help.

About halfway through their visit, Oona got very quiet. She didn't say much else until they returned to the cottage and said their goodbyes.

"Please tell me you got something." Sarah said once they had passed the gate on the path back to the manor house.

"Are ye sure ye want to hear it?" Oona asked looking back at the cottage. "It's not a nice story."

Sarah cursed under her breath. "I was afraid of that."

"It's very murky, and not because of her disease. The images are blurry and incomplete. I think she must have been drugged or drunk." They took their walk slowly wanting to finish their conversation before they reached the house.

"So, she was raped?" Sarah couldn't deal in innuendos anymore. She had to have direct answers.

"Aye. That's what I'd call it. I'm not even sure she remembered it when her memory was good." Oona said.

"Could you see who it was?"

"Oh, it was Walter Stuart." She walked on while Sarah absorbed the confirmation she'd been expecting. After a minute Oona spoke. "It's strange. I think he had feelings for her. He paid her a lot of attention, asked a lot about the prophecy and what she knew. He made several advances, but she didna bite." She blew out a long breath. "She's always been in love with Henry."

Sarah's whole body felt heavy. She kicked a rock in their path. "And now he would leave Anne for her, but she doesn't even remember who he is."

"That's a tragedy I hope ye won't repeat." Oona looped her arm in Sarah's.

"I'm trying." She had a hard time seeing her way out of her situation right now, but there had to be one. "I agreed to give James an heir."

Oona stopped and looked at her. "Then maybe ye'll be free sooner rather than later."

"What do you mean?" Goosebumps rose on her arms and the back of her neck.

Oona gave her a knowing look. "Have ye been feeling more tired than usual lately? Maybe a sour stomach, bit dizzy?"

"No." Sarah stopped in her tracks. She counted the weeks since she and James had been intimate, and since her time in the cave with Dermot. They were too close together to tell which of them might be the father. "Can you?"

As if she read Sarah's mind. Oona shook her head. "Not until it's born?"

Sarah felt herself turning red. "You must think I'm the worst."

"I think ye're a victim of circumstance in love with a man who's not yer husband." Oona put her arm around Sarah. "Actually, reminds me a bit of Da."

Sarah huffed out a breath. She fought down her rising panic. Oona must have picked up on it. Her tone was soothing when she said. "Ye're stronger than he was. And I think maybe yer man is stronger than yer mother was. There's hope."

Somehow the vote of confidence from the little sister she barely knew made her feel a little better. There was hope. They would see how much hope they had left when Sarah told Dermot what had happened to his mother.

CHAPTER FORTY-FOUR

Sarah watched Oona and Rachel throughout the evening thinking about what Oona said about her situation. They were obviously in love and free to be open about it. She couldn't help feeling a pang of jealousy. It was only amplified early Sunday afternoon when James and Dermot arrived.

"I thought I would make sure the country is as good for you as I hoped it would be." James told her as he bent to kiss her hello. They had been enjoying a lazy lunch on the veranda.

Sarah tried not to let the tension she'd been feeling over what Oona had learned show. "Don't worry. Oona has been forcing me to relax and have fun."

"Oona." He flashed his billion-dollar smile at Oona. "It's lovely to see you again."

"And I don't think you've met Oona's girlfriend Rachel Penhale." Sarah made the introduction.

James didn't seem surprised Oona had a girlfriend, which made Sarah wonder if Oona's sexuality hadn't come up in the intelligence gathering Walter had done on the three sisters of her generation. No doubt he had files on Sarah, Oona, and Bridget squirreled away somewhere.

"Rachel, it's nice to meet you." James said with his usual charm. He turned to draw Dermot who had been hanging back behind James into the conversation. "This is my brother, Dermot Sinclair."

Dermot stepped forward. "Afternoon."

"Feasgar math, a Dhiarmaid." Oona grinned at him.

"It's nice to meet you." Rachel replied.

"It's lovely to meet ye as well." He smiled at Rachel. *"Sin thu, a Oona."* (Hello there, Oona.)

"Actually, Oona and I have something we need to talk to you both about." Sarah said to James.

Henry tactfully spoke up pushing back his chair. "Rachel, have you seen the ruins near the river?"

Rachel, being very perceptive, rose to join him. "I'd love to see them."

They left, and James pulled out a chair, but Sarah stopped him. 'We should probably go to the library. We don't want Mrs. Miller strolling into this conversation."

"Alright." He pushed the chair back in and pulled Sarah's out as she rose. "After you, darling."

The library was cool and dark, with only low light filtering in through the windows. No one bothered to turn the light on. Sarah stepped into the center of the room and spun around to face the door.

Oona took her place next to her. Sarah was glad for her support. Oona gave her a reassuring look as James and Dermot followed them into the room. Dermot closed the door behind them.

"So, what do you need to tell us." James asked.

Sarah kept her focus on Dermot. "Oona and I visited your mother yesterday."

"Is she alright?" He asked, concern in his voice.

"She's fine, in fact, she's doing great. Her spirits are better than I've seen them. I think the country suits her." Sara twisted her fingers together, her nerves jumping. How did you tell the person you loved his mother had been raped? "Oona used her gift on your mother."

"What exactly is Oona's gift?" James interrupted.

Dermot froze looking at Sarah. He answered James's question. "She sees the truth."

"What does that mean?" James looked at Oona in confusion.

Oona spoke to him directly. "I see the truth about people when I look at them. The whole truth, the things they believe, the things they feel, things they hide, things they've done."

James looked alarmed, making Sarah wonder if he might be hiding something. James looked at Sarah. "You said the other sisters didn't have gifts like yours."

"I said they couldn't do what I can. It's not my place to tell you about their gifts."

"What," Dermot started to speak and stopped before looking warily at Oona. "What did you see?"

Oona took a deep breath. "Walter Stuart wanted her, but she wouldna have him. I canna be sure, but I think he drugged her and had his way with her."

The muscles in Dermot's jaw flexed, but he remained still. Sarah could almost feel the turmoil inside him. She knew in a moment, maybe two, the shell of reserve would crack.

"What makes you think she was drugged." James asked.

Oona glanced at him. "The impressions I got were in flashes of light and dark. I've seen enough drunk people through their own eyes to know what it looks like. This was something else, and she had trouble moving, like her arms and legs were too heavy."

Dermot closed his eyes as if he could block out the room while Oona talked. Every muscle was coiled. His fists clenched at his sides, and he breathed deliberately as if focusing on anything else might unleash what he was fighting so hard to keep in check. Sarah was glad Walter Stuart was miles away, otherwise she was worried Dermot would simply kill him and be done with them all. She didn't want Walter Stuart to be able to take anything else from him.

When Oona finished her explanation, Dermot turned on his heel and opened the door. He walked out into the hall. Sarah went to the door to follow him, but he held up a hand signaling her to let him go.

Her heart ached as she watched him walk out the back door, and into the garden. His back was ramrod straight under the weight he was carrying.

"I still don't understand this gift of yours." James' tone was defensive, as if he didn't want to believe Walter had done this. James and Oona squared off on either side of the Persian rug in the center of the room.

Oona cocked her head to the side and looked at him, really looked. "Maybe I should tell ye something about yerself. Like how ye were always jealous of Dermot and Seonag's relationship, or how ye really do love my sister. Or maybe I should tell ye Walter's actions with Seonag shouldna surprise ye after the conversation ye had with yer assistant on Friday."

James took a step back, shocked. "How could you know that?"

Oona held out her hands as if to say, 'because that's my gift.'

"Did the other one have a gift as well?" James asked in disbelief.

"Bridget." Sarah said, drawing his attention. "Her name was Bridget and she saw the future."

"The future." James scoffed. "But she didn't see her murderer coming."

"Our gifts dinna work on ourselves." Oona told him.

"So, you see the truth." James restated. Sarah could almost see his wheels turning trying to figure out how Oona's gift could be used to his advantage. "You'd be a useful person to have in a business meeting."

"I'm satisfied with the career I've chosen, thanks verra much." Oona said flatly. "I think I'll leave the two of ye to yerselves now."

"Thank you, Oona." Sarah knew what it cost Oona to see all the things she saw. It was a heavy responsibility. "James, I feel like you're getting distracted from the point here. Walter raped Seonag."

He looked down and his cheeks turned pink. "I am rarely surprised anymore by Walter's depravity." His brows furrowed. "But if Walter raped her while she was drugged, what does that make me? You were drugged when we—" He ran a hand through his hair looking like he was going to be sick. "Every time we—"

Sarah grabbed his hand squeezing it to get his attention. He was genuinely miserable about the perceived parallel. "You didn't know. This is not your fault."

"You have to believe I wouldn't have—" His breath hitched.

"I do. I believe you." Sarah's eyes sought his. "I believe you."

He sighed. He spent a few minutes trying to get himself together. He slumped down onto the couch. After a minute he said. "Walter will never be held to account for this. Seonag isn't exactly a reliable witness, and I don't think any court is going to accept a fae woman's truth-vision as evidence."

"So, we should do nothing?" Her tone sharpened in frustration. "Just let him keep on manipulating us all like pieces on his chess board?" Sarah threw her hands up in the air. Her voice turned sharp. "Ugh! I can't believe that's even a question. He's manipulated all of this from the time Seonag told y'all about the prophecy. He's the one who has guided everything. He took control of the company. He made an heir and a spare whether your mothers liked it or not. He's pulled all your strings from the minute you joined the company, and probably before. This is your chance to break free of him. Stop thinking about this in terms he set out and start leading."

"I am trying." James came to her rubbing his hands up and down her arms in a comforting gesture. "I'm working on blunting some of his power, but these things take time. He's not a weed we can simply pluck out and be done with. He's our COO and he's on the board. He knows more about the company than I do. Cutting him out of A.P. will be like excising a vital organ."

"What happened with Miss Lennox?" She asked him.

James dropped his hands and stepped back with a sigh. "He's been harassing her and extorting her to spy on me."

She shouldn't have been surprised, but Miss Lennox had always seemed loyal to James. There was no low Walter wouldn't stoop to. Spying on his own nephew was true to form. "That fits his M.O. Any leverage will do, even for spying on his own family."

"I wouldn't have believed it two days ago, but I do now." James's disappointment showed in every muscle. But as I said, getting him out isn't so easy."

"It is." She cut him off. "It might take time to get him out of our lives, and out of the company. But it only takes a second for you to decide to do it. As long as you keep looking at the problem through the lens he gave you, you're not going to see the solution." She tapped the side of her own head. "Once you fix your thinking, the rest will follow."

This was the moment Sarah had been working toward since they got married, the moment when James could choose to become his own man, not Walter's mouthpiece. He looked defeated. "I'm not as tough as you."

"I'm not tough." Sarah leaned down to catch his gaze. "I never had a choice. You do. But if you keep choosing the path of least resistance, nothing is going to change. He's going to keep running the show and doing God knows what in your name. You want to be a leader? Stop looking for other people to give you approval or roll out the red carpet. Lead the way. I know you can."

She needed him to believe he could lead the company without Walter's help. Uncertainty flickered on his face. "Will you help me?"

"You don't even have to ask."

***

When he was out of sight of the manor house, Dermot broke into a run and didn't stop until he was in front of his mother's cottage. It looked so peaceful with its window boxes and front garden. He paused to catch his breath with his hands braced on either side of the door. His chest heaved not only from the exertion, but the sheer pressure of all he was holding inside.

He worked to get control of his breath before he went in. He couldn't take his turmoil in to his mother. She had no idea and didn't need to know. He drew in huge breaths and counted as he exhaled. When he was finally ready, he knocked on the door and opened it.

"Halo?"

"Och, halo there, young man. His mother said with a grin when he poked his head inside. She was sitting in her usual chair with the television on and her knitting in her lap.

"Hello, Seonag. How are ye then?" He hoped he sounded cheerful, and not like a man full of rage and heartbreak.

He wondered how his mother had done it. What had she thought when she found herself pregnant without clearly remembering how it had happened? He wondered how she had managed to love him his whole life when she'd been violated. Had she ever remembered" Had she known it was Walter? If she had, how had she continued to visit Tweedholm all those years?

"Come and sit down. Tell me how ye are." She waved to the couch beside her chair.

He took a seat where she had indicated. Choking back the truth he said. "I'm all right. I've been working."

"Aye, and what kind of work are ye doing?" She asked as pleasant as she could be.

"Well, I was studying, but I'm moving more into the family business." He supposed the Stuarts were family now. That was the only way to look at it. They were all the family he had whether he wanted them or not.

"And what sort of business is that?" She asked, obviously she didn't recognize him. She rarely did these days, even in a familiar place in Seonag's mind he was still a little boy, a little boy she had chosen to have without knowing where he'd come from.

He thought about answering her question honestly, but he didn't want to bring up thoughts of the Stuarts. He didn't want any unpleasant memories to filter through. "Oh, simply business, buying and selling.'

"Is that what ye want to do?" She cocked her head. She might not remember who he was, but she could clearly read his ambivalence.

He gave her a sheepish smile and shrugged. "It pays the bills. I'll get back to school someday."

She patted his hand. "Dinna wait too long. Ye ken what they say. What can be done at any time will be done at no time."

His laugh was rueful. Trading proverbs was a game they used to play when he was a teenager. "Aye, maybe, but a proud mind and an angry purse grow ill together."

She threw her head back and laughed. "Ah, ye're a canny lad. I wish ye could meet my Dermot. Ye'd like him."

He didn't think he would. He didn't much care for the man he was becoming, bitter, angry, conflicted. He felt like he wasn't living his own life, merely hanging about James on the off chance he could be close to Sarah. He was tired of waiting for something to happen to break this stalemate. He had pledged his life for hers, and he'd never regret it. But he felt further away from her every day as he watched her grow closer to James. Now, he knew the worst of Walter's perfidy, his frustration mixed with rage in a constant undercurrent pulling at him every day.

He coasted through the rest of his visit hoping she wouldn't pick up on his mood. Then he kissed her cheek and began his walk back, but he didn't want to go into the house in his mood. He couldn't seem to string more than three thoughts together without one of them touching on Walter Stuart, and the fire he'd kept banked while visiting his mother would come roaring back to life.

He turned off the path and went into the forest toward the ruins that had been his refuge when he was a boy. It was time to burn out some of the fury building inside him.

CHAPTER FORTY-FIVE

"How do we hold a man accountable who has never been accountable for anything in his life?" His father seethed. James was clear on that now. Henry was his father because he would never claim Walter. He didn't even want to claim him publicly as his uncle anymore.

They had informed his father of the state of things after he and Rachel had returned from their walk. Rachel and Oona had retired to their room, while he, his father, and Sarah gathered in the sitting room to discuss.

Sarah stood in front of the window; her attention trained on the drive as if she was keeping watch lest Walter might arrive at any moment. Given her gift, he wondered if she knew something he didn't. She said over her shoulder. "He did this to Sconag, and harassed Miss Lennox. Who knows how many other victims he's left in his wake in the last thirty years."

He thought she wanted to say more, but her gaze turned inward, and she turned back to the window. James leaned his head against his high-backed chair. He knew she was more than likely correct. Who knew what his uncle had done in the name of restoring his family to their rightful place. It made him sick.

"I've always known he was ruthless and driven. But this is intolerable. And it's gone on too long." His father muttered.

"Yes, but how can we expose this to the board without exposing ourselves, and the prophecy? We'd be risking all our credibility."

"Now you acknowledge how ridiculous it sounds." Sarah muttered.

"I acknowledged it before, but we both know the truth of it." James leveled a censorious look on her. She couldn't still deny the prophecy after all they'd seen.

Sarah pressed her lips together and turned back to the window. James was at a loss. He didn't know how they were going to get rid of Walter. Sarah whirled around. "Do you mind if I call in some reinforcements?"

Reinforcements? "What do you have in mind?"

"You said yourself, Oona can be helpful. She can look at Walter and see everything he's up to. It will let us know what else he's done. It could give us ammunition. We need more to work with than what we have."

"The board will still need proof." James argued. "They're not going to take Oona's word for it."

"No, but what she sees can tell us where to look for proof. We can find it much faster." A spark lit her eyes as she warmed to the idea.

"Would she help?" He wasn't' sure about Sarah's enigmatic family, especially her sister.

A deadly smile grew on Sarah's face. "I'm sure she would."

Did he really want to embroil someone else in this? Then again Oona Ballantyne had already seen what he hoped was the worst of it. "Yes, I want us to be rid of him."

"Not as much as I do." Dermot's gravelly voice came from the doorway.

James turned to find his brother standing there; face grim, hands dangling at his sides. James hated that he'd even hesitated when he looked at Dermot who's been the target of so many of Walter's schemes. "We'll get free of him."

Dermot sighed, tired. His face didn't show the kind of confidence James desperately wanted to see. Dermot had always been his sounding board, the person who kept him grounded. "We'll see."

"Your hands!" Sarah went to Dermot lifting one of his hands for a closer look. His knuckles were bleeding and bruised.

"It's all right, love. Simply working out some frustration." Dermot tried to pull his hand back, but she wouldn't let go.

"Against what, rocks?" She cried. A memory flashed in his mind of a sullen Dermot in the castle ruins kicking rocks. He knew where his brother had been. Sarah pulled Dermot into the hallway. "Come to the kitchen. We've got to get some ice and antiseptic on these." Turning to James "We'll be back with Oona. Then we can make a plan."

James could only watch as his wife pulled Dermot down the hall to the kitchen to see to his injuries. He felt so impotent and, not for the first time, jealous of his brother. If he was going to keep her, he was going to have to become the leader she'd been talking about. Which made ridding them all of Walter even more vital.

"Walter would tell you to watch him when it comes to her.' His father stood at his shoulder.

James pressed his lips together in frustration. "Sarah made her choice. I trust her. And after everything Dermot has been through, I think we owe him the benefit of the doubt."

"How are things going between you and Sarah?" Henry's concern seemed genuine rather than a subtle way of asking if she was pregnant yet. James knew what Walter meant whenever he asked similar questions.

"Things were going well until she revealed her gift. I didn't take it well. I was upset she'd kept it from me, and I lost my temper. Then I compounded it by letting Walter pressure me into asking her to use her power to help Alba Petroleum." He confessed. Although she'd been helping, their relationship seemed stuck in a zone of publicly together, but privately strained. "I'm afraid that request broke something between us."

His father patted his shoulder. "She's a woman with her own mind."

"She is."

"She has a point though." Henry's tone was a little tentative, as if he wasn't sure he was qualified anymore to give fatherly advice. "I think it's time to step out of Walter's shadow."

James sighed heavily, sinking into a chair. "That's easier said than done. I'm afraid we'll never be free of his influence unless we can excise him from every part of the company and our lives."

"You're not wrong." Henry said. "I'll help you in any way I can."

***

"Did you knock what remained of the walls down?" Sarah asked as she soaked a cotton pad in peroxide. Mrs. Miller had been handy with the first aid kit when Sarah dragged him into the kitchen. Within seconds he was sitting at the table with a clean towel under his hand and Sarah tending to him.

"I hit a tree. I'm not a complete idiot." Dermot grumbled. He tried to resist the temptation to wrap his tired arms around her and never let go. The house was full of people least of all her husband, so he had to content himself with letting her sooth his sore hands.

"Did it help?" Her eyes caught his, making him feel a bit ridiculous for his fit of temper.

"I dinna want to drive back to the city and smash the monster's face in at the moment. So, aye, it helped a bit." Having burned out the rage, he could think past the fury. "Ye really dinna have to baby me like this."

"Shut up and let me take care of you." She snapped dabbing his knuckles with more force than necessary. For the first time since they'd told him, he saw past his own hurt to hers. She was hurting for him, and his mother, and herself. Surrounded by the Stuarts, this was the only outward way she could show how much she cared. *"Tha mi duilich."* (I'm sorry.)

"You don't have to apologize." She pressed her lips together and reached for the antiseptic ointment. "I don't begrudge you any outlet for what you're feeling."

"What outlet do you have?" He watched emotions flicker across her face.

She busied herself applying the ointment to the abrasions on his hand. "I don't have the luxury of venting my rage. I have to turn it into fuel for the long haul."

Guilt swamped him. There were no breaks for her. He got to go home at the end of the day and maybe feel a little bit normal. Sarah lived in captivity twenty-four hours a day. "I'm sorry."

She shook her head before pulling his other hand over the towel and beginning the process again. "You didn't do any of this."

His eyes fixed on her lips, and he recalled the feeling of them against his skin. He lowered his voice to a whisper. "My mother is safe now. Henry willna let anything happen to her."

Sarah paused and briefly closed her eyes. She matched his volume. "He can't be with her all the time, and my people aren't safe."

He leaned his head down, catching her gaze. "Ye canna sacrifice yerself forever. None of them would want that."

"Not forever." Her eyes burned like cold green flames, but she kept her voice low. "Only until James has his heir."

"Ye think that will satisfy him? He's in love with ye." He leaned closer.

"Yeah, so Oona says. I can't help his feelings only mine." She seemed confident in what she was saying.

Her focus dropped to his mouth. He was about to lean in and kiss her when Mrs. Miller bustled into the kitchen from the pantry holding a bag of frozen peas. "It took some digging, but I found just the thing for those bruised knuckles."

CHAPTER FORTY-SIX

Thirty minutes later they gathered again in the sitting room. This time they were joined by Oona and Rachel.

"Darling, I really think this is something we should keep within the family." James told her when others joined them.

Sarah started to explain, but Oona beat her to the punch. "If ye want my help, ye get Rachel's as well. Oona settled easily onto a love seat near the fireplace.

"You'll be surprised at the things I can do." Rachel sat next to Oona.

James looked unsure, but he didn't protest. "It goes without saying not a word of any of this leaves this room."

"Dinna fash, yer highness. I'm used to keeping secrets." Oona flashed him a crooked smile. She clearly enjoyed making James uncomfortable.

"Then let's get started." Henry closed the door not wanting Mrs. Miller to overhear their plans.

"Right." James stood where he could make eye contact with everyone. "I think by now we all know the goal is to extricate my uncle, Walter Stuart, from Alba Petroleum. I would love to get him out of our lives, but I doubt that will be entirely possible. However, we can cripple him financially and hurt his network of support."

"How?" Henry asked from an overstuffed chair beside the fire.

"Dermot and I have been working sympathetic board members to garner support for the clean energy initiative and rebranding. I think their support can also be counted on if we confront Walter, but we need more dirt to take to the board. We need something they can't be caught supporting or ignoring." James explained.

"Except we don't have anything but my word when it comes to assaulting your mother." Oona said glancing at Dermot.

Dermot leaned forward bracing his elbows on his knees. "But we do have James's assistant, Audra Lennox. We've learned Walter has been extorting and harassing her into spying on James for him for years."

"What?" Henry interrupted, clearly shocked.

James turned to his father. "Apparently, he placed her with me for that purpose from the start."

Henry's gaze turned inward as if he were searching his memory.

"Miss Lennox is willing to explain her situation to the board. However, it will be her word against Walter's. We still need some sort of proof of his wrongdoing." James continued laying out the situation.

"If he's done this to Seonag and Miss Lennox, chances are he's done it and worse to someone else." Sarah added looking at Oona and Rachel. "We have to find proof."

Oona looked at Sarah for a moment, no doubt watching a psychic replay of their father's death. Sarah hadn't mentioned it to James or Henry, nor had Dermot. Exposing Walter as her father's murderer would also reveal that she only married James under duress. Sarah was terrified she would lose

James's support if he knew she had been lying to him for months.

Oona must have read Sarah's thoughts. She didn't say anything about Rab's murder. "This is where we come in. I can use my gift to see what wicked deeds Walter is hiding."

"And I can find the proof." Rachel added.

"Sorry, how will ye do that?" Dermot looked doubtful.

Oona and Rachel exchanged wicked looks. Oona answered. "My lady love here is a hacker who doesna work for the government."

"Phone records, financial transactions, video evidence, if there's something electronic to be found, I can find it." Rachel blushed a little, but her voice was full of confidence.

"With me telling her what to look for, we can find it faster than anyone ye could hire." Oona said.

"And Walter doesn't consider them threats," Sarah added. "We can't trust anyone working for A.P. Security. As far as we know, Walter has no idea about Oona's gift, and Rachel keeps her activities on the down low for obvious reasons."

"To anyone looking, I work in IT at a bank." Rachel said with a shrug. I cover my digital tracks well.

"I see." Sarah could almost see his wheels turning. "Suddenly, I feel more hopeful. How do we get Oona and Walter in the same room?"

"We're not likely to invite him to dinner." Walter had been persona non grata at the Polwarth Terrace house since Anne's failed attempt at reconciliation. "I think he would suspect something if we suddenly invited him over."

"Ye could commission a portrait." Oona suggested. "It is what I do."

"Why would I commission a portrait of my estranged uncle?" James asked looking confused.

Sarah had an idea. "Because you like the one Oona gave me as a wedding gift so much you decided to get portraits of A. P. executives for the hallway in the executive suite. It's a perfect ruse, and it gives Oona a reason to look at all the executives. That way we can find out how closely each of them has been working with Walter. Added bonus."

James looked back and forth between them all as if waiting for any other suggestions. Dermot shrugged. "It's the best plan I've heard."

"Right, then." James said with a sigh. "We have a plan. The next board meeting is in a little over two weeks. Which doesn't give us much time."

"If you have a modem here, I can start poking about right now." Rachel offered.

"And I can start working on a portrait of ye to prove ye've commissioned me." Oona said.

"I can get you into the executive floor as soon as you're ready. I'll arrange it with Miss Lennox." James tapped his fingers on the arm of his chair.

Oona grinned and Sarah knew she was thinking about finally getting revenge on the man who killed her father. "I'll be there."

"I'll go tell Mrs. Miller we'll be going back to the city this evening." Sarah, Oona, and Rachel rose and went to pack their things. Sarah stopped Oona at the bottom of the stairs with a hand on her arm. "Thank you."

Oona smiled and stepped closer to Sarah. "This gift has to be good for something, right?" She leaned closer and whispered in Sarah's ear. "When are ye going to tell them about the baby?"

Sarah looked over her shoulder to where Dermot, James, and Henry stood talking softly. She finally had James and Dermot on the same page about Walter. She didn't dare shatter their alliance yet.

CHAPTER FORTY-SEVEN

Sarah stared at herself in the mirror of the bath off the downstairs hallway. Her skin felt cold and clammy, and her head was spinning. She had come out of their conversation about Walter feeling confident about their plan. But now the added complication of a baby made everything seem more risky and more important. She hadn't wanted to think about Oona's revelation about the baby until she got back to the city and confirmed it. But she couldn't deny it anymore.

The lunch she'd eaten came rushing back up and she sprinted for the toilet. The questions, scenarios, and implications running through her head were suddenly gone as she hurled up Mrs. Miller's cockaleekie soup. When she was left dry retching, she sat back against the wall and tried to catch her breath.

After a few deep breaths she was overcome by a feeling of absolute peace. The air was cool, and everything went quiet. Someone mopped her brow. Sarah sighed and opened her eyes. She expected to see Oona or Mrs. Miller, but it was neither of them. She met the dark brown eyes of Mary. She was smiling at Sarah. The peace Sarah was feeling made sense now. Mary somehow always brought her peace when she needed it.

Mary offered her hand to Sarah and helped her get up from the floor. Sarah was about to ask her advice on how to tell them about her pregnancy when a knock on the door was followed by Dermot's voice. "Are ye alright?"

"Yeah, I'll be out in a sec." Mary nodded encouragingly before fading away like smoke. Sarah's throat felt raw. She flushed the toilet and rinsed her mouth out. She needed to brush her teeth, but that would have to do for the moment. She took a couple of deep breaths before opening the door.

Dermot stood there looking concerned. "Alright then?"

"Just dandy." She quipped hoping she was convincing.

He looked at her in suspicion, but he didn't say anything.

"Excuse me." She slid past him and headed for the stairs.

As she turned to go up, she saw him lean into the powder room and sniff. "Ye're not fine."

Sarah hurried up the stairs without trying to appear like she was trying to escape him. She heard Dermot behind her. "Sarah, wait."

She didn't stop. She could barely handle the news herself; she wasn't ready to share it with anyone else, not even him. She made a beeline for her bedroom. The door was open, and James was inside, no doubt waiting for her. Sarah walked past him to the bathroom.

Behind her James said. "Can I help you, brother?"

As she picked up her toothbrush, Sarah looked back to see James and Dermot standing almost nose to nose in the doorway, eyes blazing.

She hoped a little humor would break the tension. "Good Lord, do you boys square up like this at the office every day? How do y'all get anything done?"

Dermot ignored her. "She's ill, James. She was boaking in the toilet downstairs."

"I'm fine." Sarah told James when his head swiveled her way. "Lunch didn't agree with me. That's all."

"Ye came here to get better, but it looks like ye're worse." Dermot said around James who still stood in the doorway.

"I've got it." James told him. Turning back to Sarah, he said. "Darling are you alright?"

"I'm fine." Sarah assured him.

"She's not." Dermot snapped in quick order.

"I will take care of her." James ground out to Dermot as he moved to close the door.

"Like ye have been?" Dermot blocked the door with his foot.

"Careful, brother." The muscles in James's jaw flexed as he seethed. "I might think you're still holding a candle for my wife." He emphasized the last two words.

"I'm worried about her." Dermot said through gritted teeth.

"Yes, I saw how worried you were the other day when you were fawning over her." James's voice was low and deadly.

"I'm fine, boys, really." Sarah tried to pull James further into the room so she could put the door between them.

"Someone has to have a care for her instead of using her for yer own gain." Dermot spat.

"Okay." Sarah pulled harder on James's arm, and he took a step back into the bedroom. "If you two are going to fight like a couple of dogs after a bone, you can do it in here and not the hallway."

Dermot stepped forward and closed the door hopefully shutting out anyone who might overhear them. James squeezed Sarah's hand giving her a confident smile before turning back to Dermot. "You really can't stand it, can you? You can't bear the fact that she chose me."

"Chose you?" Dermot barked, his face a mask of fury.

"Dermot, don't." Sarah hissed, but she could tell it was too late. Dermot's long fuse had finally reached its end.

"She didna choose you!" He stepped toward James lowering his voice. "Our father bought her for ye, at the cost of my life and the lives of everyone she cares about."

James reared back as if Dermot's words were a foul wind blowing right in his face.

"Dermot, please." Sarah didn't want him to say anything else, but there was no stopping him now.

"He murdered her father in front of us to prove he meant it. She didna choose ye. She chose to keep her friends and family alive."

There was only silence for several seconds as they each absorbed the gravity of what Dermot had said. James turned to her horror written on his face. "Is that true?"

Sarah sighed knowing the last of James's trust would be gone. Still, she wouldn't lie to him when asked, but she couldn't make herself say the words. Her eyes met his. They were both fighting back tears. She gave him a slight nod of confirmation.

His shoulders sank. "All this time. You..." He sank down on the bench at the end of the bed. "We..." He leaned forward, elbows on knees and covered his face with his hands. "Why didn't you tell me?"

Sarah sank to her knees in front of him. "I was protecting my family, Duff, my brother and sister, Amy, and Barrett. He threatened them all."

He dropped his hands from his face which was filled with a look of raw pain. "Tell me about your father. How did that happen?"

Sarah shot Dermot a warning look. She didn't need any more revelations from him. She would have to tell this her own way. Shifting her attention back to James. "We tried to run on my hen night."

James closed his eyes. Sarah hated telling him this, knowing it would hurt him. But there was no going back now. "Dermot's friend Des helped us navigate the South Bridge vaults. But someone tipped Walter off. He kidnapped my father and Duff and tried to make me choose between them. Dermot was right. He shot my father in front of us. He also killed Des."

"I thought your father fell down The News Steps." James said confused.

"That's where they left his body. It's the official story." Sarah said. "I have no idea how they covered up the bullet hole in his chest."

"No doubt there were bribes involved." Dermot muttered, drawing James's attention.

He looked his brother up and down before turning back to Sarah. "What about us? I know we weren't close then, but I thought we were getting closer. I thought you felt something for me."

Dermot scoffed behind her, but neither she nor James paid him any attention.

"I did. I do." She gripped his hands inching closer. "I care about you very much. I would never want to hurt you."

"But you let me think…"

"I let you think I married you for security." Sarah said. "Which is true. I let you think I want to provide you with an heir, which I do. I let you think I care about you, and I do. I have tried to be as honest as I could be without endangering people I love."

James gave her hands a gentle squeeze. "I need to think. Please excuse me."

He stood and made his way to the door. He opened it enough to slip out into the hallway, closing it behind him. The click of the latch resonated through the silent room like a whip crack.

***

Sarah remained on her knees, head hanging low as James's footsteps retreated down the hall. Dermot felt deflated. The adrenaline pumping through him as he spewed his hard truths at James had burned out. The fire was banked by Sarah's calm explanations. He regretted hurting James, but he would have learned those facts someday.

"Are you happy?" Sarah's weary question cut through the silence. "You just undid all the work I've been doing for the last three months."

She stood slowly from her place on the floor, her temper gaining steam. She whirled on him. "And you put people in danger." She pointed an angry finger toward the door stepping closer to him. "When Walter finds out James knows, he's not going to care it wasn't me who told him."

He backed away from her advance. "How am I the bad guy here?"

"That damned temper of yours!" She whisper-yelled. "I have been trying to drive a wedge between James and Walter for months, and we were on the verge of breaking free of that man." She stood directly in front of him. "Now, I'll be lucky if he doesn't go running back to Walter's arms because he thinks I've been lying to him this whole time."

'We've both been lying." He hissed back at her, keeping his voice low. "We dinna have to anymore."

"We might not have to lie to James, but we're still going to have to keep up the lies to everyone else." She tapped the side of her head. "You didn't think telling the truth would suddenly make us free, did you?"

"It could." He grabbed her hand and pulled it to him. "We could go right now. James wouldna stop us."

"Maybe not, but my face has been on every newspaper and TV in the country. Do you really think we'd get far?" She was incredulous. 'And James might not stop us, but Walter sure will. And I bet your grandfather might have something to say about it too."

She pulled away from him and sat on the bench with a sigh.

Dermot followed her but didn't sit. "What does he have to do with anything?"

"He'll want to see the prophecy come true." She looked up at him, her eyes sparkling with unshed tears. "Baby, I'm not sick. I'm pregnant."

Dermot froze, but not from shock or fear. He was overwhelmed by a pervasive sense of rightness as if the mess of their lives had settled into place like gears fitting together. He dropped to his knee in front of Sarah. "How do ye know?"

She huffed out a breath. "Oona of course."

Of course, the truth seer. He counted the weeks since they'd last been at Tweedholm, since they'd been together. Did he dare hope? "Can she tell?"

She shook her head. "Not until it's born."

"Doesna matter." He slid a hand behind her head and pulled her forehead to meet his. He whispered. "Yer child is my child whoever the father is."

She drew in a breath. "I'm relieved to hear you say that."

He released her. "Have ye told James?"

"I haven't had a chance." She gave him a rueful look. "You sort of stole my thunder."

His mind started running through the implications of this news, but the thoughts he fixed on were all about Sarah. "Ye'll see a doctor when ye're back in the city, aye? Make sure everything is all right?"

"I will." She agreed.

"Ye'll tell me if ye need anything?" Although he knew she wouldn't want for anything. James would make sure she got the best of care.

He sat on the floor beside Sarah, his hand enveloping hers. "I wish I could shout with joy, go with ye to every appointment, pick out names and nursery colors with ye. I dinna care if it's his child, but I hate that I canna be at yer side through this."

"I know." She laid her other hand on top of their joined hands. "So do I."

"D'ye think he would allow that?" He should know better than to hope.

Sarah shrugged. "I suppose it depends on how he reacts to what he just learned."

CHAPTER FORTY-EIGHT

'Is this what heartbreak feels like?' James thought, stepping onto the rocky beach at the bottom of the garden. His chest hurt, and his limbs were heavy. He had walked through the house and the garden, trying to get as far away from Sarah and Dermot as he could. But even the air around him felt thick, like walking through soup.

This was more than disappointment. She'd been forced to marry him. Despite his insistence on her consent, Walter had used whatever means he could to gain her compliance and, in the process, made James no better than a rapist. James had thought he could give her something beyond security, but all they had done was taken from her. It was no wonder she still loved Dermot.

He should be jealous. He should be furious with Dermot, but he couldn't. Now that he had the full picture, he couldn't blame Dermot any more than he could blame Sarah. Their lives had been chewed up by Walter's schemes. Yes, he wanted an independent Scotland. He believed he could lead the country to independence, but he was beginning to wonder if the ends justified the means, and if he was completely honest, why he thought he was the one to bring it about. The person telling him he should, was also a murderer, a rapist, an abuser.

The river rippled against the bank. James picked up a rock and cast it into the river watching how the current changed around it and then resolved itself into the same pattern as the rock sank. He wondered what the point of any of it was. Was he the river charging toward the sea, relentlessly moving toward its goal, or was he the rock plonked in the way but only affecting the flow for a second, irrelevant to the result.

He'd been told all his life he was meant for this. He was meant to usher Scotland toward independence, with a daughter of the old ways by his side. But no one had told him how, and it seemed no one had realized the daughter of the old ways was going to be her own person with goals, and dreams, and people to love. It was easy to talk about these things in the abstract, but the reality of it was far different.

He'd expected the politics and finances of gaining independence to be complicated, but it was nothing compared to managing the personal aspects of fulfilling this prophecy. Sarah was proving to be a worthy partner when it came to the public facing duties or supporting his efforts. But he despaired that she would ever love him. He'd thought they were forming a bond. He saw now it was a lie.

In fact, she had tried to run from him. It had taken threats and an actual murder to get her to marry him. God! He'd wondered about her grief for the father she barely knew, but now hearing he'd been murdered in front of her, it made so much more sense. And what had he done? Turned her gift into a commodity, put his hands on her in anger, expected the use of her body for his own purposes. And she'd been drugged in order for him to do that. How could she even stand to look at him? He wasn't sure he'd be able to look at himself in the mirror after today.

"Shouldn't you be preparing to go back to the city?" His father said from behind him.

"I probably should." James said, not moving. He watched the river go by as his father stood next to him. "I don't think she's ever going to love me."

"Is that what you want?" His father asked.

James's heart ached. "More than anything."

"Well, it's a good job you married her then." Henry's tone wasn't a joking one. "By the time I realized I was in love with Seonag, I was already married to your mother. I married her because she fit the expected characteristics for the wife of someone in my position, and I liked her. I was attracted to her. But I wouldn't say I was ever in love with her. We each brought something to the table, and we found a way to work together...for a time. You have the advantage of being married to Sarah. You might still win her."

"Did you know that Walter threatened her into marrying me?" James held his breath dreading his father's answer. He didn't want to believe Henry was capable of that sort of coercion.

Henry looked at him, his shock evident. "What do you mean?"

James took a beat thinking about how to explain it. "It was Sarah who broke the tie when the Nine selected me. He threatened to kill Dermot, Seonag, Sarah's family, her friends, if she didn't marry me. She changed her vote to protect them."

"He threatened to kill his own son?" Henry was as shocked as James had been. "And she believed he could do that?"

"Well, we didn't know Dermot was his son then. And I expect he was rather convincing. You know how he is."

"I do." Disappointment was heavy in his voice.

"It's worse." He had to say it, had to tell his father who Walter was. "Days before the wedding she and Dermot were going to run away." The words choked him, jamming together in his throat. "Walter murdered her father in front of her to prove how far he was willing to go."

"God!" Henry paled and turned to look at the river. They sat in silence for several minutes, the weight of this new knowledge heavy between them.

"I don't know if Walter has any connection to Cardell, but Cardell gave her a perfume that was a drug. It made her see someone else, probably Dermot, when we were...consummating our marriage." His voice cracked and he cleared his throat. "Everything I thought Sarah and I had was a lie orchestrated by him."

"Oh, son." Henry shook his head, brows creased in sympathy.

"I hate him." James said softly. "I don't simply want him out of Alba Petroleum. I want to destroy him."

"We will." Henry agreed. "But we must make sure we don't destroy everything we've built in the process. I know you feel like burning it all down right now, but you need the platform A.P. offers. Don't take the whole ship down when you can make one man walk the plank."

He made sense. "First, we get him out of the company. Then I will chip away at everything he has."

"And Sarah?" Henry asked.

James shook his head. "I don't know. She loves Dermot. I need her to accomplish what we want, but I don't think I can make her stay, not in good conscience, no matter how much I want to."

"Take it from an old man who waited until it was too late." Henry laid a hand on his shoulder. "You can't force it. I tried with your mother, but once the newness wore off, it was never right. I'm not saying you should give up without a fight, but you have to let her choose."

James felt like he couldn't breathe merely thinking of it. "What if she chooses him?"

His father put his arm around James's shoulders. "As the saying goes, 'What's for you will not go by you.' If she does choose him, I believe there will be someone for you."

***

James knocked on the bedroom door. He shouldn't have to knock on his own bedroom door, but she was in there and he wouldn't force himself on her any more than he already had. He'd half expected her to have left with Dermot and disappeared. The fact that she was still there gave him hope.

"Come in."

She was sitting next to her bags at her vanity table, looking more nervous than she had on their wedding day. He shook his head. "I have to admit, I find it a little surprising you're still here."

"I made a commitment." She said quietly.

"You were coerced. You cannot feel bound by that." James hated admitting it, but there was no avoiding the truth.

"I'm sorry you had to learn about it like that." Sarah watched him like she was waiting for him to explode.

He couldn't blame her for that either. He had put that fear there, not Walter. "You have nothing to be sorry about." He found it incredibly hard to meet her eyes. "I hope you know I would never have forced you into a marriage you didn't want."

Her voice hardened slightly. "I seem to recall you telling me after the matching ceremony that your hands were tied."

He had thought he couldn't feel more shame, but her reminder proved him wrong. He had believed there was nothing he could do, because Walter and his mother had told him so. What was it Sarah had said? He had to stop looking at things through the lens Walter had given him. "You're right. I did believe that. And you were right then, I didn't know you. I was in love with an idea I had been fed since birth."

He glanced up to find her watching him patiently. He had to tell her. "I have gotten to know you better over the past few months and I have come to love you more than I could have imagined. You have taught me to be a better man, a better leader."

"A better king?" She asked, challenge in the way she held her chin.

"I'm not even sure I'm right for Scotland anymore. That's how much you've changed me." His thumb traced the brocade pattern on the coverlet. "I still want independence, but I don't think Walter's ambitions of a restored monarchy were really for the benefit of the country. I can see now he is only out to increase his power."

"On that we can agree." She folded her hands in her lap carefully and set her jaw. She was still ill at ease. She had been for a while, but this seemed worse.

He met her eyes. It wasn't easy, but he needed her to believe him. "I don't want to hurt you any more than you already have been." He blew out a long breath. "But I need your help. We have a plan now; one I think will help us break free from Walter. You're partly responsible for that. I'm asking you to help me see it through. Help me remove Walter from the company. Without A.P.'s resources, his influence will fade. Then I can work to take him down. Will you see it through with me?"

She gave him a half-smile. "You don't even have to ask. For all our sakes, we need to be rid of him."

Relief flooded him. She wouldn't leave him yet. "Thank you." It took an effort to push the next words out, but he knew giving her the choice was the right thing to do. "When this is done, whatever you choose to do next will be up to you. If you want to leave with Dermot, or you want to stay with me, or live on your own, I won't stand in your way. I won't lie. I want you to stay with me, but I love you enough to let you go."

Sarah breathed deeply. Where he'd expected to see relief on her part, he only saw more tension. Sarah sat forward facing him directly. "That might be a more difficult choice than you think. "I'm pregnant."

Shock, joy, and anxiety ran through him in waves. The heir Walter and his mother had been pressuring him for. If she'd told him this morning, he would have been overjoyed. Now, joy warred with worry and shame at the situation they'd put her in and a bit of anger because if she chose to stay with him, he would never know if it was for his own sake or for the child's. Then another thought occurred to him. "I hope you'll pardon me for seeming indelicate, but is it mine or his?"

Her eyes narrowed on him. "Worried about your heir's legitimacy? I thought we were past that?"

He had said he wasn't concerned with restoring the monarchy. He didn't say he was unbothered by his wife being unfaithful. But then if their marriage was coerced, could he fairly be upset? "I would rather there were no secrets between us."

"That's fair." She tilted her head in acknowledgement. "I had every intention of being faithful to you when we got married. I have no excuse for it beyond the fact that I love him. I have never stopped loving him. I've been with him once since we were matched at Taigh na Damh."

"After I asked you to search for oil."

She sighed. "That doesn't justify it. I am sorry."

He couldn't be angry. She'd been forced into this. "As I said, you have done nothing to apologize for. What I said stands. When Walter is removed from the company, you can choose what you want to do. I will not hold you."

"I appreciate that, but how would we explain your pregnant wife leaving you to the public?" Her brows knit together in concern. "It would be a huge scandal which I'm sure you don't want."

"We'll cross that bridge when we come to it. For now, I suppose we have to keep up appearances. But I want you to know I won't force myself on you."

"Thank you." Sarah appeared relieved and regretful. She rose from the stool picking up her handbag. "I guess we should head back to the city if we're going to put our plan into action."

He stood and ushered her out the door. Before they joined the others for the drive back to town, pretending to be a happy couple, Sarah laughed softly.

"What's so funny?" He asked.

"Both of our families repeating history with every generation it seems."

He chuckled. "We'll have to be the ones to break the cycle."

"I like the way you think."

***

The next morning, James eyed Dermot who was sitting at the table in his office reading a report on the profit potential of wind energy. They had established a wary truce after Dermot's outburst the day before. In the way of their family, they had both issued terse apologies and then gotten back to business. Now, they sat in his office preparing for the week's meetings, which left James unsatisfied, and he hoped Dermot felt the same.

They needed to talk about their situation. He decided to take the direct approach. "Did she tell you, about the baby?"

Dermot's head shot up, and their eyes locked. His sparked with barely banked fires. "She did. What did she tell ye?"

James rested against the back of his chair trying to affect a relaxed posture. He wasn't trying to start a fight or make an accusation. "That it might be yours or mine."

"And yet I'm still here." Dermot moved to one of the chairs across from James's desk.

"I don't like the situation we find ourselves in, but we all know who is responsible for it, and it isn't the three of us." James fidgeted with his pen choosing his next words carefully. "I admit I am disappointed with both of you, but I'm the odd man out here."

Dermot looked properly guilty. "I can only say I'm sorry. I never set out to hurt ye, nor did she."

"I know." James leaned forward resting his elbows on the desk between them. "I've told Sarah as much. When we are free of Walter, she will be free to choose how she wants to go forward. I am willing to let her go if that's what she wants."

"Even if she's having your child?" Dermot looked skeptical.

"Even then." He sighed. "I've been thinking a lot about the prophecy, and I'm not sure the throne matters anymore."

"And the prophecy?" Dermot asked.

"I'm not sure we've been interpreting that correctly. This child is what's most important, not all of us. And a child needs parents who will love it. Can I trust you will love a child even if it might be mine?"

"I swore an oath to Sarah that I would always protect her children." Dermot's hand formed a fist on the arm of the chair. "Any child of hers is a child of mine. I dinna care who the father is."

"That's easy to say when the child is theoretical. I wonder if you'll feel the same when she begins to show, or once the child is born."

Dermot gritted his teeth. "I suppose we'll have to see when the time comes."

James arched an eyebrow at his brother. "I should warn you. While I will allow Sarah to choose, that doesn't mean I won't try to convince her to stay."

Dermot's voice deepened to a rumble like distant thunder. "Ye can try."

James resisted the temptation to take the bait. "There is something else I want to talk about."

"Alright." Dermot looked wary.

"When this project is complete, the company is going to need a new COO." James watched his brother's face closely. "I think we've made a good team for the past few weeks. You seem to be taking to the business well. I need a COO with integrity who can undo some of the bad culture that Walter has fostered. I would like you to consider the role."

Shock and incredulity swept over Dermot's expression. "I am not qualified for that. Ye need someone with a business background, and a lot more experience.'

"We can get someone to back you up." James waved away the concern. "I need someone I can trust."

Dermot shook his head. "Let's see how things shake out and what Sarah decides. Ye can't want us around if she chooses me."

James sighed. "I feel like I finally have a family who value me as a person and two of you are likely to leave me. I don't like it."

Dermot's face softened. "I'm sorry, mate. I wish this were all different."

Miss Lennox knocked at the door and opened it. Arguing voices came through from the hallway. "Sir, I think you may need to come out here."

"I'm here at James Stuart's request." James recognized Oona Ballantyne's sharp tongue.

He and Dermot quickly went to see what the trouble was.

"I find that hard to believe." Walter sounded superior as usual. Before he'd even stepped into the hallway, James could imagine Walter looking down his nose at Sarah's petite but fiery sister.

"What's this?" James asked. Walter stood glaring at Oona. A security guard gripped her elbow and was pulling her toward the elevator. "Let her go."

The guard immediately released her.

Walter whirled on him. "I found this…person looking at the paintings in the hallway. I'd like to know how she got past security."

"I signed her in. I asked her to come." James said coolly. He wasn't going to let his uncle rile his temper. "Don't you recognize my sister-in-law?"

Walter looked Oona up and down, distaste clear on his face. "Oh. Of course, Miss Ballantyne." He turned back to James. "Why did you invite her here?"

James grinned. 'Oona is the toast of the London art scene. She painted a portrait of Sarah as a wedding gift. I liked it so much; I've commissioned portraits of the executive team to replace these old landscapes."

"Portraits." Walter looked at James as if he'd grown another head.

"I am known for my portraits." Oona added straightening her leather jacket and looking smug.

"Are you?" Walter examined Oona again with disdain. He must have decided she looked sufficiently strange and out of place with her spiky hair and heavy boots to be a professional artist. "I wish you had told me, James."

James shrugged in response. "I made an executive decision."

"Hmm. I would prefer you check with me, before making these kinds of changes." He cast his eyes down the hall at the landscapes hanging on the walls. "I suppose we can loan these paintings to a museum. You should tell Miss Banks. Might make for some good press. When are these portraits to be ready?"

"I'll be hanging about the office this week to observe. Then it should be a few months before they are finished." Oona said in a business-like way. James supposed this was her business. "I'll need a few moments of yer time to do some sketches."

Walter looked uncomfortable, but in the end he agreed. "Very well. Arrange it with my assistant."

Walter walked down the hall shaking his head as if he thought this was all folly. James turned to Oona. "Are you alright?"

She gave him a wicked grin. "I'm grand. Sarah isna the only tough sister." She leaned close and whispered. "I saw some things we can start with. I'll look a little closer when I meet with him."

"Excellent." James smiled as she strolled to the elevator, not missing the wink she sent at Dermot on her way.

He hoped her girlfriend would be able to find something with the information Oona had gleaned. He had helped by giving her his login information to the company's network. She'd almost looked insulted that he didn't think she could get in, but he wanted her to have more time to search for dirt. He hoped Rachel was as good as she said she was.

CHAPTER FORTY-NINE

"Is this a good wine?" Sarah examined the bottle in her hands. Their driver stopped in front of the row house on Drummond Place where Oona and Rachel were staying.

James glanced at the label. "I'm not an expert, but Ratcliff picked it, so I suppose it is. Are you feeling better?"

The morning sickness or, in Sarah's case, evening sickness, had become a nightly issue over the past week. After confirming her pregnancy with Dr. Perez, Sarah started taking prenatal vitamins and keeping crackers and ginger ale handy. "Yes, much better. I only needed a bite or two to settle my stomach."

"You look beautiful." His eyes practically ate her up. He'd also been generous with his attention over the last few days although he had moved his things into another bedroom, telling the staff Sarah's pregnancy was causing her to have trouble sleeping, which was made worse by having to share a bed.

Sarah was both relieved and a little lonely. She wouldn't have thought it before he moved out, but she had gotten used to sleeping next to him. Although she had a feeling she would feel differently as the baby grew.

Fleming opened the car door. James got out and offered her his hand. He rubbed his thumb across her knuckles after she stood up. She smiled at him, then noticed Dermot holding the door of the building open. He eyed where James's hand held hers, and the muscles in his jaw flexed.

James ushered Sarah to the door with a hand at the small of her back. She didn't miss the look the brothers exchanged as they passed Dermot. James had told her they'd come to an understanding, but he hadn't said exactly what was understood. Publicly, she was Lady Sarah Stuart, and they would have to keep up appearances for the time being.

Oona's flat was on the second floor. It was beautifully furnished and spacious. It was also a location not monitored by A.P. Security where they could strategize without fear of being found out. They were meeting under the guise of a dinner party with her sister. The guests at the party happened to be involved with the plot to bring down Walter Stuart.

Rachel let the three of them in while Fleming remained stationed in the hallway. Jujhar was already there. Henry had stayed at Tweedholm and would join them when it was time for the board meeting. The only person they were missing was Audra Lennox. Oona shouted her welcome from the open kitchen where she was cooking dinner.

Sarah rushed to join her. "How can I help?"

"Salad. Things are in the refrigerator." Oona jerked her head in that direction.

"What can I do?" James followed her. Sarah grabbed the corkscrew, which was next to a half empty bottle of white wine. "You can open the wine."

He took the corkscrew and set about uncorking the bottles. He seemed eager to fit in with Oona and everyone else. Meanwhile Dermot and Jujhar were in the living room talking quietly. Dermot caught her eye and gave her a smile that said, 'We don't have to hide here.'

Sarah turned her attention to the salad and was putting the finishing touches on it when Audra Lennox arrived. She looked only slightly less buttoned-up than she did during the workday. Part of her hair was down brushing her shoulders, although it was still pulled back from her face. Her usual pencil skirt and simple blouse had been traded for a lovely, belted dress with a flared skirt in a deep wine red.

James went to take her coat, and she blushed as she switched the wine bottle, she had brought from one hand to the other as she slid her arms from the sleeves. James hung her coat on a hook before walking her to the kitchen. "Everyone, this is Audra Lennox, my executive assistant. Miss Lennox, you've met my wife. This is her sister Oona, Oona's girlfriend Rachel, and I think you already know Sarah's assistant Jujhar."

Sarah came around the kitchen island to shake Miss Lennox's hand. "Miss Lennox, it's so good to see you again. We're pretty casual here. May I call you Audra?"

Miss Lennox gave her a tentative smile. "Yes, of course, Lady Sarah."

"Great. Then you have to call me Sarah. The title always makes me uncomfortable." Sarah hoped they could be friends. She felt a lot of sympathy for Audra after hearing about Walter's harassment. "I'm so glad you've joined us."

"So am I." Audra said softly. "I'm happy to help."

"I hope we can help each other." Sarah turned to James. "Can you get Audra a glass of wine?"

"Oh, no. I couldn't let you— "Audra said.

"Don't be silly. It's nothing." James waved away her protest and poured her a glass of wine while Sarah made small talk.

Sarah didn't miss Audra's blush when James handed her the glass of Chardonnay. She wondered if James had ever noticed his assistant's crush, or maybe it was more than a crush.

"Dinner's ready." Oona slid a delicious-smelling pasta dish onto a serving plate.

By unspoken rule, they didn't discuss their plans for Walter Stuart until the meal was over. Instead, they got to know each other. They learned about Jujhar's studies in India before he'd returned to the U.K. Audra told them about her gap year in South America, and Rachel reminisced about her first job waiting tables at a seaside café. They stayed away from politics, dynasties, and hidden villages in the Highlands. They were a group of young people enjoying a satisfying meal. It reminded Sarah of dinners with her friends back in Chapel Hill. Sarah decided she liked Audra Lennox, despite the woman's shyness around her employer. James did his best to put her at ease, and by the end of the meal it appeared to have worked.

Oona, direct as ever, pushed her empty plate away. "Alright then. I reckon we should tell ye what we've found."

Everyone sat forward in anticipation. "I can tell ye Walter has been a very bad boy. In addition to Audra's situation, he's also extorted several other assistants into feeding him information." She looked at James. "Including yer father's former assistant."

"He covers his tracks well. Because he keeps the proof of what he's got on them off-line, and he gets paid in information rather than money, there isn't really a way to prove this. I found some emails with hints and veiled threats, but they could be argued away as the normal course of doing business." Rachel explained.

"What can we prove?" James asked directly.

Rachel sighed. "Not a lot. I have reason to believe he may be siphoning money from Alba Petroleum through payments to a consulting firm. I looked into the firm, whose address is in Cyprus. I can't find records of any employees, or any actual services performed by this company for A.P."

"That sounds promising." Dermot said.

"Except the ownership of this company only leads to a maze of other shell companies and I haven't traced them directly to Walter." Rachel added. "The closest I can get is Walter and one of the shell companies use the same Swiss bank."

"So, we can prove someone is being paid fraudulently, but not that he is behind it." James said, deflated.

"It's him." Oona said with certainty. "But aye, we canna prove it."

"Is there anything we can prove?" Sarah asked.

"I can prove he bribed officials in Sudan, Nigeria, Cameroon, Venezuela, and Yemen. I made a file of those records. It shouldn't be hard to present that information."

"Excellent." James processed this information. "That's the kind of thing that could come back to bite the company."

"I also found certain members of the company's security staff have been paid additional sums, large sums, off the A.P. books, but which can be traced to Walter." Rachel fidgeted with her wine glass sliding the base along the tablecloth. "He seems to be less careful about hiding those payments."

"No doubt he thinks they can be written off as moonlighting for his personal security." Jujhar suggested.

James leaned forward. "But the company could as easily provide him with a personal security detail. I have one. Sarah has one. There shouldn't be a need to pay them additionally."

"Not unless they're doing something beyond personal security." Dermot growled. "Was one of those paid a woman named Karen Douglas?"

"How did you know?" Rachel looked surprised.

Dermot cursed under his breath. "Douglas was the one who sold out Des."

"Can we prove that?" James rested his elbows on the table.

"Only the payment." Rachel said, "Not what it was for?"

"I wonder if Des's family might like to know who betrayed him." Dermot muttered. Des had been Dermot's friend from the army. He was also a scion of a local crime family. "There should be several payments around that date. There were at least four men working with him."

Rachel exchanged a look with Oona reminding everyone Oona's father had died that night. Those payments were likely part of the coverup of his death. "There were eight payments around that night, including one to the city coroner. All of them totaled around four hundred thousand pounds."

Oona cast a wan look at Sarah. "At least we know it was expensive to murder our father."

Sarah reached across the table to give her sister's hand a squeeze.

"The trouble with taking that evidence to the board is it means having to explain a lot of things I don't think we want made public." Jujhar advised them. He had a good point. Explaining why Walter shot Rab would require explaining why Sarah had felt the need to escape, which would require explaining why they were forcing her to marry in the first place. It was a Pandora's Box that would only result in all of them looking crazy to a corporate board half of whom didn't know anything about the prophecy.

"Good point." James conceded. His gaze landed back on Rachel. "Did Mark Shaw receive any of those payments?"

Rachel nodded silently, looking apologetic.

James sighed. "So, our head of security is in Walter's pocket. I'm going to need a list of those names and how much they got. We'll have to clean house once we're rid of Walter." James blew out a long breath and slumped back in his chair. "So, what we have to take to the board are sexual harassment, spying on other executives, and bribes in oil producing countries."

"Those aren't small things." Sarah tried to reassure him. "The harassment and bribery could blow back on A.P. in some very costly ways. And spying internally could create a lot of internal conflict in the leadership team."

"The harassment blow back would require the victims to go public." James pointed out.

All eyes turned to Audra who had so far been listening in silence. She looked around the table warily before speaking. "I would be willing to go on the record with my story. I might be able to get some of the others to do the same if you can give me their names."

"I'll give you a list." Rachel said.

"I can put you in touch with a solicitor who can make an affidavit of your account." Jujhar said.

"Actually, he's on the A.P. board." Dermot pointed out sure that Jujhar was thinking of Lyall Green. "We should get someone with no conflict of interest."

"Good point." Jujhar agreed. "I'm sure he can refer us to someone discreet and impartial."

"We have until a week from Monday. So, we'll need those affidavits quickly." James warned.

"I'll get to work on some of the other assistants as soon as possible." Audra promised.

"I have every confidence in you." James told her. Surveying the group. "I think we've pulled together a good argument for removing Walter. I want to thank you all for your help."

His eyes met Sarah's across the table, and she smiled at him approvingly. On their wedding day, she'd told Walter Stuart she had his king in check. That night, she finally believed it.

***

James wished they had more time to build a case that was airtight and irrefutable. He was trying to be outwardly optimistic.

"You must see some of the paintings Oona's done since she's been here in Edinburgh. They're stunning." Rachel beamed with pride.

"They dinna need to see that.' Oona scoffed looking embarrassed.

"Are you kidding?" Sarah pushed her chair back from the table grinning. "See original Oona Ballantynes before anyone else? I wouldn't miss it for the world."

"Come with me." Rachel stood motioning toward the back of the apartment where the bedrooms were. Sarah and Jujhar joined her. "There's a little room upstairs with great light she's been using for a studio. You're going to love these."

The two of them walked down the hall. Oona stood. "I'll make sure they only look at the finished ones."

Dermot went with her. "I'd best go with them."

James considered following them but noticed Miss Lennox looking down at her plate. "Are you interested in art?"

"Oh, I'm sure her paintings are lovely. I looked her up after she was in the office the other day." She smoothed a crease in her napkin resting beside her plate.

"I want to thank you, personally for your help in this. I know it won't be easy for you."

"I'm only sorry it's necessary." She looked uncomfortable. "I'm relieved I don't have to lie to you anymore. I never wanted to. You have to believe me."

"I do." He knew by now that extortion was his uncle's go-to-move. "But going forward there has to be complete honesty between us."

"Of course." A blush crept up from the high neckline of her dress. With her hair down for once rather than its usual tight knot, he wondered if she ever wore anything but the most modest clothes or was her tendency to cover up meant to prevent another situation like the one with his uncle. "Lady Sarah is very gracious."

"She also appreciates your help. My uncle has taken advantage of her as well. Not in the same way as you, but in ways that are equally as unforgiveable. He's a menace." He tightened a hand into a fist. 'We need to be rid of him."

She looked down at the table. "I'll do whatever I can to help. Hopefully, I can convince the other assistants to help. I hope their bosses will be as forgiving as you've been."

James made a mental note. He would have to do something to protect the other women who came forward. "If they are not, I'll find them positions elsewhere in the company. We shouldn't lose good people who've been embroiled in his schemes against their will."

"I'll make sure they know." She looked down into her lap, unable to meet his gaze.

"Miss Lennox," She didn't look up. "Audra." His rare use of her given name got her attention. "If we're going to continue working together, and I would prefer we do, you're going to have to forgive yourself. I know you were under duress."

She sniffed. "I'm afraid that's easier said than done. I've been under his thumb for years. I've gotten used to the undercurrent of fear. I almost don't remember what it was like before, what I was like."

It made his blood boil. Miss Lennox was a competent, thoughtful person. He had never known her without the fear of Walter. All this time she'd been captive to his schemes, exactly like Sarah. He wondered what and who in his life was his. Was there anything Walter hadn't orchestrated?

***

Oona's paintings were stunning. She had chosen people on the streets from all walks of life using her unique gift to show the similarities in their histories and inner lives. But his eyes were only for Sarah who stood in front of him gazing at a portrait of a man in a suit mid-stride walking purposefully down the street who was dreaming of decorating cakes.

Now the truth was out, it was all he could do not to touch her. He hated that publicly she was still James's wife. A small part of him worried she would get used to the luxury and security of it.

But right now, in Oona's spare bedroom studio she felt like his, like they'd never been apart. He could imagine a quiet dinner with his sister-in-law and her girlfriend talking of nothing more important than their jobs or football scores. He could pretend he and Sarah would go home and curl up in bed together. And in the morning, he'd be there with crackers and ginger-ale to settle her stomach. In weeks he could hear the baby's heartbeat, feel it move inside her. In a few months, they'd paint a nursery and put a crib together. They'd make a life.

"Will you be showing these here in Edinburgh?" Sarah asked Oona, shifting to look at a painting of a waitress serving a table at an outdoor café. She stood so close to him in the small room, he could easily touch her.

"Aye. As the ones in the gallery now sell. I'll back fill with some of these." Oona looked at the painting. Her back was to them. Rachel had gone to their bedroom to get something.

Sarah stood; head tilted to the side as she studied the painting exposing the side of her neck. Dermot imagined kissing her right there. He knew the sound she would make, what her skin smelled like. He wanted so badly to put his lips to that spot.

He had to content himself with brushing the back of his fingers against her hand hanging at her side.

"I'll go see what's holding Rachel up." Oona must have sensed the tension in the room and beat a hasty retreat.

482 · MEREDITH R. STODDARD

"I think we ran her out of her own studio." Sarah whispered.

Dermot stepped closer to her pressing himself to her back. He buried his nose in her curls. "I think the whole suggestion that we see the studio was a ruse to get us away from James."

Sarah leaned into him. The weight of her body against his felt like home. He savored the moment. He lifted a hand and spread it across her belly thinking of their child. "How are ye feeling?"

"Right now? Fantastic." She covered his hand with hers. "We'll see how I feel in the morning."

"Is the sickness bad?" He whispered in her ear.

She shook her head slightly. "It's not unbearable. As long as I keep something to nibble on nearby."

He inhaled her scent and gently nibbled her earlobe. "Like that?"

Her laugh was low and throaty. "Not quite."

"I wish I could take ye away with me." He whispered in her ear.

She sighed, tilting her head closer to his. "Soon."

"Assuming everything goes to plan." He grumbled.

"It's a good plan." She turned to face him sliding her hand along his jaw.

"It's good to get him out of the company. He deserves far worse." He pulled her closer. "I dinna want to talk about him. I only want to hold ye while I can."

"Which is only for a few minutes." She warned.

"I'll have to take what I can get." His lips took hers settling for a stolen kiss before they went into the lion's den.

CHAPTER FIFTY

"It's lovely to finally meet Scotland's own Diana. I'm afraid we didn't get a chance at your wedding." Alasdair Menzies took Sarah's hand. If he stood a little too close, Sarah wouldn't let him see she was uncomfortable.

"Oh, I'm not sure I can live up to the comparison." Instead, she shook his hand and smiled. "And I was a little busy that day."

The board members were assembling in the wide hall of the executive offices of Alba Petroleum. Sarah was acting as hostess, while the executives, board members, and their respective assistants milled about overseen by several A.P. Security staff.

"Indeed. Your charity work is quite admirable." Menzies retained her hand.

"Let's hope she can manage to avoid any scandals." Walter sidled up next to them with a narrow-eyed look before taking a sip of his coffee and drifting away to chat with the thin white-haired man James had introduced to her earlier as Giles Tait. Tait had promptly dismissed her as nothing more than James's window dressing.

Sarah watched the two of them before turning back to Menzies whose wife had jumped at the chance to join the board of Sarah's foundation. "How is Gemma?"

"She's quite well, in fact." Menzies grinned. "Very excited about the work you're doing with the foundation for the families of injured workers."

"She's been such a big help." Sarah hoped Gemma's progressive leanings had rubbed off on her husband. James had yet to confirm how he would vote.

"She's generous with her time." His tone suggested he would prefer Gemma saved more of her time for him.

"Darling, are you sure you wouldn't rather sit down?" James appeared at her elbow. He was clearly nervous about the meeting and had been soothing some of those nerves by fussing over Sarah all morning.

"I'm fine." She flashed him a smile and tried to steer him back to the task he should be focusing on, solidifying their votes for the board meeting. "I was talking with Mr. Menzies about how much help his wife has been with the foundation."

"Ah, yes." James focused on Menzies. "Brilliant work they're doing. So glad Gemma is helping."

"Yes." Menzies agreed. He and James went on chatting. Across the room, Henry arrived. Although Henry had given up his position as CEO, he had retained his position as chairman of the Alba Petroleum board. "You'll have to pardon me. I'd like a word with your father before the meeting."

"Hopefully, my father can whip his vote." James muttered watching Menzies greet his father with a friendly handshake.

"Oh, something odd happened yesterday." She said. "Your mother sent me flowers for my birthday. But when I called the chateau to thank her, Martine said she isn't there. She never arrived."

He gave her a puzzled look. "She sometimes stops in Paris on her way there. I wouldn't worry about it."

Sarah wasn't so sure, but he knew Anne better than she did. "Have you been able to wrangle Sutherland?"

James gave his head a shake. "I can't tell. He's being very cagey."

Dermot appeared beside them. "I think we have a problem."

At the same time, the elevator dinged. The doors slid open to reveal Lady Anne dressed head to foot in cream Chanel and looking like butter wouldn't melt in her mouth.

"Paris, huh?" Sarah whirled on them, keeping her voice low.

James swore under his breath.

"You said she would give her proxy vote to Henry." Dermot seethed.

"She always has." James said defensively. "The only reason she would show up here is if she means to vote against my father."

Dermot swore.

"There's nothing to be done about that now. Anne is going to do what she does." She turned to James. "Your job now is to shore up whatever other votes you can. Tait is a loss, but touch base with Sutherland, Monkton, and Bashar." Turning to Dermot. "Make sure your grandfather is on board. I'm going to check on Audra and make sure they're ready when you signal for them."

"Right." They both said.

James leaned in to kiss her cheek. "Thank you."

Sarah sent them off with encouraging nods before going to look for Miss Lennox.

***

"Can I have a word?" Dermot found Lyall Green sipping his tea and looking contemplatively at a landscape hanging at the end of the hall near the large conference room where the meeting would be held. His demeanor was as serene as ever, which set Dermot's teeth on edge.

"I heard James is planning to replace these landscapes with portraits." Green said not taking his attention off the painting.

"Portraits by Oona Ballantyne." Dermot clung to his patience. He wanted to spill everything, but he knew others might be listening.

"To which I'm sure she'll apply her unique gift." Green sipped his tea.

"That is her plan. Although I'm not sure many on the executive team would appreciate seeing their reflection through her eyes." Dermot murmured.

His grandfather chuckled. "I don't suppose they would. What would you like to speak to me about?"

Dermot wondered what Oona Ballantyne's gift would tell them about Lyall Green. Would she see the truth of his one hundred forty-seven years, or his true occupation beyond the latest cover of topflight solicitor, and investor? Either way, they needed his help. "I want to make sure we're on the same page about the votes happening today."

"I am happy to support the clean energy initiative, especially now that Lady Sarah won't be using her gift to search for oil in her delicate condition. She's too valuable to be taking such a risk."

"I should have known ye would know about that already." Dermot shook his head.

"It is my vocation." Green cocked his head to the side. "And her assistant is also my apprentice."

"So ye dinna think her gift was meant for finding oil as some others do?" He wondered why they hadn't thought to ask him before. Then again his grandfather had tried to talk them out of helping Sarah escape their engagement. His motives were always murky which made his advice suspect.

"You and I both know her value lies in more than material gain." Green sounded cool, as if they were talking about nothing more than the weather.

Dermot had wondered how much information about Sarah's activities was getting back to Green. "I suppose it was Jujhar who told ye about the baby?"

"Before you ask, I can't tell who the father is, but for legal purposes it will have to be James." His grandfather lowered his voice.

"Right." His teeth hurt from biting his tongue on that matter. Dermot hadn't even thought about asking if the old wizard could see whose child it was. He still wasn't used to thinking of the man as family. He stepped closer to Green and lowered his voice. "The other matter is to do with Walter Stuart. James is proposing to remove him as COO and from the board."

Green looked at him sharply. Dermot had thought it was impossible to surprise the old man. "On what grounds?"

"On the grounds he has been spying on the executive team by extorting their assistants, and bribing officials in some countries." Dermot kept his voice low. They intended to reveal this evidence in the meeting and hadn't told the other board members beyond Henry. They were hoping the shock value of it would compel them to make the right decisions. But Green had warned them about Walter before and he thought full disclosure would be best. "He's also embezzled funds, turned certain members of the security staff into his own private muscle, murdered Rab Ballantyne, and Desmond Thompson, but we canna prove those things. And ye probably knew them already."

Green sighed. "Sometimes we have to allow unfortunate events to keep things moving in the right direction."

Dermot gave his grandfather a narrow look. "And when he raped my mother? Did ye allow that?"

Surprise swept over Green's face. He grabbed Dermot's arm and pulled him into the conference room. "Explain."

"He drugged her and raped her. That's how I was conceived." Dermot spat. "I thought yer vocation was to watch these things."

"Would you look into your own child's sex life?" Green arched an eyebrow at him."

"I would if I thought she'd been hurt." Dermot growled.

"Your mother has always gone her own way. I thought she'd had an affair with a colleague or more likely Henry Stuart."

"Aye, that's what everyone seemed to think. Until she went to Tweedholm a few weeks ago and had a flashback." Dermot explained. "Ye ken her memory is like Swiss cheese. Something about being back there stirred something for her and brought it up. Then Oona Ballantyne confirmed it."

"But the only evidence you have is a diseased memory and a fae seer." Green said with grimness showing he finally understood their predicament.

"Exactly." Dermot's voice was flat. "But it's enough that James is done with Walter and wants him out."

"I can see why." Green stroked his beard. "I will have to think about this. The man has resources which could still be useful."

"Are ye mad?" Dermot shot.

Green made a quelling motion with his hands. "I'm merely cognizant that getting rid of him might not be as simple as voting him out."

"It's a bloody start." Seethed Dermot. "Without A.P.'s resources, his influence, and his ability to do his worst will be blunted."

"Or he'll no longer have anything to lose." Green pointed out. "If he's been embezzling money, he may have amassed more resources than you know about. We'll need to do more after today to reduce his influence."

"Aye, we've made plans for a full internal audit. A whisper campaign about some of his other activities should get him blackballed by other companies. Who will want to take on that kind of liability risk?"

"You might be surprised, my boy." Green said. "Some companies are willing to overlook egregious behavior as long as it benefits them."

"Aye, well." Dermot couldn't disagree. He'd seen countless companies getting caught doing unscrupulous or illegal things to protect their bottom lines. "Not under James's leadership, not anymore."

"Then it sounds like Lady Sarah is proving her worth in more ways than heirs and oil."

CHAPTER FIFTY-ONE

Sarah watched the conference room door close on the board, and only the board. Even the assistants of the board members were shut out. She found herself staring at the door as if she could hear right through it. Unlike the offices in Aberdeen with their glass walled conference rooms, the headquarters in Edinburgh looked as old world as could be with wood paneled walls and solid oak doors preventing anyone from seeing what was happening.

"Sit down, love." Dermot whispered to her "Ye've done all ye can."

She glanced around the now mostly empty room. The assistants of the board members had gathered in another conference room to work, leaving only the security staff and caterers who were refreshing the tea and coffee table. Audra sat at her desk eyeing the boardroom door. Sarah said. "Not everything."

She strode to Audra's desk. "Where are they?"

Audra led her to a narrow hall next to the elevator Sarah hadn't noticed before. "This way."

Sarah followed her to a break room tucked away in a corner. There was a kitchenette as well as a seating area and a dining table. It seemed to be a refuge for the executive assistants. There three women sipped tea and chatted quietly.

Their conversation stopped when Audra and Sarah entered the room.

"Ladies." Audra said. "This is Lady Sarah Stuart."

The other women rose, and Sarah stepped forward to shake their hands. "It's lovely to meet you all."

Audra made the introductions. Janice Braithwaite looked to be in her mid-thirties with curly deep brown hair and intelligent eyes. She was the assistant to the Chief Financial Officer. Wide-eyed and petite Sloane Kelly was the assistant of the Chief Technology Officer. Finally, the attractive, silver-haired, and poised Iona Stevenson was Walter's own assistant.

"I can't thank you all enough for coming forward with your stories. The kind of behavior you've been subjected to is unacceptable and I know my husband does not want this sort of thing in the company. Speaking out about this isn't going to be easy, but it's so important to prevent situations like this from happening again."

"Mr. Stuart has been at this too long. These are the lasses who are still here. I've lost count of the number of young women he's taken advantage of who have left." Ms. Stevenson said. Her steely gray eyes were like flint. "I'm glad to see Lord Caledon plans to do something about it."

"I only wish he'd known about it sooner." Sarah assured them. "He values everyone who works for the company regardless of their position."

"Miss Lennox said we wouldn't see any repercussions." Sloane said nervously.

Sarah gave her a reassuring smile. "James will do everything in his power to prevent that. You shouldn't be punished for standing up for what is right."

"I'll be glad he won't have this to hang over my head anymore." Janice muttered. "I hid it from my husband for years. This finally gave me the courage to tell him about it."

Sarah gripped her hand. "I know that was hard. You're all very brave to speak about this."

"We couldn't do it if we weren't confident in Lord Caledon's leadership." Iona said. "Maybe after us, some others will come forward."

"I hope they can find the courage you are showing. I know James appreciates it. We both do." Sarah assured them. "As I said, we'll do everything to make sure there is no blowback. If you receive any, please let us know."

Sarah hoped like hell they could live up to that promise.

***

The earnings report, projections for the next fiscal year, and impact of the rig sabotage had all been discussed. They had even discussed the new R & D project for discovering oil. Naturally, they couldn't talk about it in terms of Sarah's gift. It was simply known as Project Crow Fly and Sarah's involvement was kept secret. James had easily fielded questions on all these topics.

It was all very predictable and helped James relax into his role in this meeting rather than allowing him to dwell on the importance of the two proposals he had to present. Henry, as chairman, presided over the things keeping them organized.

"I understand James has a proposal with regard to the company's future, Son?" His father yielded the floor.

The moment of truth was at hand. James stood and buttoned his jacket, taking a moment to smooth out his jumping nerves. It wasn't as if this part was news to them. He'd been bending the ear of every board member he could meet with to discuss the rebrand as an energy company. The proposal he had put together was solid, and he'd practiced it with Dermot, Sarah, Felicia, and Miss Lennox as sounding boards. He was prepared.

He presented them with the same pitch that he'd given them individually, leaning on the idea of setting the company up for a future beyond fossil fuels. This time he presented them with numbers, the cost savings from Sarah's project, projected production of their existing wells, and the profit potential of various renewables. "I want to go beyond a few experiments with renewable energy. We can use the momentum generated by our response to the rig disaster to rebrand the company. This will signal we are forward thinking, we are environmentally conscious, and we are about more than simply oil."

He pulled back a sheet covering an easel in the corner of the room. On it was a poster of the proposed Alba Energy logo he'd had the marketing department create. He had consulted with the marketing and Public Relations departments to come up with something to represent the company's shift. It incorporated the previous logo but simplified the lines and made the colors more vibrant. It was eye-catching but similar enough to the previous logo it would call back to the company's history."

It was difficult to tell how the new logo was received. James had learned early in his career a poker face was essential in meetings like this. His father, who sat at the head of the table opposite where everyone's attention was directed gave him an approving look. James handed the reports out to the members at the table. "I've outlined here the ways I propose to reinvest the cost savings I mentioned. There is a list of renewable energy companies we can acquire along with projections for return on those investments."

He gave them a moment to skim the report, waiting for the questions he knew would inevitably come. He felt confident he was ready for them. He had been fielding those questions on an individual basis for weeks. There was little surprise in the resulting conversation. Walter didn't voice his outright resistance. He left that to Giles Tait, who questioned how this reinvestment would impact the oil part of the business.

Sutherland surprisingly expressed a dislike for the appearance of wind turbines. Bashar had asked some questions about tidal projects and Monkton asked about the offshore wind. When his father finally called for a vote, James's rebrand proposal passed six to four with Walter, Tait, Sutherland, and his mother voting against. He was disappointed in his mother and wasn't sure if her vote had been support for Walter or because she knew it was Sarah's idea. Either reason seemed petty, but then his mother's sudden interest in the company was only out of fear of losing her voice. Still, they were the minority. Hopefully, that would hold for the next vote.

***

Sarah paced across the carpet in James's office. She and the assistants had returned to the wide hall outside the boardroom to await the signal to come into the meeting. After an hour, James had opened the door and called the assistants in. Then he closed the boardroom door again.

Sarah didn't know whether it was nerves or the baby, but something caused her stomach to rebel. She beat a retreat into the private bathroom in James's office. After hurling up her breakfast, she rinsed her mouth out and touched some cold water to the back of her neck and temples. She emerged from the bathroom to find Dermot standing by the door with a cold ginger ale and pack of crackers. "You're my hero."

"I'd love to take credit, but James thought to stock these in here when he knew you'd be coming to the office." He told her.

"He's thoughtful like that." Sarah took a sip of ginger ale.

"Aye, he is." Dermot's voice went flat.

"You don't have to worry about him, you know." She nibbled the corner of a cracker.

"I'm not worried." He said not looking at her.

She cocked her head to the side watching him. "I admit. I'm a little out of practice, but I think I can still read your nonverbal cues."

He sighed heavily. "It's hard not to worry when he gets to be around ye. He gets to be thoughtful, sweet, and romantic, while I'm stuck on the fringes of yer life like some friend ye run into sometimes."

"Not for long." She set her drink and cracker down and wrapped her arms around his waist. "If everything goes right today."

He wrapped his arms around her and kissed the top of her head. "Aye, and when has everything ever gone right?"

CHAPTER FIFTY-TWO

What is the meaning of this?" Monkton asked when James opened the conference room door to invite the assistants in. "We don't need them in the boardroom."

"Actually, I do." James said. "I have some very serious issues we need to discuss, and these women have been witnesses to it."

He held out a hand, and Miss Lenox placed a stack of papers on it. James began handing out the papers to the board members as he had done with the clean energy proposals. "We have had a cancer metastasizing in our company for years. I don't know when it started or how deep it runs, but it has reached a level we cannot ignore."

He walked around the table as the board members read the reports. All but Walter. He glanced at the top page and dropped it on the table while he attempted to stare James down.

James continued. "What you are looking at is an accounting of the number of bribes paid to government officials, local warlords, and drug cartels from Pakistan to Venezuela. It has apparently been a practice spearheaded by my uncle for years."

"That is simply how things are accomplished in those places." Walter said with a shake of his head.

"Perhaps. However, it is not how things are done here. And the government has been very clear what will happen to British companies caught doing it in any part of the world." James stopped beside his father at the head of the table. He tented his fingers on the polished mahogany and leaned forward to emphasize his point. "This exposes us to legal sanctions and penalties that will damage our investments in these countries and here at home. Companies fold over issues like this."

"We're too big for that." Tait waved a hand in dismissal.

"We're not too big for sanctions." James snapped. "We're not too big for the reputational damage if this got out."

"You naïve pup." Walter blustered.

"Am I naïve, or do I merely refuse to throw my ethics out the window for money and power?" James countered. "Which brings me to my second point. My uncle's unethical behavior doesn't only extend to those outside these walls. He has been using the clerical staff to spy on the executive team for years."

"That's ridiculous!" Walter sputtered.

"He sexually harasses them and then extorts them into feeding him information about whoever they work with. I know this because he did it to my own assistant Miss Lennox."

At his invitation Miss Lennox stepped forward. "It started shortly after I was hired by the company. I was working with Mr. Shaw first, then transferred to Mr. Stuart. He pursued me relentlessly for months. Yes, I should have known better, but I was young and flattered by his attention. Eventually, we slept together, but shortly after, Mr. Stuart seemed to lose interest. Then he showed me compromising photos he'd taken of me while I was unconscious."

A flush crept up from the collar of her blouse. "Nude photos. He threatened to make them public if I didn't give him information on Mr. Shaw. Then when Lord Caledon joined as CEO, he had me assigned to his office. He continued to hold the photos over my head, and to harass me in order to get me to spy on Lord Caledon."

"Thank you, Miss Lennox." James said. "All of these ladies have similar stories."

Each of the other women shared their experiences with Walter, and with each one, James's righteous fury increased. Most were similar to Miss Lennox, a campaign of grooming and harassment followed by extortion and information sharing. With the exception of Iona Stevenson, Walter had been staring daggers at her since she had come into the room. "I am Mr. Stuart's assistant. I have been for nearly twenty years now. When I was young and working in the mail room, I went to a company holiday party. There I met Mr. Stuart. I was not someone who drank much, but I agreed to have one with Mr. Stuart. After one drink at this party, I began to feel like I was drunk. I excused myself and went toward the ladies' toilets. I never made it there."

She looked right at Walter. "I was in the hallway leading to the toilets, and everything went black. I woke up hours later in a storage closet. My clothes were askew and..." She looked down and shook her head. "My knickers were missing. The following Monday, I found an envelope on my desk."

"In it were my missing knickers and a series of photographs of me in compromising positions. Much like these other ladies. There was a note to meet the person who left the envelope for me in the same storage closet. When I did, I found Mr. Stuart there with a proposal. I would tell him whatever information I came across in the mailroom, or he would distribute those pictures to the entire office and my family. It's a slippery slope isn't it, once you're compromised? Each thing you do gives him one more thing to hold over your head. You're a fly caught in a spider's web. And I've watched him do it to more than the just ladies in this room. These are the ones brave enough to come forward."

Her story sounded so similar to Seonag's. James was sure Mrs. Stevenson had been drugged. James wondered if Walter had used the shame of exposure on Seonag as well. The pattern was easy to recognize.

Henry stood, his tone serious. "Thank you, ladies. We appreciate you bringing this to our attention."

Dismissed, the women filed out of the boardroom. Miss Lennox sent James a hopeful look. Bolstered, James continued his presentation. "Bribery, harassment, sexual assault, and corporate espionage. I don't have to tell all of you what this would do to the company if any of this became public. This sort of behavior may have been viewed as distasteful but tolerated in the past, but we cannot allow this to stand anymore. We must cut this cancer out."

"A cancer, am I?" Walter spat. "I have brought more business to this company in the decades I have been here than you ever did, Henry. I have kept the lights on, and the oil flowing when our original wells were tapped out." He thumped himself in the chest. "I have made Alba Petroleum what it is."

"Who do you think you are, you arrogant puppy, to tell us how this company should be run?" Giles Tait sneered from his seat next to Walter.

"I am the CEO this board selected." James kept his voice calm though he seethed on the inside.

"James has a point." Reza Bashar spoke up leveling a look on Tait that quieted the older man. "The government might have turned a blind eye to these sorts of things in the past. But we all know the kind of scrutiny this industry has seen after the Piper Alpha disaster, and our recent explosion means we will be in for even more of it. If these bribes are discovered, it could mean sanctions for the company and perhaps even time in prison for Mr. Stuart. If we take action before the government discovers it, then we can shield Alba Petroleum." He tilted his head to James. "Pardon me, Alba Energy from getting hit with the worst of it."

"And throw our COO under the proverbial bus?" Sutherland was incredulous. "Surely loyalty means something to you."

Bashar smirked. "Loyalty might mean something to you and Tait, Sutherland, but I didn't go to Gordonstoun, and I don't belong to the Nor Loch Club. Your sort of loyalty is why I've had to buy my way onto boards like this at a much higher cost than you. I'm not about to let your brand of loyalty bring this company to its knees."

Monkton spoke up. "The bribes could mean government sanctions, but they aren't likely to be large enough to make a dent in our bottom line. However, we should be concerned about the reputational cost of being caught out, especially right after the rig explosion."

"Or being caught knowingly harboring a rapist in our ranks." Henry added, his eyes shooting daggers at his brother.

"Or an executive the other executives can't trust." James added.

Sutherland scoffed and waved a hand as if to say it was of no consequence.

"Do you really believe anyone is going to care about a few secretaries complaining about a handsy boss." Walter's look was withering. "And if you think you can trust anyone on the executive team, you're even more naïve than I thought."

"That might have been the corporate culture you learned when you were my age, but it doesn't work like that anymore." James said, getting angrier by the second.

Walter laughed. "Of course, it does, my boy."

"I am NOT your boy." James snapped.

Walter's gaze cut between Henry and James. "No, you certainly are not."

James smiled. As if that sort of statement could hurt him. Disowned by the biological father who never should have been.

"I agree. Being caught out on any of those issues will be detrimental to the company." Menzies spoke up for the first time. His tone was thoughtful as if he hadn't heard the last exchange. "But you have to consider that summarily firing our COO and expelling him from the board will likely cause the same kind of scrutiny you are hoping to avoid?"

"Would you rather we ignore it and hope no one finds out?" Bashar asked.

"I would rather we not raise a red flag in front of the press saying, 'There's a story to be found here. You should investigate it." Menzies countered.

"We can explain it as part of the rebranding, or retirement." Henry suggested.

"Or taking responsibility for the security failure which allowed the explosion to happen." James added.

"Wouldn't it be more likely that our chief of security takes the fall for letting saboteurs get to one of our rigs?" Walter asked.

"Of course, you would let a subordinate take responsibility." James sneered. "I'll remind you Mark Shaw answers to you in more ways than this board is even aware of."

Walter's eyes narrowed on him, the realization dawning that James knew of the off-book activities of certain A.P. Security staff. James gave him a challenging look.

Lyall Green broke the tense silence. "Like many of you. I have been on this board long enough to remember when Lord Caledon joined the company. When it was suggested, we make him CEO, the agreement was that Walter Stuart would serve as COO to help him get up to speed and provide him with guidance. We have watched Lord Caledon grow and learn beside his uncle for several years now."

"I think both of his presentations today prove he is ready to take the training wheels off." Green continued. "He has become capable of taking this company into the future. He has shown he possesses the kind of integrity, fairness, and strength of purpose that will ensure the company's future in a changing world. Clinging to faulty methods or turning a blind eye to malfeasance because of some misguided loyalty will only drag this company down."

"I couldn't have said it better myself, Green." Henry leaned forward elbows on the table. "I move that Walter Stuart be dismissed as Chief Operating Officer and from this board effective immediately. All in favor?"

Henry raised his hand. James looked around the table. Bashar and Green both raised their hands confidently. James was not surprised Sutherland and Tait did not. Walter watched arrogantly.

Monkton looked back and forth between James and Walter. With a sigh he said. "It's too much change for my liking. Rebranding and a new COO is simply too much upheaval."

Menzies shifted uncomfortably and seemed like he was going to raise his hand but, in the end, did not. "I think it would be better to handle these things internally than to draw attention to them."

With his mother's vote they would be tied, and the debate would continue. But she had yet to raise her hand. "Mother?"

She met his gaze, anguish in her eyes. Then she turned to look out the window. She did not raise her hand. James's blood went cold. Would she really be so petty as to vote for Walter because he had asked her to leave his house? Clearly, she was throwing her lot in with Walter. James wondered for a moment if Walter had extorted her like he had the other women.

"Anne?" Our son needs your support." Henry said to her quietly.

"I'm sorry, but I cannot support this." She turned back to look at Henry. "Walter has never steered us wrong."

"Never?" Henry asked.

His mother blinked but held her head high. "Never."

He felt frozen. His mother's vote clinched it. Walter would remain. But they had laid out everything they could prove. All of it. What more would have moved them? Would the embezzlement be enough if they'd been able to prove it? What about the murder? His breath caught in his chest, and he shivered at the thought of continuing to be bound to Walter. He needed to cut Walter and his mother out of his life.

"If we have no further business, then we are adjourned." His father said.

"No." James's throat closed on the word. He cleared it and straightened his shoulders. "In light of today's vote. I can no longer serve as Alba Energy's CEO. I will not work at a company that would harbor such a malignant presence."

"Don't be hasty, son." Henry said.

"Don't be foolish." Walter shook his head, his tone conciliatory. "There is no reason we can't go on as we have."

"There is every reason." James focused on the blue eyes that were too like his own, and his brother's. "The things we've laid out today are only the things I can prove. I have no doubt you've committed more crimes in the name of or in the guise of this company than any of us can count. I won't be a party to it any longer."

To the table at large he said. "You'll have my resignation by the end of the day."

As he passed Monkton on his way out the door he muttered. "How's that for upheaval?"

CHAPTER FIFTY-THREE

Dermot had convinced her to sit down, but Sarah still buzzed with nervous energy. She fidgeted with a pen popping the cap off and on repeatedly, which she supposed was preferable to the leg bouncing and pacing. Dermot for his part stood stoically looking out the window. She heard a door open and close, followed by the hum of conversation in the hallway.

James appeared in the doorway looking bleak. Sarah's nerves felt electric, like she'd touched a hot wire. "What happened?"

"We won." His face looked anything but triumphant. Shock was all she could read from him. "And lost."

"What does that mean?" Alarm registered in Dermot's tone.

"They approved the rebranding and the clean energy program, but Walter is still part of the company." His shoulders slumped in defeat. "I have resigned. I can't work with him. I won't."

Sarah felt like ice was running through her veins. They had gambled big and lost. They'd been so close. They'd almost gotten away. She fought to stay in control. She couldn't freak out in the middle of the office. "Okay."

"My mother." James ground out through his teeth. "My mother was the tie breaking vote."

Reza Bashar knocked on the door frame. "Do you have a minute?"

James turned to face him. "Of course, please come in."

Bashar closed the door behind him. "I'm sorry, James. That was a disappointing vote, and I think in the end they will regret the choice to keep Walter on."

"Yes, well, it doesn't change anything." James went to the decanter he kept on the credenza. He poured liquor into two tumblers and held it over a third giving Bashar a questioning look. When Bashar shook his head, James put the stopper back. He picked up the tumblers, handing one to Dermot. "They are going to regret the decision. Walter is a ticking time bomb of malfeasance."

"I suppose they are contending with that now. The meeting adjourned, but he and your parents are still in the conference room." Bashar's face looked serious.

"I'm sure my father has a few things to say to him." James arched an ironic eyebrow.

"I get the sense there is more to this than the allegations you brought today." Bashar leaned against a chair.

"As I said, those were the allegations I could prove." James leaned back against the credenza. 'There are some strange payments to shell companies which we can't prove are his, but I have my suspicions. There is little we can do now."

"I may be able to dig into that more. I have some connections in banking." Bashar suggested.

"They're going to a shell company in Cyprus." James explained.

"And likely from there to a Swiss bank." Bashar's tone suggested he was familiar with how money was hidden and laundered. "I can see why that's hard to trace. But he should be made to account for those payments."

"I had planned an internal audit after he was no longer here to cover his tracks." James said.

"If I can get Green and some of the other board members to request an internal audit, then we may still be able to do it." Bashar eyed James. "Would you consider coming back when we have more proof?"

James thanked Bashar who said goodbye to Sarah and Dermot before leaving the room. James continued sipping his whiskey and looking stricken.

"What about Miss Lennox?" He said. "The others will quietly get settlements from the company. I'll make sure of it before I leave."

"And the company will hire another crop of assistants for Walter to harass and manipulate."

"I hope that after today, the others will be more watchful." James set his glass down on his desk and came to sit next to her on the couch looking despondent. He took her hand in his. "I'm sorry. I thought we made a good case."

"I'm sure you did." Sarah squeezed his hand to reassure him. "We were up against a lot of entrenched cronyism and misogyny."

James sighed and kissed her hand before slumping back onto the couch. He was clearly tired. He'd been working non-stop for the last week to put together both presentations for the meeting. She thought she should wait to remind him of his promise to let her choose when they were rid of Walter's yoke.

Dermot had other ideas. "What about Sarah? Will ye let her choose now?"

"Please, brother. I am exhausted. I need to think through what we will do next before I can address that." James brushed a hand over his face, clearly miserable.

Dermot started to press the issue, but Sarah shook her head warning him off. He reluctantly let it drop.

Sarah tugged on James's hand. "Let's go home. There is nothing you need to do that can't be done at home. We'll deal with all of this from there."

James took a deep breath. "I need Miss Lennox."

"I'll get her." Dermot opened the door letting Audra in.

"Miss Lennox," James stood, reclaiming some of his usual poise. "I'll be working the rest of the day from my home. I'd like you to join me there. We have a lot to do."

"Of course. I'll get my things." She left to get what they would need.

When the three of them stepped into the hall on their way to the elevators, they found James's parents having a heated but quiet argument in the corner near the boardroom. Both were red-faced with anger. Anne spotted James and broke away from Henry. "James, darling. We need to talk."

James went stiff and stone-faced. "There is not anything you could say to me that will wipe away the memory of what you did in there." He glanced at his father. "Or what you did before today."

For once, Lady Anne looked genuinely hurt. She leaned closer to him whispering, "James, please."

"Father. Will you join us at the house? I think we have much to talk about." James said, looking past his mother to Henry who nodded agreement.

The boardroom door opened. Walter stood there, white as a sheet looking more afraid than Sarah had ever seen him. Without looking at any of them, he walked through the hall and into his office, closing the door behind him.

Lyall Green walked out of the boardroom behind him looking serene. He joined them in front of the elevator. The four of them rode down the elevator in silence. Furious energy poured off of Green in waves. Sarah, Dermot, and James all resisted the temptation of asking him about his exchange with Walter.

When they reached the ground floor, Green stepped out of the elevator first. Turning back to them, he addressed James. "I'm sorry that didn't go the way you planned. I meant what I said in there. I look forward to seeing what you'll do next." He turned and walked out the door.

James asked. "What do you think he said to Walter?"

Dermot stepped out of the elevator and held the door open for them. Sarah thought she could see a hint of satisfaction in his expression. "Don't know. But I did tell him what Walter did to my mother right before the meeting. I imagine it had something to do with that."

***

"I think that's everything." James said with a sigh. "You did call the other women from this morning to tell them we'll be negotiating settlements for them."

"I spoke with them before I left the office." Miss Lennox gave him a reassuring smile.

"Of course, you did." James watched as she finished writing her notes. Her dark hair shone in the golden light in his study. "I can always rely on you." She had listened to him dictate his letter of resignation and all the steps needed to separate him from Alba Energy without once asking about her own job. "I hope you know you will always have a place with me."

Her brown eyes found his. "I'm glad to hear it. I didn't fancy job hunting."

"Even if I didn't have a position for you, you know I would have written you a glowing reference. You would have no trouble finding a new situation." He told her.

She looked down at her notepad, her cheeks turning pink. "I don't want another position."

He smiled at her. "I'm glad to hear that."

"I'll get started on these action items." She stood to leave. At the door she paused. "There is one thing."

"Yes?"

She looked shy for once. "As our arrangement is a little less formal now, do you think you might call me by my given name?"

He laughed. "Only if you call me by mine."

Her eyes sparkled with mischief. "Alright, James."

"Thank you, Audra." He smiled warmly, relieved that at least he still had capable, steadfast Audra Lennox at his side.

Now, he turned his attention to keeping Sarah beside him. He had meant it when he said he would allow Sarah to choose, but that was when he thought he would be at the head of Alba Energy.

If he was ever going to take Walter down, he was going to need Sarah. Her strength and guidance, as well as her gift were invaluable. She had shown him more about leadership in the last few months than his father or Walter ever had. It showed in the way people and the press responded to her. Since her success in Aberdeen, the tabloids had been mad for Sarah and her charity work. It was no surprise Menzies had called her Scotland's Diana. She was loved nearly as much. Not to mention, he didn't think his pride could take the hit of losing his company and his wife.

For now, he needed a break. He poured himself a whiskey and picked up the day's copy of The Scotsman. He usually only read the newspaper on weekends, knowing Miss Lennox, Audra would bring him any articles of importance during the week. Hoping for a distraction, he skimmed through the articles while the eighteen-year-old Macallan settled warmly in his stomach. There was one about Sarah's charity for injured oil workers. It mentioned the scholarships covering school fees for the children of injured workers.

The arts section included a review of Oona's show complete with a couple of photos of her best paintings. She truly made the most of her gift. Although, after the day's events, James wondered what the point of knowing the truth was, if people chose to ignore it?

It was the editorial page that caught his attention. There was a commentary regarding the coming general election. James stopped skimming and read closer. Every seat in the House of Commons would be put up to a vote. Although the campaigning wouldn't start for months, there was some buzz the Labour Party would be open to devolution for Scotland and Wales, not independence exactly, but closer to home rule.

James had watched his father and uncle work for campaigns in the past. Of course, they didn't work publicly for them. They whipped votes and support from influential people. They helped pick candidates, and push legislation benefiting the company. They'd lobbied their candidates for devolution, and in support of his leadership. Could all those years of promotion by them be put to work against Walter?

CHAPTER FIFTY-FOUR

Dermot stepped out onto the terrace inhaling the chilled air, hoping the cold would ease this tense feeling. The frigid air stung his nostrils. It had been hours since they'd returned to the house on Polwarth Terrace. Dusk was settling on the city, but there was still work to be done. He certainly wasn't going to continue working for the company if James wasn't there. He hadn't had that conversation with James or Mark Shaw yet.

He had a bad feeling about what the morning's events meant for them. He should have known something like this would happen. He'd learned the hard way too many times that Walter Stuart would never be held accountable.

The door opened behind him, but he didn't turn around. He wasn't sure he wanted to know what was coming.

"James is still closed up in the study." Sarah stopped beside him. Close enough he could smell her perfume. "Although Audra has taken up residence in the dining room with a task list a mile long."

"Who would have thought quitting yer job was so much work?" He grumbled.

She laughed beside him. "What are you doing out here?"

"Waiting for the other shoe to drop." He clasped his hands behind him mostly to keep from touching her.

"Mmm. I have that feeling too." She said softly.

"I'll be here. Ye know that. Whatever he does next."

"I know." She brushed his arm with her shoulder. "Whatever he does, we'll still be together. Even if we have to wait a bit longer."

He groaned, looking down at her, fighting the urge to take her into his arms. "Every minute feels like a bloody eternity. But I'll endure it."

She studied his profile. "Me too."

"Sarah?" James stepped out of the door onto the terrace. "Do you have a minute?"

***

"Shall we take a walk in the garden?" He suggested looking back and forth between Sarah and Dermot. He was usually supremely confident, but today had been a blow and it showed in his diminished posture.

"Sure." Sarah gave Dermot a look she hoped was encouraging. He solemnly turned toward the house leaving them alone. A second later the lights in the garden came on.

James escorted her down the steps to the terraced lawn. "You're not too cold, are you?"

"No, it's actually kind of nice." They walked down the path toward the canal. They'd been married for months, but since telling James about the baby, she'd felt awkward and tired. She'd been playing this game too long. She was impatient yet afraid of what James was about to say, so she deflected with a question about logistics. "Did you get everything squared away with Audra?"

"I did. I'm relieved she's agreed to stay with me. I don't think I could find anyone else so capable." He said, but she could tell his mind was on something else.

"She's very good at what she does." Sarah wondered if James realized Audra Lennox worked so hard for him because she cared about him in a way that was more than strictly professional. "I'm glad you have her."

They strolled on in awkward silence. The leaves had fallen from the trees around them, reminding Sarah of the first time she'd been there, the night of the Burns dinner when James had made his intentions clear. Sarah needed to know where they stood. When they reached the small dock at the canal, she bit the bullet. "James—."

"I know." He said at the same time.

They shared a nervous laugh and she said. "Go on."

"My love, I know I told you that you would be able to choose once we were free of my uncle." James began unable to look at her. Sarah had a feeling she wasn't going to like what he said next. "Today's events…"

"Mean we're not rid of him?" Sarah finished for him when he hesitated. "Except that we are. You're not working with him anymore. You're not letting him influence you. You are your own man. I know today felt like a loss, but you broke free."

"I broke free of his influence in Scotland." He paced away from her before turning back. "If anything, he's more influential now. I have no doubt his cronies on the board will make him CEO, if not permanently then at least while they search for a new one."

"After what you showed them today? How could they even think of it?" She shouldn't be surprised at the depravity hiding behind a corporate logo.

"It will be Tait, Sutherland, Menzies and probably Monkton against my father, Green and Bashar with my mother breaking the tie as she did this morning. He has the votes." Surprisingly, James didn't sound as defeated as she expected him to. His tone was one of acceptance.

"Then we go public with the bribery evidence." Sarah suggested. "Rachel can keep looking for proof of the other stuff, and Bashar said he would be looking."

James's expression went flat. "Going public would blow back as much on the company as it would on Walter. There would be sanctions which would lead to higher costs. People would lose their jobs, the same workers you care about."

Of course, he would use that angle to justify it, appealing to her principles. But she had no doubt it was his own self-interest. "And they'd never have you back as CEO if you aired the company's dirty laundry."

He tilted his head to acknowledge her point. "The fact remains, today was a victory for him, but I think I have found a way we can turn the tables and work toward our ultimate goal of independence."

She didn't miss the 'we' in his statement. Reluctantly, she asked. "How?"

He pulled his shoulders back and lifted his chin looking determined. "I'm going to stand for parliament."

Sarah shook her head blinking in surprise. That idea hadn't even crossed her mind when she considered what James might do next.

His face glowed with excitement. "There is a general election next year, and there is some speculation that a referendum on devolution will be on the Labour platform."

"Are you even in the Labour Party?" This could not be happening.

"I'm solidly Independence Party, but if Labour supports a referendum, then we will likely form a coalition with them. There's a very real chance we can help with an important step toward independence."

"Don't you think Walter will be eyeballs deep in that?"

"He might be." James agreed. "However, if not for the independence issue, Walter would be with the Tories. He's notoriously anti-Labour," He held out a hand as if presenting his argument. "Which gives me an opening to take control of the political situation. We can gain ground toward independence and if I'm elected, I can use that to affect the government's relationship with Alba Energy.

"Effectively boxing Walter out of the whole political conversation even though it's one he supports." Sarah understood. It was a smart move. If this were the chess game Walter thought it was, it would be a brilliant move. Walter couldn't attack James politically because he would damage the Stuarts' ability to restore their monarchy or at least put James in a leadership position. And it would give James some power over Walter with the added benefit of establishing James in a role of public leadership. "It sounds like the best plan forward for you."

He took her hand enveloping it in both of his. "It's the best plan forward for us. I'm going to need your help." He pulled her close, giving her a pleading look. "You have taught me so much, Sarah. I could not have done what we did today without you. You've made me a better man. And I'm going to need you beside me."

There it was. The other shoe dropped. Sarah placed her free hand over his heart choosing her words carefully. "James, you don't need me. You've always had the tools to lead, and in spite of Walter's example your heart is in the right place. All I did was show you what was already inside you."

"I wish you were right about that." He covered her hand pressing it to his chest. Suddenly Sarah was back in the study at Taigh na Damh listening to him tell her this was about Scotland, not his own ambitions. "Maybe you are, but it will be difficult to start a political career if my extremely popular and pregnant wife leaves me for my bodyguard."

Sarah froze. She should have seen it coming. "You said—"

"I said I would allow you to choose, and I will. I am not Walter. I won't force you. But I am asking you." He dropped to one knee. His tone taking on an urgency she'd never heard from him before. "I'm begging you to wait a while longer. Give me a year. Help me with this campaign. Help me gain ground over Walter. What we did to him today won't be without consequences. Let's make him pay for what he did to you, to your father. It's the best way to keep your family safe."

CHAPTER FIFTY-FIVE

May 18, 1997

Sarah and James stood in the front hall flanked by Dermot and Fleming. Sarah took a deep breath hoping to calm her nerves. She'd been dressed in a smart skirt suit and maternity top even Lady Anne would approve of, and she'd been primped, plucked, and polished until she looked like the perfect politician's wife.

She smoothed a hand over her growing belly, which seemed to ground her more than the deep breath did. There was something about the timelessness of the baby growing inside her that always brought her peace, a strange mix of expectation, dread, and rightness. Whatever happened today or over the next six weeks, it was nothing but a blip in the cycle of birth, death, and renewal all people went through.

James took her hand and flashed her his billion-dollar smile. He looked the part in his navy-blue suit with an enamel pin of the Scottish flag on his lapel. "Ready?"

"No, but there's no stopping it now." She said softly.

"Alright." Felicia Banks stood in front of the door and faced them. "Shoulders back, heads up. Smile like you can see the bright future over their heads." With that she opened the door.

They stepped out onto the stoop in front of the house on Polwarth Terrace to camera flashes, waving hands, and shouted questions. Dermot and Fleming stood beside them while James lifted a hand to quiet the crowd. The scene felt entirely too familiar, but today they were announcing his candidacy for parliament for Edinburgh South.

James held up a hand and the crowd quieted. When he spoke, his voice was strong and full of purpose. "Yesterday, Prime Minister John Major called for a general election. It's time for us, as Scots, to make our voices heard. For far too long the Tories have been in power, banging the drum for the Union."

"They call Scotland a dependent state. They say we need to be a part of the U.K., because we can't fend for ourselves. They call us freeloaders, and yet they use our oil to fuel their machines. They store their nuclear weapons in our waters." His voice grew louder and more fervent. Sarah thought Southern preachers had nothing on him.

"Do we enjoy increased benefits for that? No. We see funding for programs in Scotland cut again and again and again in favor of government programs serving the south. We give our resources to Westminster, but what we get back is a pittance, and the voices of our representatives are drowned out by Tory slurs and shouting."

He leaned forward, and some in the crowd mirrored him swept along by his speech. "I say the time has come for us to have a louder voice, one they will listen to, one that has generated economic development and spearheaded growth here in Scotland, one loud enough for them to hear. And most of all one that will tell Westminster it is time for Scotland to be ruled by Scots."

"That is why I am announcing my candidacy for the Scottish Independence Party for this constituency." He held a fist to his chest. "I will be your voice. You know me. You know my wife, Sarah, and all the charity work we have done. You know my record as a business leader. Over the next six weeks, I will show you that I am the right person to take our message to Westminster where we can deliver the referendum on devolution we've been asking for. I hope you know that I..." He cast a loving look at Sarah. "We can make them listen. I hope I can count on everyone's support."

A few shouts of 'Scotland for Scots' came from the crowd as James lifted their joined hands and camera flashes went off. Sarah turned to look at James, but just beyond him Dermot was watching them both. He wore the usual mask of indifference that was essential for a bodyguard, but for a second their eyes met. In his gaze she saw reflected all the uncertainty she felt now.

One more year. A little over seven months ago, they had told James they would give him one more year. Sarah hoped like hell they would make it.

ACKNOWLEDGMENTS

As always, I have to thank my supportive tribe starting with the Kettle Holler Literary Society, and my fellow Bookish Road Trip tour guides; Mary Helen Sheriff, Julie Valerie, Grace Sammon, Donna Norman Carbone, Linda Rosen, Josie Brown, Barbara Conrey, Lisa Roe, Hope Gibbs, Lee Bukowski, and Susan Peterson, as well as the whole Bookish Road Trip community. I love being on the road with you all.

My beta readers this round in no particular order; Stacy, Ellen, Shannon, Valerie, Candice, Cathy, Jen, Stacey, Mary, Leigh, Michelle, and Julie gave me essential feedback that contributed to making this book the best one I can give you. They kept me going when my inner critic tried to stop this book in its tracks. If you enjoyed James's perspective in this book, you can thank my friend and beta reader Ashley. It was her idea.

Last but never least, I couldn't do any of this if it weren't for the support of my husband, Eric and our wonderful kids. Also, my extended family for their lifelong support.

ONCE & FUTURE SERIES

The River Maiden

Sarah MacAlpin has plenty of ghosts. Her mother mental illness plagued her early years, and her grandmother who raised her died when she was just eighteen In spite of her difficult upbringing she's built a life for herself. One of the things that still haunts her is a song that her grandmother taught her. Growing up in the Blue Ridge mountains there were plenty of folk songs to learn, but the one Granny taught her was from her home in Scotland, in Gaelic, and unlike any other Sarah has heard.

Cauldron

Sarah's life is in shambles. Her best friend won't talk to her. The man she loves says they can't be together. She's just discovered something that destroys the main thesis of her dissertation. To top it off, she's learned that her dream fellowship in Scotland was given to her with ulterior motives by her billionaire benefactor. Sarah has to choose whether to accept the fellowship anyway and get caught up in James Stuart's web, or try to find a different path.

Thrice to Thine

After the revelations of her mother's memoir, Sarah is determined to learn everything she can about the mysterious tribe that her mother called the Auld Folk and the three "sisters" who rule them. She wants to uncover the secret that they are guarding and why it threatened her mother's happiness and her life. But their village was hidden for hundreds of years and may prove just as elusive for her. Working side by side with Dermot Sinclair, Sarah embarks on a search across the Highlands and Islands to find her people.

Nothing Good Gets Away

Sarah and Dermot are determined to put the Stuarts' ambitious schemes behind them and start a new life. When their escape plan goes awry Sarah gambles their future on a theory. One that could upend all the Stuart plans. To test her theory the Stuarts agree to let her people decide using the way that they have done matchmaking for countless generations. The Nine are willing to oblige her, but the results raise more questions than they answer. On her own and out of options Sarah must decide how she can protect herself and the people she loves.

ABOUT THE AUTHOR

Meredith R. Stoddard is the author of folklore-inspired fiction including the Once & Future Series, a contemporary fantasy series that blends Celtic legends with modern life. She is also a book coach at The Book Grower, the Communications Director of Bookish Road Trip, a community of readers, writers, and travel lovers. She hosts an Instagram Live program called Author Ride Along. She is a contributor to the Launchpad Countdown series of craft books from Red Penguin Books, and a member of Author Talk Network.

Connect with Meredith on her website.
www.meredithstoddard.com